The Existential Imagination is a collection of fictions expressing existential ideas, by seventeen authors who explore man's situation and his relationship to his self. Stripping away illusions, they offer a relevant confrontation. *The Existential Imagination* is edited and introduced by Frederick R. Karl and Leo Hamalian, two American authorities on modern fiction, who have also edited the Picador anthology of fictions for the seventies: *The naked i.*

The Existential Imagination

edited by
FREDERICK R. KARL
and
LEO HAMALIAN

PICADOR

PUBLISHED BY PAN BOOKS LIMITED

First British edition published in Picador 1973 by
Pan Books Ltd, Cavaye Place, London SW10 9PG
2nd Printing 1974
© Fawcett Publications Inc 1963
ISBN 0 330 23808 6

Printed in Great Britain by
Richard Clay (The Chaucer Press), Ltd, Bungay, Suffolk

CONTENTS

ACKNOWLEDGEMENTS AND COPYRIGHT NOTICES

The editors and publisher wish to thank the following individuals and publishers for their permission to use copyrighted material:

'Dialogue Between a Priest and a Dying Man' by the Marquis de Sade, from THE MARQUIS DE SADE: AN ESSAY by Simone de Beauvoir, with Selections from his Writings Chosen by Paul Dinnage. Translated by Paul Dinnage. Reprinted by permission.

'The Desire to be a Man' by Villiers de L'Isle-Adam. By permission of the translator, Harry Levtow.

'St Emmanuel the Good, Martyr' by Miguel de Unamuno, from ABEL SANCHEZ AND OTHER STORIES by Miguel de Unamuno. Reprinted by permission of Henry Regnery Company and F. de Unamuno.

'Cinci' by Luigi Pirandello. Copyright © 1959 by Gli Eredi, estate of Luigi Pirandello, translated by Lily Duplaix. Reprinted by permission.

'Filial Sentiments of a Parricide' from PLEASURES AND DAYS by Marcel Proust. Copyright 1948 by Lear Publishers Inc. Copyright © 1957 by F. W. Dupee and Barbara Dupee. Reprinted by permission of Librairie Gallimard.

'Moosbrugger' from THE MAN WITHOUT QUALITIES by Robert Musil, translated by Eithne Wilkins & Ernest Kaiser. Reprinted by permission of Martin Secker & Warburg Limited. Copyright © 1953 by Coward-McCann Inc.

'The Bucket Rider' reprinted from THE GREAT WALL OF CHINA by Franz Kafka, Copyright © 1953 by Schocken Books Inc. Reprinted by permission of Martin Secker & Warburg Limited.

'Socrates Wounded' by Bertolt Brecht, reprinted from TALES FROM THE CALENDAR by Bertolt Brecht. Translated by Yvonne Kapp and copyright © 1961 by Methuen & Co Limited. Reprinted by permission.

THE EXISTENTIAL IMAGINATION

Introduction

The Existential Imagination

In its literary manifestations, existentialism is varied and many-sided. We find aspects of it in writers as different as Tolstoy and Proust, Kafka and Moravia. However, even when we note that existentialism has been latent in the literature of the past 500 years, we recognize that only within the last century has it swelled into a fully compelling philosophical movement. With its emphasis upon the alienation of man from an absurd world and his estrangement from normal society, his recognition of the world as meaningless or negative, his consequent burden of soul-scarring anxieties, bringing with it his need to distinguish between his authentic and unauthentic self, his obsessive desire to confront his imminent death on one hand and his consuming passion to live on the other – with these emphases, it is not unusual that existentialism should have developed in a time of swift change when the sensitive individual finds himself fragmented and virtually destroyed by the exigencies of modern life.

To this experience, the writer may respond with a cry of nausea or with a passionate affirmation of passion itself or with the stance of rebellion, a position which perhaps fuses nausea with passion. The spirit of rebellion in the past century persuades us that man is an unwilling victim to the effacement of self. Even nihilism, as in Dostoyevsky, Kafka, and Malraux, wears the ravaged face of human protest, and the nihilist's revulsion, expressed by Moravia, Pavese, Sartre, and Beckett in their work, confirms that the individual, even at bay, stubbornly seeks human identity in an inhuman world.

It was Nietzsche who discovered that nihilism could be put to the service of the truth: 'Nihilism represents the ultimate logical conclusion of our great values and ideals – because we must experience nihilism before we can find out what value these "values" really had.' When the ego recoils passionately from the human condition, new values are created, values through which man tries to cope with his unique sense of morality and isolation.

Existentialism is a philosophy of disorientation, and the literature that has developed concomitant with its influence is a literature of despair. One of the best sources of this sense of modern despair is Coleridge's poem, 'Dejection: An Ode,' addressed to Wordsworth on his coming marriage in 1802, an odd occasion indeed for such a document. Coleridge is principally concerned not with Wordsworth or his marriage but with himself, with his own loss of creative power, what would be equivalent in an ordinary man to his loss of self or to his feelings of despair at his lack of uniqueness. Coleridge speaks of himself as suffering 'this dull pain', which the renewal of his imaginative powers might perhaps lighten. He suffers, he writes: 'A grief without a pang, void, dark, and drear, / A stifled, drowsy, unimpassioned grief, / Which finds no natural outlet, no relief, / In word, or sigh, or tear—'.

What Coleridge is experiencing is the dryness of soul that the existential philosophers beginning with Kierkegaard, forty years later, were to examine as the peculiar crises of civilized life. When, one-third through the poem, Coleridge writes, 'I may not hope from outward forms to win / The passion and the life, whose fountains are within', he is voicing an argument, since made familiar by existentialists, that only subjectivity, not objectivity and reason, can count in a world in which objects may well be meaningless and reason absurd. Within this frame of reference, the individual – stripped of tradition, custom, or belief – must make his own decisions, find his own truths, in the words of Kierkegaard, 'bloody truths,' that reveal the anguished journey of the spirit through the dark night of nothingness.

Coleridge's theme is his sense of alienation, his feeling that the world no longer 'works' for him. Itself a curious act of imagination, the poem is his attempt to resolve his estrangement and to liberate himself from his despair. With typical romantic preoccupations, Coleridge emphasized his self, as did the several philosophers who followed. Kierkegaard, the Danish philosopher who wrote towards the middle of the nineteenth century, stressed that man has lost his subjectivity, his own concrete life, and, consequently, has virtually ceased to exist. Kierkegaard found that the chief problems were not epistemological, ontological, or even metaphysical – those traditional branches of philosophy that concern themselves with man's relation to God or the universe – but human: specifically, how was the individual to come to terms with existence in a technological civilization? As a result of man's new role, his doubt and scepticism have turned inward and led to despair; man has lost most of his familiar props, and those that still remain prove insufficient. Within this frame of reference, the individual – unsupported by tradition, custom, or belief – must make his own decisions. Even the traditional baptism which the Church provides at birth is use-less, for that decision comes from without, while the chief, and sole, truth is subjective. It is only man and his consciousness which matter, and all philosophy must be in terms of man's existence, that is, existential.

The burden upon man within this view is immense. Whereas once he could turn without and find props from familiar objects, now he must seek within, in unfamiliar, unexplored territory. Accordingly, the true hero of our time is the man who can accept absolute responsibility, for this man prevents the levelling process which industrialization de-mands. As F. H. Heinemann, the English philosopher, puts it: Kierke-gaard 'introduced existence as a specifically religious category, meaning by it the single, finite, responsible, simple, suffering and guilty creature who has to make a decision in face of God and who consequently is more interested in ethical questions and in salvation than in abstract speculations.'

If the individual accepts Kierkegaard's challenge and seeks his religious centre within himself, then he begins his fierce encounter with nothing-ness. Man here floats in a foreign world in which human existence is feeble, contradictory, and contingent upon an infinity of other forces. Nothing can be certain except the individual's certainty of his own response. All he can hope to know is that he is superior to any univer-sal force, and to recognize that the universal or collective force can never understand the individual. He must be alone; for in his very aloneness is his salvation. As Nietzsche said, if all the gods are dead, then man must be mature enough to proceed from there. Man's recog-nition of this point is indeed his initial assumption of maturity and responsibility. It is, in fact, this very point that Dostoyevsky dramatizes in the character of Ivan Karamazov and that forms the substance of the Grand Inquisitor scene in *The Brothers Karamazov*. Must the indi-vidual's support come from within or without, Dostoyevsky asks, and in the Grand Inquisitor scene he ironically presents the dialectic be-tween the Inquisitor who symbolizes the 'without' and Jesus who rep-resents the 'within'. Like Nietzsche, Dostoyevsky was afraid that science and technology – and here, the materialism and mysticism of the church – by repressing human passions would alienate man from himself.

Two quotations, the first by Michael Karpovich, a Slavic scholar, the second by the poet W. H. Auden, suggest how the Grand Inquisitor passage reveals the basic concern of Dostoyevsky:

'To him, freedom meant first of all freedom of will, freedom of choice between good and evil. In this moral freedom he saw both the greatest right granted to man by God, and man's greatest responsibility. Everyone must himself make the choice between good and evil, and everyone must carry the responsibility for the choice he has made.'

'What he shows you are the depths of the soul . . . the alternating love of and terror of freedom that every human being feels . . . The importance ultimately of Dostoyevsky does seem to me to be a moral importance, in that the people who need to read him are people who are successful . . . The moment anybody is, then we all try and think, "Well, things are fine as they are, what we are doing is good," and then comes Dostoyevsky screaming, "No, it is not good enough". Society could not exist if everybody were like Dostoyevsky or his characters. But no society can ever be decent that forgets the kind of criticism Dostoyevsky offers us.'

It is possible, however, that Dostoyevsky's own words best disclose to us his most treasured secret, the ultimate formula for existence, and the slogan of all subsequent existentialists who acknowledge his influence: 'Thou shalt love life more than the meaning of life.'

Similarly, man's alienation from himself is the very problem with which Tolstoy later concerned himself: to examine situations in which man is estranged from himself because he is trapped by a society that cannot fulfil his deepest needs. In 'Memoirs of a Lunatic', as in 'The Death of Ivan Ilych' and several other pieces, Tolstoy records the feelings of a man who suffers from what Kierkegaard called 'fear and trembling', the 'sickness unto death'. In his despair, he faces the possibility of suicide, the complete nullification of his self. Tolstoy suggests, here as elsewhere, that the individual may need to face death before he can make the decision that will change his life. The 'Lunatic' finds his salvation in charity and generosity, and in a general withdrawal from the kind of behaviour society expects. As such, he is considered to be a lunatic, when, for Tolstoy, he is obviously the sole sane man in an insane world. Both Tolstoy's Lunatic and Dostoyevsky's Ivan Karamazov, the intellectual who flirts with nihilism, are nineteenth-century Hamlets who must suffer because a seemingly ordered world turns out to be disordered and meaningless, in brief, absurd.

The absurd is a condition that results when man seeking happiness and reason confronts a meaningless universe, what Camus calls the 'unreasonable silence of the world'. Put another way, the absurd results from the implicit antagonism between the individual mind and the collective world in which both strain against each other without the possibility of either satisfactory embracement or resolution.

It is the absurd world that Unamuno's 'St Emmanuel the Good, Martyr' tries to hide from his parishioners. As he tells Lázaro, the narrator's brother, 'The truth, Lázaro, is something so terrible, so unbearable, so deadly, that perhaps simple people could not live with it . . . I am here to make the souls of my faithful live, to make them happy, to make them dream they are immortal, and not to destroy them. What is needed here is for them to live in health, to live in unity of feeling, and with the truth; with my truth they would not live. Let them live. And that is what the Church does . . .' Saint Emmanuel's argument here is basically the same as Dostoyevsky's Inquisitor's: that man must not experience complete freedom but that he must sacrifice freedom for bread and illusions, both of which the Church supplies. Saint Emmanuel is of course less cynical than the Inquisitor, but nevertheless both of them indicate that an unsupported man will stagger. Since Unamuno and Dostoyevsky are Christian existentialists, they obviously find certain resolutions possible within a given area of faith, although Dostoyevsky ironically exposes the resolution of the Inquisitor as one acceptable only to slaves, not to free men. In that sense, along with Tolstoy, they are close to Kierkegaard, who was deeply religious, albeit in unorthodox terms.

What, then, about those writers, particularly of this century, who do not fall back upon the articles of Christian faith? They, too, perceive that man's position is unbearable, that his every act is meaningless in an absurd universe. They, too, recognize that freedom is a terrifying condition which man must come to accept, that in rejecting the world in a passion of nihilism, he must develop from that very spirit of negativism new and workable values, even if they are the values of despair. Several formal philosophers have tried to come to terms with this situation, among them Nietzsche, Jaspers, Heidegger, and Sartre, as well as humanists like Camus and Malraux. All of the four above-mentioned philosophers have helped define the terms of reference which appear in the fiction of the last seventy-five years, whose severe disarrangements have led to a crisis literature. All are concerned, in varying ways, with showing how man can become himself: Jaspers through a transcendence of Science, Self, and the World; Heidegger through an exhaustive analysis of human existence and what it means to *be*; Sartre through a definition of man's freedom and the terms therein.

All four assume that existentialism is a philosophy of man, that its philosophical 'answers' are not responses to technical problems in metaphysics, epistemology, or ontology, but those concerned with the welfare of man here and now, with that part of himself which he cannot escape. It provides, as Sartre feels, a new basis for humanism in which subjectivity is the sole universe man must explore.

When Sartre borrowed from Heidegger the concept that existence precedes essence, he was expressing in somewhat more intelligible language the belief in man as his own creator, responsible not only for himself but for others as well. In this view, man makes of himself what he can; he is tied to no preordained 'soul' or 'being' which, as it were, dictates the terms of his conduct. As man is to have absolute freedom, Sartre rebels against God precisely because God acts as a restrictive force on human liberty. Since man is free, he must also, as we have seen, be responsible, a position that returns us to the Kierkegaardian dictum that man's reaction to his existence must come from within. A good deal of Sartre's philosophical point of view was established during the Second World War when France suffered the Nazi occupation. Under the occupation, the resistance movement consisted of individuals, like Sartre himself, who daily had to make decisions that directly affected dozens of lives, including their own. Yet each decision had to be made in solitude. If a member of the resistance was caught, he had no redress: he had to learn for himself how much torture he could bear. In this world of intrigue and deception, there was no hope from the outside, only internal support. Man's capacity for resisting torture and death became, under these conditions, the limits of his liberty. 'Total responsibility in total solitude' Sartre gives as the very definition of liberty.

What Sartre defined is an experience that is not peculiar to himself or his writings but common to an entire generation. What he has stated in the tangled prose of *Being and Nothingness*, as well as in numerous pamphlets, essays, novels, and short stories, is nothing more than a delineation of the twentieth-century mind as it fumbles for some meaning when none is forthcoming. In his hands, existentialism becomes a philosophy of resistance and liberation; it is an attempt to set free man's authentic self from the cage-like existence of his inauthentic self.

In attempting to give man as much freedom as possible, Sartre has redefined psychoanalysis, so that man's very being rests on the freedom he gains when he chooses to make himself what he is. Sartre rejects the unconscious, which makes of man a passive being; for he considers everything that occurs to man and that is evident to his mind as an element of the conscious self and therefore controllable. Even man's negative reaction to outside phenomena demonstrates his freedom, for the ability to say No is a creative negativity in which the individual expresses his uniqueness. Thus, in 'The Room', Pierre is not simply a man chained by his lunacy to his room, but an individual who vigorously denies that anything outside even exists. In so doing, he calls into question the very sanity of those who claim he is insane: he manipulates them as much as they try to manage him, so that it becomes debatable who has more freedom. Accordingly, under the most negative of conditions – an insane man secluded in a dark room – a man can still assert himself by creating his own essence. Nothing is determined.

In replacing God with man, Sartre is careful to define what kind of man is necessary; for Sartre, it is the man of good faith, one who is reflective, conscious, aware of self and his identity. This man is free. The man of bad faith, on the contrary, is half-conscious and deceptive; he fails to reflect about himself and his role in the world. He lives sluggishly in the swampy depths of self-deception; he may accept what he should reject, or he may reject what he should accept. Sartre's novels and essays are attempts to define the man of good and bad faith and to show how he will behave in situations that demand his peculiar qualities.

In another way, then, 'The Room' may be read as a case history in self-deception or as a display of bad faith. In fact, Sartre seems obsessed with the notion of bad faith, and one critic finds in his work a prolonged effort to 'explore without the delicacy of an undue reticence the protean disguises of bad faith', in this story of a wife who lives with her insane husband on the sixth floor of an old building, refusing to let him be put in a sanatorium, seeking, through her love and sympathy, to be like him and to experience the flavour of his madness, we have a clear example of bad faith. Since she must fail in her efforts, she is forced to exist in the twilight zone which is neither madness nor health. The wife's insular, bourgeois parents illustrate another more obvious form of *mauvaise foi*; both examples are extreme, but their essence is typical, for they are simply extensions of normal reality.

Obviously, then, the existentialists, whether philosophers or men of letters, are concerned with individual conduct. Philosophy, for them, is ethical. It is clearly not the Marxist call to social action; rather it is an attempt to create individuals who can seek meaningful lives. Even put this way, the existential imagination is not heroic. Its defiance is low-keyed in modulations of character and action. The climax of an existential story is often not a traditional climax at all, but simply a ripple of behaviour, a sense of nausea overcome or experienced, a broken relationship recognized by both parties, a meaningless journey completed to nowhere.

Paradoxically, for a movement so concerned with ethics, existential fiction has provided little of an ethical theory or guide. Existentialism frequently becomes trapped by its own virtues: for if everyone is motivated ethically by his own subjectivity, then there is not only chaos, but potential immorality. If all objective values are rejected, then one's personal behaviour can be arbitrarily immoral, even though one wishes to set others free. And the latter is really the transcendent aim of existentialism. Existentialism would seem, then, to work well only for those who have a personal ethic derived from the existing legal or religious codes. It would work least well for those who have wrong responses, or bad faith, and who would simply perpetuate their subjectivity along immoral lines. Of course, the existentialist can always claim that people must transcend their baser selves, such transcendence being a mark of their maturity and responsibility. Nevertheless, most existential fiction works out without any such guide to behaviour; more often than not, as the stories show, a critical situation leads to suicide or some form of death-in-life, or perhaps to a perception of the problem without any possibility of resolution. Tolstoy and Dostoyevsky might be expected here.

None the less, despite its lack of explicit ethical basis, existentialism, as we have indicated, is entirely relevant to an age in which disorientation is the keynote. Metaphysically, we saw, it forces a concern with concrete human problems, with the condition of individuals. Further, it serves to awaken man from apathy and makes him face his true self, no matter how unpleasant that confrontation may be. Inevitably, it forces decisions which are necessary, at the same time discouraging face-saving hypocrisy and disallowing vague sentimentality. Since it focuses savagely on the individual, it is a force for truth.

As a philosophical movement, existentialism derives from continental Europe; as a crisis literature, existential fiction derives, almost wholly, from the same place. Even though isolated instances of such fiction can be found in England and the United States, these countries have not produced a body of existential literature. Some of the reasons are clear: the entire body of experience in England has been one that represents a basically forward-looking and optimistic people. Despite its many struggles and wars, England – like the United States – has not been pulled down into the muck of human degradation. Accordingly, despair in English fiction has rarely been what it is on the continent. The English philosophical movement, from Locke to Russell, has chiefly concerned itself with objects rather than subjects, and in its development contains a reasonableness and hopefulness missing from the more subjective philosophies of the continent. There is no one in England or the United States to match a Kierkegaard, a Nietzsche, a Sartre, or a Berdyaev, although Russell's definition of the good life as 'knowledge combined with benevolence' without reference to God or to human nature (essence) anticipates the more elaborate existential position.

Nevertheless, the English – and American – character shows itself to its greatest advantage in its genius for discovering practical solutions to problems. In politics, such empiricism has provided a flexible and workable system. However, the English and American distrust of pre-conceived ideas, of systems, of ideals, though politically and economically productive, has entailed some unfortunate consequences. The people who claim to be practical are in fact misrepresenting the motives of their actions and doing violence to their true natures. When a solution to a practical problem is said to require only a dispassionate assessment, it is then believed that passion or emotion plays little part in it. It is a short step from this to relegating all passion or emotion to a position where it is shrouded in secrecy, shame, and contempt. The ambivalence of mind in a situation of this kind, when it refuses to acknowledge the role of emotion as an impulse of thought and action, gives rise to hypocrisy, deep-lying neuroses, and distortions of truth. The entire existentialist movement is, in one way, a denial of such empiricism and an attempt to establish the priority of the passions.

Since existential literature responds so sensitively to underlying thoughts and feelings, not unusually it is extremely personal. Perhaps because of its very personal element, existential literature has at various times been characterized as 'despairing,' 'griping,' 'decadent,' 'atheistic,' 'communistic,' and 'pornographic.' It has often been confused with 'beat' or 'hip' literature, when in actual fact it has little connection with them. On the contrary, it is highly responsible in its attempts to give substance to the individual. In most cases, it is more 'moral' than much that passes for morality in popular literature. Frequently, existential fiction strikes through all aspects of morality to get at certain basic truths about man and his behaviour. As such, it cannot be said to stand for any one thing, or to defend any single cause. An existential victim-hero may be a communist, fascist, democrat, capitalist, socialist, business man, professor, thief, murderer; very often, he is.

In *The Man Without Qualities*, Robert Musil, an Austrian novelist of the first third of this century, wrote of a murderer named Moosbrugger.

Moosbrugger is no ordinary murderer, and his crimes are no ordinary crimes; it is Musil's point that every act must be understood as entirely unique. Moosbrugger is a carpenter of amiable and genial exterior who loathes mankind in general and women in particular, although he occasionally desires them physically. His chief wish, however, is to be left alone. He can accommodate his workmates only if they do not attempt to get close; as soon as they become chummy or familiar, he breaks out into violence, a rage intensified by his brute strength.

There are obviously forces in the man which no amount of analysis will ever reveal. There are things which Moosbrugger himself cannot ever hope to understand. The culmination of his criminal acts occurs when he virtually cuts to pieces a prostitute who will not leave him alone. The stab wounds have obviously been made by a maniac, and yet Moosbrugger is clearly not simply a maniac, but something more. As Musil writes: 'For the judge Moosbrugger was a special case; for himself he was a world, and it is very difficult to say something convincing about a world ... They [his strange shadowy arguments] came directly out of the bewildered solitude of his life, and whereas all other lives exist a hundredfold, being seen in the same way by those who lead them as by all others who confirm them, his true life existed only for himself. It was like a vapour that is always losing its shape and taking on other forms. He might, of course, have asked his judges whether their lives were essentially different.' (Volume 1, 84)

It is Musil's point, apparently, that everyone has some Moosbrugger in him, and that *his* crime is the crime that all of us at one time or another are on the verge of committing. His revulsion for mankind is the revulsion any sensitive person feels, and his desire to be left alone is a need that must be decently accommodated. Musil does not let the reader forget the Moosbrugger episode, for its substance runs like a *lietmotif* through the entire novel of over a thousand pages. If Moosbrugger is a man possessed, then his society is possessed by Moosbrugger. Musil writes that '. . . if mankind could dream collectively, it would dream Moosbrugger'.

The existential quality of the episode is evident in Moosbrugger's alienation from society and himself at the same time that society punishes him for revealing the very part of itself which it fears to confront. Wheels within wheels, the obsessed Moosbrugger finds himself in a world which is not susceptible to reason or reflection and which neither a sane nor insane man can manipulate. In brief, it is an absurd universe which sacrifices its Moosbruggers because someone has to be punished.

In this episode, as in the novel as a whole, Musil points to no resolution; on the contrary, he is content to make some indefinite point about certain aspects of nothingness. Moosbrugger, despite the horrors of his crime, is perhaps vaguely superior to those around him, for he understands his unique situation. Like Camus's Stranger, who has also committed an inexplicable murder, Moosbrugger must come to terms with several aspects of himself; there is a confrontation, a moment of truth, as it were, and in this area of self-awareness he gains a kind of freedom denied to those shackled to externalities. Moosbrugger has somehow become a free man by freeing himself of the violence within.

For Musil, as for most existentialists, recognition or self-awareness is sufficient; there is, after all, little that society can do about itself or Moosbrugger. But society can, in some way, be cautioned about its nature, so that it can be prepared to understand Moosbrugger and what he symbolizes. To elicit such recognition is to educe a moral truth.

Musil's long work becomes, as it were, a synthesis of Christian and atheistic existentialism. His characters are full of unbelief, although they proceed as though belief were possible. Ulrich himself, like a Christian knight, sets out on a quest to seek a faith which his reason tells him does not exist. Musil is well aware that all intense feelings may be illusions, and that beneath laughter and sensual delight there is disenchantment and nausea. He writes in one place of the nostalgia one feels for 'something that might best be described as nothingness'.

The Moosbrugger episode, along with Sartre's story 'The Room', Proust's 'Filial Sentiments of a Parricide', and Pirandello's 'Cinci', is revelatory about those things that lurk beneath a calm and respectable exterior. Existential literature, by definition, is concerned with this side of human existence, and perhaps more than any other mode of fiction has explored these unknown depths. Existential analysts probed these aspects of man long before Freud codified his ideas about the unconscious and subconscious; and then after Freud, existential analysts used his devices to explore the dark swamps of human behaviour. In Proust's story, there is an evident equation of the dislocated world of the parricide Henri van Blarenberghe with that of Ajax, the maddened Greek who slaughtered indiscriminately, and Orestes, who murdered his murderous mother, and Oedipus, another famous parricide who killed during a rage. Beneath the seeming joy of life, Proust tells us, there is the dying person; and often to seek the truth of things may lead to murder or suicide. Proust writes, at the end of the story, that in 'most men these painful moments of vision [when we perceive the meaninglessness of our lives] ... soon melt in the early beams of the sun which shines upon the joys of life. But what joy, what reason for living, what life can stand up to the impact of such awareness? Which is true, it or the joy of life? Which of them is the truth?'

Similarly, in Pirandello's 'Cinci', the sudden killing of the boy is not extraordinary; it is contained within the boredom of Cinci's world, and it breaks out as any violence must when there is no other outlet. Left alone by his prostitute mother, without visible guidance of any kind, feeling the deadening ennui of his existence, without any awareness of himself or his world, Cinci finds it natural to kill, even though accidentally. In an amoral universe, anything goes. After the killing, Cinci returns to his dull world, the dead boy in the woods only a memory soon to be lost amidst his next escapade.

Somewhat akin to these stories is Villiers de l'Isle-Adam's 'The Desire to Be a Man'. Villiers asks, among other questions, how does an actor distinguish his own self from his many roles? Which is the actor and which is the real man? What identity can a man have when to be convincing he must assume several identities? And in seeking one's identity, how far may one go to establish his uniqueness? These are all existential questions, based as they are on the establishment of the individual's identity. Chaudval even has several names: 'Esprit Chaudval, originally Lepeinteur, known as Monanteuil,' plus a countless number of stage names he has assumed in his long and successful career.

Chaudval suddenly desires to be himself: to feel emotions that have nothing to do with his roles. To be human means he must feel Remorse, but to feel Remorse he must commit a terrible, gratuitous crime and then throw himself into isolation. Thus, Chaudval plots his career as a feeling human being. By making his existence fit his plans, he creates his own essence. And yet such is the meaninglessness of the world that after he successfully carries through his horrible plan and retires to a deserted lighthouse to await Remorse, there is nothing. 'He felt *nothing, absolutely nothing!*' a passage that shockingly anticipates Musil's statement that 'existentially it [everything in life] was immeasurable, meaningfully it was confusion.'

Moravia's 'Back to the Sea' is full of the same nausea that permeates several of the above stories. Moravia characteristically conveys Lorenzo's feelings in terms of sexuality, employing a great many sexual images as well as the barren relationship between the frustrated man and his indifferent wife. Caught by feelings which cannot be reciprocated, filled by his guilt of a former time, unable to make contact with a woman who now sensually attracts him, feeling abused by the world and his own ambitions, Lorenzo perceives the nothingness of his existence. With his hopes and dreams lost, with his wife gone from his embrace and bed, he turns to the sea as the repository of the mystery of life. In going back to the sea, Lorenzo seeks the source of existence, the womb of life itself, and rejects a fate in which abject nausea seems his proper lot.

While Moravia makes Lorenzo unable to confront the nothingness of his existence and find a way out, the dying man in de Sade's dialogue ('Dialogue Between a Priest and a Dying Man') perceives that he can, through reason and Nature, transcend his feelings of nothingness. Rather than being awed by a world lacking God, he attempts to convince the priest that such a world is infinitely superior to one in which God rules man. In the latter world, man is ruled by fear, while in one without God, man is supreme. Man can find his identity through pleasure, and he can govern himself by reason, not superstition or hypocrisy. De Sade provides, as it were, a direct rebuttal to Villiers' Chaudval, who desires to define himself through remorse. On the contrary, de Sade's dying man counsels that barren remorse is ludicrous; crime itself must be avoided, not through fear, but through reason. Joy, happiness, pleasure – these are the qualities that Nature provides for us in this world.

De Sade, here and elsewhere, was attempting to free man through his indulgence in sensual pleasure, often the very pleasures society attempts to inhibit. In his search for man's inner freedom, de Sade foreruns a key theme of existentialism, although his work as a whole – with its emphasis upon reason – is not existential. De Sade's various libertines find that they can overcome their estrangement from a meaningless universe through their indulgence in pleasure, and the enjoyment they derive is, in a way, their means of defying death. But de Sade, in the long run, is not really ethical, for while his libertines do enjoy themselves, often their pleasure is the direct result of another's pain, even his death. De Sade argues, of course, that even the person suffering pain, or death, is himself experiencing a unique pleasure, but this point must remain debatable since his narratives are rarely concerned with the sufferer's sense of gratification. Nevertheless, de Sade's point, like Sartre's, is that 'man makes himself'. The shape may vary, but man is free to choose his own essence without any interference from above. There are no norms, de Sade indicates, and the normal shades into the abnormal so imperceptibly that frequently we cannot distinguish one from another.

At the opposite end of the spectrum, where there is no pleasure but only survival at the lowest possible level, is Samuel Beckett. Beckett's outcasts by now are famous, and the one in 'The Expelled' is typical, for he has few expectations and even smaller fulfilment. A Beckett protagonist is always in conflict with objects around him, for only he himself has reality, and even that reality comes into question. In every instance, he is divided from the rest of the world, a true stranger not only to *its* desires and needs but also to his own. Every Beckett character, like the narrator in 'The Expelled', is on a quest for his self; for Beckett, however, the quest is not tragic, but comic, the hopeless quest for a self that the protagonist knows cannot be recovered. His seekers are merely playing out what they know to be the comic game of existence.

In such a world, which neither punishes nor rewards, aspirations, hope, ambition, will itself are obviously meaningless. All endeavour is equally meaningless. No one can attain anything; no one even tries, except for his futile effort to find out who or what he is. The individual's alienation is complete, and all he can do is focus on details. Thus, at the beginning of 'The Expelled', the narrator concentrates on seemingly absurd items: the steps, his hat, the description of the house from which he is expelled; later, he stresses his gait, his toilet habits as a child, the cab ride to nowhere, the cab itself, the horse, the stable. Somehow, these details never coalesce into a meaningful experience, and they are not supposed to. They remain details, isolated from each other as much as man is isolated from objects and himself.

The stranger for Beckett is a metaphysical entity, a person so far outside 'normal' society that his actions and behaviour take place almost cosmically. By separating the character from objects around him, and further by splitting the character himself, Beckett creates a certain kind of fragmented reality. Inhabited by bums, tramps, misfits and cripples, this world is a collage of disparate images pinned together less by narrative force than by states of individual feeling. Nuances of feeling have to resolve everything, and here Beckett's relationship to existentialism is clear. The only thing that counts is subjectivity, for Beckett's outcasts are beyond all hope of salvation. Rather, isolation, alienation, lack of identity – the latter intensified to an extent perhaps equalled only by Kafka's characters – are the common stuff of his fiction.

Kafka's 'The Bucket Rider' is itself virtually surrealistic in its stress upon details, and virtually existentialist in its presentation of a frozen world in which the human will plays little or no part. The beginning, with its evocation of cold, indicates the lot of an individual who may perish for lack of a basic commodity; and yet he cannot obtain it by normal means. For Kafka's rider, the unreachable dealer becomes, as it were, a god who will dispense life-sustaining coal if only he can be reached.

In this strange story in which almost nothing occurs and yet in which everything seems to exist, Kafka exposes a cruel world in which the most ordinary things are stretched into new shapes and new meanings. Like many other Kafka protagonists, the rider must subordinate his will to the will of others: without the coal dealer's decision to give him fuel, he will not survive. Such is the absurdity of a universe which he cannot hope to understand. The absurdity, however, goes even deeper, for the rider never encounters the dealer. Like K. in *The Castle,* who is intercepted before he reaches his destination, the rider finds his plea intercepted by the dealer's wife, and it is she who relays the misinformation back to her husband. Thus, the rider does not make contact with the only person who can possibly help him. Without help, understanding, or identity, he ascends to a frozen death, locked into himself and cursing the cruelty of the world.

In Franz Kafka, man is always judged and always found guilty, in a kind of punishment without crime. He is the innocent victim of an unappeasable power, a horrible and recurrent outrage; he can only lament: 'I am here: more than that I do not know, further than that I cannot go. My bucket has no rudder and it is driven by a wind that blows in the undermost regions of death. Even this cry is to no avail, and if there is coal for some, there is only cold for me.' Kafka's vision goes beyond that of Dostoyevsky in its immutability: it denies man freedom, it denies him the terror of choice, and finally it denies him the possibility of grace. The bucket rider rebels against the order of things, but as a rebel he makes a better victim. In his universe, the bucket rider's rebellion turns into absurdity when the expression of it falls upon deaf ears. The bucket rider is the absurd victim, the aborted rebel, the cosmic fool.

The same general frozen quality is indicated in Cesare Pavese's 'Suicides', although his story is more personal and realistic than either Kafka's or Beckett's. Pavese's title is in the plural in order to indicate that the narrator as well as his mistress have 'killed' themselves, even though the former continues to live. Like Kafka's Rider, the narrator suffers from a kind of death-in-life. In his every move, he becomes aware of the absurdity of his existence, of the meaninglessness of his relationship with a woman who satisfies him neither physically nor mentally; for him, there is no such thing as real satisfaction. Even when he begins to sense enjoyment, he feels guilt; pleasure never comes freely and without entanglements. He suffers from the same nausea that afflicts Sartre's Roquentin in *Nausea*, from the same bore-dom that Tolstoy's narrator experiences before he becomes a 'lunatic', from the same ennui as Pirandello's adolescent Cinci or Villiers' ageing Chaudval.

There is no escape for Pavese's narrator; his nausea allows for no respite, and his condition does not make him a better man. He is truly possessed, without any of the powers necessary for extricating himself. He reduces his relationship with Carlotta to one of mutual torture, before finally driving her to suicide and himself to apathy. There is no person or thing to which he can turn for help; there is no help. There is here, without mitigation, not only Sartre's atmosphere of nausea but also Unamuno's tragic sense of life. In the latter's view, man lives in the grip of conflict, and his agony is a necessary condition of his existence. Of course, Unamuno carried his ideas further and taught that love can redeem the individual as well as mankind. Pavese has no such message, for, unlike Unamuno, he cannot accept the possibilities of salvation inherent in the attitude of composition. Pavese was him-self a suicide.

The content and imagery of 'Suicides', as befitting the title, indicate frustration, unrequited love, despair and death. Pavese's narrator hopes only for moments of tranquility, but even these moments become filled with doubt. He cannot really accept them, and he envies those who can glide over the surface of life. In his perception of life's darker tones, he makes himself miserable, and yet to be honest, he must grap-ple with these very feelings. Like Kierkegaard, he must experience the 'sickness unto death' and the fear and trembling implicit in self-aware-ness.

In the excerpt from Malraux's *The Royal Way*, Perken recognizes the same signs of despair and defeat, accepting the absurdity of life as he and Claude trudge through the hellish jungles of Indo-China in their quest for valuable pieces of sculpture. In their pursuit of the myster-ious Grabot — the search for whom is marked by innumerable obstacles — they try to give some form to their lives. And yet the only reality for Perken in his disenchantment is the reality of time and death. In his awareness of the human lot — what he calls a death-in-life — rests his consciousness of man's absurdity. How can one take seriously any pursuit, any hope, any illusion, any ambition when time itself defeats all? The very quality of time makes it unresponsive to man's will, and therefore in what should mean most to man he is helpless. According-ly, the sole step remaining for Perken is how to contemplate his death. If man cannot stay time, at least he can partially defeat its conquest of himself through suicide. Time defeats man's plans, but suicide defeats time, so Perken reasons. Within this frame of reference, suicide – the final shout of No – is a positive response; it is an act of defiance. Once perceiving this fact, and having rejected death, Perken knows he must face life. He has gained his peculiar kind of freedom by clearly facing the choice: life or death, and by choosing life.

Perken is obviously a prototype of the existential hero: the man who must live within the shadow of death, or else perish from boredom. Perken is a man so fascinated by the shadow death casts that life gains meaning, not from itself, but from its potential end. He says with a certain satisfaction: ' "I've been very near death. And you can't imagine the wild elation of those moments – it's the sudden glimpse of the absurdity of life that brings it – when one meets death face to face, naked" – he made a gesture as of tearing off a woman's garment – "stark naked suddenly . . ." ' Perken, of course, will not kill himself: he has chosen to live; but he cannot live without the thought of death. Malraux intuitively has put his finger on the pulse of contemporary man who claims that little exists except his unique life and yet who forces himself to live within the shadow of meaningless death. The paradox is part of the very substance of twentieth-century life: man chooses life over death, but makes death an ever-present commodity.

In the novels he wrote during the late twenties and in the thirties, we see Malraux anticipating, in the course of those stark and disillusioning struggles against oppression in China and Spain and against naked nature in Indo-China, many of the themes which call the existentialists into involvement. We meet men, like Tarrou in Camus's *The Plague*, who struggle to become saints without God, who learn the meaning of solidarity in the convulsions of their ultimate isolation, who answer the absurdity of the world with a defiant gesture.

Curiously, Malraux's reading of America literature helped him to move towards this position (although, with some exceptions, American fiction is not existential in mood). Malraux found in American literature a fundamental emphasis on the basic unity of *the act*, rather than a stress on analysis or explanation. For the existentialist, the act constitutes the unity of life. Analysis and explanation, they believe with Bergson, is not a valid means of knowledge, nor a valid approach to literature. American writers made their characters, as Sartre puts it, 'perform before our eyes acts which were complete in themselves, impossible to explain, acts which it was necessary to grasp completely, with all the obscure powers of our soul.'

The freedom that Malraux sees as implicit in man's choice to act is a freedom limited by time and circumstances and all those other aspects of destiny which mock his will to power and achievement. Malraux is Nietzschean in his awareness of man's will to power, but, even more than Nietzsche, he constantly warns of man's frailty and bafflement. He recognizes the impossibility of full achievement. Similarly, in Ilse Aichinger's 'The Bound Man', a story that seems a direct descendant of Kafka's work, the very premise is that achievement is limited; that, in fact, the greatest achievements can be gained through self-imposed limitations. The Bound Man – he has no other identity – is in much the same situation as Camus's Sisyphus: his freedom removed, his will frustrated, his energies devoted to a cause that is absurd. And yet, like Camus's hero, he finds some element of freedom within his restrictions. For Sisyphus, freedom exists in his mind, which his punishment cannot stifle; further, he gains a modicum of freedom in the very act of pushing the boulder up the mountainside, despite the fact that it will, for eternity, roll down. These elements of freedom cannot be removed, Camus argues, for they are the very substance of the human situation.

Similarly, the Bound Man awakens one morning to find himself bound from head to toes. Like a Kafka protagonist, he accepts his fate; he never questions the fact that he is bound while others are free. His limitations have been imposed by some cosmic force he does not even try to understand. He is *bound*: that is a fact of his existence, and he must confront the new situation with cunning and skill. He adapts. He makes himself a free man by working within the restrictions of his bounds. He gains his maximum freedom whenever he finds himself in harmony with his ropes, which, rather than limiting him, afford him a kind of liberty he never before enjoyed.

A further freedom that the Bound Man enjoys is his knowledge that at any time he can slip off the ropes. He has, as it were, an advantage over the man who suffers no restrictions; he can, in effect, lead a double life of intense awareness. Of course, if he unties himself, he is like everyone else: he loses his sole mark of identity. Therefore, his reluctance to undo the ropes even when sleeping is obvious. It is sufficient for him to have the knowledge of his potential freedom from the ropes; the actual fact is unimportant.

The Bound Man's decline begins when his actions are questioned and deemed impossible; his success in throttling the wolf, for example, is beyond the comprehension of people who believe in the ordinary powers of man and cannot perceive that man can transcend traditional notions of freedom. Thus, the Bound Man is brought down by the very audience which had given him the encouragement to continue. Faced by the catcalls of his former idolators, the Bound Man relinquishes his unique freedom by slipping off his ropes and escaping the infuriated mob.

The Bound Man is clearly an artist, but as soon as his art comes under question, he must live according to the mundane rules of reality. Like the Bound Man, Kafka's Hunger Artist — the analogy is very strong — similarly achieves a certain kind of freedom; by starving himself before an audience, he gains his peculiar liberty from those forces which affect everyone else. His hunger strikes are, in their way, his will to power: the length of his strike is the extent of his art. Yet the crowd becomes dissatisfied with this subtle art and turns to the more blatant circus displays, in the same way that the Bound Man's audience becomes dissatisfied with his subtle use of the ropes. In both instances, art must die for lack of appreciation. The Bound Man loses his reason for existence when he loses his freedom, and the new freedom he gains is an insufficient substitute. At the end of the story, he is frozen within himself under a moon whose colour is that of death.

The two remaining stories in the collection, 'Uncle from Heaven' and 'Socrates Wounded', are somewhat slighter pieces, which, nevertheless, cut across certain existential ideas and in themselves are finely wrought examples of ironic writing. Zieliński's story is clearly about authoritarianism in modern Poland. The political overtones are obvious, especially in the episode of the chocolate bomb plot and in the passages concerned with farsighted people who must be 'cured'. However, Zieliński transcends mere political commentary by incorporating his characters in an absurd universe in which anything may happen, and often does. Zieliński's method is one of savage parody and burlesque. In such a world, dislocation is accepted as normal, disorientation viewed as ordinary. The surface of the narrative is unreal, even surrealistic, and yet every act is treated as customary, every confrontation as usual. The narrator never questions that he must haphazardly parachute to his destination, that he must, without training, become a doctor, and that his personal wishes must be subordinated to those of his aunt. The fairy tale quality of the story recalls Kafka's, in which the supernatural appears real because existence itself no longer has either purpose or reason. Everything becomes plausible in a world in which nothing is real.

Brecht's 'Socrates Wounded' is another subtle piece of political commentary in which absurdity is the rule and order the anomaly. Brecht's immediate point is the meaninglessness of heroism in a battle when other forces besides individual actions will decide the outcome. The less obvious point is that individual will is virtually useless in a world that does not respond to heroic action. In brief, the individual is alienated almost completely from his desires, and Socrates, the coward, is temporarily Socrates the hero, only to be brought down by a ridiculous but painful thorn in his foot.

Throughout, however, Socrates never deceives himself. For Brecht, the great existential virtue is authenticity. To be an authentic person is to be one who faces the human condition, resolutely accepts his finitude and his death, creatively responds to life, and manfully assumes responsibility for all his decisions. This, Brecht implies, was the secret of Socrates' greatness.

In all seventeen stories, man experiences an encounter with nothingness – whether it be internal or external – and either succumbs to it or overcomes it through some personal resolution. The existential imagination seems particularly appropriate to a time when man has lost all familiar props and seeks new ones even while he recognizes that they too may prove insufficient. The response, obviously, must come from within; man has to transcend his pettiness and become a 'hero'. He is obliged to become worthy of his existence, and his worthiness derives from his confrontation with his situation, no matter how disenchanting, no matter how difficult and frustrating. Existential fiction is painful for the very reason that it strips life of its deceptions, while even the most realistic of us tend to hold to some illusions or believe them necessary. Joseph Conrad, although the most pitiless of realists, nevertheless wrote that man could not look directly into the heart of reality but needed the protective mask of illusions as a shield against the Medusa of existence. Clearly, to strip away illusions in order to uncover the truth is inevitably a painful process; but when man faces the truth of his existence and does react, then he is a real hero of our times.

FREDERICK R. KARL
LEO HAMALIAN

Marquis de Sade

Dialogue Between a Priest and a Dying Man

The Comte Donatien-Alphonse-François de Sade, generally known as the Marquis de Sade (1740–1814), was the author of licentious writings which have given his name to sadism. Condemned to the Bastille for criminal debauchery in 1772, he spent his captivity writing Justine, Juliette, *and several other books, which he published himself after the Revolution had freed him. He died in the Charenton lunatic asylum.*

PRIEST: Come to this fatal moment when the veil of illusion is torn away, only to leave deluded man with the remorseful picture of his errors and vices, do you not, my child, repent of the many evils that human weakness and frailty have led you to?

DYING MAN: Yes, my friend, I do repent.

PRIEST: Then take advantage of this opportune remorse to secure from heaven, in the brief space of time left you, general absolution from your sins, and bear in mind that it is only by means of the most holy sacrament of penance that it will be possible for you to obtain it from the Lord.

DYING MAN: I no more understand you than you have understood me.

PRIEST: What!

DYING MAN: I told you that I repented.

PRIEST: I heard you say so.

DYING MAN: Yes, but without understanding.

PRIEST: What interpretation?

DYING MAN: This ... Created by Nature with keen tastes and strong passions, uniquely situated in this world to indulge and satisfy them ... I only repent of not having sufficiently recognized her omnipotence; and my sole regrets are only of the indifferent use I made of the faculties – criminal in your eyes, but natural in mine – she endowed me with to serve her. At times I have resisted, and that I regret. Blinded by the absurdities of your creed, I used it to fight the whole onrush of desire that came to me by an inspiration far more divine; and I regret it. I have gathered only flowers when I might have made an abundant harvest of fruits. These are the true reasons for my sorrows; deem me wise enough not to suppose any others in me.

PRIEST: See to what your errors drag you! Where your sophisms lead you! You endow the thing created with all the potentiality of the Creator, and you do not see that these unhappy tastes that have led you astray are only the effects of this corrupted Nature to which you attribute omnipotence.

DYING MAN: My friend, it seems to me that your dialectics are as false as your thoughts. I would like you either to reason more accurately or to let me die in peace. What do you mean by 'creator', and what do you mean by 'corrupted nature'?

PRIEST: The Creator is the lord of the universe, it is He who has made all things, created all, and who keeps all simply by the working of His omnipotence.

DYING MAN: There's a great man, to be sure ... But tell me, why has this man who is so powerful made, according to you, a corrupted Nature?

PRIEST: What merit should men have, if God had not left them their free will? And what worthiness in enjoying it if on earth there were not the possibility of doing good and shunning evil?

DYING MAN: So your God would make everything awry just to tempt or to try His creature? Did He not know him then? Had He not any doubts as to the result?

PRIEST: Doubtless He did know him, but once again, He wished to leave him the credit of choosing.

DYING MAN: To what good end, since He knew the side he would take, and it only depended on Him, since you said He was omnipotent, it only depended on Him to make him take the good?

PRIEST: Who can comprehend the vast and infinite designs of God upon man, and who can understand all we see?

DYING MAN: The man who simplifies things, my friend, and especially the man who does not increase the causes the better to muddle the effects. What do you want with a second difficulty when you cannot explain the first? And since it is possible that Nature quite unaided has done all that you attribute to your God, why do you want to look for a master for her? The cause you fail to understand is perhaps the simplest thing in the world. Bring your body to perfection and you will understand Nature better. Refine your reasoning, expel your prejudices, and you will no longer need your God.

PRIEST: Do you not believe in God at all?

DYING MAN: No. And for a very plain reason, which is that it is completely impossible to believe what one does not understand.

PRIEST: But in the end you must acknowledge something after this life. It is impossible that your thoughts have not at times been pleased to penetrate the deep shadows of the fate that awaits us; and what creed can better satisfy it than that which sees infinite punishment for the man who lives evilly and an eternity of rewards for the man who lives the good life?

DYING MAN: What one, my friend? That of nothingness, because it has never frightened me, and in it I see nothing but consolation and naturalness. All others are the work of pride, and this alone comes from reason. Besides, this nothingness is neither horrible nor peremptory. Have I not under my very eyes Nature's example of perpetual generation and regeneration? Nothing dies, my friend, nothing in this world is destroyed. Today a man, tomorrow a worm, the day after a fly, is that not always existing? And why should you want me rewarded for virtues I am not worthy of, or punished for crimes I had no control over? Can you reconcile the goodness of your supposed God with this creed; can He have wanted to create me to give Himself the pleasure of punishing me, and that only as a result of choice over which I have no control?

PRIEST: You have.

DYING MAN: Yes, according to your prejudices; but reason destroys these, and the creed of man's free will was only invented to forge that of grace, so propitious to your fantasies. What man is there in the world who, seeing the scaffold side by side with the crime, would commit it if he were free not to commit it? We are swept along by an irresistible force, and are never for a moment masters enough to resolve anything other than the way our inclinations lie. There is not a single virtue that is not needed by Nature and, conversely, not a single crime that is not necessary to her. In the perfect equilibrium in which she keeps one and the other lies all her art; and can we be held guilty for the side to which she throws us? No more so than the wasp is that darts its sting into your skin.

PRIEST: So even the very greatest of all crimes should not inspire any terror in us.

DYING MAN: That is not what I said. It is enough for the law to condemn and for the sword of justice to punish to fill us with aversion or terror. But the moment we are so wretchedly committed, we must know what course to take and not abandon ourselves to barren remorse, for its action is useless since it cannot preserve us from it, void because it does not make amends for it; how absurd it is then to abandon ourselves to it; how much more absurd to fear being punished for crimes in another world, if we are so happy as to have escaped punishment in this one. Far be it from me to encourage crime on that score, for we must certainly avoid it as much as possible; but it must be avoided reasonably, and not by false fears that lead to nothing and whose effect is destroyed in a soul of any strength. Reason – yes, my friend, reason alone must tell us that injuring our brothers can never make us happy, and our heart alone must tell us that contributing to their joy is the greatest happiness Nature can give us on this earth. The whole of human morality is contained in this one saying: *make others as happy as you would wish to be yourself*, and do them no more ill than you would wish to receive. There, my friend, there are the only principles we should follow; and there is no need for a religion or a god to relish them and admit them – there need only be a sound heart. Predicant, I feel I am weakening; leave your prejudices, be a man, be human, fearless and without expectation, leave your gods and your religions; they are only good for putting swords into men's hands, and the very name of these horrors has shed more blood on earth than all other wars and scourges together. Renounce the idea of another world; there is not one. But do not renounce the pleasure of being happy and causing happiness in this world. That is the only way Nature has to offer you of doubling or lengthening your life. My friend, sensual pleasure was always the dearest of my blessings; all my life I have been a votary and have wanted to end it in her arms. My end is near. In the next room are six women, more beautiful than the dawn. I have kept them for this moment. Be firm; try to forget on their breasts the empty sophisms of superstition and all the bloody errors of hypocrisy.

NOTE

The dying man rang, the women came in, and in their arms, the predicant became a man corrupted by Nature for not knowing how to explain what corrupted Nature is.

Translated by Paul Dinnage

Feodor Dostoyevsky

The Grand Inquisitor

FROM THE BROTHERS KARAMAZOV

Born in 1821, Feodor Dostoyevsky became, together with Leo Tolstoy, the leading Russian novelist of the later nineteenth century. The novels which established his reputation are Crime and Punishment, The Idiot, The Possessed, *and* The Brothers Karamazov. *At his death in 1881, he was generally recognized as a supreme analyst of man's psychological condition.*

Dostoyevsky's sweeping genius did not accommodate itself to the short story, and the self-contained selection that best represents his existential views comes from The Brothers Karamazov. *Dostoyevsky himself regarded this chapter as the culmination of the book, and V. Rozanov, a critic and philosopher, who wrote a remarkable book on the legend of the Grand Inquisitor, affirmed that without it Dostoyevsky would never have written his masterpiece.*

The scene is laid in a screened-off corner of a shabby tavern, where, amid 'shouts for the waiters, the sound of popping corks, the click of billiard balls', Ivan Karamazov opens his heart to his younger brother, the saintly Alyosha. Ivan tells him that it is a marvel that 'the idea of the necessity of God could enter the head of such a savage, vicious beast as man.' For his own part, he is prepared to admit the actual existence of God, and even grant that all creation moves towards an ultimate harmony, but he cannot accept the ways of a Deity who includes in his scheme the suffering of the innocent. Therefore he rejects the world created by Him, and even though 'the humiliating absurdity of human contradictions' may someday vanish, he prefers to stay outside, intransigent, unreconciled, unforgiving of a small-minded God. Is there a being in the entire world, he asks, who has the right to forgive torturers of the innocent, who can justify suffering? Alyosha points to Christ. Thereupon Ivan recites the following story.

'Do you know, Alyosha – don't laugh! I made a poem about a year ago. If you can waste another ten minutes on me, I'll tell it to you.'

'You wrote a poem?'

'Oh, no, I didn't write it,' laughed Ivan, 'and I've never written two lines of poetry in my life. But I made up this poem in prose and I remembered it. I was carried away when I made it up. You will be my first reader – that is, listener. Why should an author forego even one listener?' smiled Ivan. 'Shall I tell it to you?'

'I am all attention,' said Alyosha.

'My poem is called "The Grand Inquisitor"; it's a ridiculous thing, but I want to tell it to you.'

'Even this must have a preface – that is, a literary preface,' laughed Ivan, 'and I am a poor hand at making one. You see, my action takes place in the sixteenth century, and at that time, as you probably learnt at school, it was customary in poetry to bring down heavenly powers on earth. Not to speak of Dante, in France, clerks, as well as the monks in the monasteries, used to give regular performances in which the Madonna, the saints, the angels, Christ, and God Himself were brought on the stage. In those days it was done in all simplicity. In Victor Hugo's "Notre Dame de Paris" an edifying and gratuitous spectacle was provided for the people in the *Hôtel de Ville* of Paris in the reign of Louis XI, in honour of the birth of the dauphin. It was called *Le bon jugement de la très sainte et gracieuse Vierge Marie,* and she appears herself on the stage and pronounces her *bon jugement.* Similar plays, chiefly from the Old Testament, were occasionally performed in Moscow too, up to the times of Peter the Great. But besides plays there were all sorts of legends and ballads scattered about the world, in which the saints and angels and all the powers of Heaven took part when required. In our monasteries the monks busied themselves in translating, copying, and even composing such poems – and even under the Tatars. There is, for instance, one such poem (of course, from the Greek), "The Wanderings of Our Lady through Hell", with descriptions as bold as Dante's. Our Lady visits Hell, and the Archangel Michael leads her through the torments. She sees the sinners and their punishment. There she sees among others one noteworthy set of sinners in a burning lake; some of them sink to the bottom of the lake so that they can't swim out, and "these God forgets" – an expression of extraordinary depth and force. And so Our Lady, shocked and weeping, falls before the throne of God and begs for mercy for all in Hell – for all she has seen there, indiscriminately. Her conversation with God is immensely interesting. She beseeches Him, she will not desist, and when God points to the hands and feet of her Son, nailed to the Cross, and asks, "How can I forgive His tormentors?" she bids all the saints, all the martyrs, all the angels and archangels to fall down with her and pray for mercy on all without distinction. It ends by her winning from God a respite of suffering every year from Good Friday till Trinity day, and the sinners at once raise a cry of thankfulness from Hell, chanting, "Thou art just, O Lord, in this judgement". Well, my poem would have been of that kind if it had appeared at that time. He comes on the scene in my poem, but He says nothing, only appears and passes on. Fifteen centuries have passed since He promised to come in His glory, fifteen centuries since his prophet wrote, "Behold, I come quickly", "Of that day and that hour knoweth no man, neither the Son, but the Father", as He Himself predicted on earth. But humanity awaits him with the same faith and with the same love. Oh, with greater faith, for it is fifteen centuries since man has ceased to see signs from Heaven.

No signs from Heaven come today
To add to what the heart doth say.

There was nothing left but faith in what the heart doth say. It is true there were many miracles in those days. There were saints who performed miraculous cures; some holy people, according to their biographies, were visited by the Queen of Heaven herself. But the devil did not slumber, and doubts were already arising among men of the truth of these miracles. And just then there appeared in the north of Germany a terrible new heresy. "A huge star like to a torch" (that is, to a church) "fell on the sources of the waters and they became bitter". These heretics began, blasphemously, denying miracles. But those who remained faithful were all the more ardent in their faith. The tears of humanity rose up to Him as before, awaited His coming, loved Him, hoped for Him, yearned to suffer and die for Him as before. And so many ages mankind had prayed with faith and fervour, "O Lord, our God, hasten Thy coming", so many ages called upon Him, that in His infinite mercy He deigned to come down to His servants. Before that day He had come down, He had visited some holy men, martyrs and hermits, as is written in their "Lives". Among us, Tyutchev, with absolute faith in the truth of his words, bore witness that

Bearing the Cross, in slavish dress,
Weary and worn, the Heavenly King

> *Our mother, Russia, come to bless,*
> *And through our land went wandering.*

And that certainly was so, I assure you.

'And behold, He deigned to appear for a moment to the people, to the tortured, suffering people, sunk in iniquity, but loving Him like children. My story is laid in Spain, in Seville, in the most terrible time of the Inquisition, when fires were lighted every day to the glory of God, and "in the splendid *auto da fé* the wicked heretics were burnt". Oh, of course, this was not the coming in which He will appear according to His promise at the end of time in all His heavenly glory, and which will be sudden "as lightning flashing from east to west". No, He visited His children only for a moment, and there where the flames were crackling round the heretics. In His infinite mercy He came once more among men in that human shape in which He walked among men for three years fifteen centuries ago. He came down to the "hot pavement" of the southern town in which on the day before almost a hundred heretics had, *ad majorem gloriam Dei*, been burnt by the cardinal, the Grand Inquisitor, in a magnificent *auto da fé*, in the presence of the king, the court, the knights, the cardinals, the most charming ladies of the court, and the whole population of Seville.

'He came softly, unobserved, and yet, strange to say, every one recognized Him. That might be one of the best passages in the poem. I mean, why they recognized Him. The people are irresistibly drawn to Him, they surround Him, they flock about Him, follow Him. He moves silently in their midst with a gentle smile of infinite compassion. The sun of love burns in His heart, light and power shine from His eyes, and their radiance, shed on the people, stirs their hearts with responsive love. He holds out His hands to them, blesses them, and a healing virtue comes from contact with Him, even with His garments. An old man in the crowd, blind from childhood, cries out, "O Lord, heal me and I shall see Thee!" and, as it were, scales fall from his eyes and the blind man sees Him. The crowd weeps and kisses the earth under His feet. Children throw flowers before Him, sing, and cry hosannah. "It is He — it is He!" all repeat. "It must be He, it can be no one but Him!" He stops at the steps of the Seville cathedral at the moment when the weeping mourners are bringing in a little open white coffin. In it lies a child of seven, the only daughter of a prominent citizen. The dead child lies hidden in flowers. "He will raise your child," the crowd shouts to the weeping mother. The priest, coming to meet the coffin, looks perplexed, and frowns, but the mother of the dead child throws herself at

His feet with a wail. "If it is Thou, raise my child!" she cries, holding out her hands to Him. The procession halts, the coffin is laid on the steps at His feet. He looks with compassion, and His lips once more softly pronounce, "Maiden, arise!" and the maiden arises. The little girl sits up in the coffin and looks round, smiling with wide-open wondering eyes, holding a bunch of white roses they had put in her hand.

'There are cries, sobs, confusion among the people, and at that moment the cardinal himself, the Grand Inquisitor, passes by the cathedral. He is an old man, almost ninety, tall and erect, with a withered face and sunken eyes, in which there is still a gleam of light. He is not dressed in his gorgeous cardinal's robes, as he was the day before, when he was burning the enemies of the Roman Church — at that moment he was wearing his coarse, old, monk's cassock. At a distance behind him come his gloomy assistants and slaves and the "holy guard". He stops at the sight of the crowd and watches it from a distance. He sees everything; he sees them set the coffin down at His feet, sees the child rise up, and his face darkens. He knits his thick grey brows and his eyes gleam with a sinister fire. He holds out his finger and bids the guards take Him. And such is his power, so completely are the people cowed into submission and trembling obedience to him, that the crowd immediately make way for the guards, and in the midst of deathlike silence they lay hands on Him and lead Him away. The crowd instantly bow down to the earth, like one man, before the old inquisitor. He blesses the people in silence and passes on. The guards lead their prisoner to the close, gloomy vaulted prison in the ancient palace of the Holy Inquisition and shut Him in it. The day passes and is followed by the dark, burning "breathless" night of Seville. The air is "fragrant with laurel and lemon". In the pitch darkness the iron door of the prison is suddenly opened and the Grand Inquisitor himself comes in with a light in his hand. He is alone; the door is closed at once behind him. He stands in the doorway and for a minute or two gazes into His face. At last he goes up slowly, sets the light on the table and speaks.

'"Is it Thou? Thou?" but receiving no answer, he adds at once, "Don't answer, be silent. What canst Thou say, indeed? I know too well what Thou wouldst say. And Thou hast no right to add anything to what Thou hadst said of old. Why, then, art Thou come to hinder us? For Thou hast come to hinder us, and Thou knowest that. But dost Thou know what will be tomorrow? I know not who Thou art and care not to know whether it is Thou or only a semblance of Him, but tomorrow I shall condemn Thee and burn Thee at the stake as the worst of heretics. And the very people who have today kissed Thy feet, tomorrow at the faintest sign from me will rush to heap up the embers of Thy fire. Knowest Thou that? Yes, maybe Thou knowest it,' he added with thoughtful penetration, never for a moment taking his eyes off the Prisoner.'

'I don't quite understand, Ivan. What does it mean?' Alyosha, who has been listening in silence, said with a smile. 'Is it simply a wild fantasy, or a mistake on the part of the old man – some impossible *quiproquo?*'

'Take it as the last,' said Ivan, laughing, 'if you are so corrupted by modern realism and can't stand anything fantastic. If you like it to be a case of mistaken identity, let it be so. It is true,' he went on, laughing, 'the old man was ninety; and he might well be crazy over his set idea. He might have been struck by the appearance of the Prisoner. It might, in fact, be simply his ravings, the delusion of an old man of ninety, over-excited by the *auto de fé* of a hundred heretics the day before. But does it matter to us after all whether it was a mistake of identity or a wild fantasy? All that matters is that the old man should speak out, should speak openly of what he has thought in silence for ninety years.'

'And the Prisoner too is silent? Does He look at him and not say a word?'

'That's inevitable in any case,' Ivan laughed again. 'The old man has told Him He hasn't the right to add anything to what He has said of old. One may say it is the most fundamental feature of Roman Catholicism, in my opinion at least. "All has been given by Thee to the Pope," they say, "and all, therefore, is still in the Pope's hands, and there is no need for Thee to come now at all. Thou must not meddle for the time, at least." That's how they speak and write too – the Jesuits, at any rate. I have read it myself in the works of their theologians. "Hast Thou the right to reveal to us one of the mysteries of that world from which Thou hast come?" my old man asks Him, and answers the question for Him. "No, Thou hast not; that Thou mayest not add to what has been said of old, and mayest not take from men the freedom which Thou didst exalt when Thou wast on earth. Whatsoever thou revealest anew will encroach on men's freedom of faith; for it will be manifest as a miracle, and the freedom of their faith was dearer to Thee than anything in those days fifteen hundred years ago. Didst Thou not often say then, 'I will make you free'? But now Thou hast seen these 'free' men," the old man adds suddenly, with a pensive smile. "Yes, we've paid dearly for it," he goes on, looking sternly at Him, "but at last we have completed that work in Thy name. For fifteen centuries we have been wrestling with Thy freedom, but now it is ended and over for good. Dost Thou not believe that it's over for good? Thou lookest meekly at me and deignest not even to be wroth with me. But let me tell Thee that now, today, people are more persuaded than ever that they have perfect freedom, yet they have brought their freedom to us and laid it humbly at our feet. But that has been our doing. Was this what Thou didst? Was this Thy freedom?"'

'I don't understand again,' Alyosha broke in. 'Is he ironical, is he jesting?'

'Not a bit of it! He claims it as a merit for himself and his Church that at last they have vanquished freedom and have done so to make men happy. "For now" (he is speaking of the Inquisition, of course) "for the first time it has become possible to think of the happiness of men. Man was created a rebel; and how can rebels be happy? Thou wast warned," he says to Him. "Thou hast had no lack of admonitions and warnings, but Thou didst not listen to those warnings: Thou didst reject the only way by which men might be made happy. But, fortunately, departing Thou didst hand on the work to us. Thou hast promised, Thou hast established by Thy word. Thou hast given to us the right to bind and to unbind, and now, of course, Thou canst not think of taking it away. Why, then, hast Thou come to hinder us?"'

'And what's the meaning of "no lack of admonitions and warnings"?' asked Alyosha.

'Why, that's the chief part of what the old man must say.'

' "The wise and dread spirit, the spirit of self-destruction and non-existence," the old man goes on, "the great spirit talked with Thee in the wilderness, and we are told in the books that he 'tempted' Thee. Is that so? And could anything truer be said than what he revealed to Thee in three questions and what Thou didst reject, and what in the books is called 'the temptation'? And yet if there has ever been on earth a real stupendous miracle, it took place on that day, on the day of the three temptations. The statement of those three questions was itself the miracle. If it were possible to imagine simply for the sake of argument that those three questions of the dread spirit had perished utterly from the books, and that we had to restore them and to invent them anew, and to do so had gathered together all the wise men of the earth — rulers, chief priests, learned men, philosophers, poets — and had set them the task to invent three questions, such as would not only fit the occasion, but express in three words, three human phrases, the whole future history of the world and of humanity — dost Thou believe that all the wisdom of the earth united could have invented anything in depth and force equal to the three questions which were actually put to Thee then by the wise and mighty spirit in the wilderness? From those questions alone, from the miracle of their statement, we can see that we have here to do not with the fleeting human intelligence, but with the absolute and eternal. For in those three questions the whole subsequent history of mankind is, as it were, brought together into one whole, and foretold, and in them are united all the unsolved historical contradictions of human nature. At the time it could not be so clear, since the future was unknown; but now that fifteen hundred years have passed, we see that everything in those three questions was so justly divined and foretold, and has been so truly fulfilled, that nothing can be added to them or taken from them.

' "Judge Thyself who was right – Thou or he who questioned Thee then? Remember the first question; its meaning, in other words, was this: 'Thou wouldst go into the world, and art going with empty hands, with some promise of freedom which men in their simplicity and their natural unruliness cannot even understand, which they fear and dread – for nothing has ever been more insupportable for a man and a human society than freedom. But seest Thou these stones in this parched and barren wilderness? Turn them into bread, and mankind will run after Thee like a flock of sheep, grateful and obedient, though for ever trembling, lest Thou withdraw Thy hand and deny them Thy bread.' But Thou wouldst not deprive man of freedom and didst reject the offer, thinking, what is that freedom worth, if obedience is bought with bread? Thou didst reply that man lives not by bread alone. But dost Thou know that for the sake of that earthly bread the spirit of the earth will rise up against Thee and will strive with Thee and overcome Thee and all will follow him, crying, 'Who can compare with this beast? He has given us fire from heaven!' Dost Thou know that the ages will pass, and humanity will proclaim by the lips of their sages that there is no crime, and therefore no sin; there is only hunger? 'Feed men, and then ask of them virtue!' That's what they'll write on the banner, which they will raise against Thee, and with which they will destroy Thy temple. Where Thy temple stood will rise a new building; the terrible tower of Babel will be built again, and though, like the one of old, it will not be finished, yet Thou mightest have prevented that new tower and have cut short the sufferings of men for a thousand years; for they will come back to us after a thousand years of agony with their tower. They will seek us again, hidden underground in the catacombs, for we shall be again persecuted and tortured. They will find us and cry to us, 'Feed us, for those who have promised us fire from heaven haven't given it!' And then we shall finish building their tower, for he finishes the building who feeds them. And we alone shall feed them in Thy name, declaring falsely that it is in Thy name. Oh, never, never can they feed themselves without us! No science will give them bread so long as they remain free. In the end they will lay their freedom at our feet, and say to us, 'Make us your slaves, but feed us.' They will understand themselves, at last, that freedom and bread enough for all are inconceivable together, for never, never will they be able to share between them! They will be convinced, too, that they can never be free, for they are weak, vicious, worthless and rebellious. Thou didst promise them the bread of Heaven, but, I repeat again, can it compare with earthly bread in the eyes of the weak, ever sinful and ignoble race of man? And if for the sake of the bread of Heaven thousands and tens of thousands shall follow Thee, what is to become of the millions and tens of thousands of millions of creatures who will not have the strength to forego the earthly bread for the sake of the heavenly? Or dost Thou care only for the tens of thousands of the great and strong, while the millions, numerous as the sands of the sea, who are weak but love Thee, must exist only for the sake of the great and strong? No, we care for the weak too. They are sinful and rebellious, but in the end they too will become obedient. They will marvel at us and look on us as gods, because we are ready to endure the freedom which they have found so dreadful and to rule over them – so awful it will seem to them to be free. But we shall tell them that we are Thy servants and rule them in Thy name. We shall deceive them again, for we will not let Thee come to us again. That deception will be our suffering, for we shall be forced to lie.

' "This is the significance of the first question in the wilderness, and this is what Thou hast rejected for the sake of that freedom which Thou hast exalted above everything. Yet in this question lies hid the great secret of this world. Choosing 'bread', Thou wouldst have satisfied the universal and everlasting craving of humanity – to find some one to worship. So long as man remains free he strives for nothing so incessantly and so painfully as to find some one to worship. But man seeks to worship what is established beyond dispute, so that all men would agree at once to worship it. For these pitiful creatures are concerned not only to find what one or the other can worship, but to find something that all would believe in and worship; what is essential is that all may be *together* in it. This craving for *community* of worship is the chief misery of every man individually and of all humanity from the beginning of time. For the sake of common worship they've slain each other with the sword. They have set up gods and challenged one another, 'Put away your gods and come and worship ours, or we will kill you and your gods!' And so it will be to the end of the world, even when gods disappear from the earth; they will fall down before idols just the same. Thou didst know, Thou couldst not but have known, this fundamental secret of human nature, but Thou didst reject the one infallible banner which was offered Thee to make all men bow down to Thee alone — the banner of earthly bread; and Thou hast rejected it for the sake of freedom and the bread of Heaven. Behold what Thou didst further. And all again in the name of freedom! I tell Thee that man is tormented by no greater anxiety than to find some one quickly to whom he can hand over that gift of freedom with which the ill-fated creature is born. But only one who can appease their conscience can take over their freedom. In bread there was offered Thee an invincible banner; give bread, and man will worship Thee, for nothing is more certain than bread. But if some one else gains possession of his conscience — oh! then he will cast away Thy bread and follow after him who has ensnared his conscience. In that Thou wast right. For the secret of man's being is not only to live but to have something to live for. Without a stable conception of the object of life, man would not consent to go on living, and would rather destroy himself than remain on earth, though he had bread in abundance. That is true. But what happened? Instead of taking men's freedom from them, Thou didst make it greater than ever! Didst Thou forget that man prefers peace, and even death, to freedom of choice in the knowledge of good and evil? Nothing is more seductive for man than his freedom of conscience, but nothing is a greater cause of suffering. And behold, instead of giving a firm foundation for setting the conscience of man at rest for ever, Thou didst choose all that is exceptional, vague and enigmatic; Thou didst choose what was utterly beyond the strength of men, acting as though Thou didst not love them at all — Thou who didst come to give Thy life for them! Instead of taking possession of men's freedom, Thou didst increase it, and burdened the spiritual kingdom of mankind with its sufferings for ever. Thou didst desire man's free love, that he should follow Thee freely, enticed and taken captive by Thee. In place of the rigid ancient law, man must hereafter with free heart decide for himself what is good and what is evil, having only Thy image before him as his guide. But didst Thou not know he would at last reject even Thy image and Thy truth, if he is weighed down with the fearful burden of free choice? They will cry aloud at last that the truth is not in Thee, for they could not have been left in greater confusion and suffering than Thou hast caused, laying upon them so many cares and unanswerable problems.

'"So that, in truth, Thou didst Thyself lay the foundation for the destruction of Thy kingdom, and no one is more to blame for it. Yet what was offered Thee? There are three powers, three powers alone, able to conquer and to hold captive for ever the conscience of these impotent rebels for their happiness — those forces are miracle, mystery and authority. Thou hast rejected all three and hast set the example for doing so. When the wise and dread spirit set Thee on the pinnacle of the temple and said to Thee, 'If Thou wouldst know whether Thou art the Son of God then cast Thyself down, for it is written: the angels shall hold him up lest he fall and bruise himself, and Thou shalt know then whether Thou art the Son of God and shalt prove then how great is Thy faith in Thy Father.' But Thou didst refuse and wouldst not cast Thyself down. Oh! of course, Thou didst proudly and well, like God; but the weak, unruly race of men, are they gods? Oh, Thou didst know then that in taking one step, in making one movement to cast Thyself down, Thou wouldst be tempting God and have lost all Thy faith in Him, and wouldst have been dashed to pieces against that earth which Thou didst come to save. And the wise spirit that tempted Thee would have rejoiced. But I ask again, are there many like Thee? And couldst Thou believe for one moment that men, too, could face such a temptation? Is the nature of men such, that they can reject miracle, and at the great moments of their life, the moments of their deepest, most agonizing spiritual difficulties, cling only to the free verdict of the heart? Oh, Thou didst know that Thy deed would be recorded in books, would be handed down to remote times and the utmost ends of the earth, and Thou didst hope that man, following Thee, would cling to God and not ask for a miracle. But Thou didst not know that when man rejects miracle he rejects God too; for man seeks not so much God as the miraculous. And as man cannot bear to be without the miraculous, he will create new miracles of his own for himself, and will worship deeds of sorcery and witchcraft, though he might be a hundred times over a rebel, heretic and infidel. Thou didst not come down from the Cross when they shouted to Thee, mocking and reviling Thee, 'Come down from the cross and we will believe that Thou art He.' Thou didst not come down, for again Thou wouldst not enslave man by a miracle, and didst crave faith given freely, not based on miracle. Thou didst crave for free love and not the base raptures of the slave before the might that has overawed him for ever. But Thou didst think too highly of men therein, for they are slaves, of course, though rebellious by nature. Look round and judge; fifteen centuries have passed, look upon them. Whom hast Thou raised up to Thyself? I swear, man is weaker and baser by nature than Thou hast believed him! Can he, can he do what Thou didst? By showing him so much respect, Thou didst, as it were, cease to feel for him, for Thou didst ask far too much from him – Thou who hast loved him more than Thyself! Respecting him less, Thou wouldst have asked less of him. That would have been more like love, for his burden would have been lighter. He is weak and vile. What though he is everywhere now rebelling against our power, and proud of his rebellion? It is the pride of a child and a schoolboy. They are little children rioting and barring out the teacher at school. But their childish delight will end; it will cost them dear. They will cast down temples and drench the earth with blood. But they will see at last, the foolish children, that, though they are rebels, they are impotent rebels, unable to keep up their own rebellion. Bathed in their foolish tears, they will recognize at last that He who created them rebels must have meant to mock at them. They will say this in despair, and their utterance will be a blasphemy which will make them more unhappy still, for man's nature cannot bear blasphemy, and in the end always avenges it on itself. And so unrest, confusion and unhappiness – that is the present lot of man after Thou didst bear so much for their freedom! Thy great prophet tells in vision and in image, that he saw all those who took part in the first resurrection and that there were of each tribe twelve thousand. But if there were so many of them, they must have been not men but gods. They had borne Thy cross, they had endured scores of years in the barren, hungry wilderness, living upon locusts and roots – and Thou mayest indeed point with pride at those children of freedom, of free love, of free and splendid sacrifice for Thy name. But remember that they were only some thousands; and what of the rest? And how are the other weak ones to blame, because they could not endure what the strong have endured? How is the weak soul to blame that it is unable to receive such terrible gifts? Canst Thou have simply come to the elect and for the elect? But if so, it is a mystery and we cannot understand it. And if it is a mystery, we too have a right to preach a mystery, and to teach them that it's not the free judgement of their hearts, not love that matters, but a mystery which they must follow blindly, even against their conscience. So we have done. We have corrected Thy work and have founded it upon *miracle, mystery* and *authority*. And men rejoiced that they were again led like sheep, and that the terrible gift that had brought them such suffering, was, at last, lifted from their hearts. Were we right teaching them this? Speak! Did we not love mankind, so meekly acknowledging their feebleness, lovingly lightening their burden, and permitting their weak nature even sin with our sanction? Why hast Thou come now to hinder us? And why dost Thou look silently and searchingly at me with Thy mild eyes? Be angry. I don't want Thy love, for I love Thee not. And what use is it for me to hide anything from Thee? Don't I know to Whom I am speaking? All that I can say is known to Thee already. And is it for me to conceal from Thee our mystery? Perhaps it is Thy will to hear it from my lips. Listen, then. We are not working with Thee, but with *him* — that is our mystery. It's long — eight centuries — since we have been on *his* side and not on Thine. Just eight centuries ago, we took from him what Thou didst reject with scorn, that last gift he offered Thee, showing Thee all the kingdoms of the earth. We took from his Rome and the sword of Cæsar, and proclaimed ourselves sole rulers of the earth, though hitherto we have not been able to complete our work. But whose fault is that? Oh, the work is only beginning, but it has begun. It has long to await completion and the earth has yet much to suffer, but we shall triumph and shall be Cæsars, and then we shall plan the universal happiness of man. But Thou mightest have taken even then the sword of Cæsar. Why didst Thou reject that last gift? Hadst Thou accepted that last counsel of the mighty spirit, Thou wouldst have accomplished all that man seeks on earth — that is, someone to worship, someone to keep his conscience, and some means of uniting all in one unanimous and harmonious ant-heap, for the craving for universal unity is the third and last anguish of men. Mankind as a whole has always striven to organize a universal state. There have been many great nations with great histories, but the more highly they were developed the more unhappy they were, for they felt more acutely than other people the craving for worldwide union. The great conquerors, Timours and Ghenghis-Khans, whirled like hurricanes over the face of the earth striving to subdue its people, and they too were but the unconscious expression of the same craving for universal unity. Hadst Thou taken the world and Cæsar's purple, Thou wouldst have founded the universal state and have given universal peace. For who can rule men if not he who holds their conscience and their bread in his hands? We have taken the sword of Cæsar, and in taking it, of course, have rejected Thee and followed *him*. Oh, ages are yet to come of the confusion of free thought, of their science and cannibalism. For having begun to build their tower of Babel without us, they will end, of course, with cannibalism. But then the beast will crawl to us and lick our feet and spatter them with tears of blood. And we shall sit upon the beast and raise the cup, and on it will be written, 'Mystery'. But then, and only then, the reign of peace and happiness will come for men. Thou art proud of Thine elect, but Thou hast only the elect, while we give rest to all. And besides, how many of those elect, those mighty ones who could become elect, have grown weary waiting for Thee, and have transferred and will transfer the powers of their spirit and the warmth of their heart to the other camp, and end by raising their *free* banner against Thee. Thou didst Thyself lift up that banner. But with us all will be happy and will no more rebel nor destroy one another as under Thy freedom. Oh, we shall persuade them that they will only become free when they renounce their freedom to us and submit to us. And shall we be right or shall we be lying? They will be convinced that we are right, for they will remember the horrors of slavery and confusion to which Thy freedom brought them. Freedom, free thought and science, will lead them into such straits and will bring them face to face with such marvels and insoluble mysteries, that some of them, the fierce and rebellious, will destroy themselves, others, rebellious but weak, will destroy one another, while the rest, weak and unhappy, will crawl fawning to our feet and whine to us: 'Yes, you were right, you alone possess His mystery, and we come back to you, save us from ourselves!'

'"Receiving bread from us, they will see clearly that we take the bread made by their hands from them, to give it to them, without any miracle. They will see that we do not change the stones to bread, but in truth they will be more thankful for taking it from our hands than for the bread itself! For they will remember only too well that in old days, without our help, even the bread they made turned to stones in their hands, while since they have come back to us, the very stones have turned to bread in their hands. Too, too well they know the value of complete submission! And until men know that, they will be unhappy. Who is most to blame for their not knowing it, speak? Who scattered the flock and sent it astray on unknown paths? But the flock will come together again and will submit once more, and then it will be once for all. Then we shall give them the quiet humble happiness of weak creatures such as they are by nature. Oh, we shall persuade them at last not to be proud, for Thou didst lift them up and thereby taught them to be proud. We shall show them that they are weak, that they are only pitiful children, but that childlike happiness is the sweetest of all. They will become timid and will look to us and huddle close to us in fear, as chicks to the hen. They will marvel at us and will be awestriken before us, and will be proud at our being so powerful and clever, that we have been able to subdue such a turbulent flock of thousands of millions. They will tremble impotently before our wrath, their minds will grow fearful, they will be quick to shed tears like women and children, but they will be just as ready at a sign from us to pass to laughter and rejoicing, to happy mirth and childish song. Yes, we shall set them to work, but in their leisure hours we shall make their life like a child's game, with children's songs and innocent dance. Oh, we shall allow them even sin, they are weak and helpless, and they will love us like children because we allow them to sin. We shall tell them that every sin will be expiated, if it is done with our permission, that we allow them to sin because we love them, and the punishment for these sins we take upon ourselves. And we shall take it upon ourselves, and they will adore us as their saviours who have taken on themselves their sins before God. And they will have no secrets from us. We shall allow or forbid them to live with their wives and mistresses, to have or not to have children — according to whether they have been obedient or disobedient — and they will submit to us gladly and cheerfully. The most painful secrets of their conscience, all, all they will bring to us, and we shall have an answer for all. And they will be glad to believe our answer, for it will save them from the great anxiety and terrible agony they endure at present in making a free decision for themselves. And all will be happy, all the millions of creatures except the hundred thousand who rule over them. For only we, we who guard the mystery, shall be unhappy. There will be thousands of millions of happy babes, and a hundred thousand sufferers who have taken upon themselves the curse of the knowledge of good and evil. Peacefully they will die, peacefully they will expire in Thy name, and beyond the grave they will find nothing but death. But we shall keep the secret, and for their happiness we shall allure them with the reward of heaven and eternity. Though if there were anything in the other world, it certainly would not be for such as they. It is prophesied that Thou wilt come again in victory, Thou wilt come with Thy chosen, the proud and strong, but we will say that they have only saved themselves, but we have saved all. We are told that the harlot who sits upon the beast, and holds in her hands the *mystery*, shall be put to shame, that the weak will rise up again, and will rend her royal purple and will strip naked her loathsome body. But then I will stand up and point out to Thee the thousand millions of happy children who have known no sin. And we who have taken their sins upon us for their happiness will stand up before Thee and say: 'Judge us if Thou canst and darest'. Know that I fear Thee not. Know that I too have been in the wilderness, I too have lived on roots and locusts, I too prized the freedom with which Thou hast blessed men, and I too was striving to stand among Thy elect, among the strong and powerful, thirsting 'to make up the number'. But I awakened and would not serve madness. I turned back and joined the ranks of those *who have corrected Thy work*. I left the proud and went back to the humble, for the happiness of the humble. What I say to Thee will come to pass, and our dominion will be built up. I repeat, tomorrow Thou shalt see that obedient flock who at a sign from me will hasten to heap up the hot cinders about the pile on which I shall burn Thee for coming to hinder us. For if any one has ever deserved our fires, it is Thou. Tomorrow I shall burn Thee. Dixi."

'. . . When the Inquisitor ceased speaking, he waited some time for his prisoner to answer him. His silence weighed down upon him. He saw that the prisoner had listened intently all the time, looking gently in his face and evidently not wishing to reply. The old man longed for Him to say something, however bitter and terrible. But he suddenly approached the old man in silence and softly kissed him on his bloodless aged lips. That was all his answer. The old man shuddered. His lips moved. He went to the door, opened it, and said to him: "Go, and come no more . . . come not at all, never!" And he let Him out into the dark alleys of the town. The prisoner went away.'

'And the old man?'

'The kiss glows in his heart, but the old man adheres to his idea.'

'And you with him, you too?' cried Alyosha, mournfully.

Ivan laughed.

'Why, it's all nonsense, Alyosha. It's only a senseless poem of a senseless student, who could never write two lines of verse. Why do you take it so seriously? . . .'

Translated by Constance Garnett

Leo Tolstoy

Memoirs of a Lunatic

The world-famous novelist Leo Tolstoy was born in Tula, Russia, in 1828 and gained his fame with War and Peace *(1866) and* Anna Karenina *(1877) before undergoing a period of spiritual turmoil that lasted until his death in 1910. He represented his monumental personal upheaval in a novel,* Resurrection, *in several long essays and autobiographical memoirs, and in stories and novellas like 'Memoirs of a Lunatic' and 'The Death of Ivan Ilych'.*

This morning I underwent a medical examination in the government council room. The opinions of the doctors were divided. They argued among themselves and came at last to the conclusion that I was not mad. But this was due to the fact that I tried hard during the examination not to give myself away. I was afraid of being sent to the lunatic asylum, where I would not be able to go on with the mad undertaking I have on my hands. They pronounced me subject to fits of excitement, and something else, too, but nevertheless of sound mind. The doctor prescribed a certain treatment, and assured me that by following his directions my trouble would completely disappear. Imagine, all that torments me disappearing completely! Oh, there is nothing I would not give to be free from my trouble. The suffering is too great!

I am going to tell explicitly how I came to undergo that examination; how I went mad, and how my madness was revealed to the outside world.

Up to the age of thirty-five I lived like the rest of the world, and nobody had noticed any peculiarities in me. Only in my early childhood, before I was ten, I had occasionally been in a mental state similar to the present one, and then only at intervals, whereas now I am continually conscious of it.

I remember going to bed one evening, when I was a child of five or six. Nurse Euprasia, a tall, lean woman in a brown dress, with a double chin, was undressing me, and was just lifting me up to put me into bed.

'I will get into bed myself,' I said, preparing to step over the net at the bedside.

'Lie down, Fedinka. You see, Mitinka is already lying quite still,' she said, pointing with her head to my brother in his bed.

I jumped into my bed still holding nurse's hand in mine. Then I let it go, stretched my legs under the blanket and wrapped myself up. I felt so nice and warm! I grew silent all of a sudden and began thinking: 'I love nurse, nurse loves me and Mitinka, I love Mitinka too, and he loves me and nurse. And nurse loves Taras; I love Taras too, and so does Mitinka. And Taras loves me and nurse. And mother loves me and nurse, nurse loves mother and me and father; everybody loves everybody, and everybody is happy.'

Suddenly the housekeeper rushed in and began to shout in an angry voice something about a sugar basin she could not find. Nurse got cross and said she did not take it. I felt frightened; it was all so strange. A cold horror came over me, and I hid myself under the blanket. But I felt no better in the darkness under the blanket. I thought of a boy who had got a thrashing one day in my presence – of his screams, and of the cruel face of Foka when he was beating the boy.

'Then you won't do it any more; you won't!' he repeated and went on beating.

'I won't,' said the boy; and Foka kept on repeating over and over, 'You won't, you won't!' and did not cease to strike the boy.

That was when my madness came over me for the first time. I burst into sobs, and they could not quiet me for a long while. The tears and despair of that day were the first signs of my present trouble.

I well remember the second time my madness seized me. It was when aunt was telling us about Christ. She told His story and got up to leave the room. But we held her back: 'Tell us more about Jesus Christ!' we said.

'I must go,' she replied.

'No, tell us more, please!' Mitinka insisted, and she repeated all she had said before. She told us how they crucified Him, how they beat and martyred Him, and how He went on praying and did not blame them.

'Auntie, why did they torture Him?'

'They were wicked.'

'But wasn't He God?'

'Be still – it is nine o'clock, don't you hear the clock striking?'

'Why did they beat Him? He had forgiven them. Then why did they hit Him? Did it hurt Him? Auntie, did it hurt?'

'Be quiet, I say. I am going to the dining-room to have tea now.'

'But perhaps it never happened, perhaps He was not beaten by them?'

'I am going.'

'No, Auntie, don't go! ...' And again my madness took possession of me. I sobbed and sobbed, and began knocking my head against the wall.

Such had been the fits of madness in my childhood. But after I was fourteen, from the time the instincts of sex awoke and I began to give way to vice, my madness seemed to have passed, and I was a boy like other boys. Just as happens with all of us who are brought up on rich, over-abundant food, and are spoiled and made effeminate, because we never do any physical work, and are surrounded by all possible temptations, which excite our sensual nature when in the company of other children similarly spoiled, so I had been taught vice by other boys of my age and I indulged in it. As time passed other vices came to take the place of the first. I began to know women, and so I went on living, up to the time I was thirty-five, looking out for all kinds of pleasures and enjoying them. I had a perfectly sound mind then, and never a sign of madness. Those twenty years of my normal life passed without leaving any special record on my memory, and now it is only with a great effort of mind and with utter disgust, that I can concentrate my thoughts upon that time.

Like all the boys of my set, who were of sound mind, I entered school, passed on to the university and went through a course of law studies. Then I entered the State service for a short time, married, and settled down in the country, educating – if our way of bringing up children can be called educating – my children, looking after the land, and filling the post of a Justice of the Peace.

It was when I had been married ten years that one of those attacks of madness I suffered from in my childhood made its appearance again. My wife and I had saved up money from her inheritance and from some Government bonds* of mine which I had sold, and we decided that with that money we would buy another estate. I was naturally keen to increase our fortune, and to do it in the shrewdest way, better than anyone else would manage it. I went about inquiring what estates were to be sold, and used to read all the advertisements in the papers. What

* These government bonds were of a peculiar kind: At the moment of the abolition of serfdom, the Russian Government handed to the owners of serfs State bonds instead of money, called in Russia 'the redemption bonds'. The money due by the Government on these papers was paid off at fixed periods – and the owners of these bonds sold them often like ordinary Government papers.

I wanted was to buy an estate, the produce or timber of which would cover the cost of purchase, and then I would have the estate practically for nothing. I was looking out for a fool who did not understand business, and there came a day when I thought I had found one. An estate with large forests attached to it was to be sold in the Pensa Government. To judge by the information I had received the proprietor of that estate was exactly the imbecile I wanted, and I might expect the forests to cover the price asked for the whole estate. I got my things ready and was soon on my way to the estate I wished to inspect.

We had first to go by train (I had taken my man-servant with me), then by coach, with relays of horses at the various stations. The journey was very pleasant, and my servant, a good-natured youth, liked it as much as I did. We enjoyed the new surroundings and the new people, and having now only about two hundred miles more to drive, we decided to go on without stopping, except to change horses at the stations. Night came on and we were still driving. I had been dozing, but presently I awoke, seized with a sudden fear. As often happens in such a case, I was so excited that I was thoroughly awake and it seemed as if sleep were gone for ever. 'Why am I driving? Where am I going?' I suddenly asked myself. It was not that I disliked the idea of buying an estate at a bargain, but it seemed at that moment so senseless to journey to such a far away place, and I had a feeling as if I were going to die there, away from home. I was overcome with horror.

My servant Sergius awoke, and I took advantage of the fact to talk to him. I began to remark upon the scenery around us; he had also a good deal to say, of the people at home, of the pleasure of the journey, and it seemed strange to me that he could talk so gaily. He appeared so pleased with everything and in such good spirits, whereas I was annoyed with it all. Still, I felt more at ease when I was talking with him. Along with my feelings of restlessness and my secret horror, however, I was fatigued as well, and longed to break the journey somewhere. It seemed to me uneasiness would cease if I could only enter a room, have tea, and, what I desired most of all, sleep.

We were approaching the town Arzamas.

'Don't you think we had better stop here and have a rest?'

'Why not? It's an excellent idea.'

'How far are we from the town?' I asked the driver.

'Another seven miles.'

The driver was a quiet, silent man. He was driving rather slowly and wearily.

We drove on. I was silent, but I felt better, looking forward to a rest and hoping to feel the better for it. We drove on and on in the darkness, and the seven miles seemed to have no end. At last we reached the town. It was sound asleep at that early hour. First came the small houses, piercing the darkness, and as we passed them, the noise of our jingling bells and the trotting of our horses sounded louder. In a few places the houses were large and white, but I did not feel less dejected for seeing them. I was waiting for the station, and the samovar, and longed to lie down and rest.

At last we approached a house with pillars in front of it. The house was white, but it seemed to me very melancholy. I felt even frightened at its aspect and stepped slowly out of the carriage. Sergius was busying himself with our luggage, taking what we needed for the night, running about and stepping heavily on the doorsteps. The sound of his brisk tread increased my weariness. I walked in and came into a small passage. A man received us; he had a large spot on his cheek and that spot filled me with horror. He asked us into a room which was just an ordinary room. My uneasiness was growing.

'Could we have a room to rest in?' I asked.

'Oh, yes, I have a very nice bedroom at your disposal. A square room, newly whitewashed.'

The fact of the little room being square was – I remember it so well – most painful to me. It had one window with a red curtain, a table of birch wood and a sofa with a curved back and arms. Sergius boiled the water in the samovar and made the tea. I put a pillow on the sofa in the meantime and lay down. I was not asleep; I heard Sergius busy with the samovar and urging me to have tea. I was afraid to get up from the sofa, afraid of driving away sleep; and just to be sitting in that room seemed awful. I did not get up, but fell into a sort of doze. When I started up out of it, nobody was in the room and it was quite dark. I woke up with the very same sensation I had the first time and knew sleep was gone. 'Why am I here? Where am I going? Just as I am I must be for ever. Neither the Pensa nor any other estate will add to or take anything away from me. As for me, I am unbearably weary of myself. I want to go to sleep, to forget – and I cannot, I cannot get rid of self.'

I went out into the passage. Sergius was sleeping there on a narrow bench, his hand hanging down beside it. He was sleeping soundly, and the man with the spot on his cheek was also asleep. I thought, by going out of the room, to get away from what was tormenting me. But *it* followed me and made everything seem dark and dreary. My feeling of horror, instead of leaving me, was increasing.

'What nonsense!' I said to myself. 'Why am I so dejected? What am

I afraid of?' 'You are afraid of me' – I heard the voice of Death – 'I am here.'

I shuddered. Yes, – Death! Death will come, it will come and it ought not to come. Even in facing actual death I would certainly not feel anything of what I felt now. Then it would be simply fear, whereas now it was more than that. I was actually seeing, feeling the approach of death, and along with it I felt death ought not to exist.

My entire being was conscious of the necessity of the right to live, and at the same time of the inevitability of dying. This inner conflict was causing me unbearable pain. I tried to shake off the horror; I found a half-burnt candle in a brass candlestick and lighted it. The candle with its red flame burnt down until it was not much taller than the low candlestick. The same thing seemed to be repeated over and over; nothing lasts, life is not, all is death – but death ought not to exist. I tried to turn my thoughts to what had interested me before, to the estate I was to buy and to my wife. Far from being a relief, these seemed nothing to me now. To feel my life doomed to be taken from me was terror shutting out any other thought. 'I must try to sleep,' I decided. I went to bed, but the next instant I jumped up, seized with horror. A sickness overcame me, a spiritual sickness not unlike the physical uneasiness preceding actual illness – but in the spirit, not in the body. A terrible fear similar to the fear of death, when mingled with the recollections of my past life, developed into a horror as if life were departing. Life and death were flowing into one another. An unknown power was trying to tear my soul into pieces, but could not bend it. Once more I went out into the passage to look at the two men asleep; once more I tried to go to sleep. The horror was always the same – now red, now white and square. Something was tearing within but could not be torn apart. A torturing sensation! An arid hatred deprived me of every spark of kindly feeling. Just a dull and steady hatred against myself and against that which had created me. What did create me? God? We say God ... 'What if I tried to pray?' I suddenly thought. I had not said a prayer for more than twenty years and I had no religious sentiment, although just for formality's sake I fasted and partook of the communion every year. I began saying prayers; 'God, forgive me', 'Our Father', 'Our Lady', I was composing new prayers, crossing myself, bowing to the earth, looking around me all the while for fear I might be discovered in my devotional attitude. The prayers seemed to divert my thoughts from the previous terror, but it was more the fear of being seen by somebody that did it. I went to bed again. But the moment I shut my eyes the very same feeling of terror made me jump up. I could not stand it any longer. I called the hotel servant, roused Sergius from his sleep, ordered him to harness the horses to the carriage and we were soon driving on once more. The open air and the drive made me feel much better. But I realized that something new had come into my soul, and had poisoned the life I had lived up to that hour.

We reached our destination in the evening. The whole day long I remained struggling with despair, and finally conquered it; but a horror remained in the depth of my soul. It was as if a misfortune had happened to me, and although I was able to forget it for a while, it remained at the bottom of my soul, and I was entirely dominated by it.

The manager of the estate, an old man, received us in a very friendly manner, though not exactly with great joy; he was sorry that the estate was to be sold. The clean little rooms with upholstered furniture, a new, shining samovar on the tea-table, nice large cups, honey served with the tea – everything was pleasant to see. I began questioning him about the estate without any interest, as if I were repeating a lesson learned long ago and nearly forgotten. It was so uninteresting. But that night I was able to go to sleep without feeling miserable. I thought this was due to having said my prayers again before going to bed.

After that incident I resumed my ordinary life; but the apprehension that this horror would again come upon me was continual. I had to live my usual life without any respite, not giving way to my thoughts, just like a schoolboy who repeats by habit and without thinking the lesson learned by heart. That was the only way to avoid being seized again by the horror and the despair I had experienced in Arzamas.

I had returned home safe from my journey; I had not bought the estate – I had not enough money. My life at home seemed to be just as it had always been, save for my having taken to saying prayers and to going to church. But now, when I recollect that time, I see that I only imagined my life to be the same as before. The fact was I merely continued what I had previously started, and was running with the same speed on rails already laid; but I did not undertake anything new.

Even in those things which I had already taken in hand my interest had diminished. I was tired of everything, and was growing very religious. My wife noticed this, and was often vexed with me for it. No new fit of distress occurred while I was at home. But one day I had to go unexpectedly to Moscow, where a lawsuit was pending. In the train I entered into conversation with a land-owner from Kharkov. We were talking about the management of estates, about bank business, about the hotels in Moscow, and the theatres. We both decided to stop at the 'Moscow Court', in the Miasnizkaia Street, and go that evening to the opera, to *Faust*. When we arrived I was shown into a small room, the heavy smell of the passage being still in my nostrils. The porter brought in my portmanteau, and the maid lighted the candle, the flame of which burned up brightly and then flickered, as it usually does. In the room next to mine I heard somebody coughing, probably an old man. The maid went out, and the porter asked whether I wished him to open my bag. In the meanwhile the candle flame had flared up, throwing its light on the blue wallpaper with yellow stripes, on the partition, on the shabby table, on the small sofa in front of it, on the mirror hanging on the wall, and on the window. I saw what the small room was like, and suddenly felt the horror of the Arzamas night awakening within me.

'My God! Must I stay here for the night? How can I?' I thought. 'Will you kindly unfasten my bag?' I said to the porter, to keep him longer in the room. 'And now I'll dress quickly and go to the theatre,' I said to myself.

When the bag had been untied I said to the porter, 'Please tell the gentleman in Number 8 – the one who came with me – that I shall be ready presently, and ask him to wait for me.'

The porter left, and I began to dress in haste, afraid to look at the walls. 'But what nonsense!' I said to myself. 'Why am I frightened like a child? I am not afraid of ghosts—' Ghosts! – To be afraid of ghosts is nothing to what I was afraid of! 'But what is it? Absolutely nothing. I am only afraid of myself ... Nonsense!'

I slipped into a cold, rough, starched shirt, stuck in the studs, put on evening dress and new boots, and went to call for the Kharkov land-owner, who was ready. We started for the opera house. He stopped on the way to have his hair curled, while I went to a French hairdresser to have mine cut, where I talked a little to the Frenchwoman in the shop and bought a pair of gloves. Everything seemed all right. I had com-pletely forgotten the oblong room in the hotel, and the walls.

I enjoyed the *Faust* performance very much, and when it was over my companion proposed that we should have supper. This was con-trary to my habits; but just at that moment I remembered the walls in my room, and accepted.

We returned home after one. I had had two glasses of wine – an unusual thing for me – in spite of which I was feeling quite at ease.

But the moment we entered the passage with the lowered lamp lighting it, the moment I was surrounded by the peculiar smell of the hotel, I felt a cold shudder of horror running down my back. But there was nothing to be done. I shook hands with my new friend, and stepped into my room.

I had a frightful night – much worse than the night at Arzamas; and it was not until dawn, when the old man in the next room was coughing again, that I fell asleep – and then not in bed, but, after getting in and out of it many times, on the sofa.

I suffered the whole night unbearably. Once more my soul and my body were tearing themselves apart within me. The same thoughts came again: 'I am living, I have lived up till now, I have the right to live; but around me is death and destruction. Then why live? Why not die? Why not kill myself immediately? No; I could not. I am afraid. Is it better to wait for death to come when it will? No, that is even worse; and I am also afraid of that. Then, I must live. But what for? In order to die?' I could not get out of that circle. I took a book, and began reading. For a moment it made me forget my thoughts. But then the same questions and the same horror came again. I got into bed, lay down, and shut my eyes. That made the horror worse. God had created things as they are. But why? They say, 'Don't ask; pray.' Well, I did pray; I was praying now, just as I did at Arzamas. At that time I had prayed simply, like a child. Now my prayers had a definite meaning: 'If Thou exist, reveal Thy existence to me. To what end am I created? What am I?' I was bowing to the earth, repeating all the prayers I knew, composing new ones; and I was adding each time, 'Reveal Thy existence to me!' I became quiet, waiting for an answer. But no answer came, as if there were nothing to answer. I was alone with myself and was answering my own questions in place of Him who would not answer. 'What am I created for?' 'To live in a future life,' I answered. 'Then why this uncertainty and torment? I cannot believe in future life. I did believe when I asked, but not with my whole soul. Now I cannot, I cannot! If Thou didst exist, Thou wouldst reveal it to me, to all men. But Thou dost not exist, and there is nothing true but distress.' But I cannot accept that! I rebelled against it; I implored Him to reveal His existence to me. I did all that everybody does, but He did not reveal Himself to me. 'Ask and it shall be given unto you,' I remembered, and began to entreat; in doing so I felt no real comfort, but just surcease of despair. Perhaps it was not entreaty on my part, but only denial of Him. You retreat a step from Him, and He goes from you a mile. I did not believe in Him, and yet here I was entreating Him. But He did not reveal Himself. I was balancing my accounts with Him, and was blaming Him. I simply did not believe.

The next day I used all my endeavours to get through with my affairs somehow during the day, in order to be saved from another night in the hotel room. Although I had not finished everything, I left for home in the evening.

That night at Moscow brought a still greater change into my life, which had been changing ever since the night at Arzamas. I was now paying less attention to my affairs, and grew more and more indifferent to everything around me. My health was also getting bad. My wife urged me to consult a doctor. To her my continual talk about God and religion was a sign of ill-health, whereas I knew I was ill and weak, because of the unsolved questions of religion and of God.

I was trying not to let that question dominate my mind, and continued living amid the old unaltered conditions, filling up my time with incessant occupations. On Sundays and feast days I went to church; I even fasted as I had begun to do since my journey to Pensa, and did not cease to pray. I had no faith in my prayers, but somehow I kept the demand note in my possession instead of tearing it up, and was always presenting it for payment, although I was aware of the impossibility of getting paid. I did it just on the chance. I occupied my days, not with the management of the estate – I felt disgusted with all business because of the struggle it involved – but with the reading of papers, magazines, and novels and with card-playing for small stakes. The only outlet for my energy was hunting. I had kept that up from habit, having been fond of this sport all my life.

One day in winter, a neighbour of mine came with his dogs to hunt wolves. Having arrived at the meeting place we put on snowshoes to walk over the snow and move rapidly along. The hunt was unsuccessful; the wolves contrived to escape through the stockade. As I became aware of that from a distance, I took the direction of the forest to follow the fresh track of a hare. This led me far away into a field. There I spied the hare, but he had disappeared before I could fire. I turned to go back, and had to pass a forest of huge trees. The snow was deep, the snowshoes were sinking in, and the branches were entangling me. The wood was getting thicker and thicker. I wondered where I was, for the snow had changed all the familiar places. Suddenly I realized that I had lost my way. How should I get home or reach the hunting party? Not a sound to guide me! I was tired and bathed in perspiration. If I stopped, I would probably freeze to death; if I walked on, my strength would forsake me. I shouted, but all was quiet, and no answer came. I turned in the opposite direction, which was wrong again, and looked round. Nothing but the wood on every hand. I could not tell which was east or west. I turned back again, but I could hardly move a step. I was frightened, and stopped. The horror I had experienced in Arzamas and in Moscow seized me again, only a hundred times greater. My heart was beating, my hands and feet were shaking. Am I to die here? I don't want to! Why death? What is death? I was about to ask again, to reproach God, when I suddenly felt I must not; I ought not. I had not the right to present any account to Him; He had said all that was necessary, and the fault was wholly mine. I began to implore His forgiveness for I felt disgusted with myself. The horror, however, did not last long. I stood still one moment, plucked up courage, took the direction which seemed to be the right one, and was actually soon out of the wood. I had not been far from its edge when I lost my way. As I came out on the main road, my hands and feet were still shaking, and my heart was beating violently. But my soul was full of joy. I soon found my party, and we all returned home together. I was not quite happy but I knew there was a joy within me which I would understand later on; and that joy proved real. I went to my study to be alone and prayed remembering my sins, and asking for forgiveness. They did not seem to be numerous; but when I thought of what they were they were hateful to me.

Then I began to read the Scriptures. The Old Testament I found incomprehensible but enchanting, the New touching in its meekness. But my favourite reading was now the lives of the saints; they were consoling to me, affording example which seemed more and more possible to follow. Since that time I have grown even less interested in the management of affairs and in family matters. These things even became repulsive to me. Everything was wrong in my eyes. I did not quite realize why they were wrong, but I knew that the things of which my whole life had consisted, now counted for nothing. This was plainly revealed to me again on the occasion of the projected purchase of an estate, which was for sale in our neighbourhood on very advantageous terms. I went to inspect it. Everything was very satisfactory, the more so because the peasants on that estate had no land of their own beyond their vegetable gardens. I grasped at once that in exchange for the right of using the landowner's pasture-ground, they would do all the harvesting for him; and the information I was given proved that I was right. I saw how important that was, and was pleased, as it was in accordance with my old habits of thought. But on my way home I met an old woman who asked her way, and I entered into a conversation with her, during which she told me about her poverty. On returning home, when telling my wife about the advantages the estate afforded, all at once I felt ashamed and disgusted. I said I was not going to buy that estate, for its profits were based on the sufferings of the peasants. I was struck at that moment with the truth of what I was saying, the truth of the peasants having the same desire to live as ourselves, of their being our equals, our brethren, the children of the Father, as the Gospel says. But unexpectedly something which had been gnawing within me for a long time became loosened and was torn away, and something new seemed to be born instead.

My wife was vexed with me and abused me. But I was full of joy. This was the first sign of my madness. My utter madness began to show itself about a month later.

This began by my going to church; I was listening to the Mass with great attention and with a faithful heart, when I was suddenly given a wafer; after which everyone began to move forward to kiss the Cross, pushing each other on all sides. As I was leaving church, beggars were standing on the steps. It became instantly clear to me that this ought not to be, and in reality was not. But if this is not, then there is no death and no fear, and nothing is being torn asunder within me, and I am not afraid of any calamity which may come.

At that moment the full light of the truth was kindled in me, and I grew into what I am now. If all this horror does not necessarily exist around me, then it certainly does exist within me. I distributed on the spot all the money I had among the beggars in the porch, and walked home instead of driving in my carriage as usual, and all the way I talked with the peasants.

Translated by Constance Garnett

Villiers de l'Isle-Adam

The Desire to be a Man

Villiers de l'Isle-Adam was born in Brittany in 1838, the scion of a noble family. During his career as a novelist, playwright, and short story writer, his name was linked with both the Decadent and Symbolist movements in France. Among his several collections of fantastic and macabre tales, his best known works are Contes cruels *and* Axël. *He died in 1889.*

Midnight struck at the Exchange, under a sky filled with stars. In those days, the rigours of martial law still weighed on the city, and in compliance with curfew regulations, waiters of establishments where lights still showed were hurrying to close down. In the cafés along the boulevards, the gaslight butterflies flew swiftly up from the chandeliers, one by one, into the darkness. From outside came the clatter of chairs being stacked in fours on the marble tables; it was the psychological moment when every bartender deems it proper to point, with napkined arm, down the straight and narrow path his last customers must take to the street.

The sad October wind was whistling that Sunday. Sparse yellowed leaves, dusty and rustling, raced along in the gusts, brushing the stones and scraping the paved road, then, like bats, disappeared into the night, reminding one of banal days, spent forever. The theatres of the Boulevard du Crime, where at the evening performance Medicis, Salviatis and Montefeltres had poignarded each other to their hearts' content, loomed like the very haunts of Silence, their mute entrances guarded by caryatids. Carriages and pedestrians became scarcer by the moment. Here and there already gleamed will-o'-the-wisp lanterns of ragpickers, phosphorescences rising from the heaps of refuse over which they rummaged.

At the corner of the Rue Hauteville, under a lamp post by a café of quite elegant appearance, a tall passer-by with saturnine face, a smooth chin, and a somnambulistic gait – long greying hair under a felt hat of Louis XIII style, black-gloved hands clasping an ivory-headed cane and wrapped in an old royal-blue cloak lined with questionable astrakhan – had stopped, as if mechanically hesitating to cross the street that separated him from the Boulevard Bonne-Nouvelle.

Was this late stroller returning home? Had the mere vagaries of a nocturnal walk led him to that street corner? It was hard to tell by his look. In any event, noticing suddenly on his right one of those public mirrors, narrow and long like his own figure, which are sometimes attached to the fronts of showy bars – he came to an abrupt stop, planted himself face to face before his own image, and examined himself from head to toe. Then, suddenly, he raised his hat with a gesture that recalled the past and gave himself a rather ceremonious salute.

His head, thus unexpectedly bared, showed him to be the celebrated tragedian Esprit Chaudval, born Lepeinteur, called Monanteuil, scion of a very respectable family of Saint-Malo pilots, whom the mysteries of Destiny had led to become a leading player in the provinces, a star of productions abroad, and a rival (often with success) of our great Frédéric Lemaître.

While he stared at himself in this sort of stupor, the waiters of the café were helping the last habitués into their coats and getting their hats down off the hooks for them; others noisily spilled the contents of their metal cash-boxes and piled up the day's coins in cylinders on a tray. This haste and fluster was produced by the ominous presence of two unexpected policemen, who stood in the doorway, arms crossed, and harassed the laggard barkeeper with their cold stare. In a little while the shutters were bolted into their iron frames – except the one for the mirror, which by a strange oversight was neglected in the midst of the general rush.

Then the boulevard grew very quiet. Chaudval alone, heedless of all these disappearances, remained in his trance-like attitude at the corner of the Rue Hauteville, on the pavement before the forgotten mirror.

This pale lunary mirror seemed to give the artist the sensation of bathing in a pond; Chaudval shivered.

Alas! let us admit it, in that cruel, sombre crystal the actor had just perceived himself growing old.

He noted that his hair, yesterday only sprinkled with grey, was turning silvery. Well, that was that! Farewell curtain-calls and wreaths, farewell roses of Thalia and Melpomene's laurels. He must take leave forever, with shaking of hands and with tears, of beaux and grisettes, of noble liveries and shapely curves, of valets and ingenues.

He must get down at once from the chariot of Thespis and watch it disappear in the distance, bearing his comrades! Watch the tinsel and the pennants which, in the morning, had fluttered in the sun even on the very wheels of the chariot, playthings of the joyous wind of Hope – watch them disappear into the twilight at the distant bend in the road.

Chaudval, rudely awakened to his fifty years (he was really a good fellow), sighed. A mist passed before his eyes; a kind of wintry fever seized him, and hallucinations dilated his pupils.

The wild fixity with which his gaze plumbed the mirror providence had placed before him finally gave his pupils the faculty of magnifying objects and suffusing them with solemnity, which physiologists have noted in individuals affected by a very intense emotion.

The long mirror thus took on different shapes under those eyes filled with troubled, amorphous thoughts. Memories of childhood, of beaches and silvery waves, danced in his brain. And the mirror, doubtless because of the stars, which lent depth to its surface, at first gave him the sensation of the somnolent waters of a bay. Then, swelling further, through the old fellow's sighs, it took on the aspect of the sea and the night, those two age-old friends of desolate hearts.

He intoxicated himself for some time on this vision, but the street lamp, which from overhead cast a red glow on the cold drizzle behind him, came back to him reflected from the depth of that fearful glass as the flare of a blood-coloured beacon, pointing the way to shipwreck for the lost vessel of his future.

He shook off this spell and drew himself up to his full height with a nervous burst of forced, bitter laughter which made the two policemen under the trees shiver. Fortunately for the artist, they thought him some harmless drunk or some disappointed lover, and they continued their round without giving the miserable Chaudval another thought.

'All right, then, we renounce,' he said simply and in a low voice, as the man condemned to die, awakened suddenly, says to the executioner: 'I am yours, friend.'

Thereupon the old actor, in dazed dejection, wandered off into a monologue:

'I acted wisely the other night when I asked my old friend Mlle Pinson, who shares the good will, not to speak of the bed, of the Minister, to get me, between two burning avowals of passion, that position of lighthouse-keeper which my ancestors held on the Breton coast. Ah, hold it! now I understand the strange effect the street light produced on me in the mirror! ... It expressed my subconscious thought ... Pinson is going to send me my appointment, that's sure. And then I retire into my lighthouse, like a rat into a cheese. I shall light the way for distant ships at sea. A lighthouse! There's always something of a stage-set about one. I am all alone in the world; what better refuge could there be for my old days?'

Chaudval suddenly interrupted his reverie.

'Well, I'll be ... !' he said, feeling in his breast beneath his cloak, 'Why ... that letter the mailman gave me just as I was going out ... it must be the reply! What the devil, I was just going into this café to read it, and I forgot all about it! I'm really in a bad way. Ah! here we are.'

Chaudval took a large envelope out of his pocket, from which there fell, as soon as he opened it, an official looking letter. He snatched it up feverishly and ran through it in a glance by the red glare of the street lamp.

'My lighthouse! my appointment!' he cried. 'Saved, oh my God!' he added mechanically, as though from old habit, and in a falsetto voice so sudden and so different from his own that he looked about him for a third person present.

'Here now, let's be calm, and ...' he added a moment later, *'be a man!'*

But at these words, Esprit Chaudval, born Lepeinteur, known as Monanteuil, stopped as if turned to a statue; the word seemed to have immobilized him.

'What?' he continued after a pause, 'What was that I just wished? To be a Man? ... After all, why not?'

He folded his arms and reflected.

'Here it is nearly half a century that I have been *impersonating*, that I have been *play-acting* the passions of others, without ever feeling them myself – for, deep down, I myself have never felt anything. It's a joke to think I'm anything like those others! Am I then only a *shadow*? Passions! Feelings! Real acts! REAL ONES! That's it, that's what constitutes a MAN in the true sense of the word! Well, since age forces me to rejoin the human race, I must find some passions for myself, some *real* feeling ..., since that is the condition *sine qua non*, without which one cannot possibly pretend to the title of Man. There's solid reasoning for you; the logic stares you in the face. Now what emotion would be most in keeping with my true nature, at last brought back to life?'

He thought awhile, then went on sadly:

'Love? – Too late. Glory? – I've had my share! Ambition? – Let's leave that trash to politicians.'

Suddenly he cried out.

'I have it' he said: 'REMORSE! There's something that goes with my dramatic temperament.'

He looked at himself in the mirror, putting on a face convulsed and contorted as if by an inhuman horror.

'That's it!' he concluded: 'Nero! Macbeth! Orestes! Hamlet! Erostratus! – Ghosts! Ah yes! I too want to see *true* ghosts, like all those fellows who were lucky enough to be hardly able to take a step without ghosts.'

He struck his forehead.

'But *how?* I am as innocent as a newly-born lamb.'

And, after another stage-pause:

'Let that be no obstacle!' he went on: 'where there's a will, there's a way! ... I certainly have the right to become, at any cost, what I *ought* to be. I have a right to my Humanity. To feel remorse one must have committed crimes? Very well, crimes we shall have. What does it matter, once it is for ... the good cause. Yes – so be it.' (And here he fell into dialogue): 'I shall commit horrifying ones.' 'When?' 'Right away. Let's not put off to tomorrow!' 'What crimes?' 'Just one! ... But a great one, of the wildest atrocity, of a kind to loose all the Furies of hell!' 'Which?' 'Why, the most dazzling ... Bravo! I've got it! ARSON! The steps are simple: I set fire, pack my trunks, return properly crouched behind the window of some cab to enjoy my triumph in the midst of the horror-stricken crowd, carefully gather up the curses of the dying – then catch the northwest train, with enough remorse stocked up to last me the rest of my days. After that, I go into hiding in my lighthouse! In the very heart of the spotlight, right in the middle of the ocean! Where the police will consequently never be able to find me, my crime being *gratuitous*. And there I shall writhe in solitude.' (At this point Chaudval straightened up and improvised a line positively worthy of Corneille):

Guarded from suspicion by the grandeur of the crime!

'Is is said. And now,' concluded the great artist, picking up a cobblestone and looking around to make sure he was alone, 'and now, as for you, you shall never again reflect anyone.'

And he hurled the stone against the mirror, which broke into a thousand gleaming slivers.

This first duty accomplished, Chaudval made off hurriedly, as if satisfied with this preliminary but energetic feat of daring, and hastened towards the boulevards, where a few minutes later he signalled a carriage, jumped in, and disappeared.

Two hours later, the flames of an immense conflagration, leaping from large warehouses of kerosene, oil, and matches, were reflected from all the windowpanes of the Temple quarter. Soon companies of firemen, dragging and pushing their equipment, converged from all sides and the dismal blasts of their horns startled awake the inhabitants of this crowded neighbourhood. Innumerable hurrying footsteps rang out on the pavements; the crowd jammed the large Place du Château d'Eau and the adjoining streets. Bucket brigades were already hastily forming. Within fifteen minutes, a detachment of troops had thrown up a cordon around the scene of the blaze. Policemen working by the bloody glare of torches kept back the crowd.

Vehicles, trapped, no longer moved. Everyone was shouting. Distant cries could be made out amidst the terrible crackling of the fire. The victims, caught in this inferno, screamed, and the roofs of the houses crashed in on them. A hundred families of workmen employed in the burning factories were left destitute and homeless.

Off to a side, a solitary carriage loaded with two large trunks stood behind the crowd thronging the square. And in that carriage sat Esprit Chaudval, born Lepeinteur, called Monanteuil; from time to time he pulled aside the blind and contemplated his handiwork.

'Ah!' he said to himself softly, 'What an object of horror I feel I am before God and man! That, that is the true mark of Cain!'

The face of the good old actor beamed.

'O wretch,' he muttered, 'what sleepless nights I shall savour, surrounded by the vengeful ghosts of my victims! I feel welling in me the soul of Nero, burning Rome for artistic exaltation! Of Erostratus, burning the temple of Ephesus for love of glory! Of Rostopchin, burning Moscow through patriotism! Of Alexander, burning Persepolis as a chivalrous gesture to his immortal Thaïs! ... As for me, I burn from duty, having no other method of *existence*! I burn because I owe myself to myself! I am squaring accounts! What a Man I'm going to be! How I shall live! Yes, at last I am going to know what it feels like to be tormented. What nights, magnificent with horror, I am going to spend deliciously! ... Ah! I breathe again! I am reborn! I exist! When I think that I have been an actor ...! Now that I am, in the gross eyes of mortals, only gallows-game, it is time to flee like lightning and shut myself up in my lighthouse, to enjoy my remorse in peace.'

The day after next, in the evening, Chaudval arrived at his destination without incident and took possession of his old desolate lighthouse, a flame fallen into disuse, over a ruined pile of masonry, which official compassion had relit for him.

The signal could scarcely be of any use; it was a mere superfluity, a sinecure, a dwelling with a light overhead, which the whole world could have done without, except Chaudval.

So the worthy tragedian, having brought there his bed, supplies of food, and a large mirror in which to study his facial expressions, shut himself up at once, far from all human suspicion.

Around him moaned the sea, in which the ancient abyss of the heavens bathed its starry brilliance. He watched the waves, driven by the windy gusts, assail his tower, as Stylites might have contemplated the sands swirling around his column in the breath of the hot desert wind.

In the distance he followed with an empty stare the smoke of steamers or the sails of fishing boats.

Every other moment, the fire he had set kept slipping this dreamer's mind. He went up and down his stone staircase.

On the evening of the third day, then, Lepeinteur sat in his room, sixty feet above the billows, rereading in a Paris newspaper the story of the great disaster that had occurred two days before.

An unknown criminal had tossed some matches into stores of inflammable fluids. An enormous fire, which had kept firemen and residents of neighbouring districts up all night, had broken out in the Temple quarter.

Nearly a hundred victims had perished; whole families of unfortunates had been plunged into darkest misery.

The entire square, still smoking, was in mourning.

The identity of the wretch who had committed the foul crime was unknown, and above all the criminal's *motive*.

Upon reading this, Chaudval jumped for joy and feverishly rubbed his hands, shouting: 'What a success! What a marvellous scoundrel I am! Am I going to be haunted enough? What ghosts I shall see! I knew I would become a Man! ... Ah, the means were drastic, I admit, but it had to be! . . . It had to be!'

Reading over the Paris paper again, he came across mention of a special benefit performance to be given on behalf of the victims of the fire.

'Indeed,' Chaudval murmured, 'I should have offered the collaboration of my talent for the benefit of my victims! It would have been my farewell performance. I would have recited *Orestes*. I'd have been absolutely convincing . . .'

Thereupon Chaudval began life in his lighthouse.

And the evenings fell, succeeded one another, and the nights.

Something happened that dumbfounded the artist. Something dreadful!

Contrary to his hopes and expectations, his conscience gave him no pangs of remorse at all. Not a single ghost appeared. He felt *nothing – but absolutely nothing!*

The silence was beyond belief. He could not get over it.

Sometimes, as he looked into the mirror, he noticed that his good-natured expression had not changed at all. Furious then, he would rush to his signals and mix them up, in the fervent hope of causing some distant ship to sink, in order to stir up, activate, and prod his stubborn remorse – to rouse the ghosts.

All in vain!

Sterile crimes! Wasted efforts! He felt *nothing*. He saw not a single threatening phantom. He could no longer sleep, so choked was he by despair and *shame*. So much so that one night, suffering a cerebral seizure in his luminous solitude, he cried out in his death agony, amidst the roar of the ocean, while the great winds of the open sea lashed his tower lost in the infinite:

'Ghosts! For the love of God ... Let me see even one Ghost! *Haven't I earned it?*'

But the God whom he invoked did not grant him this favour, and the old player died still declaiming futilely in his emphatic style his great wish to see ghosts – *without understanding that he himself was what he was looking for.*

Translated by Harry Levtow

Miguel de Unamuno

Saint Emmanuel the Good, Martyr

> *Miguel de Unamuno was born in Bilbao, Spain, in 1864. A well-known philosopher* (The Tragic Sense of Life) *and teacher, Unamuno wrote several short novels such as* Abel Sanchez *and* The Madness of Dr Montarco, *in which the individual is pitted in a death struggle against the rest of society. He died in 1936.*

If with this life only in view we have had hope in Christ, we are of all men the most to be pitied.

Saint Paul: 1 Cor. 15:19

Now that the bishop of the diocese of Renada, to which this my beloved village of Valverde de Lucerna belongs, is seeking (according to rumour), to initiate the process of beatification of our Don Manuel, or more correctly, Saint Emmanuel the Good, who was parish priest here, I want to state in writing, by way of confession (although to what end only God, and not I can say), all that I can vouch for and remember of that matriarchal man who pervaded the most secret life of my soul, who was my true spiritual father, the father of my spirit, the spirit of myself, Angela Carballino.

The other, my flesh-and-blood temporal father, I scarcely knew, for he died when I was still a very young girl. I know that he came to Valverde de Lucerna from the outside world – that he was a stranger – and that he settled here when he married my mother. He had brought a number of books with him: *Don Quixote*, some plays from the classic theatre, some novels, a few histories, the *Bertoldo*, everything all mixed together. From these books (practically the only ones in the entire village), I nurtured dreams as a young girl, dreams which in turn devoured me. My good mother gave me very little account either of the words or the deeds of my father. For the words and deeds of Don Manuel, whom she worshipped, of whom she was enamoured, in common with all the rest of the village – in an exquisitely chaste manner, of course – had obliterated the memory of the words and deeds of her husband; him she commended to God, with full fervour, as she said her daily rosary.

Don Emmanuel I remember as if it were yesterday, from the time when I was a girl of ten, just before I was taken to the convent school in the cathedral city of Renada. At that time Don Emmanuel, our saint, must have been about thirty-seven years old. He was tall, slender, erect; he carried himself the way our Buitre Peak carries its crest, and his eyes had all the blue depth of our lake. As he walked he commanded all eyes, and not only the eyes but the hearts of all; gazing round at us he seemed to look through our flesh as through glass and penetrate our hearts. We all of us loved him, especially the children. And the things he said to us! Not words, things! The villagers could scent the odour of sanctity, they were intoxicated with it.

It was at this time that my brother Lazarus, who was in America, from where he regularly sent us money with which we lived in decent leisure, had my mother send me to the convent school, so that my education might be completed outside the village; he suggested this move despite the fact that he had no special fondness for the nuns. 'But since, as far as I know,' he wrote us, 'there are no lay schools there yet – especially not for young ladies – we will have to make use of the ones that do exist. The important thing is for Angelita to receive some polish and not be forced to continue among village girls.' And so I entered the convent school. At one point I even thought I would become a teacher; but pedagogy soon palled upon me.

At school I met girls from the city and I made friends with some of them. But I still kept in touch with people in our village, and I received frequent reports and sometimes a visit.

And the fame of the parish priest reached as far as the school, for he was beginning to be talked of in the cathedral city. The nuns never tired of asking me about him.

Ever since early youth I had been endowed, I don't very well know from where, with a large degree of curiosity and restlessness, due at least in part to that jumble of books which my father had collected, and these qualities were stimulated at school, especially in the course of a relationship which I developed with a girl friend, who grew excessively attached to me. At times she proposed that we enter the same convent together, swearing to an everlasting 'sisterhood' – and even that we seal the oath in blood. At other times she talked to me, with eyes half closed, of sweethearts and marriage adventures.

Strangely enough, I have never heard of her since, or of what became of her, despite the fact that whenever our Don Manuel was spoken of, or when my mother wrote me something about him in her letters – which happened in almost every letter – and I read it to her, this girl would exclaim, as if in rapture: 'What luck, my dear, to be able to live near a saint like that, a live saint, of flesh and blood, and to be able to kiss his hand; when you go back to your village write me everything, everything, and tell me about him.'

Five years passed at school, five years which now have evanesced in memory like a dream at dawn, and when I became fifteen I returned to my own Valverde de Lucerna. By now everything revolved around Don Emmanuel: Don Emmanuel, the lake and the mountain. I arrived home anxious to know him, to place myself under his protection, and hopeful he would set me on my path in life.

It was rumoured that he had entered the seminary to become a priest so that he might thus look after the sons of a sister recently widowed and provide for them in place of their father; that in the seminary his keen mind and his talents had distinguished him and that he had subsequently turned down opportunities for a brilliant career in the church because he wanted to remain exclusively a part of his Valverde de Lucerna, of his remote village which lay like a brooch between the lake and the mountain reflected in it.

How he did love his people! His life consisted in salvaging wrecked marriages, in forcing unruly sons to submit to their parents, or reconciling parents to their sons, and, above all, of consoling the embittered and the weary in spirit; meanwhile he helped everyone to die well.

I recall, among other incidents, the occasion when the unfortunate daughter of old aunt Rabona returned to our town. She had been in the city and lost her virtue there; now she returned unmarried and cast off, and she brought back a little son. Don Emmanuel did not rest until he had persuaded an old sweetheart, Perote by name, to marry the poor girl and, moreover, to legitimize the little creature with his own name. Don Emmanuel told Perote:

'Come now, give this poor waif a father, for he hasn't got one except in heaven.'

'But, Don Emmanuel, it's not my fault . . .!'

'Who knows, my son, who knows . . .! And besides, it's not a question of guilt.'

And today, poor Perote, inspired on that occasion to saintliness by Don Emmanuel, and now a paralytic and invalid, has for staff and consolation of his life the son he accepted as his own when the boy was not his at all.

On Midsummer's Night, the shortest night of the year, it was a local custom here (and still is) for all the old crones, and a few old men, who thought they were possessed or bewitched (hysterics they were, for the most part, or in some cases epileptics) to flock to the lake. Don Emmanuel undertook to fulfil the same function as the lake, to serve as a pool of healing, to treat his charges and even, if possible, to cure them. And such was the effect of his presence, of his gaze, and above all of his voice – the miracle of his voice! – and the infinitely sweet authority of his words, that he actually did achieve some remarkable cures. Whereupon his fame increased, drawing all the sick of the environs to our lake and our priest. And yet once when a mother came to ask for a miracle in behalf of her son, he answered her with a sad smile:

'Ah, but I don't have my bishop's permission to perform miracles.'

He was particularly interested in seeing that all the villagers kept themselves clean. If he chanced upon someone with a torn garment he would send him to the church: 'Go and see the sacristan, and let him mend that tear.' The sacristan was a tailor, and when, on the first day of the year, everyone went to congratulate him on his saint's day – his holy patron was Our Lord Jesus Himself – it was by Don Emmanuel's wish that everyone appeared in a new shirt, and those that had none received the present of a new one from Don Emmanuel himself.

He treated everyone with the greatest kindness; if he favoured anyone, it was the most unfortunate, and especially those who rebelled. There was a congenital idiot in the village, the fool Blasillo, and it was towards him that Don Emmanuel chose to show the greatest love and concern; as a consequence he succeeded in miraculously teaching him things which had appeared beyond the idiot's comprehension. The fact was that the embers of understanding feebly glowing in the idiot were kindled whenever, like a pitiable monkey, he imitated his Don Emmanuel.

The marvel of the man was his voice; a divine voice which brought one close to weeping. Whenever he officiated at Solemn High Mass and intoned the prelude, a tremor ran through the congregation and all within sound of his voice were moved to the depths of their being. The sound of his chanting, overflowing the church, went on to float over the lake and settle at the foot of the mountain. And when on Good Friday he intoned 'My God, my God, my God, why hast Thou forsaken me?' a profound shudder swept through the multitude, like the lash of a north-easter across the waters of the lake. It was as if these people heard the Lord Jesus Christ himself, as if the voice sprang from the ancient crucifix, at the foot of which generations of mothers had offered up their sorrows. And it happened that on one occasion his mother heard him and was unable to contain herself, and cried out to him right in the church, 'My son!', calling her child. And the entire congregation was visibly affected. It was as if the mother's cry had issued from the half-open lips of the Mater Dolorosa – her heart transfixed by seven swords – which stood in one of the chapels of the nave. Afterwards, the fool Blasillo went about piteously repeating, as if he were an echo, 'My God, my God, my God, why hast Thou forsaken me?' with such effect that everyone who heard him was moved to tears, to the great satisfaction of the fool, who prided himself on this triumph of imitation.

The priest's effect on people was such that no one ever dared to tell him a lie, and everyone confessed themselves to him without need of a confessional. So true was this that on one occasion, when a revolting crime had been committed in a neighbouring village, the judge – a dull fellow who badly misunderstood Don Emmanuel – called on the priest and said:

'Let us see, Don Manuel, if you can get this bandit to admit the truth.'

'So that afterwards you may punish him?' asked the saintly man. 'No, Judge; I will not extract from any man a truth which could be the death of him. That is a matter between him and his God ... Human justice is none of my affair. "Judge not that ye be not judged," said our Lord.'

'But the fact is, Father, that I, a judge ...'

'I understand. You, Judge, must render unto Caesar that which is Caesar's, while I shall render unto God that which is God's.'

And, as Don Emmanuel departed, he gazed at the suspected criminal and said:

'Make sure, only, that God forgives you, for that is all that matters.'

Everyone went to Mass in the village, even if it were only to hear him and see him at the altar, where he appeared to be transfigured, his countenance lit from within. He introduced one holy practice to the popular cult; it consisted in assembling the whole town inside the church, men and women, ancients and youths, some thousand persons; there we recited the Creed, in unison, so that it sounded like a single voice: 'I believe in God, the Almighty Father, Creator of heaven and earth ...' and all the rest. It was not a chorus, but a single voice, a simple united voice, all the voices based on one on which they formed a kind of mountain, whose peak, lost at times in the clouds, was Don Emmanuel. As we reached the section, 'I believe in the resurrection of the flesh and life everlasting'. the voice of Don Emmanuel was submerged, drowned in the voice of the populace as in a lake. In truth, he was silent. And I could hear the bells of that city which is said hereabouts to be at the bottom of the lake – bells which are also said to be audible on Midsummer's Night – the bells of the city which is submerged in the spiritual lake of our populace; I was hearing the voice of our dead, resurrected in us by the communion of saints. Later, when I had learned the secret of our saint, I understood that it was as if a caravan crossing the desert lost its leader as they approached the goal of their trek, whereupon his people lifted him on their shoulders to bring his lifeless body into the promised land.

When it came to dying themselves, most of the villagers refused to die unless they were holding on to Don Emmanuel's hand, as if to an anchor chain.

In his sermons he never inveighed again unbelievers, Masons, liberals or heretics. What for, when there were none in the village? Nor did it occur to him to speak against the wickedness of the press. On the other hand, one of his most frequent themes was gossip, against which he lashed out.

'Envy,' he liked to repeat, 'envy is nurtured by those who prefer to think they are envied, and most persecutions are the result of a persecution complex rather than of an impulse to persecute.'

'But Don Emmanuel, just listen to what that fellow was trying to tell me ...'

'We should concern ourselves less with what people are trying to tell us than with what they tell us without trying ...'

His life was active rather than contemplative, and he constantly fled from idleness, even from leisure. Whenever he heard it said that idleness was the mother of all the vices, he added: 'And also of the greatest vice of them all, which is to think idly.' Once I asked him what he meant and he answered: 'Thinking idly is thinking as a substitute for doing, or thinking too much about what is already done instead of about what must be done. What's done is done and over with, and one must go on to something else, for there is nothing worse than remorse without possible relief.' Action! Action! Even in those early days I had already begun to realize that Don Emmanuel fled from being left to think in solitude, and I guessed that some obsession haunted him.

And so it was that he was always occupied, sometimes even occupied in searching for occupations. He wrote very little on his own, so that he scarcely left us anything in writing, even notes; on the other hand, he acted as scrivener for everyone else, especially mothers, for whom he composed letters to their absent sons.

He also worked with his hands, pitching in to help with some of the village tasks. At threshing time he reported to the threshing floor to flail and winnow, meanwhile teaching and entertaining the workers by turn. Sometimes he took the place of a worker who had fallen sick. One day in the dead of winter he came upon a child, shivering with the bitter cold. The child's father had sent him into the woods to bring back a strayed calf.

'Listen,' he said to the child, 'you go home and get warm, and tell your father that I am bringing back the calf.' On the way back with the animal he ran into the father, who had come out to meet him, thoroughly ashamed of himself.

In winter he chopped wood for the poor. When a certain magnificent walnut tree died – 'that matriarchal walnut', he called it, a tree under whose shade he had played as a boy and whose fruit he had eaten for so many years – he asked for the trunk, carried it to his house and, after he had cut six planks from it, which he put away at the foot of his bed, he made firewood of the rest to warm the poor. He also was in the habit of making handballs for the boys and a goodly number of toys for the younger children.

Often he used to accompany the doctor on his rounds, adding his presence and prestige to the doctor's prescriptions. Most of all he was interested in maternity cases and the care of children; it was his opinion that the old wives' sayings 'from the cradle to heaven' and the other one about 'little angels belong in heaven' were nothing short of blasphemy. The death of a child moved him deeply.

'A child stillborn,' I once heard him say, 'or one who dies soon after birth, is the most terrible of mysteries to me. It's as if it were suicide. Or as if the child were crucified.'

And once, when a man had taken his own life and the father of the suicide, an outsider, asked Don Emmanuel if his son could be buried in consecrated ground, the priest answered:

'Most certainly, for at the last moment, in the very last throes, he must certainly have repented. There is no doubt of it whatsoever in my mind.'

From time to time he would visit the local shop to help the teacher, to teach alongside him – and not only the catechism. The simple truth was that he fled relentlessly from idleness and from solitude. He went so far in this desire of his to mingle with the villagers, especially the youth and the children, that he even attended the village dances. And more than once he played the drum to keep time for the young men and women dancing; this kind of activity, which in another priest would have seemed like a grotesque mockery of his calling, in him somehow took on the appearance of a holy and religious exercise. When the Angelus would ring out, he would put down the drum and sticks, take off his hat (all the others doing the same) and pray: 'The angel of the Lord declared unto Mary: Hail Mary ...' And afterwards: 'Now, let us rest until tomorrow.'

'First of all,' he would say, 'the village must be happy; everyone must be happy to be alive. To be satisfied with life is of first importance. No one should want to die until it is God's will.'

'I want to die now,' a recently widowed woman once told him, 'I want to be with my husband ...'

'And why now?' he asked. 'Stay here and pray God for his soul.'

One of his well-loved remarks was made at a wedding: 'Ah, if I could only change all the water in our lake into wine, into a dear little wine which, no matter how much of it one drank, would always make one joyful without intoxicating ... or, if intoxicating, would make one joyfully drunk.'

Once upon a time a band of poor acrobats came through the village. The leader – who arrived on the scene with a gravely ill and pregnant wife and three sons to help him – played the clown. While he was in the village square making all the children, and even some of the adults, laugh with glee, his wife suddenly fell desperately ill and had to leave; she went off accompanied by a look of anguish from the clown and a howl of laughter from the children. Don Emmanuel hurried after, and, a little later, in a corner of the inn's stable, he helped her give up her soul in a state of grace. When the performance was over and the villagers and the clown learned of the tragedy, they came to the inn, and there the poor bereaved clown, in a voice choked with tears, told Don Emmanuel, as he took his hand and kissed it: 'They are quite right, Father, when they say you are a saint.' Don Emmanuel took the clown's hand in his and replied before everyone:

'It's you who are the saint, good clown. I watched you at your work and understood that you do it not only to provide bread for your children, but also to give to the children of others. And I tell you now that your wife, the mother of your children, whom I sent to God while you worked to give joy, is at rest in the Lord, and that you will join her there, and that the angels, whom you will make laugh with happiness in heaven, will reward you with their laughter.'

And everyone present wept, children and elders alike, as much from sorrow as from a mysterious joy in which all sorrow was drowned. Later, recalling that solemn hour, I have come to realize that the imperturbable joyousness of Don Emmanuel was merely the temporal, earthly form of an infinite, eternal sadness which the priest concealed from the eyes and ears of the world with heroic saintliness.

His constant activity, his ceaseless intervention in the tasks and diversions of everyone, had the appearance, in short, of a flight from himself, of a flight from solitude. He confirmed this suspicion: 'I have a fear of solitude,' he would say. And still, from time to time he would go off by himself, along the shores of the lake, to the ruins of the abbey where the souls of pious Cistercians seem still to repose, although history has long since buried them in oblivion. There, the cell of the so-called Father-Captain can still be found, and it is said that the drops of blood spattered on the walls as he flagellated himself can still be seen. What thoughts occupied our Don Emmanuel as he walked there? I remember a conversation we held once in which I asked him, as he was speaking of the abbey, why it had never occurred to him to enter a monastery, and he answered me:

'It is not at all because of the fact that my sister is a widow and I have her children and herself to support – for God looks after the poor – but rather because I simply was not born to be a hermit, an anchorite; the solitude would crush my soul; and, as far as a monastery is concerned, my monastery is Valverde de Lucerna. I was not meant to live alone, or die alone. I was meant to live for my village, and die for it too. How should I save my soul if I were not to save the soul of my village as well?'

'But there have been saints who were hermits, solitaries . . .' I said.

'Yes, the Lord gave them the grace of solitude which He has denied me, and I must resign myself. I must throw away my village to win my soul. God made me that way. I would not be able to resist the temptations of the desert. I would not be able, alone, to carry the cross of birth . . .'

I have summoned up all these recollections, from which my faith was fed, in order to portray our Don Emmanuel as he was when I, a young girl of sixteen, returned from the convent of Renada to our 'monastery of Valverde de Lucerna', once more to kneel at the feet of our 'abbot'.

'Well, here is the daughter of Simona,' he said as soon as he saw me, 'made into a young woman, and knowing French, and how to play the piano, and embroider, and heaven knows what else besides! Now you must get ready to give us a family. And your brother Lazarus;

when does he return? Is he still in the New World?'

'Yes, Father, he is still in the New World.'

'The New World! And we in the Old. Well then, when you write him, tell him for me, on behalf of the parish priest, that I should like to know when he is returning from the New World to the Old, to bring us the latest from over there. And tell him that he will find the lake and the mountain as he left them.'

When I first went to him for confession, I became so confused that I could not enunciate a word. I recited the 'Forgive me, Father, for I have sinned', in a stammer, almost a sob. And he, observing this, said:

'Good heavens, my dear, what are you afraid of, or of whom are you afraid? Certainly you're not trembling now under the weight of your sins, nor in the fear of God. No, you're trembling because of me, isn't that so?'

At this point I burst into tears.

'What have they been telling you about me? What fairy tales? Was it your mother, perhaps? Come, come, please be calm; you must imagine you are talking to your brother ...'

At this I plucked up courage and began to tell him of my anxieties, doubts and sorrows.

'Bah! Where did you read all this, Miss Intellectual. All this is literary nonsense. Don't succumb to everything you read just yet, not even to Saint Theresa. If you need to amuse yourself, read the *Bertoldo*, as your father before you did.'

I came away from my first confession to that holy man deeply consoled. The initial fear – simple fright more than respect – with which I had approached him, turned into a profound pity. I was at the time a very young woman, almost a girl still; and yet, I was beginning to be a woman, in my innermost being I felt the juice and stirrings of maternity, and when I found myself in the confessional at the side of the saintly priest, I sensed a kind of unspoken confession on his part in the soft murmur of his voice. And I remembered how when he had intoned in the church the words of Jesus Christ: 'My God, my God, why hast Thou forsaken me?' his own mother had cried out in the congregation: 'My son!'; and I could hear the cry that had rent the silence of the temple. And I went to him again for confession – and to comfort him.

Another time in the confessional I told him of a doubt which assailed me, and he responded:

'As to that, you know what the catechism says. Don't question me about it, for I am ignorant; in Holy Mother Church there are learned doctors of theology who will know how to answer you.'

'But you are the learned doctor here.'

'Me? A learned doctor? Not even in thought! I, my little doctress, am only a poor country priest. And those questions ... do you know who whispers them into your ear? Well ... the Devil does!'

Then, making bold, I asked him point-blank:

'And suppose he were to whisper these questions to you?'

'Who? To me? The Devil? No, we don't even know each other, my daughter, we haven't met at all.'

'But if he did whisper them? ...'

'I wouldn't pay any attention. And that's enough of that; let's get on, for there are some people, really sick people, waiting for me.'

I went away thinking, I don't know why, that our Don Emmanuel, so famous for curing the bedevilled, didn't really even believe in the Devil. As I started home, I ran into the fool Blasillo, who had probably been hovering around outside; as soon as he saw me, and by way of treating me to a display of his virtuosity, he began the business of repeating – and in what a manner! – 'My God, my God, why hast Thou forsaken me?' I arrived home utterly saddened and locked myself in my room to cry, until finally my mother arrived.

'With all these confessions, Angelita, you will end by going off to a nunnery.'

'Don't worry, Mother,' I answered her. 'I have plenty to do here in the village, and it will be my only convent.'

'Until you marry.'

'I don't intend to,' I rejoined.

The next time I saw Don Emmanuel I asked him, looking straight into his eyes:

'Is there really a Hell, Don Emmanuel?'

And he, without altering his expression, answered:

'For you, my daughter, no.'

'For others, then?'

'Does it matter to you, if you are not to go there?'

'It matters for the others, in any case. Is there a Hell?'

'Believe in Heaven, the Heaven we can see. Look at it there' – and he pointed to the heavens above the mountain, and then down into the lake, to the reflection.

'But we are supposed to believe in Hell as well as in Heaven,' I said.

'That's true. We must believe everything believed and taught by our Holy Mother Church, Catholic, Apostolic, and Roman. And now, that will do!'

I thought I read a deep unknown sadness in his eyes, eyes which were as blue as the waters of the lake.

Those years passed as if in a dream. Within me, a reflected image of Don Emmanuel was unconsciously taking form. He was an ordinary enough man in many ways, of such daily use as the daily bread we asked for in our Paternoster. I helped him whenever I could with his tasks, visiting the sick, his sick, the girls at school, and helping, too, with the church linen and the vestments; I served in the role, as he said, of his deaconess. Once I was invited to the city for a few days by a school friend, but I had to hurry home, for the city stifled me – something was missing, I was thirsty for a sight of the waters of the lake, hungry for a sight of the peaks of the mountain; and even more, I missed my Don Emmanuel, as if his absence called to me, as if he were endangered by my being so far away, as if he were in need of me. I began to feel a kind of maternal affection for my spiritual father; I longed to help him bear the cross of birth.

My twenty-fourth birthday was approaching when my brother Lazarus came back from America with the small fortune he had saved up. He came back to Valverde de Lucerna with the intention of taking me and my mother to live in a city, perhaps even Madrid.

'In the country,' he said, 'in these villages, a person becomes stupefied, brutalized and spiritually impoverished.' And he added: 'Civilization is the very opposite of everything countrified. The idiocy of village life! No, that's not for us; I didn't have you sent away to school so that later you might spoil here, among these ignorant peasants.'

I said nothing, though I was disposed to resist emigration. But our mother, already past sixty, took a firm stand from the start: 'Change pastures at my age?' she demanded at once. A little later she made it quite clear that she could not live out of sight of her lake, her mountain, and, above all, of her Don Emmanuel.

'The two of you are like those cats that get attached to houses,' my brother muttered.

When he realized the complete sway exercised over the entire village – especially over my mother and myself – by the saintly priest, my brother began to resent him. He saw in this situation an example of the obscurantist theocracy which, according to him, smothered Spain. And he commenced to spout the old anti-clerical commonplaces, to which he added anti-religious and 'progressive' propaganda brought back from the New World.

'In the Spain of sloth and flabby useless men, the priests manipulate the women, and the women manipulate the men. Not to mention the idiocy of the country, and this feudal backwater!'

'Feudal,' to him, meant something frightful. 'Feudal' and 'medieval' were the epithets he employed to condemn something completely.

The failure of his diatribes to move us and their total lack of effect upon the village – where they were listened to with respectful indifference – disconcerted him no end. 'The man does not exist who could move these clods.' But, he soon began to understand – for he was an intelligent man, and therefore a good one – the kind of influence exercised over the village by Don Emmanuel, and he came to appreciate the effect of the priest's work in the village.

'This priest is not like the others,' he announced. 'He is, in fact, a saint.'

'How do you know what the others are like,' I asked. To which he answered:

'I can imagine.'

In any case, he did not set foot inside the church nor did he miss an opportunity to parade his incredulity – though he always exempted Don Emmanuel from his scorning accusations. In the village, an unconscious expectancy began to build up, the anticipation of a kind of duel between my brother Lazarus and Don Emmanuel – in short, it was expected that Don Emmanuel would convert my brother. No one doubted but that in the end the priest would bring him into the fold. On his side, Lazarus was eager (he told me himself, later) to go and hear Don Emmanuel, to see and hear him in the church, to get to know him and to talk with him, so that he might learn the secret of his spiritual hold over our souls. And he let himself be coaxed to this end, so that finally – 'out of curiosity,' as he said – he went to hear the preacher.

'Now, this is something else again,' he told me as soon as he came from hearing Don Emmanuel for the first time. 'He's not like the others; still, he doesn't fool me, he's too intelligent to believe everything he must teach.'

'You mean you think he's a hypocrite?'

'A hypocrite ... no! But he has a job by which he must live.'

As for me, my brother undertook to see that I read the books he brought me, and others which he urged me to buy.

'So your brother Lazarus wants you to read,' Don Emmanuel queried. 'Well, read, my daughter, read and make him happy by doing so. I know you will read only worthy books. Read even if only novels; they are as good as the books which deal with so-called "reality". You are better off reading than concerning yourself with village gossip and old wives' tales. Above all, though, you will do well to read devotional books which will bring you contentment in life, a quiet, gentle contentment, and peace.'

And he, did he enjoy such contentment?

It was about this time that our mother fell mortally sick and died. In her last days her one wish was that Don Emmanuel should convert Lazarus, whom she expected to see again in heaven, in some little corner among the stars from where they could see the lake and the mountain of Valverde de Lucerna. She felt she was going there now, to see God.

'You are not going anywhere,' Don Emmanuel would tell her; 'you are staying right here. Your body will remain here, in this land, and your soul also, in this house, watching and listening to your children though they do not see or hear you.'

'But, Father,' she said, 'I am going to see God.'

'God, my daughter, is all around us, and you will see Him from here, right from here. And all of us in Him, and He in all of us.'

'God bless you,' I whispered to him.

'The peace in which your mother dies will be her eternal life,' he told me.

And, turning to my brother Lazarus: 'Her heaven is to go on seeing you, and it is at this moment that she must be saved. Tell her you will pray for her.'

'But—'

'But what? ... Tell her you will pray for her, to whom you owe your life. And I know that once you promise her, you *will* pray, and I know that once you pray ...'

My brother, his eyes filled with tears, drew near our dying mother and gave her his solemn promise to pray for her.

'And I, in heaven, will pray for you, for all of you,' my mother responded. And then, kissing the crucifix and fixing her eyes on Don Emmanuel, she gave up her soul to God.

'Into Thy hands I commend my spirit,' prayed the priest.

My brother and I stayed on in the house alone. What had happened at the time of my mother's death had established a bond between Lazarus and Don Emmanuel. The latter seemed even to neglect some of his charges, his patients and his other needy to look after my brother. In the afternoons, they would go for a stroll together, walking along the lake or toward the ruins, overgrown with ivy, of the old Cistercian abbey.

'He's an extraordinary man,' Lazarus told me. 'You know the story they tell of how there is a city at the bottom of the lake, submerged beneath the water, and that on Midsummer's Night the sound of its church bells can be heard . . .'

'Yes, a city "feudal and medieval" . . .'

'And I believe,' he went on, 'that at the bottom of Don Emmanuel's soul there is a city, submerged and inundated, and that sometimes the sound of its bells can be heard . . .'

'Yes . . . And this city submerged in Don Emmanuel's soul, and per-haps – why not – in yours as well, is certainly the cemetery of the souls of our ancestors, the ancestors of our Valverde de Lucerna . . ."feudal and medieval"!'

In the end, my brother began going to Mass. He went regularly to hear Don Emmanuel. When it became known that he was prepared to comply with his annual duty of receiving Communion, that he would receive when the others received, an intimate joy ran through the town, which felt that by this act he was restored to his people. The rejoicing was of such nature, moreover, so openhanded and honest, that Lazarus never did feel that he had been 'vanquished' or 'over-come'.

The day of his Communion arrived; of Communion before the entire village, with the entire village. When it came time for my brother's turn, I saw Don Emmanuel – white as January snow on the mountain, and moving like the surface of the lake when it is stirred by the north-east wind – come up to him with the holy wafer in his hand, which trembled violently as it reached out to Lazarus's mouth; at that mo-ment the priest had an instant of faintness and the wafer dropped to the ground. My brother himself recovered it and placed it in his mouth. The people saw the tears on Don Emmanuel's face, and everyone wept, saying: 'What great love he bears!' And then, because it was dawn, a cock crowed.

On returning home I locked myself in with my brother; alone with him I put my arms around his neck and kissed him.

'Lazarus, Lazarus, what joy you have given us all today; the entire village, the living and the dead, and especially our mother. Did you see how Don Emmanuel wept for joy? What joy you have given us all!'

'It was for that reason that I did what I did,' he answered me.

'For what? To give us pleasure? Surely you did it for your own sake, first of all; because of your conversion.'

And then Lazarus, my brother, grown as pale and tremulous as Don Emmanuel when he was giving Communion, bade me sit down, in the very chair where our mother used to sit. He took a deep breath, and, in the intimate tone of a familiar and domestic confession, he told me:

'Angelita, the time has come when I must tell you the truth, the absolute truth, and I shall tell you because I must, because I cannot, I ought not, conceal it from you, and because, sooner or later, you are bound to intuit it anyway, if only halfway – which would be worse.'

Thereupon, serenely and tranquilly, in a subdued voice, he recounted a tale that drowned me in a lake of sorrow. He told how Don Emmanuel had appealed to him, particularly during the walks to the ruins of the old Cistercian abbey, to set a good example, to avoid scandalizing the townspeople, to take part in the religious life of the community, to feign belief even if he did not feel any, to conceal his own ideas – all this without attempting in any way to catechize him, to instruct him in religion, or to effect a true conversion.

'But is it possible?' I asked in consternation.

'Possible and true. When I said to him: "Is this you, the priest, who suggests I dissimulate?" he replied, hesitatingly: "Dissimulate? Not at all! That is not dissimulation. 'Dip your fingers in the holy water, and you will end by believing,' as someone said." And I, gazing into his eyes, asked him: "And you, celebrating the Mass, have you ended by believing?" He looked away and stared out at the lake, until his eyes filled with tears. And it was in this way that I came to understand his secret.'

'Lazarus!' I cried out, incapable of another word.

At that moment the fool Blasillo came along our street, crying out his: 'My God, my God, why hast Thou forsaken me?' And Lazarus shuddered, as if he had heard the voice of Don Emmanuel, or of Christ.

'It was then,' my brother at length continued, 'that I really understood his motives and his saintliness; for a saint he is, Sister, a true saint. In trying to convert me to his holy cause – for it is a holy cause – he was not attempting to score a triumph, but rather was doing it to protect the peace, the happiness, the illusions, perhaps, of his charges. I understood that if he thus deceives them – if it *is* deceit – it is not for his own advantage. I submitted to his logic – and that was my conversion.

'I shall never forget the day on which I said to him: "But Don Emmanuel, the truth, the truth, above all!"; and he, all a-tremble, whispered in my ear – though we were all alone in the middle of the countryside – "The truth? The truth, Lazarus, is perhaps something so unbearable, so terrible, something so deadly, that simple people could not live with it!"

' "And why do you show me a glimpse of it now, here, as if we were in the confessional?" I asked. And he said: "Because if I did not, I would be so tormented by it, so tormented, that I would finally shout it in the middle of the plaza, which I must never, never, never do ... I am put here to give life to the souls of my charges, to make them happy, to make them dream they are immortal – and not to destroy them. The important thing is that they live sanely, in concord with each other – and with the truth, with my truth, they could not live at all. Let them live. That is what the Church does, it lets them live. As for true religion, all religions are true as long as they give spiritual life to the people who profess them, as long as they console them for having been born only to die. And for each people the truest religion is their own, the religion that made them ... And mine? Mine consists in consoling myself by consoling others, even though the consolation I give them is not ever mine." I shall never forget his words.'

'But then this Communion of yours has been a sacrilege,' I dared interrupt, regretting my words as soon as I said them.

'Sacrilege? What about the priest who gave it to me? And his Masses?'

'What martyrdom!' I exclaimed.

'And now,' said my brother, 'there is one more person to console the people.'

'To deceive them, you mean?' I said.

'Not at all,' he replied, 'but rather to confirm them in their faith.'

'And they, the people, do they really believe, do you think?'

'About that, I know nothing! ... They probably believe without trying, from force of habit, tradition. The important thing is not to stir them up. To let them live their thin sentiments, without acquiring the torments of luxury. Blessed are the poor in spirit!'

'That then is the sentiment you have learned from Don Emmanuel ... And tell me, do you feel you have carried out your promise to our mother on her deathbed, when you promised to pray for her?'

'Do you think I *could* fail her? What do you take me for, sister? Do you think I would go back on my own word, my solemn promise made at the hour of death to a mother?'

'I don't know ... You might have wanted to deceive her so she could die in peace.'

'The fact is, though, that if I had not lived up to my promise, I would be totally miserable.'

'And ...'

'I carried out my promise and I have not neglected for a single day to pray for her.'

'Only for her?'

'Well, now, for whom else?'

'For yourself! And now, for Don Emmanuel.'

We parted and went to our separate rooms. I to weep through the night, praying for the conversion of my brother and of Don Emmanuel. And Lazarus, to what purpose, I know not.

From that day on I was fearful of finding myself alone with Don Emmanuel, whom I continued to aid in his pious works. And he seemed to sense my inner state and to guess at its cause. When at last I came to him in the confessional's penitential tribunal (who was the judge, and who the offender?) the two of us, he and I, bowed our heads in silence and began to cry. It was he, finally, Don Emmanuel, who broke the terrible silence, with a voice which seemed to issue from the tomb:

'Angelita, you have the same faith you had when you were ten, don't you? You believe, don't you?'

'I believe, Father.'

'Then go on believing. And if doubts come to torment you, suppress them utterly, even to yourself. The main thing is to live ...'

I summoned up courage, and dared to ask, trembling:

'But, Father, do you believe?'

For a brief moment he hesitated, and then, mastering himself, he said:

'I believe!'

'In what, Father, in what? Do you believe in the after life? Do you believe that in dying we do not die in every way, completely? Do you believe that we will see each other again, that we will love each other in a world to come? Do you believe in another life?'

The poor saint was sobbing.

'My child, leave off, leave off!'

Now, when I come to write this memoir, I ask myself: Why did he not deceive me? Why did he not deceive me as he deceived the others? Why did he afflict himself? Why could he not deceive himself, or why could he not deceive me? And I want to believe that he was afflicted because he could not deceive himself into deceiving me.

'And now,' he said, 'pray for me, for your brother, and for yourself – for all of us. We must go on living. And giving life.'

And, after a pause:

'Angelita, why don't you marry?'

'You know why I do not.'

'No, no; you must marry. Lazarus and I will find you a suitor. For it would be good for you to marry, and rid yourself of these obsessions.'

'Obsessions, Don Emmanuel?'

'I know well enough what I am saying. You should not torment yourself for the sake of others, for each of us has more than enough to do answering for himself.'

'That it should be you, Don Emmanuel, who says this! That you should advise me to marry and answer for myself alone and not suffer over others! That it should be you!'

'Yes, you are right, Angelita. I am no longer sure of what I say. I am no longer sure of what I say since I began to confess to you. Only, one must go on living. Yes! One must live!'

And when I rose to leave the church, he asked me:

'Now, Angelita, in the name of the people, do you absolve me?'

I felt pierced by a mysterious and priestly prompting and said:

'In the name of the Father, the Son and the Holy Ghost, I absolve you, Father.'

We quitted the church, and as I went out I felt the quickening of maternity within me.

My brother, now totally devoted to the work of Don Emmanuel, had become his closest and most zealous collaborator and companion. They were bound together, moreover, by their common secret. Lazarus accompanied the priest on his visits to the sick, and to schools, and he placed his resources at the disposition of the saintly man. A little more zeal, and he would have learned to help celebrate Mass. All the while he was sounding deeper in the unfathomable soul of the priest.

'What manliness!' he exclaimed to me once. 'Yesterday, as we walked along the lake he said: "There lies my direst temptation." When I interrogated him with my eyes, he went on: "My poor father, who was close to ninety when he died, was tormented all his life, as he confessed to me himself, by a temptation to suicide, by an instinct to self-destruction which had come to him from a time before memory – from birth, from his *nation*, as he said – and was forced to fight against it always. And this fight grew to be his life. So as not to succumb to this temptation he was forced to take precautions, to guard his life. He told me of terrible episodes. His urge was a form of madness – and I have inherited it. How that water beckons me in its deep quiet! ... an apparent quietude reflecting the sky like a mirror – and beneath it the hidden current! My life, Lazarus, is a kind of continual suicide, or a struggle against suicide, which is the same thing ... Just so long as our people go on living!" And then he added: "Here the river eddies to form a lake, so that later, flowing down the plateau, it may form into cascades, waterfalls, and torrents, hurling itself through gorges and chasms. Thus does life eddy in the village; and the temptation to suicide is the greater beside the still waters which at night reflect the stars, than it is beside the crashing falls which drive one back in fear. Listen, Lazarus, I have helped poor villagers to die well, ignorant, illiterate villagers, who had scarcely ever been out of their village, and I have learned from their own lips, or divined it when they were silent, the real cause of their sickness unto death, and there at the head of their deathbed I have been able to see into the black abyss of their life-weariness. A weariness a thousand times worse than hunger! For our part, Lazarus, let us go on with our kind of suicide of working for the people, and let them dream their life as the lake dreams the heavens."

'Another time,' said my brother, 'as we were coming back, we spied a country girl, a goat-herd, standing erect on a height of the mountain slope overlooking the lake and she was singing in a voice fresher than its waters. Don Emmanuel took hold of me, and pointing to her said: "Look, it's as though time had stopped, as though this country girl had always been there just as she is, singing in the way she is, and as though she would always be there, as she was before my consciousness began, as she will be when it is past. That girl is a part of nature – not of history – along with the rocks, the clouds, the trees, and the waters." He has such a subtle feeling for nature, he infuses it with spirit!

'I shall not forget the day when snow was falling and he asked me: "Have you ever seen a greater mystery, Lazarus, than the snow falling, and dying, in the lake, while a hood is laid upon the mountain?"'

Don Emmanuel had to moderate and temper my brother's zeal and his neophyte's rawness. As soon as he heard that Lazarus was going about inveighing against some of the popular superstitions he told him forcefully:

'Leave them alone! It's difficult enough making them understand where orthodox belief leaves off and where superstition begins. It's hard enough, especially for us. Leave them alone, then, as long as they get some comfort ... It's better for them to believe everything, even things that contradict one another, than to believe nothing. The idea that someone who believes too much ends by not believing in anything is a Protestant notion. Let us not protest! Protestation destroys contentment and peace.'

My brother told me, too, about one moonlit night when they were returning to town along the lake (whose surface a mountain breeze was stirring, so that the moonbeams topped the whitecaps), Don Emmanuel turned to him and said:

'Look, the water is reciting the litany and saying: *ianua caeli, ora pro nobis;* gate of heaven, pray for us.'

Two evanescent tears fell from his lashes to the grass, where the light of the full moon shone upon them like dew.

And time went hurrying by, and my brother and I began to notice that Don Emmanuel's spirits were failing, that he could no longer control completely the deep rooted sadness which consumed him; perhaps some treacherous illness was undermining his body and soul. In an effort to rouse his interest, Lazarus spoke to him of the good effect the organization of a type of Catholic agrarian syndicate would have.

'A syndicate?' Don Emmanuel repeated sadly. 'A syndicate? And what is that? The Church is the only syndicate I know. And you have certainly heard "My kingdom is not of this world." Our Kingdom, Lazarus, is not of this world ...'

'And of the other?'

Don Emmanuel bowed his head:

'The other is here. Two kingdoms exist in this world. Or rather, the other world ... Ah, I don't really know what I'm saying. But as for the syndicate, that's a vestige from your days of "progressivism". No, Lazarus, no; religion does not exist to resolve the economic or political conflicts of this world, which God handed over to men for their disputes. Let men think and act as they will, let them console themselves for having been born, let them live as happily as possible in the illusion that all this has a purpose. I don't propose to advise the poor to submit to the rich, nor to suggest to the rich that they subordinate themselves to the poor; but rather to preach resignation in everyone, and charity towards everyone. For even the rich man must resign himself – to his riches, and to life; and the poor man must show charity – even to the rich. The Social Question? Ignore it, for it is none of our business. So, a new society is on the way, in which there will be neither rich nor poor, in which wealth will be justly divided, in which everything will belong to everyone – and so, what then? Won't this general well-being and comfort lead to even greater tedium and weariness of life? I know well enough that one of those chiefs of what they call the Social Revolution has already said that religion is the opium of the people. Opium ... Opium ... Yes, opium it is. We should give them opium, and help them sleep, and dream. I, myself, with my mad activity, give myself opium. And still I don't manage to sleep well, let alone dream well ... What a fearful nightmare! ... I, too, can say, with the Divine Master: "My soul is weary unto death". No, Lazarus, no; no syndicates for us. If *they* organize them, well and good – they would be distracting themselves in that way. Let them play at syndicates, if that makes them happy.'

The entire village began to realize that Don Emmanuel's spirit was weakening, that his strength was waning. His very voice – that miracle of a voice – acquired a kind of quaking. Tears came into his eyes for any reason whatever – or for no reason. Whenever he spoke to people about the other world, about the other life, he was compelled to pause at frequent intervals, and he would close his eyes. 'It is a vision,' people would say, 'he has a vision of what lies ahead.' At such moments the fool Blasillo was the first to break into tears. He wept copiously these days, crying now more than he laughed, and even his laughter had the sound of tears.

The last Easter Week which Don Emmanuel was to celebrate among us, in this world, in this village of ours, arrived, and all the village sensed the impending end of tragedy. And how the words did strike home when for the last time Don Emmanuel cried before us: 'My God, my God, why hast Thou forsaken me?'! And when he repeated the words of the Lord to the Good Thief ('All thieves are good,' Don Emmanuel used to tell us): 'Tomorrow shalt thou be with me in Paradise.' ...! And then, the last general Communion which our saint was to give! When he came to my brother to give him the Host – his hand steady this time – just after the liturgical '.. *in vitam aeternam*,' he bent down and whispered to him: 'There is no other life but this, no life more eternal ... let them dream it eternal ... let it be eternal for a few years ...'

And when he came to me he said: 'Pray, my child, pray for us all.' And then, something so extraordinary happened that I carry it now in my heart as the greatest of mysteries: he bent over and said, in a voice which seemed to belong to the other world: '. . . and pray, too, for our Lord Jesus Christ.'

I stood up, going weak as I did so, like a somnambulist. Everything around me seemed dream-like. And I thought: 'Am I to pray, too, for the lake and the mountain?' And next: 'Am I bewitched, then?' Home at last, I took up the crucifix my mother had held in her hands when she had given up her soul to God, and, gazing at it through my tears and recalling the 'My God, my God, why hast Thou forsaken me?' of our two Christs, the one of this earth and the other of this village, I prayed: 'Thy will be done on earth as it is in heaven,' and then, 'And lead us not into temptation. Amen.' After this I turned to the statue of the Mater Dolorosa – her heart transfixed by seven swords – which had been my poor mother's most sorrowful comfort, and I prayed again: 'Holy Mary, Mother of God, pray for us sinners, now and in the hour of our death. Amen.' I had scarcely finished the prayer, when I asked myself: 'Sinners? Sinners are we? And what is our sin, what is it?' And all day I brooded over the question.

The next day I presented myself before Don Emmanuel – Don Emmanuel now in the full sunset of his magnificent religiosity – and I said to him:

'Do you remember, my Father, years ago when I asked you a certain question you answered: "That question you must not ask me; for I am ignorant; there are learned doctors of the Holy Mother Church who will know how to answer you"?'

'Do I remember? . . . Of course. And I remember I told you those were questions put to you by the Devil.'

'Well, then, Father, I have come again, bedevilled, to ask you another question put to me by my Guardian Devil.'

'Ask it.'

'Yesterday, when you gave me Communion, you asked me to pray for all of us, even for . . .'

'That's enough! . . . Go on.'

'I arrived home and began to pray; when I came to the part "Pray for us sinners, now and at the hour of our death", a voice in me asked: "Sinners? Sinners are we? And what is our sin?" What is our sin, Father?'

'Our sin?' he replied. 'A great doctor of the Spanish Catholic Apostolic Church has already explained it; the great doctor of *Life is a Dream* has written "The greatest sin of man is to have been born." That, my child, is our sin; to have been born.'

'Can it be atoned, Father?'

'Go and pray again. Pray once more for us sinners, now and at the hour of our death ... Yes, at length the dream is atoned ... at length life is atoned ... at length the cross of birth is expiated and atoned, and the drama comes to an end ... And as Calderón said, to have done good, to have feigned good, even in dreams, is something which is not lost.'

The hour of his death arrived at last. The entire village saw it come. And he made it his finest lesson. For he would not die alone or at rest. He died preaching to his people in the church. But first, before being carried to the church (his paralysis made it impossible for him to move), he summoned Lazarus and me to his bedside. Alone there, the three of us together, he said:

'Listen to me: watch over these poor sheep; find some comfort for them in living, and let them believe what I could not. And Lazarus, when your hour comes, die as I die, as Angela will die, in the arms of the Holy Mother Church, Catholic, Apostolic, and Roman; that is to say, of the Holy Mother Church of Valverde de Lucerna. And now, farewell; until we never meet again, for this dream of life is coming to an end ...'

'Father, Father,' I cried out.

'Do not grieve, Angela, only go on praying for all sinners, for all who have been born. Let them dream, let them dream ... O, what a longing I have to sleep, to sleep, sleep without end, sleep for all eternity, and never dream! Forgetting this dream! ... When they go to bury me, let it be in a box made from the six planks I cut from the old walnut tree – poor old tree! – in whose shade I played as a child, when I began the dream ... In those days, I did really believe in life everlasting. That is to say, it seems to me now that I believed. For a child, to believe is the same as to dream. And for a people, too ... You'll find those six planks I cut at the foot of the bed.'

He was seized by a sudden fit of choking, and then, composing himself once more, he went on:

'You will recall that when we prayed together, animated by a common sentiment, a community of spirit, and we came to the final verse of the Creed, you will remember that I would fall silent ... When the Israelites were coming to the end of their wandering in the desert, the Lord told Aaron and Moses that because they had not believed in Him they would not set foot in the Promised Land with their people; and he bade them climb the height of Mount Hor, where Moses ordered Aaron stripped of his garments, so that Aaron died there, and then Moses went up from the plains of Moab to Mount Nebo, to the top of Pisgah, looking into Jericho, and the Lord showed him all of the land promised to His people, but said to him: "You will not go there". And there Moses died, and no one knew his grave. And he left Joshua to be chief in his place. You, Lazarus, must be my Joshua, and if you can make the sun stand still, make it stop, and never mind progress. Like Moses, I have seen the face of God — our supreme dream — face to face, and as you already know, and as the Scripture says, he who sees God's face, he who sees the eyes of the dream, the eyes with which He looks at us, will die inexorably and forever. And therefore, do not let our people, so long as they live, look into the face of God. Once dead, it will no longer matter, for then they will see nothing . . .'

'Father, Father, Father,' I cried again.

And he said:

'Angela, you must pray always, so that all sinners may go on dreaming, until they die, of the resurrection of the flesh and the life everlasting . . .'

I was expecting 'and who knows it might be . . .' But instead, Don Emmanuel had another attack of coughing.

'And now,' he finally went on, 'and now, in the hour of my death, it is high time to have me brought, in this very chair, to the church, so that I may take leave there of my people, who await me.'

He was carried to the church and brought, in his armchair, into the chancel, to the foot of the altar. In his hands he held a crucifix. My brother and I stood close to him, but the fool Blasillo wanted to stand even closer. He wanted to grasp Don Emmanuel by the hand, so that he could kiss it. When some of the people nearby tried to stop him, Don Emmanuel rebuked them and said:

'Let him come closer . . . Come, Blasillo, give me your hand.'

The fool cried for joy. And then Don Emmanuel spoke:

'I have very few words left, my children; I scarcely feel I have strength enough left to die. And then, I have nothing new to tell you, either. I have already said everything I have to say. Live with each other in peace and contentment, in the hope that we will all see each other again some day, in that other Valverde de Lucerna up there among the night-time stars, the stars which the lake reflects over the image of the reflected mountain. And pray, pray to the Most Blessed Mary, and to our Lord. Be good . . . that is enough. Forgive me whatever wrong I may have done you inadvertently or unknowingly. After I give you my blessing, let us pray together, let us say the Paternoster, the Ave Maria, the Salve, and the Creed.'

Then he gave his blessing to the whole village, with the crucifix held in his hand, while the women and children cried and even some of the men wept softly. Almost at once the prayers were begun. Don Emmanuel listened to them in silence, his hand in the hand of Blasillo the fool, who began to fall asleep to the sound of the praying. First the Paternoster, with its 'Thy will be done on earth as it is in heaven'; then the Ave Maria, with its 'Pray for us sinners, now and in the hour of our death'; followed by the Salve, with its 'mourning and weeping in this vale of tears'; and finally, the Creed. On reaching 'The resurrection of the flesh and life everlasting' the people sensed that their saint had yielded up his soul to God. It was not necessary to close his eyes even, for he died with them closed. When an attempt was made to wake Blasillo, it was found that he, too, had fallen asleep in the Lord forever. So that later there were two bodies to be buried.

The village immediately repaired en masse to the house of the saint to carry away holy relics, to divide up pieces of his garments among themselves, to carry off whatever they could find as a memento of the blessed martyr. My brother preserved his breviary, between the pages of which he discovered a carnation, dried as in a herbarium and mounted on a piece of paper, and upon the paper a cross and a certain date.

No one in the village seemed able to believe that Don Emmanuel was dead; everyone expected to see him – perhaps some of them did – taking his daily walk along the side of the lake, his figure mirrored in the water, or silhouetted against the background of the mountain. They continued to hear his voice, and they all visited his grave, around which a veritable cult sprang up, old women 'possessed by devils' came to touch the cross of walnut, made with his own hands from the tree which had yielded the six planks of his casket.

The ones who least of all believed in his death were my brother and I. Lazarus carried on the tradition of the saint, and he began to compile a record of the priest's words. Some of the conversations in this account of mine were made possible by his notes.

'It was he,' said my brother, 'who made me into a new man. I was a true Lazarus whom he raised from the dead. He gave me faith.'

'Ah, faith ...'

'Yes, faith, faith in the charity of life, in life's joy. It was he who cured me of my delusion of "progress", of my belief in its political implications. For there are, Angela, two types of dangerous and harmful men: those who, convinced of life beyond the grave, of the resurrection of the flesh, torment other people – like the inquisitors they are – so that they will despise this life as a transitory thing and work for the other life; and then, there are those who, believing only in this life . . .'

'Like you, perhaps . . .'

'Yes, and like Don Emmanuel. Believing only in this world, this second group looks forward to some vague future society and exerts every effort to prevent the populace finding consoling joy from belief in another world . . .'

'And so . . .'

'The people should be allowed to live with their illusion.'

The poor priest who came to the parish to replace Don Emmanuel found himself overwhelmed in Valverde de Lucerna by the memory of the saint, and he put himself in the hands of my brother and myself for guidance. He wanted only to follow in the footsteps of the saint. And my brother told him: 'Very little theology, Father, very little theology. Religion, religion, religion.' Listening to him, I smiled to myself, wondering if this was not a kind of theology, too.

I had by now begun to fear for my poor brother. From the time Don Emmanuel died it could scarcely be said that he lived. Daily he went to the priest's tomb; for hours on end he stood gazing into the lake. He was filled with nostalgia for deep, abiding peace.

'Don't stare into the lake so much,' I begged him.

'Don't worry. It's not the lake which draws me, nor the mountain. Only, I cannot live without his help.'

'And the joy of living, Lazarus, what about the joy of living?'

'That's for others. Not for those of us who have seen God's face, those of us on whom the Dream of Life has gazed with His eyes.'

'What; are you preparing to go and see Don Emmanuel?'

'No, sister, no. Here at home now, between the two of us, the whole truth – bitter as it may be, bitter as the sea into which the sweet waters of our lake flow – the whole truth for you, who are so set against it . . .'

'No, no, Lazarus. You are wrong. Your truth is not the truth.'

'It's my truth.'

'Yours, perhaps, but surely not . . .'

'His, too.'

'No, Lazarus. Not now, it isn't. Now, he must believe otherwise; now he must believe . . .'

'Listen, Angela, once Don Emmanuel told me that there are truths which, though one reveals them to oneself, must be kept from others;

and I told him that telling me was the same as telling himself. And then he said, he confessed to me, that he thought that more than one of the great saints, perhaps the very greatest himself, had died without believing in the other life.'

'Is it possible?'

'All too possible! And now, sister, you must be careful that here, among the people, no one even suspects our secret . . .'

'Suspect it?' I cried in amazement. 'Why even if I were to try, in a fit of madness, to explain it to them, they wouldn't understand it. The people do not understand your words, they understand your actions much better. To try and explain all this to them would be like reading some pages from Saint Thomas Aquinas to eight-year-old children, in Latin.'

'All the better. In any case, when I am gone, pray for me and for him and for all of us.'

At length, his own time came. A sickness which had been eating away at his robust nature seemed to flare with the death of Don Emmanuel.

'I don't so much mind dying,' he said to me in his last days, 'as the fact that with me another piece of Don Emmanuel dies too. The remainder of him must live on with you. Until, one day, even we dead will die forever.'

When he lay in the throes of death, the people of the village came in to bid him farewell (as is customary in our towns) and they commended his soul to the care of Don Emmanuel the Good, Martyr. My brother said nothing to them; he had nothing more to say. He had already said everything there was to say. He had become a link between the two Valverde de Lucernas – the one at the bottom of the lake and the one reflected in its surface. He was already one more of us who had died of life, and, in his way, one more of our saints.

I was desolate, more than desolate; but I was, at least, among my own people, in my own village. Now, having lost my Saint Emmanuel, the father of my soul, and my own Lazarus, my more than carnal brother, my spiritual brother, now it is I realize that I have aged. But, have I really lost them then? Have I grown old? Is my death approaching?

I must live! And he taught me to live, he taught us to live, to feel life, to feel the meaning of life, to merge with the soul of the mountain, with the soul of the lake, with the soul of the village, to lose ourselves in them so as to remain in them forever. He taught me by his life to lose myself in the life of the people of my village, and I no longer felt the passing of the hours, and the days, and the years, any more than I felt the passage of the water in the lake. It began to seem that my life would always be thus. I no longer felt myself growing old. I no longer lived in myself, but in my people, and my people lived in me. I tried to speak as they spoke, as they spoke without trying. I went into the street – it was the one highway – and, since I knew everyone, I lived in them and forgot myself (while, on the other hand, in Madrid, where I went once with my brother, I had felt a terrible loneliness, since I knew no one, and had been tortured by the sight of so many unknown people).

Now, as I write this memoir, this confession of my experience with saintliness, with a saint, I am of the opinion that Don Emmanuel the Good, my Don Emmanuel, and my brother, too, died believing they did not believe, but that, without believing in their belief, they actually believed, with resignation and in desolation.

But why, I have asked myself repeatedly, did not Don Emmanuel attempt to convert my brother deceitfully, with a lie, pretending to be a believer himself without being one? And I have finally come to think that Don Emmanuel realized he would not be able to delude him, that with him a fraud would not do, that only through the truth, with his truth, would he be able to convert him; that he knew he would accomplish nothing if he attempted to enact the comedy – the tragedy rather – which he played out for the benefit of the people. And thus did he win him over, in effect, to his pious fraud; thus did he win him over to the cause of life with the truth of death. And thus did he win me, who never permitted anyone to see through his divine, his most saintly, game. For I believed then, and I believe now, that God – as part of I know not what sacred and inscrutable purpose – caused them to believe they were unbelievers. And that at the moment of their passing, perhaps, the blindfold was removed.

And I, do I believe?

As I write this – here in my mother's old house, and I past my fiftieth year and my memories growing as dim and blanched as my hair – outside it is snowing, snowing upon the lake, snowing upon the mountain, upon the memory of my father, the stranger, upon the memory of my mother, my brother Lazarus, my people, upon the memory of my Saint Emmanuel, and even on the memory of the poor fool Blasillo, my Saint Blasillo – and may he help me in heaven! The snow effaces corners and blots out shadows, for even in the night it shines and illuminates. Truly, I do not know what is true and what is false, nor what I saw and what I merely dreamt – or rather, what I dreamt and and what I merely saw –, nor what I really knew or what I merely believed to be true. Neither do I know whether or not I am transferring to this paper, white as the snow outside, my consciousness, for it to remain in writing, leaving me without it. But why, any longer, cling to it?

Do I really understand any of it? Do I really believe in any of it? Did what I am writing about here actually take place, and did it take place in just the way I tell it? Is it possible for such things to happen? Is it possible that all this is more than a dream dreamed within another dream? Can it be that I, Angela Carballino, a woman in her fifties, am the only one in this village to be assailed by far-fetched thoughts, thoughts unknown to everyone else? And the others, those around me, do they believe? And what does it mean, to believe? At least they go on living. And now they believe in Saint Emmanuel the Good, Martyr, who, with no hope of immortality for himself, preserved their hope in it.

It appears that our most illustrious bishop, who set in motion the process for beatifying our saint from Valverde de Lucerna, is intent on writing an account of Don Emmanuel's life, something which would serve as a guide for the perfect parish priest, and with this end in mind he is gathering information of every sort. He has repeatedly solicited information from me; more than once he has come to see me; and I have supplied him with all sorts of facts. But I have never revealed the tragic secret of Don Emmanuel and my brother. And it is curious that he has never suspected. I trust that what I have set down here will never come to his knowledge. For, all temporal authorities are to be avoided; I fear all authorities on this earth – even when they are church authorities.

But this is an end to it. Let its fate be what it will . . .

How, you ask, did this document, this memoir of Angela Carballino fall into my hands? That, reader, is something I must keep secret. I have transcribed it for you just as it is written, just as it came to me, with only a few, a very few editorial emendations. It recalls to you other things I have written? This fact does not gain-say its objectivity, its originality. Moreover, for all I know, perhaps I created real, actual beings, independent of me, beyond my control, characters with immortal souls. For all I know, Augusto Perez in my novel *Mist** was

---

* In the denouement of *Mist*, the protagonist Augusto Perez turns on Unamuno, and tells him that he, a creation of human thought and genius, is more real than his author, a product of blind animality.

right when he claimed to be more real, more objective than I myself, who had thought to have invented him. As for the reality of this Saint Emmanuel the Good, Martyr — as he is revealed to me by his disciple and spiritual daughter Angela Carballino — of his reality it has not occurred to me to doubt. I believe in it more than the saint himself did. I believe in it more than I do in my own reality.

And now, before I bring this epilogue to a close, I wish to recall to your mind, patient reader, the ninth verse of the Epistle of the forgotten Apostle, Saint Judas — what power in a name! — where we are told how my heavenly patron, St Michael Archangel (Michael means 'Who such as God?' and archangel means archmessenger) disputed with the Devil (Devil means accuser, prosecutor) over the body of Moses, and would not allow him to carry it off as a prize, to damnation. Instead, he told the Devil: 'May the Lord rebuke thee'. And may he who wishes to understand, understand!

I would like also, since Angela Carballino injected her own feelings into her narrative — I don't know how it could have been otherwise — to comment on her statement to the effect that if Don Emmanuel and his disciple Lazarus had confessed their convictions to the people, they, the people, would not have understood. Nor, I should like to add, would they have believed the pair. They would have believed in their works and not their words. And works stand by themselves, and need no words to back them up. In a village like Valverde de Lucerna one makes one's confession by one's conduct.

And as for faith, the people scarce know what it is, and care less.

I am well aware of the fact that no action takes place in this narrative, this *novelistic* narrative, if you will — the novel is, after all, the most intimate, the truest history, so that I scarcely understand why some people are outraged to have the Bible called a novel, when such a designation actually sets it above some mere chronicle or other. In short, nothing happens. But I hope that this is because everything that takes place happens, and, instead of coming to pass, and passing away, remains forever, like the lakes and the mountains and the blessed simple souls fixed firmly beyond faith and despair, the blessed souls who, in the lakes and the mountains, outside history, in their divine novel, take refuge.

Translated by Anthony Kerrigan

Luigi Pirandello

Cinci

Born in 1867 and raised in Sicily, Luigi Pirandello is best known for his plays (Six Characters in Search of an Author, As You Desire Me), *although he was a prolific writer of stories and novels as well. He died shortly after receiving the Nobel Prize, in 1936.*

The dog sat patiently on his hind legs before the closed door and waited for it to open. Every so often he lifted a paw and scratched; every so often he let out a low whine.

Cinci, back from school with his books, strapped together, slung over his shoulder, found the dog still sitting there in the street. The boy was annoyed by this patient waiting and gave the dog a kick. Then he kicked the door for good measure, knowing that it was locked and that no one was home. Finally, he threw his books at the door, as if he expected them to pass right through it and land on the floor inside. But they came flying back at him with the same force with which he had hurled them. Surprised, as if the door were playing with him, Cinci threw the books back again. Then, as there were already three in the game – Cinci, the door and the books – the dog wanted to play too. He jumped at every throw and barked with each rebound.

People stopped to look. A few of them smiled, almost in spite of themselves, at the silliness of the game and at the dog's delight. Others were indignant to see expensive books treated with so little regard. Cinci soon tired of the sport and dropped his books on the ground, then lowered himself to a sitting position by scraping his spine along the wall. He had planned to sit on the books, but they slipped out from under him and he found himself coming down hard on the ground. He looked around with a foolish grin while the dog jumped back, eyeing him.

All the mischief that passed through Cinci's head showed clearly in that thatch of straw-coloured hair and in his sparkling green eyes. He was at the awkward age, gawky and bristling. Having forgotten his handkerchief when he returned to school in the afternoon, he now sat on the ground snuffling, his long legs exposed because he still wore short pants though he was too big for them, his knobby knees pulled up almost level with his face. No shoes could withstand the treatment he gave them. The ones he had on were already done for.

He was bored. Above all, he was bored. Hugging his knees, he snorted, then dragged his back up along the wall again. Fox leaped up, expectant. Where are we off to? A walk in the country, perhaps, to swipe a couple of figs or apples? Cinci was not yet sure. He listlessly tied up his books and replaced them over his shoulder.

The paved street ended beyond his house where the dirt road began, and it led deeper and deeper into the open country. What a wonderful sensation it must be, when you're riding in a carriage, to feel the horse's hoofs and the wheels pass from the hard pavement on to the soft, silent dirt road! It must be a little like when the teacher, after being provoked and flying into a rage, suddenly speaks in a quiet, gentle voice once more and the dread of punishment decreases. To get into the open country, you followed the dirt road past the last houses of their stinking suburb until it widened out into the little square on the outskirts of town. A new hospital had just been built there, its whitewashed walls still so fresh and glaring that they blinded you in the sun.

All the patients had recently been moved from the old hospital in ambulances and on stretchers. It was like a parade when they filed by, the ambulances first, their curtains fluttering at the little windows, then the bed cases carried by on beautiful hammocklike stretchers.

By the time Cinci and his dog reached the square, it was growing late. The sun had already set, and the convalescents in their grey shorts and white nightcaps no longer leaned out of the large windows to stare sadly at the old church opposite where it rose amid a cluster of dilapidated houses and a few straggling trees.

Cinci stopped, uncertain, then lounged against a paling, filled with helpless bitterness at so many things he could not understand. First there was his mother. How did she live and what did she live on? She was never at home and insisted on sending him to that school — that cursed school so far away. Every day he had to run for at least half an hour to get there on time; then at noon he came back only to rush again after bolting a couple of mouthfuls. His mother always said he was a loafer who wasted his time playing with the dog. She was for-ever reproaching him: he did not study, he was dirty, he always got cheated when she sent him to buy something, he brought back food that wasn't fresh ...

Now where was Fox?

There he was, poor little dog, mutely waiting for him to make up his mind. Anyway *he* knew what was expected of him: follow your master! Cinci wanted to do something, but there was always the same problem – he didn't know what to do. His mother could at least have given him the key when she went out to sew by the day in gentlemen's houses – for that's what she gave him to understand she was doing. But no. She said he was not to be trusted and that, if she had not returned by the time he got back from school, she would not be long and he could wait. Where? In front of the door? Sometimes he had waited two hours in the cold and even in the rain. Then, instead of taking shelter, he would go to the corner and stand under the rain-spout on purpose so that he would be wringing wet. Finally, she would appear, all out of breath, carrying a borrowed umbrella, her face flaming, her eyes very bright and shifty, so nervous she could never find the latch key in her purse.

'You're soaked! Now just be patient. I was kept late!'

Cinci frowned as he kept on walking uphill. There were things he didn't want to think about – his father, for instance. He had never known his father. When he was little he had been told that his father had died before he was born, but no one had ever said who his father was; now he no longer cared to ask or to find out. He might even be that cripple over there, paralysed down the right side, who still managed to drag himself along to the saloon. Fox went up and barked at him. It was the crutch he didn't like.

All those women standing around in a circle, bulging in front but not pregnant – well, maybe one of them was, the one with the skirt hiked up in the front and nearly dragging on the ground in back. That other one with the baby in her arms, reaching into her blouse – ugh! What a blob of flesh! His own mother was beautiful, still young and slender. She too had nursed him at her breast when he was a baby, perhaps in a house in the country or out in the sun on a threshing floor. He vaguely remembered a house in the country when he was little – if he had not dreamed it, or seen it somewhere. Who knows? When evening came and the oil lamps were lit, one could feel a shadow obscure those country houses as the lamp was carried from room to room and the light faded from one window only to reappear at another.

Beyond the square, the road meandered up the side of a hill and continued on into the country. He looked up and could see the whole vast expanse of the sky. The last rays of the dying sun had disappeared and above the darkened hill there was the softest blue. Evening shadows fell across the earth, dimming the white glare of the hospital wall.

An old woman hurried towards the little church for evening prayers. Cinci suddenly made up his mind to go in too, and Fox stopped, looking up at him because he well knew he was not allowed inside churches. At the entrance, the old woman, who was already late, was panting and whimpering as she struggled to lift the heavy leather curtain. Cinci held it aside for her, but she frowned instead of thanking him, sensing he had not come there to worship. It was cold as a cave in that little church. On the main altar two candles burned fitfully, and here and there a few stray lamps glimmered. The dust of ages lay in the penetrating dampness. Echoes lurked in the gloomy silence, ready to spring out at the least noise. The pews were lined with devout old women, each in her accustomed place. Cinci felt an impulse to let out a howl to make them jump. Not a howl perhaps, but what about throwing down his heavy load of books, as if by accident! Why not? He let them drop and, like a shot, the echoes jumped out to his great delight, thundering and crashing about him. Cinci had often tried this experiment of raising echoes. There was now no further need to gall the patience of those poor scandalized old worshippers. He walked out of the church and found Fox ready to follow along the path uphill. He longed to bite into some fruit and climbed over a low wall to grope his way through the dark trees. But he could not be certain whether this impulse was prompted by hunger or by an urge just to do *something*.

The steep country road was deserted and full of little stones loosened by the hoofs of the passing donkeys and sent rolling down and over and over. Cinci kicked a couple into the air with the toe of his shoe. The slopes on either side were covered with long green, plumed oats, so pleasant to chew on. The little plumes came off and clung together like a bouquet in your hand. If they were thrown at someone, the oats that clung were counted as future wives or husbands. Cinci decided to try this out on Fox. Seven wives, no less! But then, nearly all of them stuck fast in Fox's fur, so it didn't count. Fox, the old stupid, just stood there with his eyes closed, not understanding the joke about the seven wives on his back!

Cinci did not feel like going any further. He was tired and as bored as before. He went to the left of the road and sat on the wall. From there he looked up at the new moon, its pale gold just beginning to shine in the faint green of the sky. He saw it and he didn't see it – like things that slip through the mind, one flowing into another, then all receding farther and farther from his young body sitting there so still that he was no longer aware of it. If he had put his own hand on his knee, or on his foot hanging down in its dirty, scuffed shoe, it would have seemed like a stranger's. He was no longer *in* his body. He had joined the things he saw and did not see – the darkening sky, the brightening moon, that mass of dark trees which seemed suspended in thin air, the fresh, black earth so newly tilled, still exhaling the odour of damp rot of these last sunny October days.

All of a sudden, absorbed as he was, he was distracted and instinctively lifted his hand to his ear. A shrill little laugh had come from beneath the wall. A country boy about his own age had hidden himself on the side of the wall bordering the fields. He had picked and stripped a blade of oats too and, slipping a loose knot in one end, he was stealthily lifting up his arm to loop it over Cinci's ear. As soon as Cinci turned, the boy quickly signalled to him to be still. Then he moved the blade of oats along the wall towards the head of a little lizard peeping out from between the stones. The boy had been hoping to trap it for an hour. Cinci leaned down anxiously to watch. Without realizing it, the lizard had slipped its own head into the noose but not quite far enough to be caught. The head must advance a trifle more, and even now, if the hand holding the trap should tremble and alarm the lizard, it might escape. Yes, yes, but wait! Easy now! He must be prepared to give a jerk at just the right moment. It was the work of a second. There! The lizard was flashing like a fish at the end of that long blade of oats.

Cinci eagerly jumped down from the wall, but the other boy, holding the noose and probably fearing he would take the lizard from him, swung his arm around several times in the air and then brought the creature down with a dull slap on a big stone which lay among the weeds.

'No!' screamed Cinci, but too late.

The lizard lay motionless on the stone, its white stomach gleaming in the light. Cinci was angry. He too had wanted to see the lizard caught, prompted by the natural instinct of the hunter in all of us. But to kill it like that, without first looking closely at those quick little eyes, watching it up to the last convulsion, those twitching legs, that all-over quiver of its green body – no, it was too stupid and shameful! Cinci went up to the boy and punched him in the chest with all his might, sending him sprawling. The boy jumped right up again, furious, and grabbed a handful of dirt from the nearest furrow which he flung at Cinci's face, blinding him. Cinci was all the more outraged and infuriated by the taste of dirt in his mouth. He took a clod of earth and threw it back. The fight grew desperate. The country boy was quicker and had a surer aim. He never missed, moving in closer and closer with those missiles of dirt which did not wound but struck with a dull thud and fell like hail on Cinci's chest, in his face and hair, in his ears and even into his shoes. Suffocated, unable to protect or defend himself, Cinci leaped up with his arm raised to snatch a stone from the wall. Something scurried away — was it Fox? He hurled the stone and, all of a sudden, where before everything had been spinning around, striking his eyes, now nothing moved — the clump of trees, the thin crescent moon. It was as if time itself had stopped in stupefied amazement at the sight of the boy stretched on the ground.

Still panting, his heart pounding, terror flooding him as he leaned against the wall in the unbelievable silken repose of the countryside under the moonlight, Cinci foundered in a backwash of man's eternal solitude from which he wanted to flee. He had not done it! He had not meant to do it! He knew nothing about it! Then, as though he were actually someone else drawing near only out of curiosity, he took a step, then another, and bent down to look. The boy's head was bashed in; blood still dripped from his gaping mouth onto the ground. Part of his leg showed between his cotton sock and his pants leg. He looked as if he had always been dead. It was like a dream. The lizard lay stomach up on the stone with the blade of oats caught around its throat. Cinci knew he must wake up and go away. He quickly vaulted the wall, picked up his bundle of books and started off. Fox followed him, as usual.

On the way back downhill, Cinci's confidence increased as the distance lengthened so that he did not hurry at all. He reached the empty square. The moon shone here too, but it was another moon, unheeding, which lit up the white façade of the hospital.

Now once again along the road through the suburbs, back to the house — to which, of course, his mother had not yet returned. No need to give any explanation of his whereabouts; he had simply waited here for her. And this — which would be true for his mother — became the truth for him too. In fact, he stood with his shoulders against the wall beside the door just as before.

It was enough that he be found there, waiting.

Translated by Lily Duplaix

Marcel Proust

Filial Sentiments of a Parricide

Marcel Proust, who was born near Paris in 1871, wrote several stories and essays before settling down to his long, monumental work, The Remembrance of Things Past. *He worked on the several parts of this novel until his death in 1922.*

When, some months ago, Monsieur van Blarenberghe died, I remembered that my mother had known his wife very well. Ever since the death of my parents, I have become (in a sense which this is not the place to discuss) less myself and more their son. Though I have not turned my back on my own friends, I very much prefer to cultivate theirs, and the letters which I now write are, for the most part, those I think they would have written, those they can no longer write. I write, in their stead, letters of congratulation, letters, especially, of condolence, addressed to friends of theirs whom I scarcely know. When, therefore, Madame von Blarenberghe lost her husband, I wanted her to receive some small token of the sadness which my parents would have felt. I remembered that, many years before, I had occasionally met her son at the houses of mutual friends. It was to him, now, that I wrote, but in the name, so to speak, of my vanished parents rather than in my own. I received the following reply. It was a beautiful letter, eloquent of filial affection. I feel that such a piece of evidence, in view of the significance which it assumes in the light of the drama which followed so hard upon its heels and of the light which it throws upon that drama, ought to be made public. Here it is:

Les Timbrieux, par Josselin   (Morbihan)
September 24, 1904

My Dear Sir,
It is a matter of regret to me that I have been so long in thanking you for your sympathy in my great sorrow. I trust that you will for-

give me. So crushing has been my loss that, on the advice of my doctors, I have spent the last four months in travelling. It is only now, and with extreme difficulty, that I am beginning to resume my former way of life.

However dilatory I may have been, I should like you to know that I deeply appreciate your remembering our former pleasant relations, and that I am touched by the impulse that led you to write to me – and to my mother – in the name of those parents who have been so untimely taken from you. I never had the honour of knowing them except very slightly, but I am aware how warmly my father felt for yours, and how pleased my mother always was to see Madame Proust. It shows great delicacy and sensibility on your part thus to convey to me a message from beyond the grave.

I shall shortly be back in Paris, and if, between now and then, I can overcome that desire to be left to myself which, up to the present, I have felt as the result of the disappearance of one in whom my whole life was centred and who was the source of all my happiness, it will give me much pleasure to shake your hand and talk with you about the past.

Yours most sincerely,
H. van Blarenberghe

I was much touched by this letter. I felt full of pity for a man who was suffering so acutely – of pity and of envy. He still had a mother left to him, and in consoling her could find consolation for himself. If I could not respond to the efforts he wished to make to bring about a meeting, it was because of purely material difficulties. But, more than anything else, his letter made pleasanter the memories I had of him. The happy relationship to which he referred had, as a matter of fact, been the most ordinary of social contacts. I had had few opportunities of talking to him when we had happened to meet one another at dinners, but the intellectual distinction of our hosts had been, and still was, a guarantee that Henri van Blarenberghe, beneath an appearance that was slightly conventional, and representative more of the circle in which he moved than of his own personality, concealed an original and lively nature. Among the strange snapshots of memory which our brains, so small and yet so vast, collect by the thousand, the one that is the clearest to me when I rummage among those in which Henri van Blarenberghe appears, is that of a smiling face and of the curious amused look he had, with mouth hanging half open, when he had discharged a witty repartee. It is thus that I, as one so rightly says, 'see' him, always charming, always moderately distinguished. Our eyes play a greater part than we are prepared to admit in that active exploration of the past to which we give the name of memory. If, when someone is scrutinizing an incident of his past in an endeavour to fix it, to make it once again a living reality, we look at his eyes as he tries to recollect, we see that they are emptied of all consciousness of what is going on around him, of the scene which, but a moment earlier, they reflected. 'You're not there at all,' we say; 'you're far away.' Yet what we see is but the reverse side of what is going on within his mind. At such moments the loveliest eyes in the world are powerless to move us by their beauty, are no more – to misinterpret a phrase of Wells – than 'time machines', than telescopes focused upon the invisible, which see further the older we grow. When we watch the rusted gaze of old men – wearied by the effort to adapt themselves to the conditions of a time so different from their own – grow blind in an effort to remember, we feel, with extraordinary certainty, that the trajectory of their glance, passing over life's shadowed failures, will come to earth not some few feet in front of them – as they think – but, in reality, fifty or sixty years behind. I remember how the charming eyes of Princesse Mathilde took on a more than ordinary beauty when they became fixed on some image which had come unbidden to the retina when, in memory, she saw this or that great man, this or that great spectacle dating back to the early years of the century. It was *that* she saw: something we shall never see. At such moments, when my glance met hers, I got a vivid impression of the supernatural, because with a curious and mysterious nearsightedness and as the result of an act of resurrection, she was linking past and present.

Charming and moderately distinguished. Those are the words I used when thinking back to my memories of him. But after his letter had come I put a few added touches to the picture thus preserved, interpreting as evidence of a deeper sensibility, of a less wholly 'social' mentality, certain ways he had of looking, certain characteristics which might lend themselves to a more interesting, a more generous 'reading' than the one I had at first accorded him.

When, somewhat later, I asked him to tell me about one of the staff of the Eastern Railway (Monsieur van Blarenberghe was chairman of the board), in whom a friend of mine was taking an interest, I received the following reply. It had been written on the twelfth of last January but, in consequence of my having changed my address, unknown to him, did not reach me until the seventeenth, that is to say, not a fort-night, barely eight days, before the date of the drama.

48 Rue de la Bienfaisance
January 12, 1907

Dear Sir,

Thinking it possible that the man X might still be employed by the Eastern Railway Company, I have made inquiries at their offices and have asked them to let me know where he may be found. Nothing is known of him. If you have the name right, its owner has disappeared, leaving no trace. I gather that he was, in any case, only tem-porarily in their employ and that he occupied a very subordinate position.

I am much disturbed by the news you give me of the state of your health ever since the premature and cruel death of your parents. If it is any consolation, let me tell you that I, too, have suffered physically as well as emotionally from the shock of my father's death. But hope springs eternal ... What the year 1907 may have in store for me I do not know, but it is my dearest wish that it may bring some alleviation to you as well as to me and that in the course of the next few months we may be able to meet.

I should like you to know how deeply I sympathize with you.

Yours sincerely,
H. van Blarenberghe

Five or six days after receiving this letter, I remembered, one morning on waking, that I wanted to answer it. One of those unexpected spells of cold had set in which are like the high tides of heaven, submerging all the dikes raised by great cities between ourselves and nature, thrusting at our closed windows, creeping into our very rooms, making us realize, when they lay a bracing touch upon our shoulders, that the elements have returned to attack in force. The days were disturbed by sudden changes in the temperature and by violet barometric shocks. Nor did this display of nature's powers bring any sense of joy. One bemoaned in advance the snow that was on the way, and even inani-mate objects, as in André Rivoire's lovely poem, seemed to be 'waiting for the snow'. A 'depression' has only to 'advance towards the Balearics', as the newspapers put it, Jamaica has only to experience an earthquake tremor for people in Paris who are subject to headaches, rheumatism, and asthma, and probably lunatics as well, to have a crisis — so closely linked are nervous temperaments with the furthest points upon the earth's surface by bonds whose strength they must often wish was less compulsive. If the influence of the stars upon some at least of such cases be ever recognized (see Framery and Pelletean as quoted by Monsieur Brissaud), to whom could the lines of the poet be held to be more applicable:

Et de longs fils l'unissent aux étoiles?

No sooner was I awake than I sat down to answer Henri van Blaren-berghe. But before doing so, I wanted just to glance at *Le Figaro*, to proceed to that abominable and voluptuous act known as *reading the paper*, thanks to which all the miseries and catastrophes of the world during the past twenty-four hours – battles that have cost the lives of fifty-thousand men, crimes, strikes, bankruptcies, fires, poisonings, suicides, divorces, the shattering emotions of statesmen and actors alike – are transmuted for our own particular use, though we are not ourselves involved, into a daily feast that seems to make a peculiarly exciting and stimulating accompaniment to the swallowing of a few mouthfuls of coffee brought in response to our summons. No sooner have we broken the fragile band that wraps *Le Figaro* and alone sep-arates us from the miseries of the world, and hastily glanced at the first sensational paragraphs of which the wretchedness of so many human beings 'forms an element', those sensational paragraphs, the contents of which we shall later retail to those who have not yet read their papers, than we feel a delightful sense of being once again in contact with that life with which, when we awoke, it seemed so useless to renew acquaintance. And if, from time to time, something like a tear starts from our gorged and glutted eyes, it is only when we come on a passage like this: 'An impressive silence grips all hearts: the drums roll out a salute, the troops present arms, and a great shout goes up – "Vive Fallières!" ...' At that we weep, though a tragedy nearer home would have us dry-eyed. Vile actors that we are who can be moved to tears only by the sorrows of Hercules or, at a still lower level, by the state progresses of the President of the Republic! But on this particular morning the reading of *Le Figaro* moved me to no easy responses. I had just let my fascinated eyes skim the announcements of volcanic eruptions, ministerial crises, and gang fights and was just beginning to read a paragraph, the heading of which, 'Drama of a Lunatic', promised a more than usually sharp stimulus for my morning faculties, when I suddenly saw the victim of this particular episode had been Madame van Blarenberghe, that the murderer, who had later committed suicide, was the man whose letter lay within reach of my hand, waiting to be answered. *'Hope springs eternal . . . What the year 1907 may have in store for me I do not know, but it is my dearest wish that it may bring some alleviation to you as well as to me . . .'* etc. 'Hope springs eternal! What the year 1907 may have in store for me I do not know'! Well, life's answer had not been long delayed; 1907 had not yet dropped the first of its months into the past, and already it had brought him his present – a gun, a revolver, a dagger, and that blindness with which Athene once struck the mind of Ajax, driving him to slaughter shepherds and flocks alike on the plains of Greece, not knowing what he did. 'I it was who set lying images before his eyes. And he rushed forth, striking to right and left, thinking it was the Atrides whom he slew, falling first on one, then on another. I it was who goaded on this man caught in the toils of a murderous madness, I who set a snare for his feet, and even now he is returned, his brow soaked in sweat, his hands reeking with blood.' Madmen, in the fury of their onslaught, are without knowledge of what they do, but, the crisis once past, then comes agony. Tekmessa, the wife of Ajax, said: 'His madness is diminished, his fury fallen to stillness like the breath of Motos. But now that his wits are recovered, he is tormented by a new misery, for to look on horrors for which no one but oneself has been responsible adds bitterness to grief. Ever since he realized what has happened, he has been howling in a black agony – he who used to say that tears are unworthy of a man. He sits, not moving, uttering his cries, and I know well that he is planning against himself some dark design.' But when with Henri van Blarenberghe the fit had passed, it was no scene of slaughtered flocks and shepherds that he saw before him. Grief does not kill in a moment. He did not fall dead at sight of his murdered mother lying there at his feet. He did not fall dead at the sound of her dying voice, when she said, like Tolstoy's Princesse Andrée: 'Henri, what have you done to me! What have you done to me!' . . . 'On reaching the landing of the stairs between the first and second floors, they,' said the *Matin* (the servants who, in this account – which may not have been accurate – are represented as being in a panic and running down into the hall four steps at a time), 'saw Madame van Blarenberghe, her face contorted with terror, descending the first few stairs, and heard her cry out: "Henri! Henri! What have you done?" Then the wretched woman, her head streaming with blood, threw up her arms and fell forward on her face. The terrified servants rushed for help. Soon afterwards, four policemen, who had been summoned, forced the locked door of the murderer's room. There were dagger wounds on his body, and the left side of his face had been ripped open by a pistol shot. *One eye was hanging out on the pillow.*' I thought, reading this, not of Ajax. In the 'eye hanging out on the pillow' I saw, remembering that most terrible act which the history of human suffering has ever recorded, the eye of the wretched Oedipus ... 'and Oedipus, rushing forth with a great cry, called for a sword ... With terrible moaning he dashed himself against the double doors, tore them from their sunken hinges, and stormed into the room, where he saw Jocasta hanging from the strangling rope. Finding her thus, the wretched man groaned in horror and loosened the cord. His mother's body, no longer supported, fell to the ground. Then he snatched the golden brooches from Jocasta's dress and thrust them into his open eyes, saying that no longer should they look upon the evils he had suffered, the miseries he had caused; and, bellowing curses, he struck his staring eyes again and again, and the bleeding pupils ran down his cheeks in a rain, in a hail of black blood. Then he cried out, bidding those who stood by to show the parricide to the race of Cadmus, urging them to drive him from the land. Ah! thus is ancient felicity given its true name. But from that day has been no dearth of all the evils that are named among men; groans and disasters, death and obloquy.' And, thinking of Henri van Blarenberghe's torment when he saw his mother lying dead before him, I thought, too, of another wretched madman, of Lear, holding in his arms the body of his daughter, Cordelia:

> *She's dead as earth ...*
> *No, no, no life.*
> *Why should a dog, a horse, a rat have life*
> *And thou no breath at all? Thou'lt come no more,*
> *Never, never, never, never, never ...*
> *Do you see this? Look on her, look, her lips,*
> *Look there, look there!*

In spite of his terrible wounds, Henri van Blarenberghe did not die at once. I cannot but think abominably cruel (though there may have been purpose in it. Does one really know what lay behind the drama? Remember the Brothers Karamazov) the behaviour of the police inspector. 'The wretched man was not dead. The inspector took him by the shoulders, and spoke to him. "Can you hear me? Answer." ... The murderer opened his one remaining eye, blinked a few times, and relapsed into a coma.' I am tempted to address to that brutal inspector the words uttered by Kent in that same scene of *King Lear* from which I have just quoted, when he stopped Edgar from bringing Lear round from his fainting fit:

Vex not his ghost: O, let him pass! he hates him much
That would upon the rack of this tough world
Stretch him out longer.

If I have dwelt upon those great names of tragedy, Ajax and Oedipus, I wish the reader to understand why and why, too, I have published these letters and written this essay. I want to show in what a pure, in what a religious atmosphere of moral beauty this explosion of blood and madness could occur and bespatter without soiling. I want to bring into the room of the crime something of the breath of heaven, to show that what this newspaper paragraph recorded was precisely one of those Greek dramas, the performance of which was almost a sacred ceremony; that the poor parricide was no criminal brute, no moral leper beyond the pale of humanity, but a noble example, a tender and a loving son whom an ineluctable fate – or, let us say, pathological, and so speak the language of today – had driven to crime, and to its expiation, in a manner that should forever be illustrious. 'I find it difficult to believe in death,' wrote Michelet in a fine passage. True, he was speaking only of a jellyfish, about whose death – so little different from its life – there is nothing incredible, so that one is inclined to wonder whether Michelet was not merely making use of one of those hackneyed 'recipes' on which all great writers can lay their hands at need and so serve to their customers at short notice, just the dish for which they have asked. But if I find no difficulty in crediting the death of a jellyfish, I do not find it easy to believe in the death of a person, nor even in the mere eclipse, the mere toppling of his reason. Our sense of the continuity of the human consciousness is too strong. A short while since, and that mind was master of life and death, could move us to a feeling of respect; and now, both life and death have mastered it. It has become feebler than our own, which, for all its weakness, can now no longer bow before what so quickly has become almost nothing. For this, madness is to blame, madness which is like an old man's loss of his faculties, like death itself. What, today, is the man who, only yesterday, could write the wise and high-minded letter I have already quoted? And even – to move for a moment to the lower level of those trivial matters which, nevertheless, are so important – the man who was so moderate and so sober in what he asked of life, who loved the little things of existence, answered a letter with such charm, was so scrupulous in doing what was demanded of him, valued the opinions of others, and wanted to appear in their eyes as someone, if not of in-fluence, at least of easy friendliness, playing the social game so sensi-tively, so loyally ... These things, I say, are very important, and if I quoted, a while back, the first part of his second letter, which really concerned only my personal affairs, it was because the practical good sense which it displays seems even more at variance with what after-wards occurred than does the admirable and profound melancholy expressed in its final lines. Often, when a mind has been brought low, it is the main limbs of the tree, its top, that live on, when all the tangle of its lower branches has been eaten away by disease. In the present case, the spiritual core was left intact. I felt, as I was copying those letters, how very much I should have liked to be able to make my readers realize the extreme delicacy, nay, more – the quite incredible firmness of the hand which must have been needed to produce such neat and exquisite calligraphy.

What have you done to me! What have you done to me! If we let ourselves think for a few moments we shall, I believe, agree that there is probably no devoted mother who could not, when her last day dawns, address the same reproach to her son. The truth is that, as we grow older, we kill the heart that loves us by reason of the cares we lay on it, by reason of that uneasy tenderness that we inspire and keep forever stretched upon the rack. Could we but see in the beloved body the slow work of destruction that is the product of the painful tenderness which is the mainspring of its being, could we but see the faded eyes, the hair against whose valiant blackness time had so long been powerless, now sharing in the body's general defeat and suddenly turned white; could we but see the hardened arteries, the congested kidneys, the over-worked heart; could we but watch courage failing under the blows of life, the slowing movements, the heavy step, the spirit once so tireless and unconquerable, now conscious of hope gone forever, and that former gaiety, innate and seemingly immortal, so sweet a consort for sad moments, now finally withered – perhaps, seeing all this in a flash of that lucidity now come too late, which even lives spent in a long illusion may sometimes have, as Don Quixote once had his – perhaps, then, like Henri van Blarenberghe when he stabbed his mother to death, we should recoil before the horror of our lives, and seize the nearest gun, and make an end. In most men these painful moments of vision (even assuming they can gain the heights from which such seeing is possible) soon melt in the early beams of the sun which shines upon the joys of life. But what joy, what reason for living, what life can stand up to the impact of such awareness? Which is true, it or the joy of life? Which of them is the truth?

Translated by Gerard Hopkins

Robert Musil

Moosbrugger

FROM THE MAN WITHOUT QUALITIES, VOLUME I

*Born in Klagenfurt, Austria, in 1880, Robert Musil is almost
unknown except to a small circle of readers who regard him as one
of the greatest figures in German literature. In 1906, he gained a
measure of notice with a novel called* Young Torless. *In the early
Twenties, he began work on the long novel (unfinished at his
death) which was to occupy him for the rest of his life,* The Man
Without Qualities. *Musil was rewriting the third volume,* The
Criminals, *when he died in Switzerland, in 1942, an exile from his
Nazi-dominated homeland.*

*A synopsis of the first seventeen chapters of Volume I (of which
the 'Moosbrugger' excerpt is chapter eighteen) is difficult, not
only because of the book's complexity and satirical comedy, but
also because the real action lies not on the surface, in what the
characters do, but within their states of mind, the shifts of their
emotions, their ideas, and the contrast between their thoughts
and their behaviour. However, if we were to trace Musil's deliberate and meandering trail, we would find that there are two main
themes bound up with each other. The first involves Ulrich, the
protagonist, and the second Moosbrugger, the sexual maniac and
murderer. Ulrich, the son of a Viennese professor, for a display of
intellectual 'impertinence', is sent to be educated at an obscure
Belgian school which 'does a roaring trade in the black sheep of
other schools, at a low fee'. Like the author himself, Ulrich later
rejects a career in mathematics and turns towards music and
philosophy. At the time of the Moosbrugger episode, Ulrich has
given up his 'qualities' and, against his intentions, is drifting towards the post of honorary secretary to a patriotic movement
called* The Collateral Campaign. *Ulrich subconsciously recognizes*

the danger of drifting from moral action and recognizes in Moos-
brugger the extreme example of such moral waywardness. He has
nightmares about the criminal and, later on, pleads mercy for him.

At this time the Moosbrugger case was attracting much public attention.

Moosbrugger was a carpenter, a big, broad-shouldered man without
any superfluous fat, with hair like brown lamb's-skin and harmless-
looking great fists. His face also expressed good-hearted strength and
the wish to do right, and if one had not seen these qualities, one would
have smelt them, in the rough-and-ready, straightforward, dry, work-
aday smell that went with this thirty-four-year-old man, from his
having to do with wood and a kind of work that called for steadiness
as much as for exertion.

One stopped as though rooted to the spot, when for the first time
one encountered this face so blessed by God with all the signs of goodness, for Moosbrugger was usually accompanied by two armed gend-
armes and had his hands shackled before him to a strong steel chain,
the grip of which was held by one of his escorts.

When he noticed that one was looking at him, a smile passed over
his broad, kindly face with the unkempt hair and the moustache and
little imperial. He wore a short black jacket and light grey trousers. He
carried himself in a straddling, military way. But it was chiefly this
smile that had kept the law-court reporters busy. It might have been an
embarrassed smile, or a cunning one, an ironical, treacherous, grieved,
mad, blood-thirsty, or uncanny one: one could see them groping for
contradictory expressions, and they seemed to be desperately searching
for something in this smile, something that they obviously found
nowhere else in the whole honest look of the man.

For Moosbrugger had killed a street-woman, a prostitute of the
lowest type, in a horrifying manner. The reporters had described in
detail a throat-wound extending from the larynx to the back of the
neck, as well as the two stab-wounds in the breast, which had pierced
the heart, the two others on left side of the back, and the cutting off
of the breasts, which could almost be detached from the body. They
had expressed their abhorrence of it, but they did not leave off until
they had counted thirty-five stabs in the abdomen and described the
long slash from the navel to the sacrum, which continued up the back
in a multitude of smaller slashes, while the throat showed the marks of
throttling. From such horrors they could not find their way back to
Moosbrugger's kind face, although they themselves were kind men

and yet had described what had happened in a matter-of-fact, expert way and obviously breathless with excitement. They made little use even of the most obvious explanation: that here they were confronted with a madman – Moosbrugger had already been in lunatic asylums several times on account of similar crimes – although nowadays a good reporter is very well up on such matters. It looked as though they were still reluctant to give up the idea of the villain and to dismiss the incident from their own world into that of the insane, an attitude in keeping with that of the psychiatrists, who had declared him normal quite as often as they had declared him not responsible for his actions. And there was, furthermore, the remarkable circumstance that, even when the facts had scarcely become publicly known, Moosbrugger's insane excesses had been felt to be 'something interesting, for once' by thousands of people who deplored the sensationalism of the newspapers, by busy officials as by fourteen-year-old schoolboys and housewives wrapped in the haze of their domestic cares. Although indeed one sighed over such a monstrosity, one was inwardly more preoccupied with it than with one's own affairs. Indeed, it was quite likely to happen that some staid assistant under-secretary or bank-manager would say to his sleepy wife as they were going to bed: 'What would you do now if I were a Moosbrugger?'

When Ulrich's gaze fell on this face that bore the marks of being in God's own keeping, and on the shackles, he turned swiftly on his heel and gave a sentry at the *Landesgericht* nearby some cigarettes, asking about the convoy that must only just have left the gates, so discovering ... Well, anyway, something of the sort must have happened at some time, or else one would not so frequently find it described in this manner. Ulrich almost believed in it himself; but the historical truth of that particular situation was that he had merely read it all in the newspaper. It was to be a long time yet before he got to know Moosbrugger personally, and previous to that he only once succeeded in seeing him in the flesh during the trial. The probability of learning something unusual from a newspaper is far greater than that of experiencing it; in other words, it is in the realm of the abstract that the more important things happen in these times, and it is the unimportant that happens in real life.

What Ulrich in this way learnt about Moosbrugger's history was approximately the following.

As a boy Moosbrugger had been a poverty-stricken wretch, a shepherd-lad in a hamlet so small that it did not even have a village street; and he was so poor that he never spoke to a girl. Girls were something that he could always only look at, even later when he was an apprentice, and even on his wanderings as a journeyman. Now, one must just imagine what that means. Something that one craves for just as naturally as one craves for bread or water is only there to be looked at. After a time one's desire for it becomes unnatural. It walks past, the skirts swaying round its ankles. It climbs over a stile, becoming visible right up to the knees. One looks into its eyes, and they become opaque. One hears it laughing, turns round swiftly, and looks into a face that is round and unmoving as a hole in the ground where a mouse has just disappeared.

So it was understandable that even after the murder of the first girl Moosbrugger had vindicated himself by saying that he was continually haunted by spirits, which called him day and night. They would throw him out of bed when he was asleep, and disturbed him at his work. Then he would hear them talking to each other and quarrelling all day and all night long. That was not insanity, and Moosbrugger extremely disliked hearing it spoken of as such, although he himself did some-times embroider it all with reminiscences of sermons or 'pile it on' according to the advice one gets in prison on how to simulate. The material, however, was always there, ready, waiting — only fading out a little whenever one did not happen to be paying attention to it.

That was the way it had been on his journeyings, too. It is difficult for a carpenter to find work in winter, and Moosbrugger was often without a roof over his head for weeks. Now supposing one has been walking all day, and arrives at a village and cannot get shelter. One has to go on and on walking, far into the night. One has no money for a meal, so one drinks schnapps until two candles light up behind one's eyes and the body walks on its own. One doesn't want to ask for a doss-down at 'the station', in spite of the hot soup, partly because of the bugs and partly because of the insulting fuss they make; and so one collects a few coppers by begging, instead, and crawls into some farmer's haystack. Without asking him, of course — for what's the sense of asking and asking and only getting insulted? Of course in the morn-ing there's likely to be a row and a charge of assault, vagrancy and begging, and the outcome is that there's a thicker and thicker file of such previous convictions, opened up by each new judge with a great air of importance, as though Moosbrugger himself were explained in it.

And who thinks of what it means not to be able to have a proper wash for days and weeks on end? One's skin becomes so stiff that it stops one from making any but rough movements, even supposing one wanted to make gentle, loving ones — the living soul sets and hardens under such a crust. It may not affect the mind so much; one goes on doing what is necessary quite sensibly. The mind is quite likely to keep burning like a little lamp in a huge walking lighthouse that is full of crushed earthworms or grasshoppers – but everything personal in it is squashed, and what walks about is only the fermenting organic substance. Then Moosbrugger on his wanderings, passing through the villages, or even on the lonely road, met with whole processions of women. First there was one, and then it might be half an hour before there was another woman, but even if they came at such long intervals and had nothing to do with one another, still, as a whole they were processions. They would be going from one village to the other or would just have slipped out of the house for a moment, they wore thick shawls or jackets that stood out in a stiff snaky line round their hips, they came into warm rooms or drove their children along in front of them or they were so alone on the road that one could have dropped them with a stone, like a crow. Moosbrugger insisted that he could not have committed murder for the pleasure of it, because he had always been inspired with feelings of disgust for all these females. And that seems not improbable, considering that one thinks one understands even the cat sitting in front of a cage in which a fat, fair-feathered canary is hopping up and down, or striking a mouse, letting it go, and striking it again, just for the sake of seeing it run away once more – and what is going on in a dog that runs after a turning wheel, biting at it, he, the friend of man? This relation to the living, moving, silently bowling or flitting things points to a secret aversion from a fellow-creature delighting in its own existence.

And after all what was one to do when she screamed? One could either come to one's senses or, if one was simply incapable of that, press her face to the ground and stuff earth into her mouth.

Moosbrugger was only a journeyman carpenter, an utterly solitary man, and although he was well liked by his mates in all the places where he worked, he had no friend. An irresistible urge from time to time cruelly turned his personality inside-out. Perhaps he would really have needed, as he said himself, only the upbringing, and the opportunity, to make something quite different of it and become a destroying Angel, slaughtering thousands, an incendiary, setting theatres on fire, or a great anarchist (those anarchists who leagued themselves together in secret societies he referred to with contempt as 'impostors'). He was clearly not normal; but although obviously it was his diseased nature that was the cause of his behaviour and set him apart from other human beings, to him it felt like a stronger and

higher awareness of his own personality. His whole life was a struggle
– laughably and horribly clumsy – to extort acknowledgement of this.
As an apprentice, he had broken the fingers of a master who had tried
to beat him. From another master he ran away with money – for the
sake of necessary justice as he himself put it. He never stood it long
in any place. So long as he could keep the men in awe, as he always
did at first, huge-shouldered as he was, with his kindly calm ways and
his taciturn manner of going about his work, he stayed. As soon as
they became matey and began to treat him without respect, as though
now they had seen through him, he cleared out, for then he was seized
by an uncanny feeling as though he were not quite firmly fixed inside
his own skin. Once he had left it too late. Then four bricklayers on the
site had plotted to make him feel their superiority and to throw him
down the scaffolding from the top storey. He even heard them tittering
as they came up behind his back, and then he hurled himself on them
with all his extraordinary strength, threw one of them down two flights
and cut right through the arm-sinews of two others. That he had been
punished for this had been a shock to his feelings, as he said. He went
abroad. He made his way to Turkey, and then back again, for everywhere the world was in league against him; no magic formula was a
match for this conspiracy, and no benevolence either.

Such expressions he had picked up eagerly in mental hospitals and
prisons, with scraps of French and Latin that he stuck in at the most
unsuitable places in his speeches, since he had found out that it was
the possession of these languages that gave those in power the right to
'arrive at findings' where his fate was concerned. For the same reason
he did his utmost to use educated speech during the trial, saying, for
instance, 'this must serve as the basis of my brutality,' or 'I had
imagined her even crueller than I habitually estimate women of that
sort.' But when he saw that even this failed to make an impression, he
not infrequently rose to the heights of an immense theatrical pose,
scornfully declaring himself a 'theoretical anarchist' who could get
himself rescued by the Social-Democrats at any moment if he were prepared to accept anything from the hands of those worst of Jewish
exploiters of the ignorant working class. In this he too had his
'science', a field on to which the learned presumption of his judges
could not follow him.

This usually earned him the comment 'intelligence – remarkable' in
the opinion of the courts, respectful attention during the proceedings,
and severer sentences; but fundamentally his flattered vanity regarded
these proceedings as the highlights of his life. Hence too he hated no

one as fervently as the psychiatrists who believed they could dispose of his entire difficult personality with a few long Latin or Greek words, as though for them it were an every-day matter. As always happens in such cases, medical opinion as to his mental state fluctuated under pressure from the juristic body of ideas, which superimposed itself upon it. And Moosbrugger missed none of these opportunities during the public proceedings to prove his superiority to the psychiatrists and unmask them as swelled-headed dunces and charlatans, who knew absolutely nothing and would have to take him into the asylum if he chose to simulate, instead of sending him to jail, where he really ought to be. For he did not deny these acts of his. He wanted them understood as mishaps arising out of a grand attitude to life. Above all, the giggling womenfolk were in a conspiracy against him; they all had their fancy-boys, and a steady man's straightforward way of talking was something they despised, if they did not take it for a downright insult. He kept out of their way as much as he could, so as not to be irritated; but this was not always possible. Days came when a man got quite stupid in his head and could not get a proper hold on anything, with his hands sweating from restlessness. And then, when one had to give in, one could be sure that at the very first step, far off, like an advance patrol sent out by the others, such walking poison would cross one's path, a cheat, secretly laughing at the man while she was weakening him and playing her tricks on him, if indeed she didn't do something far worse to him, being utterly unscrupulous as they all are.

And so it had come to the end of that night, a night spent in listless drinking – with a lot of shouting to keep down one's inner uneasiness. The world is sometimes quite unsteady even when one is not drunk. The walls that are the street sway like stage scenery, with something waiting behind it to step out at its cue. On the fringe of the town everything grows quieter, there where one comes out into the open fields lit up by the moon. There Moosbrugger had to turn back in order to get home by the long way round, and there it was, at the iron bridge, that the girl accosted him. She was the kind of girl that hires herself out to men down there by the meadows, an out-of-work, runaway servant girl, a little thing of whom there was nothing to be seen but two inveigling mouse-eyes gazing out from under her kerchief. Moosbrugger waved her away and quickened his steps. But she kept on begging him to take her home with him. Moosbrugger walked on, straight ahead, round the corner, and finally round and round, not knowing what to do. He took long strides, and she ran along beside him. He stopped, and there she stood like a shadow. He was drawing her along after him, that was it. Then he made one more attempt to scare her off: he turned round and spat into her face, twice. But it did not help; nothing could affront her.

This happened in the vast park that they had to cross at its narrowest part. Then Moosbrugger became certain that some fancy-man of the girl's must be somewhere about – for else how would she have had the courage to follow him in spite of his annoyance? He reached for the knife in his trouser pocket, for surely he was being got at, perhaps they were again about to attack him. Behind the women there was always the other man, sneering at one. And, come to think of it, didn't she look like a man in disguise? He saw shadows moving and heard a crackling in the bushes. And always the sneaking female at his side, like the pendulum of a huge clock, time and again repeating her request. But there was nothing there on which he could have rushed with all his giant's strength, and he began to be frightened of this uncanny way in which nothing was happening.

When they began to go down the first, still very gloomy street, there was sweat on his forehead, and he was trembling. He kept his eyes fixed straight ahead. Then he went into the café that happened to be still open. He tossed off a black coffee and three brandies one after the other and was able to sit quietly for a while, perhaps as long as a quarter of an hour. But when he paid, there again the thought was: What was he to do if she was still waiting outside? There are such thoughts that are like string winding itself in endless nooses round one's arms and legs. And he had taken only a few steps out into the dark street when he felt the girl at his side. Now she was no longer humble, but brazen and self-confident; nor did she plead any more; she was merely silent. There and then he realized that he would never get rid of her, because it was he himself who was drawing her along after him. His throat filled up with tearful disgust. He walked on, and, again, the thing half behind him was himself. It was just the same way that he always met processions. He had once cut a big splinter of wood out of his leg himself, because he was too impatient to wait for the doctor; it was very much the same, the way he felt his knife now, lying long and hard in his pocket.

But with an almost more than earthly exertion of his conscience Moosbrugger hit upon yet another way out. Behind the hoarding along which the street now led there was a sports-ground; there one could not be seen, and so he entered. In the small ticket-booth he rolled up, with his head pushed into the corner where it was darkest. And the soft, accursed second self lay down beside him. So he pretended to go to sleep at once, in order to be able to slip away later.

When he began quietly crawling out, feet first, there it was again, winding its arms round his neck. And then he felt something hard in her or his pocket. He tugged it out. He was not clear about whether it was a scissors or a knife; he struck home with it. She had insisted that it was only a scissors, but it was his knife. She fell with her head inside the booth; he hauled her some way out, on to the soft earth, and stabbed and stabbed at her until he had cut her completely away from himself. Then he stood beside her for perhaps another quarter of an hour, gazing at her, while the night again grew calmer and strangely, wonderfully smooth. Now she could never insult a man again, clutching at him. Finally he had carried the corpse over the street and laid it down by a bush so that it could be more easily found and buried, as he declared, for now one couldn't blame her any more.

During the proceedings Moosbrugger made quite unpredictable difficulties for his counsel. He sat there at huge ease on his bench, like an onlooker, calling out 'Hear! Hear!' to the public prosecuter whenever he made a point of Moosbrugger's being a public menace and did it in a way that Moosbrugger considered worthy of himself. He gave good marks to witnesses who declared that they had never noticed anything about him that pointed to his being not responsible for his actions. 'You're a queer customer,' the presiding judge said from time to time, in a flattering way, and conscientiously pulled tighter the noose that the accused had laid round his own neck. Then Moosbrugger would stand astonished for an instant, like a harried bull in the arena, his eyes straying, and seeing from the faces of those sitting around him – what he could not understand – that yet once again he had worked himself one layer deeper down into his guilt.

What attracted Ulrich particularly was that Moosbrugger's own defence was obviously based on an obscurely perceptible plan. He had not gone out with the intention of killing, neither did his dignity permit him to be insane; there could not be any talk of sexual 'gratification', but only of disgust and contempt: and therefore the act could only be manslaughter, into which he had been lured by the suspicious behaviour of the woman – 'this caricature of a woman,' as he expressed it. It even seemed that he was demanding to have his murder regarded as a political crime, and he sometimes conveyed the impression that he was fighting, not for himself at all, but for this interpretation of the legal situation. The tactics that the judge employed against this were the usual ones of seeing in everything a murderer's clumsily sly efforts to divert himself of his responsibility.

'Why did you wipe your bloodstained hands? – Why did you throw the knife away? – Why did you change into a clean suit and underclothes after the crime? – Because it was Sunday? Not because they were bloodstained? – Why did you go to an entertainment? Evidently the crime did not prevent you from doing so? Did you feel no remorse whatsoever?'

Ulrich well understood the deep resignation that Moosbrugger felt when in such moments he regretted his insufficient education, which made it impossible for him to untie the knots in this net of incomprehension. But from the judge this only drew the emphatic reproof: 'You always manage to shift the blame on to other people!' This judge rolled everything up into one, starting with the police-reports and the vagrancy, and then presented it to Moosbrugger as his guilt. But for Moosbrugger it all consisted of separate incidents that had nothing to do with each other, each of them with a different cause, which lay outside Moosbrugger and somewhere in the world as a whole. In the judge's eyes his acts were something that issued from him; in his, they had come towards him the way birds come flying along. For the judge Moosbrugger was a special case; for himself he was a world, and it is very difficult to say something convincing about a world. There were two kinds of tactics fighting each other, two kinds of unity and of logical consistency; but Moosbrugger had the less favourable position, for even a cleverer man could not have expressed his strange shadowy arguments. They came directly out of the bewildered solitude of his life, and whereas all other lives exist a hundredfold, being seen in the same way by those who lead them as by all the others who confirm them, his true life existed only for himself. It was like a vapour that is always losing its shape and taking on other forms. He might, of course, have asked his judges whether their lives were essentially different. But such things never occurred to him. Before the law, all that had been so natural while it was one thing happening after the other now lay within him, one thing beside the other, without any sense at all; and he made the greatest efforts, struggling to get sense into it, a sense that would be in no way inferior to the dignity of the gentlemen opposing him. The judge made an almost kindly impression in his attempts to support him in this and to put expressions at his disposal, even though they were such as would deliver Moosbrugger up to the most terrible consequences.

It was like a shadow fighting with a wall, and in the end, Moosbrugger's shadow was only just a ghastly flickering. On this last day of the trial Ulrich was present. When the president of the court read the findings that declared him responsible for his action, Moosbrugger rose and addressed the court: 'I am satisfied, I have attained my object.' Scornful incredulity in the eyes round about answered him, and he added angrily: 'As a result of having forced the court to try me, I am satisfied with the conduct of the case!' The president of the court, who had now become all severity and condemnation, rebuked him, remarking that the court was not concerned with whether he was satisfied or not. Then he read out the death sentence to him, exactly as though the nonsense that Moosbrugger had been talking all through the trial, to the delight of all present, had now for once to be accorded a serious answer. To that Moosbrugger said nothing, lest it might look as though he were frightened. Then the proceedings were concluded, and it was all over. At this moment, however, his mind staggered, reeling back, powerless, before the high-and-mightiness of those who did not understand. He turned round as the warders were already leading him out, he fought for words, stretched his hands above his head and shouted in a voice that shook itself free of his guards' grip: 'I am satisfied, even though I must confess to you that you have condemned a madman!'

This was an inconsistency. Ulrich sat breathless. This was clearly madness, and just as clearly it was merely the distorted pattern of our own elements of existence. It was disjointed and steeped in darkness. Yet somehow Ulrich could not help thinking: if mankind could dream collectively, it would dream Moosbrugger. He came back to the present only when the 'miserable clown of a lawyer', as Moosbrugger had once ungratefully called his counsel in the course of the trial, announced, on account of some details or other, that he would submit a plea of nullity, while his – and Ulrich's – gigantic client was led away.

Translated by Eithne Wilkins
and Ernst Kaiser

Franz Kafka

The Bucket Rider

Franz Kafka was born in Prague in 1883. He lived only until 1924 and never saw his major novels in print. Since then, the publication of The Castle, The Trial, Amerika, *and his shorter fiction has given him an international reputation. His themes of anxiety, frustration, and cosmic disunity seem particularly appropiate to a time when little — either personal or public — can be certain.*

Coal all spent; the bucket empty; the shovel useless; the stove breathing out cold; the room freezing; the leaves outside the window rigid, covered with rime; the sky a silver shield against anyone who looks for help from it. I must have coal; I cannot freeze to death; behind me is the pitiless stove, before me the pitiless sky, so I must ride out between them and on my journey seek aid from the coal-dealer. But he has already grown deaf to ordinary appeals; I must prove irrefutably to him that I have not a single grain of coal left, and that he means to me the very sun in the firmament. I must approach like a beggar who, with the death-rattle already in his throat, insists on dying on the doorstep, and to whom the grand people's cook accordingly decides to give the dregs of the coffee-pot; just so must the coal-dealer, filled with rage, but acknowledging the command, 'Thou shalt not kill,' fling a shovelful of coal into my bucket.

My mode of arrival must decide the matter; so I ride off on the bucket. Seated on the bucket, my hands on the handle, the simplest kind of bridle, I propel myself with difficulty down the stairs; but once down below my bucket ascends, superbly, superbly; camels humbly squatting on the ground do not rise with more dignity, shaking themselves under the sticks of their drivers. Through the hard frozen streets we go at a regular canter; often I am upraised as high as the first storey of a house; never do I sink as low as the house doors. And at last I float at an extraordinary height above the vaulted cellar of the dealer, whom I see far below crouching over his table, where he is writing; he has opened the door to let out the excessive heat.

'Coal-dealer!' I cry in a voice burned hollow by the frost and muffled in the cloud made by my breath, 'please, coal-dealer, give me a little coal. My bucket is so light that I can ride on it. Be kind. When I can I'll pay you.'

The dealer puts his hand to his ear. 'Do I hear rightly?' He throws the question over his shoulder to his wife. 'Do I hear rightly? A customer.'

'I hear nothing,' says his wife, breathing in and out peacefully while she knits on, her back pleasantly warmed by the heat.

'Oh, yes, you must hear,' I cry. 'It's me, an old customer; faithful and true; only without means at the moment.'

'Wife,' says the dealer, 'it's someone, it must be; my ears can't have deceived me so much as that; it must be an old, a very old customer, that can move me so deeply.'

'What ails you, man?' says his wife, ceasing from her work for a moment and pressing her knitting to her bosom. 'It's nobody, the street is empty, all our customers are provided for; we could close down the shop for several days and take a rest.'

'But I'm sitting up here on the bucket,' I cry, and unfeeling frozen tears dim my eyes, 'please look up here, just once; you'll see me directly; I beg you, just a shovelful; and if you give me more it'll make me so happy that I won't know what to do. All the other customers are provided for. Oh, if I could only hear the coal clattering into the bucket!'

'I'm coming,' says the coal-dealer, and on his short legs he makes to climb the steps of the cellar, but his wife is already beside him, holds him back by the arm and says: 'You stay here; seeing you persist in your fancies I'll go myself. Think of the bad fit of coughing you had during the night. But for a piece of business, even if it's one you've only fancied in your head, you're prepared to forget your wife and child and sacrifice your lungs. I'll go.'

'Then be sure to tell him all the kinds of coal we have in stock; I'll shout out the prices after you.'

'Right,' says his wife, climbing up to the street. Naturally she sees me at once. 'Frau Coal-dealer,' I cry, 'my humblest greetings; just one shovelful of coal; here in my bucket; I'll carry it home myself. One shovelful of the worst you have. I'll pay you in full for it, of course, but not just now, not just now.' What a knell-like sound the words 'not just now' have, and how bewilderingly they mingle with the evening chimes that fall from the church steeple nearby!

'Well, what does he want?' shouts the dealer. 'Nothing,' his wife shouts back, 'there's nothing here; I see nothing, I hear nothing; only six striking, and now we must shut up the shop. The cold is terrible; tomorrow we'll likely have lots to do again.'

She sees nothing and hears nothing; but all the same she loosens her apron-strings and waves her apron to waft me away. She succeeds, unluckily. My bucket has all the virtues of a good steed except powers of resistance, which it has not; it is too light; a woman's apron can make it fly through the air.

'You bad woman!' I shout back, while she, turning into the shop, half-contemptuous, half-reassured, flourishes her fist in the air. 'You bad woman! I begged you for a shovelful of the worst coal and you would not give me it.' And with that I ascend into the regions of the ice mountains and am lost forever.

Translated by
Willa and Edwin Muir

Bertolt Brecht

Socrates Wounded

Bertolt Brecht (1889–1956), poet, playwright, novelist, and the-
atrical director, left his native Germany for the United States in
1935. In 1947, he returned to East Germany and soon became
director of an experimental theatre, producing his own plays, such
as Mother Courage, Galileo, The Good Woman of Setzuan, *and*
The Caucasian Chalk-Circle, *as well as several other* avant-garde
works. Upon his death, he was generally considered among the
greatest of twentieth-century playwrights.

Socrates, the midwife's son, who was able in his dialogues to deliver
his friends of well-proportioned thoughts so soundly and easily and
with such hearty jests, thus providing them with children of their own,
instead of, like other teachers, foisting bastards on them, was considered not only the cleverest of all Greeks but also one of the bravest.
His reputation for bravery strikes us as quite justified when we read
in Plato how coolly and unflinchingly he drained the hemlock which the
authorities offered him in the end for services rendered to his fellow-
citizens. Some of his admirers, however, have felt the need to speak
of his bravery in the field as well. It is a fact that he fought at the
battle of Delium, and this in the light infantry, since neither his standing, a cobbler's, nor his income, a philosopher's, entitled him to enter
the more distinguished and expensive branches of the service. Nevertheless, as you may suppose, his bravery was of a special kind.

On the morning of the battle Socrates had primed himself as best he
could for the bloody business by chewing onions which, in the soldier's
view, induced valour. His scepticism in many spheres led to credulity
in many others; he was against speculative thought and in favour of
practical experience and so he did not believe in the gods, but he did
believe in onions.

Unfortunately he felt no real effect, at least no immediate one, and
so he traipsed glumly in a detachment of swordsmen who were march-

ing in single file to take up their position in a reaped field somewhere. Behind and ahead stumbled Athenian boys from the suburbs, who pointed out that the shields from the Athenian arsenals were too small for fat people like him. He had been thinking the same thing, but in terms of *broad* people who were less than half covered by the absurdly narrow shields.

The exchange of views between the man in front of him and the man behind on the profits made by the big armourers out of small shields was cut short by the order: 'Fall out'.

They dropped on to the stubble and a captain reprimanded Socrates for trying to sit on his shield. He was less upset by the reprimand than by the hushed voice in which it was given. It looked as though the enemy were thought to be near.

The milky morning haze completely obscured the view. Yet the noise of tramping and of clanking arms indicated that the plain was peopled.

With great disquiet Socrates remembered a conversation he had had the previous evening with a fashionable young man whom he had once met behind the scenes and who was a cavalry officer.

'A capital plan!' the young puppy had explained. 'The infantry just waits drawn up, loyal and steadfast, and takes the brunt of the enemy's attack. And meanwhile the cavalry advances in the valley and falls on him from the rear.'

The valley must lie fairly far to the right, somewhere in the mist. No doubt the cavalry was advancing there now.

The plan had struck Socrates as good, or at any rate not bad. After all, plans were always made, particularly when your strength was inferior to the enemy's. When it came to brass tacks, it was simply a matter of fighting, that is, slashing away. And there was no advance according to plan, but merely according to where the enemy let you.

Now, in the grey dawn, the plan struck Socrates as altogether wretched. What did it mean: the infantry takes the enemy's attack? Usually one was glad to evade an attack, now, all of a sudden, the art lay in taking the brunt of it. A very bad thing that the general himself was a cavalryman.

The ordinary man would need more onions than there were on the market.

And how unnatural it was, instead of lying in bed, to be sitting here on the bare ground in the middle of a field so early in the morning, carrying at least ten pounds of iron about your person and a butcher's knife in your hand. It was quite right to defend the city if it was attacked, for otherwise you would be exposed to gross inconveniences;

but why was the city attacked? Because the shipowners, vineyard proprietors and slave-traders in Asia Minor had put a spoke in the wheel of Persian shipowners, vineyard proprietors and slave-traders. A fine reason!

Suddenly everyone sat up.

Through the mist on the left came a muffled roar accompanied by the clang of metal. It spread fairly rapidly. The enemy's attack had begun.

The detachment stood up. With bulging eyes they stared into the mist before them. Ten paces away a man fell on his knees and gibbered an appeal to the gods. Too late, in Socrates' view.

All at once, as if in answer, a fearful roar issued from further to the right. The cry for help seemed to have merged into a death cry. Socrates saw a little iron rod come flying out of the mist. A javelin.

And then massive shapes, indistinct in the haze, appeared in front: the enemy.

Socrates, with an overpowering sense that perhaps he had already waited too long, turned about awkwardly and took to his heels. His breastplate and heavy greaves hampered him a good deal. They were far more dangerous than shields, because you could not throw them away.

Panting, the philosopher ran across the stubble. Everything depended on whether he could get a good enough start. If only the brave lads behind him were taking the attack for a bit.

Suddenly a fiendish pain shot through him. His left sole stung till he felt he simply could not bear it. Groaning, he sank to the ground, but leapt up again with another yell of pain. With frantic eyes he looked about him and realized what was up. He had landed in a field full of thorns.

There was a tangle of low undergrowth with sharp thorns. A thorn must have stuck in his foot. Carefully, with streaming eyes, he searched for a spot on the ground where he could sit down. He hobbled a few steps in a circle on his sound foot before lowering himself for the second time. He must pull the thorn out at once.

He listened intently to the noise of battle: it extended pretty far on both sides, though straight ahead it was at least a hundred paces away. However, it seemed to be coming nearer, slowly but unmistakably.

Socrates could not get his sandal off. The thorn had pierced the thin leather sole and was deeply embedded in his flesh. How dared they supply soldiers, who were supposed to defend their country against the enemy, with such thin shoes? Each tug at the sandal was attended by searing pain. Exhausted, the poor man's massive shoulders drooped. What now?

His dejected eye fell on the sword at his side. A thought flashed through his mind, more welcome than any that ever came to him in debate. Couldn't the sword be used as a knife? He grabbed it.

At that moment he heard heavy footsteps. A small squad broke through the scrub. Thank the gods, they were his own side! They halted for a few seconds when they saw him. 'That's the cobbler,' he heard them say. Then they went on.

But now there was a noise from the left too. And then orders in a foreign language rang out. The Persians!

Socrates tried to get to his feet again, that is, to his right foot. He leant on his sword, which was only a little too short. And then, to the left, in the small clearing, he saw a cluster of men locked in combat. He heard heavy groans and the impact of dull iron on iron or leather.

Desperately he hopped backwards on his sound foot. Twisting it he came down again on the injured one and dropped with a moan. When the battling cluster – it was not large, a matter of perhaps twenty or thirty men – had approached to within a few paces, the philosopher was sitting on his backside between two briars looking helplessly at the enemy.

It was impossible for him to move. Anything was better than to feel that pain in the ball of his foot even once more. He did not know what to do and suddenly he started to bellow.

To be precise it was like this: he heard himself bellowing. He heard his voice roaring from the mighty barrel of his thorax: 'Over here, Third Battalion! Let them have it, lads!'

And simultaneously he saw himself gripping the sword and swinging it round him in a circle, for in front of him, appearing from the scrub, stood a Persian soldier with a spear. The spear was knocked sideways, tearing the man down with it.

And Socrates heard himself bellowing again and saying:

'Not another step back, lads! Now we've got them where we want them, the sons of bitches! Crapolus, bring up the Sixth! Nullus, to the right! If anyone retreats I'll tear him to shreds!'

To his surprise he saw two of his own side standing by gaping at him in terror. 'Roar!' he said softly, 'for heaven's sake, roar!' One of them let his jaw drop with a fright, but the other actually started roaring something. And the Persian in front of them got up painfully and ran into the brush.

A dozen exhausted men came stumbling out of the clearing. The yelling had made the Persians turn tail. They feared an ambush.

'What's going on here?' one of his fellow countrymen asked Socrates, who was still sitting on the ground.

'Nothing,' he said. 'Don't stand about like that gaping at me. You'd better run to and fro giving orders, so that over there they don't realize how few we are.'

'We'd better retreat,' said the man hesitantly.

'Not one step!' Socrates protested. 'Have you got cold feet?'

And as a soldier needs to have not only fear, but also luck, they suddenly heard from some way off, but quite clearly, the trampling of horses and wild shouts, and these were in Greek! Everyone knows how overwhelmingly the Persians were routed that day. It finished the war.

As Alcibiades at the head of the cavalry reached the thorn field, he saw a group of foot soldiers carrying a stout man shoulder high.

Reining in his horse, he recognized Socrates, and the soldiers told him how, by his unflinching resistance, he had made the wavering battle line stand firm.

They bore him in triumph to the baggage train. There, despite his protests, he was put on one of the forage wagons and, surrounded by soldiers streaming with sweat and shouting excitedly, he made his return to the capital.

He was carried shoulder high to his little house.

Xantippe, his wife, made bean soup for him. Kneeling at the hearth and blowing at the fire with puffed out cheeks, she glanced at him from time to time. He was still sitting on the chair where his comrades had set him down.

'What's the matter with *you?*' she asked suspiciously.

'Me,' he muttered, 'nothing.'

'What's all this talk about your heroic deeds?' she wanted to know.

'Exaggeration,' he said. 'It smells first class.'

'How can it smell when I haven't got the fire going yet? I suppose you've made a fool of yourself again,' she said angrily. 'And tomorrow when I go for the bread I shall find myself a laughingstock again.'

'I've not made a fool of myself at all. I gave battle.'

'Were you drunk?'

'No. I made them stand firm when they were retreating.'

'You can't even stand firm yourself,' she said, getting up, for the fire had caught. 'Pass me the salt-cellar from the table.'

'I'm not sure,' he said slowly and reflectively, 'I'm not sure if I wouldn't prefer on the whole not to eat anything. My stomach's a little upset.'

'Just as I said; you're drunk. Try standing up and walking about the room a bit. We'll soon see.'

Her unfairness exasperated him. But in no circumstances did he intend to stand up and show her that he could not put his foot to the ground. She was uncannily sharp when it came to nosing out something discreditable to him. And it would be discreditable if the underlying reason for his steadfastness in battle came to light.

She went on busying herself round the stove with the pot and in between let him know her mind.

'I haven't any doubt that your fine friends found you some funk-hole again, well in the rear, near the cook-house. It's all a fiddle.'

In torment he looked out of the little window on to the street where a lot of people with white lanterns were strolling about, for the victory was being celebrated.

His grand friends had tried to do nothing of the sort, nor would he have agreed to it; at all events, not straight off.

'Or did they think it quite in order for the cobbler to march in the ranks? They won't lift a finger for you. He's a cobbler, they say, and let him stay a cobbler. Otherwise we shouldn't be able to visit him in his filthy dump and jabber with him for hours on end and hear the whole world say: what do you think of that, he may be a cobbler, but these grand people sit about with him and talk philersophy. Filthy lot!'

'It's called philerphoby,' he said equably.

She gave him an unfriendly look.

'Don't keep on correcting me. I know I'm uneducated. If I weren't you wouldn't have anybody to bring you a tub of water now and again to wash your feet.'

He winced and hoped she had not noticed it. On no account must there be any question of washing his feet today. Thank the gods, she was off again on her harangue.

'Well, if you weren't drunk and they didn't find a funk-hole for you either, then you must have behaved like a butcher. So there's blood on your hands, eh? But if I squash a spider, you start shouting. Not that I believe you really fought like a man, but you must have done something crafty, something a bit underhand or they wouldn't be slapping you on the back like this. I'll find out sooner or later, don't you worry.'

The soup was now ready. It smelled enticing. The woman took the pot and, holding the handles with her skirt, set it on the table and began to ladle it out.

He wondered whether, after all, he had not better recover his appetite. The thought that he would then have to go to the table restrained him just in time.

He did not feel at all easy. He was well aware that the last word had not yet been said. There was bound to be a lot of unpleasantness before long. You could hardly decide a battle against the Persians and be left in peace. At the moment, in the first flush of victory, no one, of course, gave a thought to the man responsible for it. Everyone was fully occupied proclaiming his own glorious deeds from the housetops. But tomorrow or the day after, everyone would wake up to the fact that the other fellow was claiming all the credit, and then they would be anxious to push him forward. So many would be able to score off so many others if the cobbler were proclaimed the real hero in chief. They couldn't stand Alcibiades as it was. What pleasure it would give them to throw in his teeth: Yes, you won the battle, but a cobbler fought it.

And the thorn hurt more savagely than ever. If he did not get his sandal off soon, it might mean blood poisoning.

'Don't smack your lips like that,' he said absentmindedly.

The spoon remained stuck in his wife's mouth.

'Don't do what?'

'Nothing,' he hastened to assure her in alarm. 'I was miles away.'

She stood up, beside herself, banged the pot down on the stove and went out.

He heaved a deep sigh of relief. Hastily he levered himself out of the chair and hopped to his couch at the back, looking round nervously. As she came back to fetch her wrap to go out she looked suspiciously at the way he lay motionless on the leather-covered hammock. For a moment she thought there must be something the matter with him after all. She even considered asking him, for she was very devoted to him. But she thought better of it and left the room sulkily to watch the festivities with the woman from next door.

Socrates slept badly and restlessly and woke up feeling worried. He had got his sandal off, but had not been able to get hold of the thorn. His foot was badly swollen.

His wife was less sharp this morning.

She had heard the whole city talking about her husband the evening before. Something really must have happened to impress people so deeply. That he had held up an entire Persian battle line she certainly could not accept. Not him, she told herself. Yes, hold up an entire public meeting with his questions, he could do that all right. But not a battle line. So what had happened?

She was so uncertain that she brought him his goat's milk in bed.

He had made no attempt to get up.

'Aren't you going out?' she asked.

'Don't feel like it,' he growled.

That is not the way to answer a civil question from your wife, but she thought that perhaps he only wanted to avoid being stared at and let the answer pass.

Visitors began arriving early: a few young men, the sons of well-off parents, his usual associates. They always treated him as their teacher and some of them even made notes while he talked, as though it were something quite special.

Today they told him at once that Athens resounded with his fame. It was a historic date for philosophy (so she had been right after all: it was called philersophy and not something else). Socrates had demonstrated, they said, that the great thinker could also be the great man of action.

Socrates listened to them without his usual mockery. As they spoke he seemed to hear, still far away, as one hears a distant thunderstorm, stupendous laughter, the laughter of a whole city, even of a whole country, far away, but drawing nearer, irresistibly approaching, infecting everyone: the passers-by in the streets, the merchants and politicians in the market place, the artisans in their little workshops.

'That's all rubbish what you're saying,' he said with a sudden resolve. 'I didn't do anything at all.'

They looked at each other and smiled. Then one of them said:

'That's just what we said. We knew you'd take it like that. What's this hullabaloo all of a sudden, we asked Eusopulos outside the gymnasium. For ten years Socrates has been performing the greatest intellectual feats and no one so much as turned his head to look at him. Now he's won a battle and the whole of Athens is talking about him. Don't you see how disgraceful it is, we said.'

Socrates groaned.

'But I didn't win it at all. I defended myself because I was attacked. I wasn't interested in this battle. I neither trade in arms nor do I own vineyards in the area. I wouldn't know what to fight battles for. I found myself amongst a lot of sensible men from the suburbs, who have no interest in battles, and I did exactly what they all did, at the most, a few seconds before them.'

They were dumbfounded.

'There you are!' they exclaimed, 'that's what we said too. He did nothing but defend himself. That's his way of winning battles. With your permission we'll hurry back to the gymnasium. We interrupted a discussion on this subject only to wish you good morning.'

And off they went, wallowing deeply in discussion.

Socrates lay propped up on his elbows in silence and gazed at the smoke-blackened ceiling. His gloomy forebodings had been right.

His wife watched him from a corner of the room. Mechanically she went on mending an old dress.

All of a sudden she asked softly: 'Well, what's behind it all?'

He gave a start. He looked at her uncertainly.

She was a worn-out creature, flat-chested as a board and sad-eyed. He knew he could depend on her. She would still be standing up for him when his pupils would be saying: 'Socrates? Isn't that the vile cobbler who repudiates the gods?' He'd been a bad bargain for her, but she did not complain — except to him. And there had never yet been an evening without some bread and a bit of bacon for him on the shelf when he came home hungry from his rich pupils.

He wondered whether he should tell her everything. But then he realized that before long, when people, like those just now, came to see him and talked about his heroic deeds, he would have to utter a whole lot of lies and hypocrisies in her hearing, and he could not bring himself to do that if she knew the truth, for he respected her.

So he let it be and just said: 'Yesterday's cold bean soup is stinking the whole place out again.'

She only shot him another suspicious look.

Naturally they were in no position to throw food away. He was only trying to find something to sidetrack her. Her conviction that there was something wrong with him grew. Why didn't he get up? He always got up late, but simply because he went to bed late. Yesterday he had gone to bed very early. And today, with victory celebrations, the whole city was on the go. All the shops in the street were shut. Some of the cavalry that had been pursuing the enemy had got back at five o'clock in the morning, the clatter of horses' hoofs had been heard. He adored tumultuous crowds. On occasions like this he ran round from morning till night, getting into conversation with people. So why wasn't he getting up?

The threshold darkened and in came four officials. They remained standing in the middle of the room and one of them said in a business-like but exceedingly respectful tone that he was instructed to escort Socrates to the Areopagus. The general, Alcibiades himself, had proposed that a tribute be paid to him for his martial feats.

A hum of voices from the street showed that the neighbours were gathering outside the house.

Socrates felt sweat breaking out. He knew that now he would have to get up and, even if he refused to go with them, he would at least have to get on his feet, say something polite and accompany these men to the door. And he knew that he would not be able to take more than two steps at the most. Then they would look at his foot and know what was up. And enormous laughter would break out, there and then.

So, instead of getting up, he sank back on his hard pillow and said cantankerously:

'I require no tribute. Tell the Areopagus that I have an appointment with some friends at eleven o'clock to thrash out a philosophical question that interests us, and therefore, much to my regret, I cannot come. I am altogether unfitted for public functions and feel much too tired.'

This last he added because he was annoyed at having dragged in philosophy, and the first part he said because he hoped that rudeness was the easiest way to shake them off.

The officials certainly understood this language. They turned on their heels and left, treading on the feet of the people standing outside.

'One of these days they'll teach you to be polite to the authorities,' said his wife angrily and went into the kitchen.

Socrates waited till she was outside. Then he swiftly swung his heavy body round in the bed, seated himself on the edge of it, keeping a wary eye on the door, and tried with infinite caution to step on the bad foot. It seemed hopeless.

Streaming with sweat he lay back again.

Half an hour passed. He took up a book and read. So long as he kept his foot still he felt practically nothing.

Then his friend Antisthenes turned up.

He did not remove his heavy coat, remained standing at the foot of the couch, coughed in a rather forced way and scratched his throat with its bristly beard as he looked at Socrates.

'Still in bed? I thought I should only find Xantippe at home. I got up specially to enquire after you. I had a bad cold and that was why I couldn't come along yesterday.'

'Sit down,' said Socrates monosyllabically.

Antisthenes fetched a chair from the corner and sat down by his friend.

'I'm starting the lessons again tonight. No reason to interrupt them any longer.'

'No.'

'Of course, I asked myself whether they'd turn up. Today there are the great banquets. But on the way here I ran into young Phaeston and when I told him that I was taking algebra tonight, he was simply delighted. I told him he could come in his helmet. Protagoras and the others will hit the ceiling with rage when it's known that on the night after the battle they just went on studying algebra at Antisthenes'.'

Socrates rocked himself gently in his hammock, pushing himself off the slightly crooked wall with the flat of his hand. His protuberant eyes looked searchingly at his friend.

'Did you meet anybody else?'

'Heaps of people.'

Socrates gazed sourly at the ceiling. Should he make a clean breast of it to Antisthenes? He felt pretty sure of him. He himself never took money for lessons and was therefore not in competition with Antisthenes. Perhaps he really ought to lay the difficult case before him.

Antisthenes looked with his sparkling cricket's eyes inquisitively at his friend and told him:

'Giorgius is going about saying to everyone that you must have been on the run and in the confusion gone the wrong way, that's to say, forwards. A few of the more decent young people want to thrash him for it.'

Unpleasantly surprised, Socrates looked at him.

'Rubbish,' he said with annoyance. He realized in a flash what trumps his opponents would hold if he declared himself.

During the night, towards morning, he had wondered whether he might not present the whole thing as an experiment and say he had wanted to see just how gullible people were. 'For twenty years I've been teaching pacifism in every back street, and one rumour was enough for my own pupils to take me for a berserker,' and so on and so on. But then the battle ought not to have been won. Patently this was an unfavourable moment for pacifism. After a defeat even the top dogs were pacifists for a while; after a victory even the underdogs approved of war, at any rate for a while, until they noticed that for them there wasn't all that difference between victory and defeat. No, he couldn't cut much ice with pacifism just now.

There was a clatter of horses in the street. The riders halted in front of the house and in came Alcibiades with his buoyant step.

'Good morning, Antisthenes, how's the philosophy business going? They're in a great state,' he cried, beaming. 'There's an uproar in the Areopagus over your answer, Socrates. As a joke I've changed my proposal to give you a laurel wreath to the proposal to give you fifty strokes. Of course, that annoyed them, because it exactly expressed their feelings. But you'll have to come along, you know. We'll go together, on foot.'

Socrates sighed. He was on very good terms with young Alcibiades. They had often drunk together. It was very nice of him to call. It was certainly not only his wish to rile the Areopagus. And that wish itself was an honourable one and deserved every support.

At last he said cautiously as he went on rocking himself in his hammock: 'Haste is the wind that blows the scaffolding down. Take a seat.'

Alcibiades laughed and drew up a chair. Before he sat down he bowed politely to Xantippe, who stood at the kitchen door wiping her wet hands on her skirt.

'You philosophers are funny people,' he said a little impatiently. 'For all I know you may be regretting now that you helped us win the battle. I daresay Antisthenes has pointed out to you that there weren't enough good reasons for it.'

'We've been talking about algebra,' said Antisthenes quickly and coughed again.

Alcibiades grinned.

'Just as I expected. For heaven's sake, no fuss about a thing of this sort, what? Now to my mind it was sheer bravery. Nothing remarkable, if you like; but what's so remarkable about a handful of laurel leaves? Grit your teeth and go through with it, old man. It'll soon be over, and it won't hurt. And then we can go and have one.'

He looked searchingly at the broad powerful figure, which was now rocking rather violently.

Socrates thought fast. He had hit on something that he could say. He could say that he had sprained his foot last night or this morning. When the men had lowered him from their shoulders, for instance. There was even a moral to it: the case demonstrated how easily you could come to grief through being honoured by your fellow citizens.

Without ceasing to swing himself, he leant forward so that he was sitting upright, rubbed his bare left arm with his right hand and said slowly:

'It's like this. My foot . . .'

As he spoke the word his glance, which was not quite steady – for now it was a matter of uttering the first real lie in this affair; so far he had merely kept silence – fell upon Xantippe at the kitchen door.

Socrates' speech failed him. All of a sudden he no longer wanted to produce his tale. His foot was not sprained.

The hammock came to a standstill.

'Listen, Alcibiades,' he said forcefully and in a quite different voice, 'there can't be any talk of bravery in this matter. As soon as the battle started, that's to say, as soon as I caught sight of the first Persian, I ran for it and, what's more, in the right direction – in retreat. But there was a field full of thorns. I got a thorn in my foot and couldn't go on. Then I laid about me like a savage and almost struck some of our own men. In desperation I yelled something about other units, to make the Persians believe there were some, which was absurd because of course they don't understand Greek. At the same time they seemed to be a bit nervous themselves. I suppose they just couldn't stand the roaring at that stage, after all they'd had to go through during the advance. They stopped short for a moment and at that point our cavalry turned up. That's all.'

For a few seconds it was quiet in the room. Alcibiades stared at him unblinkingly. Antisthenes coughed behind his hand, this time quite naturally. From the kitchen door, where Xantippe was standing, came a loud peal of laughter.

Then Antisthenes said drily:

'And so of course you couldn't go to the Areopagus and limp up the steps to receive the laurel wreath. I can understand that.'

Alcibiades leant back in his chair and contemplated the philosopher on the couch with narrowed eyes. Neither Socrates nor Antisthenes looked at him.

He bent forward again and clasped one knee with his hands. His narrow boyish face twitched a little, but it betrayed nothing of his thoughts or feelings.

'Why didn't you say you had some other sort of wound?' he asked.

'Because I've got a thorn in my foot,' said Socrates bluntly.

'Oh, that's why?' said Alcibiades. 'I see.'

He rose swiftly and went up to the bed.

'Pity I didn't bring my own wreath with me. I gave it to my man to hold. Otherwise I should leave it here for you. You can take my word for it, I think you're brave enough. I don't know anybody who in this situation would have told the story you've just told.'

And he went out quickly.

As Xantippe was bathing his foot later and extracting the thorn she said acrimoniously:

'It could have meant blood poisoning.'

'If nothing worse,' said the philosopher.

Translated by Yvonne Kapp

André Malraux

The Royal Way

PART III, CHAPTER I

*André Malraux (1901–   ), the French novelist and essayist, has
successfully combined a career of letters and action. His novels,
based upon his own experiences, deal with the Chinese revolution
(The Conquerors and Man's Fate), an archeological adventure in
the Cambodian jungles (The Royal Way), the events of the Spanish
Civil War (Man's Hope), and the early battles of World War II
(The Walnut Trees of Altenburg).*

The following selection comes from The Royal Way *(1935), a
novel of adventure which ferments into philosophy without becoming philosophical. It opens aboard a ship bound for Indo-
China. One of the passengers, Claude Vannec, a French arch-
eologist escaping the tedium of home, decides to invade the
Cambodian jungle with a legendary adventurer called Perken, a
Kurtz-like figure driven by lust and ambition, whom he meets in a
Djibouti brothel. Together they plan to seek archeological trea-
sures (huge stone sculptures for which London dealers pay a
fortune) among the lost temples of Cambodia, at the same time
exploring the regions lying along the Royal Way of the ancient
Khmers. Perken, it turns out, is also looking for a certain Grabot,
a deserter from the French army who has been serving as a
Siamese agent among the savages of the Cambodian interior. A
guide tells them that a white man is somewhere in the region, and
Claude, who has never met Grabot, finds himself eager to encounter this man whom Perken describes as '. . . the genuine
article, a really brave man' who puts out his own eye and permits
himself to be bitten by a black scorpion to prove his strength of
will. As the following excerpt begins, Perken and Claude are about
to enter the village where they hope to find Grabot (they do find
him later, a slave tethered to a grindstone).*

In the midst of these half-savage tribes which had successfully with-stood inclusion in a protectorate, life was no less uncertain, no less precarious than in the forest. In the village where the bartering took place, a village even more dilapidated than the temples, what few Cambodians there were seemed terror-stricken, and parried every question about the other villages, about the tribal chiefs, about Grabot. Perken's name, however, was not unknown to them, or so it seemed. They had not a trace of the sensual, easy-going temperament of the Laos and Lower Cambodians. Here were real savages; one smelled their meaty smell. At last the messengers reported that, in return for two bottles of European spirit, the party would be permitted to travel through the tribe's territory and be given a guide. They were unable to discover from whom the permit came. But, as they moved up-country to the Stieng headquarters, a far more pressing problem forced itself upon their minds. Claude was brought up sharply by a blow on the arm from Perken.

'Look down. Don't move.'

Less than three inches from his right foot two extremely sharp splinters of bamboo protruded from the ground, like the prongs of a fork. Perken pointed again.

'What else?' Claude asked.

Perken's only answer was a low whistle. Then he flung his cigarette in front of him. Through the green air, turbid with the shadows of impending night, it described a fiery red parabola, and fell on to the soft mould lining the side of the cart track. Near the place where it had fallen Claude saw two more bamboo spikes.

'What gadgets are those?'

'War spikes.'

Claude glanced at the Moi tribesman who was waiting for them – they had changed guides at the village – leaning on his cross-bow.

'That fellow should have warned us, shouldn't he?' Claude asked.

'I don't like the look of things at all.'

They shuffled along the track, hardly daring to lift their feet from the ground, following the yellow object in front of them – their guide. His sarong was incredibly filthy: it seemed mottled with blood. Claude felt that the man was neither wholly human nor altogether bestial. Each time he had to lift his foot – to cross a tree trunk or a root – he felt the sinews of his leg contract, dreading to take an over-hasty step. He groped his way ahead like a blind man, his muscles shrinking from the hidden dangers of the way. Try as he might to see, his eyes were practically useless; his sense of smell replaced them and he sniffed

uneasily the gusts of tepid air, reeking with heavy fumes of mould.
How could he see the spikes, if rotting leaves all but covered up the
track? He was helpless as a slave; his legs seemed shackled. For all
his efforts to master a desire to tread with extreme circumspection, the
spasms in his calves were more imperious than his will.

'What about the bullocks, Perken? Supposing one of them's brought
down?'

'There's not much danger of that. They feel the spikes much sooner
than we can.'

He thought of riding in one of the carts behind, of which Xa was the
only driver. But, if he did so, he would be incapable of resisting an
attack.

They crossed the dry bed of a stream. The crossing was a welcome
respite; in that pebbly surface anyhow, nothing could lurk hidden. A
few yards away they saw three Mois standing on a bank of clayey soil,
one above the other, staring at them with blank, inhuman fixity; their
eyes seemed dead and stony, facets of the universal silence.

'If things turn out badly,' Perken observed, 'some of these blighters
will be taking us in the rear.'

The eyes of the savages followed their retreat, impassive as before.
Only one of them had a crossbow. The track was getting less dark; the
trees did not stand quite so thickly together. They were still obliged to
walk warily, but the obsession of the war spikes was losing its hold on
them. At last a glade, open to the declining sun, showed up in front.

The guide halted. Some thin strands of rattan were stretched neck-
high across the track, covered with tiny thorns which glistened in the
sun and tapered off into invisibility. The guide unfastened the strands.
Claude had failed to notice them. 'If,' he said to himself, 'we land in a
mess, it'll be none too easy getting away.'

When they had passed, the Moi carefully replaced the saw-like
strands as he had found them.

No track was visible across the glade. Still one, at least, must lead
away from it, continuing the track which had brought them there. For
all its air of peacefulness, there was something sinister about the glade,
their camping place for the coming night. Half of it was already submerged in darkness, and the other half lit only by the bright yellow
glow which precedes the nightfall. No palm trees were to be seen; Asia
was manifest only in the heat, in the huge bulk of some red tree trunks,
and in the brooding silence, which the hum of myriads of insects and,
now and then, the lone cry of a bird swooping down on a lofty branch,
seemed to render vaster still, still more impressive. Like stagnant water

the heavy silence closed down on all these vagrant sounds, while high aloft the bough swayed gently, gently swaying in the dusk. Beyond the trackless masses of vegetation cataracting down steep declivities that fell away into the evening mist, the mountains stood out sharply against the dying sky. The Mois, like the woodworms that infest the giant trees, fought with small but deadly weapons. In the great hush of the forest their furtive methods, their inexplicable wariness, seemed all the more ominous. They had only to deal with three men without an escort, led by a guide whom the tribesmen had provided of their own accord; what possible need was there for those spikes or rattan strands? Why should the glade have been defended in this manner? 'Does it mean that Grabot is sparing no pains to keep his liberty of action?' Claude asked himself. And, as though the very rarity of thoughts in this oasis of the forest had made Claude's silent question audible, Perken answered it.

'I'm convinced that he isn't alone.'

'What do you mean?'

'Not the only *chief*. Or else it would mean that he's gone native, through and through ...'

He paused. The implications of his words seemed to permeate the dreaming forest, to find their illustration in the squatting guide busily scratching a knee blotched by the scabs of some foul skin disease.

'... that he has become another man, in fact,' Perken concluded.

Once more they had come up against the unknown. Their venture was urging them towards this man as it had led them along the invisible alignment of the Royal Way. And now he, too, stood between them and their appointed destiny. Still, he had granted them the right of way ...

The photographs which Perken had brought from Bangkok loomed as vividly in Claude's remembrance as if a fixed idea had limned them there. He saw a sturdy, jovial, one-eyed adventurer who roamed the jungle and haunted the Chinese bars of Siam, his topee on the back of his head, his mouth agape and eyelids puckered with gargantuan laughter. Claude had seen faces in which, across the grossness of maturity, there somehow showed a hint of childish candour. It showed itself in a laugh, in the way the eyes grew rounded with surprise, in carefree gestures. Thus he could picture Grabot slamming a topee down over the ears of a pal, or of an enemy. But, in these primitive surroundings, how much of the townsman would have survived? As Perken said, he well might have 'gone native'.

Claude went to look for the guide. He found him crooning a native chant, for the benefit of Xa alone, beside the motionless oxen. The fires they had kindled for the night were making little explosive noises not far from the camp beds which had been set up under mosquito nets. The tents had not been pitched, on account of the heat.

'Better take down the mosquito nets,' Perken said. 'It's bad enough knowing that blasted fire will keep us in full view. At least let's try to get a sight of anyone attacking us.'

The glade was wide, and an assailant would have to cross a patch of open ground.

'If anything happens,' Perken continued, 'the one who's on watch shoots down the guide; then we'll slip behind that bush there on the right, so as to get out of the light of the fire.'

'But, even if we beat them off, how can we carry on without a guide?'

Whatever might be threatening them seemed to depend on Grabot; he held the master cards that would decide their fate.

'Have you any idea what his game can be?' Claude asked.

'Grabot's?'

'Obviously.'

'Now that we're so close to him, so near what we've been expecting of him, I've almost lost faith in my theories . . .'

The fire went on sputtering, but the flames rose straight and bright. They were almost pink, and lit up only the leaping spirals of their own smoke. The glow the fire cast on the walls of leafage all around was hardly distinguishable from the sky. Now that Perken was confronted with the last move of the game on which he had staked so much, he realized he did not know his man.

'After all the spikes we've seen, do you still suppose he means to let us through?'

'If he's on his own, yes.'

'And you're sure he has no notion of the value of our stones?'

Perken shrugged his shoulders.

'That's quite beyond him,' he replied. 'Why, I myself . . .'

'But, if he's not on his own, mayn't there be someone with him who knows?'

'Well, it certainly isn't a white man . . . Anyhow, fellows who have nerve enough to come up into these parts usually stand by each other. What's more, I've done Grabot a good turn or two.' He paused, lost in thought, his eyes fixed on the grass beside his feet. 'I'd like to know what it can be that he's trying to ward off,' he said at last. 'It's with his early dreams, his sense of degradation that a man keeps his passions alive.'

'It depends on what his passions are.'

'I told you of a fellow who used to get women at Bangkok to tie him up naked. That was Grabot. After all it isn't so very much sillier than to propose to sleep and live – to live! – with another human creature. But he feels damnably humiliated by it.'

'Because other people know?'

'Nobody knows about it. Because of himself, because he does it. So he tries *to make up for it*. That, I imagine, is the chief reason that brought him here. Courage atones for a great deal. And then – don't all the little things we are ashamed of seem insignificant beside all this?'

As if the sweep of an arm were utterly inadequate to indicate the majesty about them, he contented himself with a quick jerk of his chin towards the clearing and the far mountains dissolving into darkness. Now the tall barrier of trees was drenched in shadow and above the great primeval forest brooding round them a host of stars outshone their leaping fire; the slow, tremendous progress of the night overwhelmed Claude with a sense of supreme loneliness, making him feel once more a hunted thing at bay. And in the lambent darkness he discerned an ineluctable indifference, an immanence of death.

'Yes, I can understand he doesn't care a damn about dying.'

'That's not it. It's not the death that he doesn't fear – death is something quite outside his range. It's this; he's not afraid of being killed ... Of course there's nothing much in that – not being afraid of getting a bullet in one's head.' He lowered his voice. 'But, if the bullet gets you in the belly, it's less agreeable. A long drawn out business; pretty beastly. You know as well as I do that life is meaningless; when a man lives alone he can't help brooding over the problem of his destiny. And death is always there, you see, ahead of him, like ... like a standing proof of the futility of life.'

'For each of us.'

'For nobody! It exists for nobody. Very few of us could go on living if ... But everyone bears in mind the fact that – how'm I to make you see what I'm driving at? – that he may be killed. That's what I mean. To be killed – that's of no importance. But death, death is different; it's the exact opposite in fact. You're too young, of course ... I realized it the first time I saw a woman growing old, a woman whom ... well, a woman I knew. (But I've told you about Sarah, haven't I?) Then, too, as if that warning wasn't enough, there was the time – the first time – when I found that I was impotent.' The words forced their way out painfully; to rise to the surface they had to wrench their way through a mesh of strangling roots. 'No,' Perken continued, 'I never got that feeling from the sight of a dead body. To grow old, that's it – to peter out. Especially when one's cut off from others. A death-in-life. What weighs on me is – how shall I put it? – my human lot, my limitations; that I must grow old, and time, that loathsome thing, spread through me like a cancer, inevitably. Time – there you have it! D'you see all those damn fool insects making for our lamp, obeying the call of the light? The termites, too, obey the law of the anthill. I ... *I will not obey.*'

The forest had awakened with the great stir of nightfall; the wild life of the earth rose with the darkness. Claude felt incapable of putting further questions. The words formed in his mind passed over Perken's as above a subterranean river. By all the immensity of the forest such a man was sundered from those to whom reason and truth are real; could he appeal to any human aid in fighting down the phantoms massed around him in the gloom? He had just drawn his revolver; a glint of light flickered along the barrel.

'My whole life depends on how I regard the act of pressing this trigger when I put the barrel between my lips. The point is: do I then believe I am destroying myself, or that I am taking a definite step forward? Life is so much raw material; what is one making of it? – that's the question. It's true one never can make anything of it, really; still there are several methods of making nothing of it. And, in order to live one's life *according to plan*, one must have a short way with life's threats, the threat of growing old, of wearing out, and so forth. So a revolver is an excellent life insurance, for it's easy enough to kill oneself when death is a means ... That's where Grabot's strength lies.'

The last glow had left the sky. All Asia had passed into the night, the dark dominion of solitude and silence. Above the faint crackling of the fire, they could hear the voices of the two natives, monotonous and shrill, but devoid of resonance – imprisoned voices. Near at hand the steady tick of an alarm clock meted out the silence of the jungle, and, more than the campfire, more even than the voices, its punctual tick brought Claude back to the world of living men. Here, anyhow, was something precise and clear-cut, functioning with the stolid perseverance of every reliable machine. His thoughts rose to the plane of full awareness, but enriched by all that they had drawn from the depths whence they emerged, and still in thrall to the elemental influences of darkness and the sun-scorched earth. It was as if all things, even the earth itself, were seeking to convince him of the futility of human life.

'And the *other* death, the death that is within us ...?'

'To live on in defiance of all that' – Perken's eyes indicated the tremendous menace of the night – 'can you realize what that means? To live defying death is the same thing. It seems to me sometimes that I am staking myself, all that I am, on a single moment – my last. And, very likely, it will come quite soon; some more or less filthy arrow will settle the business, once for all.'

'One doesn't choose one's death.'

'No doubt. And, having waived my choice of death, I've had to choose my life.'

The red glint on his shoulder flickered; he had made an unseen gesture in the darkness. A puny gesture, as puny as the little human speck whose feet were hidden in shadow, whose fitful voice floated up into the starry depths. A man's voice, lonely and remote, poised between the shining sky, and death, and darkness; yet in it there was something so inhuman that Claude felt as isolated from it as he would have been by incipient madness.

'Then you want to die,' Claude asked, 'with an intense awareness of death, and yet without . . . flinching?'

'I've been very near death. And you can't imagine the wild elation of those moments – it's the sudden glimpse of the absurdity of life that brings it – when one meets death face to face, naked' – he made a gesture as of tearing off a woman's garments – 'stark naked suddenly . . .'

Keeping his eyes fixed on the glittering sky, Claude answered:

'Nearly everyone bungles his death, one way or other.'

'I spend my life with death in view. But I know what you mean – for you, too, are afraid – and it's true enough. Very likely when my time comes I'll fail to rise to the occasion . . . So much the worse! And, anyhow, there's something satisfactory in the mere thought that life is being annihilated.'

'You've never thought seriously of killing yourself?'

'When I think about my death it's with a view to living – not to dying.'

There could be no mistaking the tension in his voice; it expressed a bitter joy, emptied of every hope, like wave-worn jetsam drawn up from sea depths deep as the dark night around them.

Translated by Stuart Gilbert

Jean-Paul Sartre

The Room

Perhaps the most famous contemporary philosopher of existentialism, Jean-Paul Sartre was born in France in 1905. His first novel, Nausea *(1938), established his main themes, and since then he has been a prolific essayist, novelist and playwright. In all of his representative works, he has been concerned with defining the limits of man's freedom. In the 1940's, he founded the now influential* Le Temps Moderne, *a periodical which reflects his social and political views.*

Mme Darbedat held a *rahat-loukoum* between her fingers. She brought it carefully to her lips and held her breath, afraid that the fine dust of sugar that powdered it would blow away. 'Just right,' she told herself. She bit quickly into its glassy flesh and a scent of stagnation filled her mouth. 'Odd how illness sharpens the sensations.' She began to think of mosques, of obsequious Orientals (she had been to Algeria for her honeymoon) and her pale lips started in a smile: the *rahat-loukoum* was obsequious too.

Several times she had to pass the palm of her hand over the pages of her book, for in spite of the precaution she had taken they were covered with a thin coat of white powder. Her hand made the little grains of sugar slide and roll, grating on the smooth paper: 'That makes me think of Arcachon, when I used to read on the beach.' She had spent the summer of 1907 at the seashore. Then she wore a big straw hat with a green ribbon; she sat close to the jetty, with a novel by Gyp or Colette Yver. The wind made swirls of sand rain down upon her knees, and from time to time she had to shake the book, holding it by the corners. It was the same sensation: only the grains of sand were dry while the small bits of sugar stuck a little to the ends of her fingers. Again she saw a band of pearl grey sky above a black sea. 'Eve wasn't born yet.' She felt herself all weighted down with memories and precious as a coffer of sandalwood. The name of the book she used to read suddenly came back to mind: it was called *Petite Madame*, not at all boring. But ever since an unknown illness had confined her to her room she preferred memoirs and historical works.

She hoped that suffering, heavy readings, a vigilant attention to her memories and the most exquisite sensations would ripen her as a lovely hothouse fruit.

She thought, with some annoyance, that her husband would soon be knocking at her door. On other days of the week he came only in the evening, kissed her brow in silence and read *Le Temps*, sitting in the armchair across from her. But Thursday was M Darbedat's *day*: he spent an hour with his daughter, generally from three to four. Before going he stopped in to see his wife and both discussed their son-in-law with bitterness. These Thursday conversations, predictable to their slightest detail, exhausted Mme Darbedat. M Darbedat filled the quiet room with his presence. He never sat, but walked in circles about the room. Each of his outbursts wounded Mme Darbedat like a glass splintering. This particular Thursday was worse than usual: at the thought that it would soon be necessary to repeat Eve's confessions to her husband, and to see his great terrifying body convulse with fury, Mme Darbedat broke out in a sweat. She picked up a *loukoum* from the saucer, studied it for a while with hesitation, then sadly set it down: she did not like her husband to see her eating *loukoums*.

She heard a knock and started up. 'Come in,' she said weakly.

M Darbedat entered on tiptoe. 'I'm going to see Eve,' he said, as he did every Thursday. Mme Darbedat smiled at him. 'Give her a kiss for me.'

M Darbedat did not answer and his forehead wrinkled worriedly: every Thursday at the same time, a muffled irritation mingled with the load of his digestion. 'I'll stop in and see Franchot after leaving her, I wish he'd talk to her seriously and try to convince her.'

He had made frequent visits to Dr Franchot. But in vain. Mme Darbedat raised her eyebrows. Before, when she was well, she shrugged her shoulders. But since sickness had weighted down her body, she replaced the gestures which would have tired her by plays of emotion in the face: she said *yes* with her eyes, *no* with the corners of her mouth: she raised her eyebrows instead of her shoulders.

'There should be some way to take him away from her by force.'

'I told you already it was impossible. And besides, the law is very poorly drawn up. Only the other day Franchot was telling me that they have a tremendous amount of trouble with the families: people who can't make up their mind, who want to keep the patient at home; the doctors' hands are tied. They can give their advice, period. That's all. He would,' he went on, 'have to make a public scandal or else she would have to ask to have him put away herself.'

'And that,' said Mme Darbedat, 'isn't going to happen tomorrow.'

'No.' He turned to the mirror and began to comb his fingers through his beard. Mme Darbedat looked at the powerful red neck of her husband without affection.

'If she keeps on,' said M Darbedat, 'she'll be crazier than he is. It's terribly unhealthy. She doesn't leave his side, she only goes out to see you. She has no visitors. The air in their room is simply unbreathable. She never opens the window because Pierre doesn't want it open. As if you should ask a sick man. I believe they burn incense, some rubbish in a little pan, you'd think it was a church. Really, sometimes I wonder ... she's got a funny look in her eyes, you know.'

'I haven't noticed,' Mme Darbedat said. 'I find her quite normal. She looks sad, obviously.'

'She has a face like an unburied corpse. Does she sleep? Does she eat? But we aren't supposed to ask her about those things. But I should think with a fellow like Pierre next to her, she wouldn't sleep a wink all night.' He shrugged his shoulders. 'What I find amazing is that we, her parents, don't have the right to protect her against herself. Understand that Pierre would be much better cared for by Franchot. There's a big park. And besides, I think,' he added, smiling a little, 'he'd get along much better with people of his own type. People like that are children; you have to leave them alone with each other; they form a sort of freemasonry. That's where he should have been put the first day and for his own good, I'd say. Of course it's in his own best interest.

After a moment, he added, 'I tell you I don't like to know she's alone with Pierre, especially at night. Suppose something happened. Pierre has a very sly way about him.'

'I don't know,' Mme Darbedat said, 'if there's any reason to worry. He always looked like that. He always seemed to be making fun of the world. Poor boy,' she sighed, 'to have had his pride and then come to that. He thought he was cleverer than all of us. He had a way of saying "You're right" simply to end the argument ... It's a blessing for him that he can't see the state he's in.'

She recalled with displeasure the long, ironic face, always turned a little to the side. During the first days of Eve's marriage, Mme Darbedat asked nothing more than a little intimacy with her son-in-law. But he had discouraged her: he almost never spoke, he always agreed quickly and absentmindedly.

M Darbedat pursued his idea. 'Franchot let me visit his place,' he said. 'It was magnificent. The patients have private rooms with leather armchairs, if you please, and day-beds. You know, they have a tennis court and they're going to build a swimming pool.'

He was planted before the window, looking out, rocking a little on his bent legs. Suddenly he turned lithely on his heel, shoulders lowered, hands in his pockets. Mme Darbedat felt she was going to start perspiring: it was the same thing every time: now he was pacing back and forth like a bear in a cage and his shoes squeaked at every step.

'Please, please won't you sit down. You're tiring me.' Hesitating, she added, 'I have something important to tell you.'

M Darbedat sat in the armchair and put his hands on his knees; a slight chill ran up Mme Darbedat's spine: the time had come, she had to speak.

'You know,' she said with an embarrassed cough, 'I saw Eve on Tuesday.'

'Yes.'

'We talked about a lot of things, she was very nice, she hasn't been so confiding for a long time. Then I questioned her a little, I got her to talk about Pierre. Well, I found out,' she added, again embarrassed, 'that she is *very* attached to him.'

'I know that too damned well,' said M Darbedat.

He irritated Mme Darbedat a little: she always had to explain things in such detail. Mme Darbedat dreamed of living in the company of fine and sensitive people who would understand her slightest word.

'But I mean,' she went on, 'that she is attached to him *differently* than we imagined.'

M Darbedat rolled furious, anxious eyes, as he always did when he never completely grasped the sense of an allusion or something new.

'What does that all mean?'

'Charles,' said Mme Darbedat, 'don't tire me. You should understand a mother has difficulty in telling certain things.'

'I don't understand a damned word of anything you say,' M Darbedat said with irritation. 'You can't mean . . .'

'Yes,' she said.

'They're still . . . now, still . . .?'

'Yes! Yes! Yes!' she said, in three annoyed and dry little jolts.

M Darbedat spread his arms, lowered his head and was silent.

'Charles,' his wife said worriedly, 'I shouldn't have told you. But I couldn't keep it to myself.'

'Our child,' he said slowly. 'With this madman! He doesn't even recognize her any more. He calls her Agatha. She must have lost all sense of her own dignity.'

He raised his head and looked at his wife severely. 'You're sure you aren't mistaken?'

'No possible doubt. Like you,' she added quickly, 'I couldn't believe her and I still can't. The mere idea of being touched by that wretch ... So ...' she sighed, 'I suppose that's how he holds on to her.'

'Do you remember what I told you,' M Darbedat said, 'when he came to ask for her hand? I told you I thought he pleased Eve *too much*. You wouldn't believe me.' He struck the table suddenly, blushing violently. 'It's perversity! He takes her in his arms, kisses her and calls her Agatha, selling her on a lot of nonsense about flying statues and God knows what else! Without a word from her! But what in heaven's name's between those two? Let her be sorry for him, let her put him in a sanatorium and see him every day – fine. But I never thought ... I considered her a widow. Listen, Jeannette,' he said gravely, 'I'm going to speak frankly to you; if she had any sense, I'd rather see her take a lover!'

'Be quiet, Charles!' Mme Darbedat cried.

M Darbedat wearily took his hat and the cane he had left on the stool. 'After what you've just told me,' he concluded, 'I don't have much hope left. In any case, I'll have a talk with her because it's my duty.'

Mme Darbedat wished he would go quickly.

'You know,' she said to encourage him, 'I think Eve is more headstrong than ... than anything. She knows he's incurable but she's obstinate, she doesn't want to be in the wrong.'

M Darbedat stroked his beard absently.

'Headstrong? Maybe so. If you're right, she'll finally get tired of it. He's not always pleasant and he doesn't have much to say. When I say hello to him he gives me a flabby handshake and doesn't say a word. As soon as they're alone, I think they go back to his obsessions: she tells me sometimes he screams as though his throat were being cut because of his hallucinations. He sees statues. They frighten him because they buzz. He says they fly around and make fishy eyes at him.'

He put on his gloves and continued, 'She'll get tired of it, I'm not saying she won't. But suppose she goes crazy before that? I wish she'd go out a little, see the world: she'd meet some nice young man – well, someone like Schroeder, an engineer with Simplon, somebody with a future, she could see him a little here and there and she'd get used to the idea of making a new life for herself.'

Mme Darbedat did not answer, afraid of starting the conversation up again. Her husband bent over her.

'So,' he said, 'I've got to be on my way.'

'Goodbye, Papa,' Mme Darbedat said, lifting her forehead up to him. 'Kiss her for me and tell her for me she's a poor dear.'

Once her husband had gone, Mme Darbedat let herself drift to the bottom of her armchair and closed her eyes, exhausted. 'What vitality,' she thought reproachfully. As soon as she got a little strength back, she quietly stretched out her pale hand and took a *loukoum* from the saucer, groping for it without opening her eyes.

Eve lived with her husband on the sixth floor of an old building on the Rue du Bac. M Darbedat slowly climbed the 112 steps of the stairway. He was not even out of breath when he pushed the bell. He remembered with satisfaction the words of Mlle Dormoy: 'Charles, for your age, you're simply marvellous.' Never did he feel himself stronger and healthier than on Thursday, especially after these invigorating climbs.

Eve opened the door: that's right, she doesn't have a maid. No girls *can* stay with her. I can put myself in their place. He kissed her. 'Hello, poor darling.'

Eve greeted him with a certain coldness.

'You look a little pale,' M Darbedat said, touching her cheek. 'You don't get enough exercise.'

There was a moment of silence.

'Is Mamma well?' Eve asked.

'Not good, not too bad. You saw her Tuesday? Well, she's just the same. Your Aunt Louise came to see her yesterday, that pleased her. She likes to have visitors, but they can't stay too long. Aunt Louise came to Paris for that mortgage business. I think I told you about it, a very odd sort of affair. She stopped in at the office to ask my advice. I told her there was only one thing to do: sell. She found a taker, by the way: Bretonnel. You remember Bretonnel. He's retired from business now.'

He stopped suddenly: Eve was hardly listening. He thought sadly that nothing interested her any more. It's like the books. Before you had to tear them away from her. Now she doesn't even read any more.

'How is Pierre?'

'Well,' Eve said. 'Do you want to see him?'

'Of course,' M Darbedat said gaily, 'I'd like to pay him a little call.'

He was full of compassion for this poor young man, but he could not see him without repugnance. *I detest unhealthy people.* Obviously, it was not Pierre's fault: his heredity was terribly loaded down. M Darbedat sighed: *All the precautions are taken in vain, you find out those things too late.* No, Pierre was not responsible. But still he had always carried that fault in him; it formed the base of his character; it wasn't like cancer or tuberculosis, something you could always put aside when you wanted to judge a man as he is. His nervous grace, the subtlety which pleased Eve so much when he was courting her were the flowers of madness. He was already mad when he married her only you couldn't tell.

It makes you wonder, thought M Darbedat, *where responsibility begins, or rather, where it ends.* In any case, he was always analysing himself too much, always turned in on himself. But was it the cause or effect of his sickness? He followed his daughter through a long, dim corridor.

'This apartment is too big for you,' he said. 'You ought to move out.'

'You say that every time, Papa,' Eve answered, 'but I've already told you Pierre doesn't want to leave his room.'

Eve was amazing. Enough to make you wonder if she realized her husband's state. He was insane enough to be in a strait-jacket and she respected his decisions and advice as if he still had good sense.

'What I'm saying is for your own good.' M Darbedat went on, somewhat annoyed, 'It seems to me that if I were a woman I'd be afraid of these badly lighted old rooms. I'd like to see you in a bright apartment, the kind they're putting up near Auteuil, three airy little rooms. They lowered the rents because they couldn't find any tenants; this would be just the time.'

Eve quietly turned the doorknob and they entered the room. M Darbedat's throat tightened at the heavy odour of incense. The curtains were drawn. In the shadows he made out a thin neck above the back of an armchair: Pierre's back was turned. He was eating.

'Hello, Pierre,' M Darbedat said, raising his voice. 'How are we today?' He drew near him: the sick man was seated in front of a small table: he looked sly.

'I see we had soft boiled eggs,' M Darbedat said, raising his voice higher. 'That's good!'

'I'm not deaf,' Pierre said quietly.

Irritated, M Darbedat turned his eyes towards Eve as his witness. But Eve gave him a hard glance and was silent. M Darbedat realized he had hurt her. Too bad for her. It was impossible to find just the right tone for this boy. He had less sense than a child of four and Eve wanted him treated like a man. M Darbedat could not keep himself from waiting with impatience for the moment when all this ridiculous business would be finished. Sick people always annoyed him a little – especially madmen because they were wrong. Poor Pierre, for example, was wrong all along the line, he couldn't speak a reasonable word and yet it would be useless to expect the least humility from him, or even temporary recognition of his errors.

Eve cleared away the eggshells and the cup. She put a knife and fork in front of Pierre.

'What's he going to eat now,' M Darbedat said jovially.

'A steak.'

Pierre had taken the fork and held it in the ends of his long, pale fingers. He inspected it minutely and then gave a slight laugh.

'I can't use it this time,' he murmured, setting it down, 'I was warned.'

Eve came in and looked at the fork with passionate interest.

'Agatha,' Pierre said, 'give me another one.'

Eve obeyed and Pierre began to eat. She had taken the suspect fork and held it tightly in her hands, her eyes never leaving it; she seemed to make a violent effort. How suspicious all their gestures and relationships are! thought M Darbedat.

He was uneasy.

'Be careful, Pierre, take it by the middle because of the prongs.'

Eve sighed and laid the fork on the serving table. M Darbedat felt his gall rising. He did not think it well to give in to all this poor man's whims – even from Pierre's viewpoint it was pernicious. Franchot had said: 'One must never enter the delirium of a madman.' Instead of giving him another fork, it would have been better to have reasoned quietly and made him understand that the first was like all the others.

He went to the serving table, took the fork ostentatiously and tested the prongs with a light finger. Then he turned to Pierre. But the latter was cutting his meat peacefully: he gave his father-in-law a gentle, inexpressive glance.

'I'd like to have a little talk with you,' M Darbedat said to Eve.

She followed him docilely into the salon. Sitting on the couch, M Darbedat realized he had kept the fork in his hand. He threw it on the table.

'It's much better here,' he said.

'I never come here.'

'All right to smoke?'

'Of course, Papa,' Eve said hurriedly. 'Do you want a cigar?'

M Darbedat preferred to roll a cigarette. He thought eagerly of the discussion he was about to begin. Speaking to Pierre he felt as embarrassed about his reason as a giant about his strength when playing with a child. All his qualities of clarity, sharpness, precision, turned against him; *I must confess it's somewhat the same with my poor Jeannette.* Certainly Mme Darbedat was not insane, but this illness had .., stultified her. Eve, on the other hand, took after her father ... a straight, logical nature; discussion with her was a pleasure; *that's why I don't want them to ruin her.* M Darbedat raised his eyes. Once again he wanted to see the fine intelligent features of his daughter. He was disappointed with this face; once so reasonable and transparent, there was now something clouded and opaque in it. Eve had always been beautiful. M Darbedat noticed she was made up with great care, almost with pomp. She had blued her eyelids and put mascara on her long lashes. This violent and perfect make-up made a painful impression on her father.

'You're green beneath your rouge,' he told her. 'I'm afraid you're getting sick. And the way you make yourself up now! You used to be so discreet.'

Eve did not answer and for an embarrassed moment M Darbedat considered this brilliant, worn-out face beneath the heavy mass of black hair. He thought she looked like a tragedian. *I even know who she looks like. That woman ... that Roumanian who played* Phèdre *in French at the Mur d'Orange.* He regretted having made so disagreeable a remark: *It escaped me! Better not worry her with little things.*

'Excuse me,' he said smiling, 'you know I'm an old purist. I don't like all these creams and paints women stick on their face today. But I'm in the wrong. You must live in your time.'

Eve smiled amiably at him. M Darbedat lit a cigarette and drew several puffs.

'My child,' he began, 'I wanted to talk with you: the two of us are going to talk the way we used to. Come, sit down and listen to me nicely; you must have confidence in your old Papa.'

'I'd rather stand,' Eve said. 'What did you want to tell me?'

'I am going to ask you a single question,' M Darbedat said a little more dryly. 'Where will all this lead you?'

'All this?' Eve asked astonished.

'Yes ... all this whole life you've made for yourself. Listen,' he went on, 'don't think I don't understand you (he had a sudden illumination) but what you want to do is beyond human strength. You want to live solely by imagination, isn't that it? You don't want to admit he's sick. You don't want to see the Pierre of today, do you? You have eyes only for the Pierre of before. My dear, my darling little girl, it's an impossible bet to win,' M Darbedat continued. 'Now I'm going to tell you a story which perhaps you don't know. When we were at Sables-d'Olonne – you were three years old – your mother made the acquaintance of a charming young woman with a superb little boy. You played on the beach with this little boy, you were thick as thieves, you were engaged to marry him. A while later, in Paris, your mother wanted to see this young woman again; she was told she had had a terrible accident. That fine little boy's head was cut off by a car. They told your mother, "Go and see her, but above all don't talk to her about the death of her child, she *will not* believe he is dead." Your mother went, she found a half-mad creature: she lived as though her boy was still alive; she spoke to him, she set his place at the table. She lived in such a state of nervous tension that after six months they had to take her away by force to a sanitorium where she was obliged to stay three years. No, my child,' M Darbedat said, shaking his head, 'these things are impossible. It would have been better if she had recognized the truth courageously. She would have suffered once, then time would have erased with its sponge. There is nothing like looking things in the face, believe me.'

'You're wrong,' Eve said with effort. 'I know very well that Pierre is . . .'

The word did not escape. She held herself very straight and put her hands on the back of the armchair: there was something dry and ugly in the lower part of her face.

'So . . .?' asked M Darbedat, astonished.

'So . . .?'

'You . . .?'

'I love him as he is,' said Eve rapidly and with an irritated look.

'Not true,' M Darbedat said forcefully. 'It isn't true: you don't love him, you can't love him. You can only feel that way about a healthy, normal person. You pity Pierre, I don't doubt it, and surely you have the memory of three years of happiness he gave you. But don't tell me you love him. I won't believe you.'

Eve remained wordless, staring at the carpet absently.

'You could at least answer me,' M Darbedat said coldly. 'Don't think this conversation has been any less painful for me than it has for you.'

'More than you think.'

'Well then, if you love him,' he cried, exasperated, 'it is a great misfortune for you, for me and for your poor mother because I'm going to tell you something I would rather have hidden from you: before three years Pierre will be sunk in complete dementia, he'll be like a beast.'

He watched his daughter with hard eyes: he was angry at her for having compelled him, by stubbornness, to make this painful revelation.

Eve was motionless; she did not so much as raise her eyes.

'I knew.'

'Who told you?' he asked stupified.

'Franchot. I knew six months ago.'

'And I told him to be careful with you,' said M Darbedat with bitterness. 'Maybe it's better. But under those circumstances you must understand that it would be unpardonable to keep Pierre with you. The struggle you have undertaken is doomed to failure, his illness won't spare him. If there were something to be done, if we could save him by care, I'd say yes. But look: you're pretty, intelligent, gay, you're destroying yourself willingly and without profit. I know you've been admirable, but now it's over . . . done, you've done your duty and more; now it would be immoral to continue. We also have duties to ourselves, child. And then you aren't thinking about us. You must,' he repeated, hammering the words, 'send Pierre to Franchot's clinic. Leave this apartment where you've had nothing but sorrow and come home to us. If you want to be useful and ease the sufferings of someone else, you have your mother. The poor woman is cared for by nurses, she needs someone closer to her, and *she*,' he added, 'can appreciate what you do for her and be grateful.'

There was a long silence. M Darbedat heard Pierre singing in the next room. It was hardly a song, rather a sort of sharp, hasty recitative. M Darbedat raised his eyes to his daughter.

'It's no then?'

'Pierre will stay with me,' she said quietly. 'I get along well with him.'

'By living like an animal all day long?'

Eve smiled and shot a glance at her father, strange, mocking and almost gay. *It's true*, M Darbedat thought furiously, *that's not all they do; they sleep together*.

'You are completely mad,' he said, rising.

Eve smiled sadly and murmured, as if to herself, 'Not enough so.'

'Not enough? I can only tell you one thing, my child. You frighten me.'

He kissed her hastily and left. Going down the stairs he thought: *we should send out two strong-arm men who'd take the poor imbecile away and stick him under a shower without asking his advice on the matter.*

It was a fine autumn day, calm and without mystery; the sunlight gilded the faces of the passers-by. M Darbedat was struck with the simplicity of the faces; some weather-beaten, others smooth, but they reflected all the happiness and care with which he was so familiar.

I know exactly what I resent in Eve, he told himself, entering the Boulevard St Germain. *I resent her living outside the limits of human nature. Pierre is no longer a human being: in all the care and all the love she gives him she deprives human beings of a little. We don't have the right to refuse ourselves to the world; no matter what, we live in society.*

He watched the faces of the passers-by with sympathy; he loved their clear, serious looks. In these sunlit streets, in the midst of mankind, one felt secure, as in the midst of a large family.

A woman stopped in front of an open-air display counter. She was holding a little girl by the hand.

'What's that?' the little girl asked, pointing to a radio set.

'Mustn't touch,' her mother said. 'It's a radio; it plays music.'

They stood for a moment without speaking, in ecstasy. Touched, M Darbedat bent down to the little girl and smiled.

'He's gone.' The door closed with a dry snap. Eve was alone in the salon. *I wish he'd die.*

She twisted her hands around the back of the armchair: she had just remembered her father's eyes. M Darbedat had bent over Pierre with a competent air; he had said 'That's good!' the way someone says when they speak to invalids. He had looked and Pierre's face had been painted in the depths of his sharp, bulging eyes. *I hate him when he looks at him because I think he sees him.*

Eve's hands slid along the armchair and she turned to the window. She was dazzled. The room was filled with sunlight, it was everywhere, in pale splotches on the rug, in the air like a blinding dust. Eve was not accustomed to this diligent, indiscreet light which darted from everywhere, scouring all the corners, rubbing the furniture like a busy housewife and making it glisten. However, she went to the window and raised the muslin curtain which hung against the pane. Just at that

moment M Darbedat left the building. Eve suddenly caught sight of his
broad shoulders. He raised his head and looked at the sky, blinking,
then with the stride of a young man he walked away. *He's straining
himself*, thought Eve, *soon he'll have a stitch in the side*. She hardly
hated him any longer: there was so little in that head; only the tiny
worry of appearing young. Yet rage took her again when she saw him
turn the corner of the Boulevard St Germain and disappear. *He's
thinking about Pierre*. A little of their life had escaped from the closed
room and was being dragged through the streets, in the sun, among the
people. *Can they never forget about us?*

The Rue du Bac was almost deserted. An old lady crossed the street
with mincing steps; three girls passed, laughing. Then men, strong,
serious men carrying briefcases and talking among themselves. *Normal
people*, thought Eve, astonished at finding such a powerful hatred in
herself. A handsome, fleshy woman ran heavily towards an elegant
gentleman. He took her in his arms and kissed her on the mouth. Eve
gave a hard laugh and let the curtain fall.

Pierre sang no more but the woman on the fourth floor was playing
the piano; she played a Chopin Etude. Eve felt calmer; she took a step
towards Pierre's room but stopped almost immediately and leaned
against the wall in anguish; each time she left the room, she was panic-
stricken at the thought of going back. Yet she knew she could live
nowhere else: she loved the room. She looked around it with cold
curiosity as if to gain a little time: this shadowless, odourless room
where she waited for her courage to return. *You'd think it was a
dentist's waiting room*. Armchairs of pink silk, the divan, the tabourets
were sombre and discreet, a little fatherly; man's best friends. Eve
imagined those grave gentlemen dressed in light suits, all like the ones
she saw at the window, entering the room, continuing a conversation
already begun. They did not even take time to reconnoitre, but
advanced with firm step to the middle of the room; one of them,
letting his hand drag behind him like a wake in passing knocked over
cushions, objects on the table, and was never disturbed by their
contact. And when a piece of furniture was in their way, these poised
men, far from making a detour to avoid it, quietly changed its place.
Finally they sat down, still plunged in their conversation, without even
glancing behind them. *A living-room for normal people*, thought Eve.
She stared at the knob of the closed door and anguish clutched her
throat: *I must go back. I never leave him alone so long*. She would have
to open the door, then stand for a moment on the threshold, trying to
accustom her eyes to the shadow and the room would push her back

with all its strength. Eve would have to triumph over this resistance and enter all the way into the heart of the room. Suddenly she wanted violently to see Pierre; she would have liked to make fun of M Darbedat with him. But Pierre had no need of her; Eve could not foresee the welcome he had in store for her. Suddenly she thought with a sort of pride that she had no place anywhere. *Normal people think I belong with them. But I couldn't stay an hour among them. I need to live out there, on the other side of the wall. But they don't want me out there.*

A profound change was taking place around her. The light had grown old and greying: it was heavy, like the water in a vase of flowers that hasn't been changed since the day before. In this aged light Eve found a melancholy she had long forgotten: the melancholy of an autumn afternoon that was ending. She looked around her, hesitant, almost timid: all that was so far away: there was neither day nor night nor season nor melancholy in the room. She vaguely recalled autumns long past, autumns of her childhood, then suddenly she stiffened: she was afraid of memories.

She heard Pierre's voice. 'Agatha! Where are you?'

'Coming!' she cried.

She opened the door and entered the room.

The heavy odour of incense filled her mouth and nostrils as she opened her eyes and stretched out her hands – for a long time the perfume and the gloom had meant nothing more to her than a single element, acrid and heavy, as simple, as familiar as water, air or fire – and she prudently advanced towards a pale stain which seemed to float in the fog. It was Pierre's face: Pierre's clothing (he dressed in black ever since he had been sick) melted in obscurity. Pierre had thrown back his head and closed his eyes. He was handsome. Eve looked at his long, curved lashes, then sat close to him on the low chair. *He seems to be suffering*, she thought. Little by little her eyes grew used to the darkness. The bureau emerged first, then the bed, then Pierre's personal things: scissors, the pot of glue, books, the herbarium which shed its leaves onto the rug near the armchair.

'Agatha?'

Pierre had opened his eyes. He was watching her, smiling. 'You know, that fork?' he said. 'I did it to frighten that fellow. There was *almost* nothing the matter with it.'

Eve's apprehensions faded and she gave a light laugh. 'You succeeded,' she said. 'You drove him completely out of his mind.'

Pierre smiled. 'Did you see? He played with it a long time, he held it right in his hands. The trouble is,' he said, 'they don't know how to take hold of things; they grab them.'

'That's right,' Eve said.

Pierre tapped the palm of his left hand lightly with the index of his right.

'They take with that. They reach out their fingers and when they catch hold of something they crack down on it to knock it out.'

He spoke rapidly and hardly moving his lips; he looked puzzled.

'I wonder what they want,' he said at last, 'that fellow has already been here. Why did they send him to me? If they wanted to know what I'm doing all they have to do is read it on the screen, they don't even need to leave the house. They make mistakes. They have the power but they make mistakes. I never make any, that's my trump card. *Hoffka!*' he said. He shook his long hands before his forehead. 'The bitch Hoffka, Paffka! Suffka! Do you want any more?'

'Is it the bell?' asked Eve.

'Yes. It's gone.' He went on severely. 'This fellow, he's just a subordinate. You know him, you went into the living-room with him.'

Eve did not answer.

'What did he want?' asked Pierre. 'He must have told you.'

She hesitated an instant, then answered brutally. 'He wanted you locked up.'

When the truth was told quietly to Pierre he distrusted it. He had to be dealt with violently in order to daze and paralyse his suspicions. Eve preferred to brutalize him rather than lie: when she lied and he acted as if he believed it she could not avoid a very slight feeling of superiority which made her horrified at herself.

'Lock me up!' Pierre repeated ironically. 'They're crazy. What can walls do to me. Maybe they think that's going to stop me. I sometimes wonder if there aren't two groups. The real one, the negro — and then a bunch of fools trying to stick their noses in and making mistake after mistake.'

He made his hand jump up from the arm of the chair and looked at it happily.

'I can get through walls. What did you tell them?' he asked, turning to Eve with curiosity.

'Not to lock you up.'

He shrugged. 'You shouldn't have said that. You made a mistake too ... unless you did it on purpose. You've got to call their bluff.'

He was silent. Eve lowered her head sadly: *They grab things!* How *scornfully he said that — and he was right. Do I grab things too? It*

*doesn't do any good to watch myself, I think most of my movements
annoy him. But he doesn't say anything.* Suddenly she felt as miserable
as when she was fourteen and Mme Darbedat told her. 'You don't
know what to do with your hands.' She didn't dare make a move and
just at that time she had an irresistible desire to change her position.
Quietly she put her feet under the chair, barely touching the rug. She
watched the lamp on the table – the lamp whose base Pierre had
painted black – and the chess set. Pierre had left only the black pawns
on the board. Sometimes he would get up, go to the table and take the
pawns in his hand one by one. He spoke to them, called them Robots
and they seemed to stir with a mute life under his fingers. When he set
them down, Eve went and touched them in her turn (she always felt
somewhat ridiculous about it). They had become little bits of dead
wood again but something vague and incomprehensible stayed in them,
something like understanding. *These are his things,* she thought. *There
is nothing of mine in the room.* She had had a few pieces of furniture
before; the mirror and the little inlaid dresser handed down from her
grandmother and which Pierre jokingly called '*your* dresser'. Pierre had
carried them away with him; things showed their true face to Pierre
alone. Eve could watch them for hours: they were unflaggingly stubborn and determined to deceive her, offering her nothing but their
appearance – as they did to Dr Franchot and M Darbedat. *Yet,* she told
herself with anguish, *I don't see them quite like my father. It isn't
possible for me to see them exactly like him.*

She moved her knees a little: her legs felt as though they were
crawling with ants. Her body was stiff and taut and hurt her; she felt
it too alive, too demanding. *I would like to be invisible and stay here
seeing him without his seeing me. He doesn't need me; I am useless in
this room.* She turned her head slightly and looked at the wall above
Pierre. Threats were written on the wall. Eve knew it but she could not
read them. She often watched the big red roses on the wallpaper until
they began to dance before her eyes. The roses flamed in shadow. Most
of the time the threat was written near the ceiling, a little to the left of
the bed; but sometimes it moved. *I must get up. I can't ... I can't sit
down any longer.* There were also white discs on the wall that looked
like slices of onion. The discs spun and Eve's hands began to tremble:
Sometimes I think I'm going mad. But no, she thought, *I can't go mad.
I get nervous, that's all.*

Suddenly she felt Pierre's hand on hers.

'Agatha,' Pierre said tenderly.

He smiled at her but he held her hand by the ends of his fingers with a sort of revulsion, as though he had picked up a crab by the back and wanted to avoid its claws.

'Agatha,' he said, 'I would so much like to have confidence in you.'

She closed her eyes and her breast heaved. *I mustn't answer anything, if I do he'll get angry, he won't say anything more.*

Pierre had dropped her hand. 'I like you, Agatha,' he said, 'but I can't understand you. Why do you stay in the room all the time?'

Eve did not answer.

'Tell me why.'

'You know I love you,' she said dryly.

'I don't believe you,' Pierre said. 'Why should you love me? I must frighten you: I'm haunted.' He smiled but suddenly became serious. 'There is a wall between you and me. I see you, I speak to you, but you're on the other side. What keeps us from loving? I think it was easier before. In Hamburg.'

'Yes,' Eve said sadly. Always Hamburg. He never spoke of their real past. Neither Eve nor he had ever been to Hamburg.

'We used to walk along the canal. There was a barge, remember? The barge was black; there was a dog on the deck.'

He made it up as he went along; it sounded false.

'I held your hand. You had another skin. I believed all you told me. Be quiet!' he shouted.

He listened for a moment. 'They're coming,' he said mournfully.

Eve jumped up. 'They're coming? I thought they wouldn't ever come again.'

Pierre had been calmer for the past three days; the statues did not come. Pierre was terribly afraid of the statues even though he would never admit it. Eve was not afraid: but when they began to fly, buzzing, around the room, she was afraid of Pierre.

'Give me the ziuthre,' Pierre said.

Eve got up and took the ziuthre: it was a collection of pieces of cardboard Pierre had glued together; he used it to conjure the statues. The ziuthre looked like a spider. On one of the cardboards Pierre had written 'Power over ambush' and on the other, 'Black'. On a third he had drawn a laughing face with wrinkled eyes: it was Voltaire.

Pierre seized the ziuthre by one end and looked at it darkly.

'I can't use it any more,' he said.

'Why?'

'They turned it upside down.'

'Will you make another?'

He looked at her for a long while. 'You'd like me to, wouldn't you,' he said between his teeth.

Eve was angry at Pierre. *He's warned every time they come: how does he do it? He's never wrong.*

The ziuthre dangled pitifully from the ends of Pierre's fingers. *He always finds a good reason not to use it. Sunday when they came he pretended he'd lost it but I saw it behind the paste pot and he couldn't fail to see it. I wonder if he isn't the one who brings them.* One could never tell if he were completely sincere. Sometimes Eve had the impression that despite himself Pierre was surrounded by a swarm of unhealthy thoughts and visions. But at other times Pierre seemed to invent them. *He suffers. But how much does he* believe *in the statues and the negro. Anyhow, I know he doesn't see the statues, he only hears them: when they pass he turns his head away; but he still says he sees them; he describes them.* She remembered the red face of Dr Franchot: 'But my dear madame, all mentally unbalanced persons are liars; you're wasting your time if you're trying to distinguish between what they really feel and what they pretend to feel.' She gave a start. *What is Franchot doing here? I don't want to start thinking like him.*

Pierre had got up. He went to throw the ziuthre into the waste-basket: *I want to think like you,* she murmured. He walked with tiny steps, on tiptoe, pressing his elbows against his hips so as to take up the least possible space. He came back and sat down and looked at Eve with a closed expression.

'We'll have to put up black wallpaper,' he said. 'There isn't enough black in this room.'

He was crouched in the armchair. Sadly Eve watched his meagre body, always ready to withdraw, to shrink: he arms, legs and head looked like retractable organs. The clock struck six. The piano downstairs was silent. Eve sighed: the statues would not come right away; they had to wait for them.

'Do you want me to turn on the light?'

She would rather not wait for them in darkness.

'Do as you please,' Pierre said.

Eve lit the small lamp on the bureau and a red mist filled the room. Pierre was waiting too.

He did not speak but his lips were moving, making two dark stains in the red mist. Eve loved Pierre's lips. Before, they had been moving and sensual; but they had lost their sensuality. They were wide apart, trembling a little, coming together incessantly, crushing against each other only to separate again. They were the only living things in this blank face; they looked like two frightened animals. Pierre could mutter like that for hours without a sound leaving his mouth and Eve often let herself be fascinated by this tiny, obstinate movement. *I love his mouth.* He never kissed her any more; he was horrified at contacts: at night they touched him – the hands of men, hard and dry, pinched him all over; the long-nailed hands of women caressed him. Often he went to bed with his clothes on but the hands slipped under the clothes and tugged at his shirt. Once he heard laughter and puffy lips were placed on his mouth. He never kissed Eve after that night.

'Agatha,' Pierre said, 'don't look at my mouth.'

Eve lowered her eyes.

'I am not unaware that people can learn to read lips,' he went on insolently.

His hand trembled on the arm of the chair. The index finger stretched out, tapped three times on the thumb and the other fingers curled: this was a spell. *It's going to start*, she thought. She wanted to take Pierre in her arms.

Pierre began to speak at the top of his voice in a very sophisticated tone.

'Do you remember Sao Paulo?'

No answer. Perhaps it was a trap.

'I met you there,' he said, satisfied. 'I took you away from a Danish sailor. We almost fought but I paid for a round of drinks and he let me take you away. All that was only a joke.'

He's lying, he doesn't believe a word of what he says. He knows my name isn't Agatha. I hate him when he lies. But she saw his staring eyes and her rage melted. *He isn't lying*, she thought, *he can't stand it any more. He feels them coming; he's talking to keep from hearing them.* Pierre dug both hands into the arm of the chair. His face was pale; he was smiling.

'These meetings are often strange,' he said, 'but I don't believe it's by chance. I'm not asking who sent you. I know you wouldn't answer. Anyhow, you've been smart enough to bluff me.'

He spoke with great difficulty, in a sharp, hurried voice. There were words he could not pronounce and which left his mouth like some soft and shapeless substance.

'You dragged me away right in the middle of the party, between the rows of black automobiles, but behind the car there was an army with red eyes which glowed as soon as I turned my back. I think you made signs to them, all the time hanging on my arm, but I didn't see a thing, I was too absorbed by the great ceremonies of the Coronation.'

He looked straight ahead, his eyes wide open. He passed his hand over his forehead very rapidly, in one spare gesture, without stopping his talking. He did not want to stop talking.

'It was the Coronation of the Republic,' he said stridently, 'an impressive spectacle of its kind because of all the species of animals that the colonies sent for the ceremony. You were afraid to get lost among the monkeys. I said among the monkeys,' he repeated arrogantly, looking around him, 'I could say *among the negroes!* The abortions sliding under the tables, trying to pass unseen, are discovered and nailed to the spot by my Look. The password is silence. To be silent. Everything in place and attention for the entrance of the statues, that's the countersign. Tralala ...' he shrieked and cupped his hands to his mouth. 'Tralalala, tralalalala!'

He was silent and Eve knew that the statues had come into the room. He was stiff, pale and distrustful. Eve stiffened too and both waited in silence. Someone was walking in the corridor: it was Marie the housecleaner, she had undoubtedly just arrived. Eve thought, *I have to give her money for the gas.* And then the statues began to fly; they passed between Eve and Pierre.

Pierre went 'Ah!' and sank down in the armchair, folding his legs beneath him. He turned his face away; sometimes he grinned, but drops of sweat pearled his forehead. Eve could stand the sight no longer, this pale cheek, this mouth deformed by a trembling grimace; she closed her eyes. Gold threads began to dance on the red background of her eyelids; she felt old and heavy. Not far from her Pierre was breathing violently. *They're flying, they're buzzing, they're bending over him.* She felt a slight tickling, a pain in the shoulder and right side. Instinctively her body bent to the left as if to avoid some disagreeable contact, as if to let a heavy, awkward object pass. Suddenly the floor creaked and she had an insane desire to open her eyes, to look to her right, sweeping the air with her hand.

She did nothing; she kept her eyes closed and a bitter joy made her tremble: *I am afraid too*, she thought. Her entire life had taken refuge in her right side. She leaned towards Pierre without opening her eyes. The slightest effort would be enough and she would enter this tragic world for the first time. *I'm afraid of the statues*, she thought. It was a violent, blind affirmation, an incantation. She wanted to believe in their presence with all her strength. She tried to make a new sense, a sense of touch out of the anguish which paralysed her right side. She *felt* their passage in her arm, in her side and shoulder.

The statues flew low and gently; they buzzed. Eve knew that they had an evil look and that eyelashes stuck out from the stone around their eyes; but she pictured them badly. She knew, too, that they were not quite alive but that slabs of flesh, warm scales appeared on their great bodies; the stone peeled from the ends of their fingers and their palms were eaten away. Eve could not *see* all that: she simply thought of enormous women sliding against her, solemn and grotesque, with a human look and compact heads of stone. *They are bending over Pierre –* Eve made such a violent effort that her hands began trembling – *they are bending over me.* A horrible cry suddenly chilled her. They had touched him. She opened her eyes: Pierre's head was in his hands, he was breathing heavily. Eve felt exhausted: *a game,* she thought with remorse; *it was only a game. I didn't sincerely believe it for an instant. And all that time he suffered as if it were real.*

Pierre relaxed and breathed freely. But his pupils were strangely dilated and he was perspiring.

'Did you see them?' he asked.

'I can't see them.'

'Better for you. They'd frighten you,' he said. 'I am used to them.'

Eve's hands were still shaking and the blood had rushed to her head. Pierre took a cigarette from his pocket and brought it up to his mouth. But he did not light it:

'I don't care whether I see them or not,' he said, 'but I don't want them to touch me: I'm afraid they'll give me pimples.'

He thought for an instant, then asked, 'Did you hear them?'

'Yes,' Eve said, 'it's like an aeroplane engine.' (Pierre had told her this the previous Sunday.)

Pierre smiled with condescension. 'You exaggerate,' he said. But he was still pale. He looked at Eve's hands. 'Your hands are trembling. That made quite an impression on you, my poor Agatha. But don't worry. They won't come back again before tomorrow.' Eve could not speak. Her teeth were chattering and she was afraid Pierre would notice it. Pierre watched her for a long time.

'You're tremendously beautiful,' he said, nodding his head. 'It's too bad, too bad.'

He put out his hand quickly and toyed with her ear. 'My lovely devil-woman. You disturb me a little, you are too beautiful: that distracts me. If it weren't a question of recapitulation ...'

He stopped and looked at Eve with surprise.

'That's not the word ... it came ... it came,' he said, smiling vaguely. 'I had another on the tip of my tongue ... but this one ... came in its place. I forget what I was telling you.'

He thought for a moment, then shook his head.

'Come,' he said, 'I want to sleep.' He added in a childish voice, 'You know, Agatha, I'm tired. I can't collect my thoughts any more.'

He threw away his cigarette and looked at the rug anxiously. Eve slipped a pillow under his head.

'You can sleep too,' he told her, 'they won't be back.'

... *Recapitulation* ...

Pierre was asleep, a candid, half-smile on his face; his head was turned to one side: one might have thought he wanted to caress his cheek with his shoulder. Eve was not sleepy, she was thoughtful: *Recapitulation*. Pierre had suddenly looked stupid and the word had slipped out of his mouth, long and whitish. Pierre had stared ahead of him in astonishment, as if he had seen the word and didn't recognize it; his mouth was open, soft: something seemed broken in it. He stammered. *That's the first time it ever happened to him: he noticed it, too. He said he couldn't collect his thoughts any more.* Pierre gave a voluptuous little whimper and his hand made a vague movement. Eve watched him harshly: *how is he going to wake up*. It gnawed at her. As soon as Pierre was asleep she had to think about it. She was afraid he would wake up wild-eyed and stammering. *I'm stupid*, she thought, *it can't start before a year; Franchot said so*. But the anguish did not leave her; a year: a winter, a springtime, a summer, the beginning of another autumn. One day his features would grow confused, his jaw would hang loose, he would half open his weeping eyes. Eve bent over Pierre's hand and pressed her lips against it. *I'll kill you before that.*

Translated by Lloyd Alexander

Samuel Beckett

The Expelled

Samuel Beckett was born in Dublin in 1906, although he has lived most of his adult life in France. Before he made his international reputation with 'Waiting for Godot', he had written several novels which pursue similar themes of desolation and hopelessness, Murphy, Watt, Molloy, Malone Dies, *and* The Unnamable.

There were not many steps. I had counted them a thousand times, both going up and coming down, but the figure has gone from my mind. I have never known whether you should say one with your foot on the sidewalk, two with the following foot on the first step, and so on, or whether the sidewalk shouldn't count. At the top of the steps I met with the same dilemma. In the other direction, I mean from top to bottom, it was the same, the word is not too strong. I did not know where to begin nor where to end, that's the truth of the matter. I arrived therefore at three totally different figures, without ever knowing which of them was right. And when I say that the figure has gone from my mind, I mean that none of the three figures is with me any more, in my mind. It is true that if I were to find, in my mind, where it is certainly to be found, one of these figures, I would find it and it alone, without being able to deduce from it the other two. And even were I to recover two, I would not know the third. No, I would have to find all three, in my mind, in order to know all three. Memories are killing. So you must not think of certain things, of those that are dear to you, or rather you must think of them, for if you don't there is the danger of finding them, in your mind, little by little. That is to say, you must think of them for a while, a good while, every day several times a day, until they sink forever in the mud. That's an order.

After all it is not the number of steps that matters. The important thing to remember is the fact that there were not many steps, and that I have remembered. Even for the child there were not many, compared to other steps he knew, from seeing them every day, from going up them and coming down, and playing on them at knuckle-bones and other games the very names of which he has forgotten. What must it have been like then for the man I had overgrown into?

The fall was therefore not serious. Even as I fell I heard the door slam, which brought me a little comfort, in the midst of my fall. For that meant they were not pursuing me down into the street with a stick, to beat me in full view of the passers-by. For if that had been their intention they would not have shut the door, but left it open, so that the persons assembled in the vestibule might enjoy my chastisement and be edified. So, for once, they had confined themselves to throwing me out, and no more about it. I had time, before coming to rest in the gutter, to conclude this piece of reasoning.

Under these circumstances, nothing compelled me to get up immediately. I rested my elbow on the sidewalk, funny the things you remember, settled my ear in the cup of my hand and began to reflect on my situation, notwithstanding its familiarity. But the sound, fainter but unmistakable, of the door slammed again, roused me from my reverie, in which already a whole landscape was taking form, charming with hawthorn and wild roses, most dreamlike, and made me look up in alarm, my hands flat on the sidewalk and my legs braced for flight. But it was merely my hat sailing towards me through the air, rotating as it came. I caught it and put it on. They were most correct, according to their god. They could have kept this hat, but it was not theirs, it was mine, so they gave it back to me. But the spell was broken.

How describe this hat? And why? When my head had attained I shall not say its definitive but its maximum dimensions, my father said to me, Come, son, we are going to buy your hat, as though it had pre-existed from time immemorial in a pre-established place. He went straight to the hat. I personally had no say in the matter, nor had the hatter. I have often wondered if my father's purpose was not to humiliate me, if he was not jealous of me who was young and handsome, fresh at least, while he was already old and all bloated and purple. It was forbidden me, from that day forth, to go out bareheaded, my pretty brown hair blowing in the wind. Sometimes, in a secluded street, I took it off and held it in my hand, but trembling. I was required to brush it morning and evening. Boys my age with whom, in spite of everything, I was obliged to mix occasionally, mocked me. But I said to myself, It is not really the hat, they simply make merry at the hat because it is a little more glaring than the rest, for they have no finesse. I have always been amazed at my contemporaries' lack of finesse, I whose soul writhed from morning to night, in the mere quest of itself. But perhaps they were simply being kind, like those who make game of the hunchback's big nose. When my father died I could have got rid of this hat, there was nothing more to prevent me, but not I. But how describe it? Some other time, some other time.

I got up and set off. I forget how old I can have been. In what had just happened to me there was nothing in the least memorable. It was neither the cradle nor the grave of anything whatever. Or rather it resembled so many other cradles, so many other graves, that I'm lost. But I don't believe I exaggerate when I say that I was in the prime of life, what I believe is called the full possession of one's faculties. Ah yes, them I possessed all right. I crossed the street and turned back towards the house that had just ejected me, I who never turned back when leaving. How beautiful it was! There were geraniums in the windows. I have brooded over geraniums for years. Geraniums are artful customers, but in the end I was able to do what I liked with them. I have always greatly admired the door of this house, up on top of its little flight of steps. How describe it? It was a massive green door, encased in summer in a kind of green and white striped housing, with a hole for the thunderous wrought-iron knocker and a slit for letters, this latter closed to dust, flies and tits by a brass flap fitted with springs. So much for that description. The door was set between two pillars of the same colour, the bell being on that to the right. The curtains were in unexceptional taste. Even the smoke rising from one of the chimney pots seemed to spread and vanish in the air more melancholy than the neighbours', and bluer. I looked up at the third and last floor and saw my window outrageously open. A thorough cleaning was in full swing. In a few hours they would close the window, draw the curtains and spray the whole place with disinfectant. I knew them. I would have gladly died in that house. In a sort of vision, I saw the door open and my feet come out.

I wasn't afraid to look, for I knew they were not spying on me from behind the curtains, as they could have done if they had wished. But I knew them. They had all gone back into their dens and resumed their occupations.

And yet I had done them no harm.

I did not know the town very well, scene of my birth and of my first steps in this world, and then of all the others, so many that I thought all trace of me was lost, but I was wrong. I went out so little! Now and then I would go to the window, part the curtains and look out. But then I hastened back to the depths of the room, where the bed was. I felt ill at ease with all this air about me, lost before the confusion of innumerable prospects. But I still knew how to act at this period, when it was absolutely necessary. But first I raised my eyes to the sky, whence cometh our help, where there are no roads, where you wander freely, as in a desert, and where nothing obstructs your vision, wherever you turn your eyes, but the limits of vision itself. That is why I always raise my eyes, in times of great trouble, to this sky which is such a rest, no matter how cloudy, or leaden, or veiled by the rain, from the viewless confusion of the town, the country, the earth. It gets monotonous in the end, but I can't help it. When I was younger I thought life would be good in the middle of a plain, and I went to the Lüneburg heath. With the plain in my head I went to the heath. There were other heaths far less remote, but a voice kept saying to me, It's the Lüneburg heath you need. The element lüne must have had something to do with it. As it turned out the Lüneburg heath was most unsatisfactory, most unsatisfactory. I came home disappointed, and at the same time relieved. Yes, I don't know why, but I have never been disappointed, and I often was in the early days, without feeling at the same time, or a moment later, an undeniable relief.

I set off. What a gait. Stiffness of the lower limbs, as if nature had denied me knees, extraordinary splaying of the feet to right and left of the line of march. The trunk, on the contrary, as if by the effect of a compensatory mechanism, was as flabby as an old ragbag, tossing wildly to the unpredictable jolts of the pelvis. I have often tried to correct these defects, to stiffen my bust, flex my knees and walk with my feet in front of one another, for I had at least five or six, but it always ended in the same way, I mean by a loss of equilibrium, followed by a fall. A man must walk without paying attention to what he's doing, as he sighs, and when I walked without paying attention to what I was doing I walked in the way I have just described, and when I began to pay attention I managed a few steps of creditable execution and then fell. I decided therefore to be myself. This carriage is due, in my opinion, in part at least, to a certain leaning from which I have never been able to free myself completely and which left its stamp, as was only to be expected, on my impressionable years, those which govern the fabrication of character, I refer to the period which extends, as far as the eye can see, from the first totterings, behind a chair, to the third form, in which I concluded my studies. I had then the deplorable habit, having pissed in my trousers, or having shat there, which I did fairly regularly early in the morning, about ten or half past ten, of persisting in going on and finishing my day as if nothing had happened. The very idea of changing my trousers, or of confiding in mother, who goodness knows asked nothing better than to help me, was unbearable, I don't know why, and till bedtime I dragged on with burning and stinking between my little thighs, or sticking to my bottom, the result of my incontinence. Whence this wary way of walking, with the legs stiff and wide apart, and this desperate rolling of the bust, no doubt intended to put people off the scent, to make them think I was full of gaiety and high spirits, without a care in the world, and to lend plausibility to my explanations concerning my nether rigidity, which I ascribed to hereditary rheumatism. My youthful ardour, in so far as I had any, spent itself in this effort, I became sour and mistrustful, a little before my time, in love with hiding and the prone position. Poor juvenile solutions, explaining nothing. No need then for caution, we may reason on to our heart's content, the fog won't lift.

The weather was fine. I advanced down the street, keeping as close as I could to the sidewalk. The widest sidewalk is never wide enough for me, once I set myself in motion, and I hate to inconvenience strangers. A policeman stopped me and said, The street for vehicles, the sidewalk for pedestrians. Like a bit of the Old Testament. So I got back on the sidewalk, almost apologetically, and persevered there, in spite of an indescribable jostle, for a good twenty steps, till I had to fling myself to the ground to avoid crushing a child. He was wearing a little harness, I remember, with little bells, he must have taken himself for a pony, or a Clydesdale, why not. I would have crushed him gladly, I loathe children, and it would have been doing him a service, but I was afraid of reprisals. Everyone is a parent, that is what keeps you from hoping. One should reserve, on busy streets, special tracks for these dirty little creatures, their prams, hoops, sweets, scooters, skates, grandpas, grandmas, nannies, balloons and balls, all their foul little happiness in a word. I fell then and brought down with me an old lady covered with spangles and lace, who must have weighed about sixteen stone. Her screams soon drew a crowd. I had high hopes she had broken her femur, old ladies break their femur easily, but not enough, not enough. I took advantage of the confusion to make off, muttering unintelligible oaths, as if I were the victim, and I was, but I couldn't have proved it. They never lynch children, babies, no matter what they do they are whitewashed in advance. I personally would lynch them with the utmost pleasure, I don't say I'd lend a hand, no, I am not a violent man, but I'd encourage the others and stand them drinks when it was done. But no sooner had I begun to reel on than I was stopped by a second policeman, similar in all respects to the first, so much so that I wondered whether it was not the same one. He pointed out to me that the sidewalk was for everyone, as if it was quite obvious that I could not be assimilated to that category. Would you like me, I said, without thinking for a single moment of Heraclitus, to get down in the gutter? Get down wherever you want, he said, but leave some room for others. If you can't bloody well get about like every one else, he said, you'd do better to stay at home. It was exactly my feeling. And that he should attribute to me a home was no small satisfaction. At that moment a funeral passed, as sometimes happens. There was a great flurry of hats and at the same time a flutter of countless fingers. Personally if I were reduced to making the sign of the cross I would set my heart on doing it right, nose navel, left nipple, right nipple. But the way they did it, slovenly and wild, he seemed crucified all of a heap, no dignity, his knees under his chin and his hands anyhow. The more fervent stopped dead and muttered. As for the policeman he stiffened to attention, closed his eyes and saluted. Through the windows of the cabs I caught a glimpse of the mourners conversing with animation, no doubt scenes from the life of their late dear brother in Christ, or sister. I seem to have heard that the hearse trappings are not the same in both cases, but I never could find out what the difference consists in. The horses were farting and shitting as if they were going to the fair. I saw no one kneeling.

But with us the last journey is quickly done, it is in vain you quicken your pace, the last cab containing the domestics soon leaves you behind, the respite is over, the people come back to life, you may look to yourself again. So I stopped a third time, of my own free will, and took a cab. Those I had just seen pass, crammed with people hotly arguing, must have made a strong impression on me. It's a big black box, rocking and swaying on its springs, the windows are small, you curl up in a corner, it smells musty. I felt my hat grazing the roof. A little later I leant forward and closed the windows. Then I sat down again with my back to the horse. I was dozing off when a voice made me jump, the cabman's. He had opened the door, no doubt despairing of making himself heard through the window. All I saw was his moustache. Where to? he said. He had climbed down from his seat on purpose to ask me that. And I who thought I was far away already. I reflected, searching in my memory for the name of a street, or a monument. Is your cab for sale? I said. I added, Without the horse. What would I do with a horse? But what would I do with a cab? Could I as much as stretch out in it? Who would bring me food? To the Zoo, I said. It is rare for a capital to be without a Zoo. I added, Don't go too fast. He laughed. The suggestion that he might go too fast to the Zoo must have amused him. Unless it was the prospect of being cabless. Unless it was simply myself, my own person, whose presence in the cab must have transformed it, so much so that the cabman, seeing me there with my head in the shadows of the roof and my knees against the window, had wondered perhaps if it was really his cab, really a cab. He hastens to look at his horse, and is reassured. But does one ever know oneself why one laughs? His laugh in any case was brief, which suggested I was not the joke. He closed the door and climbed back to his seat. It was not long then before the horse got under way.

Yes, surprising though it may seem, I still had a little money at this time. The small sum my father had left me as a gift, with no restrictions, at his death, I still wonder if it wasn't stolen from me. Then I had none. And yet my life went on, and even in the way I wanted, up to a point. The great disadvantage of this condition, which might be defined as the absolute impossibility of all purchase, is that it compels you to bestir yourself. It is rare, for example, when you are completely penniless, that you can have food brought to you from time to time in your retreat. You are therefore obliged to go out and bestir yourself, at least one day a week. You can hardly have a home address under these circumstances, it's inevitable. It was therefore with a certain delay that I learnt they were looking for me, for an affair concerning me. I forget through what channel. I did not read the newspapers, nor do I remember having spoken with anyone during these years, except perhaps three or four times, on the subject of food. At any rate, I must have had wind of the affair one way or another, otherwise I would never have gone to see the lawyer, Mr Nidder, strange how one fails to forget certain names, and he would never have received me. He verified my identity. That took some time. I showed him the metal initials in the lining of my hat, they proved nothing but they increased the probabilities. Sign, he said. He played with a cylindrical ruler, you could have felled an ox with it. Count, he said. A young woman, perhaps venal, was present at this interview, as a witness no doubt. I stuffed the wad in my pocket. You shouldn't do that, he said. It occurred to me that he should have asked me to count before I signed, it would have been more in order. Where can I reach you, he said, if necessary? At the foot of the stairs I thought of something. Soon after I went back to ask him where this money came from, adding that I had a right to know. He gave me a woman's name that I've forgotten. Perhaps she had dandled me on her knees while I was still in swaddling clothes, and there had been some lovey-dovey. Sometimes that suffices.

I repeat, in swaddling clothes, for any later it would have been too late, for lovey-dovey. It is thanks to this money then that I still had a little. Very little. Divided by my life to come it was negligible, unless my conjectures were unduly pessimistic. I knocked on the partition beside my hat, right in the cabman's back if my calculations were correct. A cloud of dust rose from the upholstery. I took a stone from my pocket and knocked with the stone, until the cab stopped. I noticed that, unlike most vehicles, which slow down before stopping, the cab stopped dead. I waited. The whole cab shook. The cabman, on his high seat, must have been listening. I saw the horse as with my eyes of flesh. It had not lapsed into the drooping attitude of its briefest halts, it remained alert, its ears pricked up. I looked out of the window, we were again in motion. I banged again on the partition, until the cab stopped again. The cabman got down cursing from his seat. I lowered the window to prevent his opening the door. Faster, faster. He was redder than ever, purple in other words. Anger, or the rushing wind. I told him I was hiring him for the day. He replied that he had a funeral at three o'clock. Ah, the dead. I told him I had changed my mind and no longer wished to go to the Zoo. Let us not go to the Zoo, I said. He replied that it made no difference to him where we went, provided it wasn't too far, because of his animal. And they talk to us about the specificity of primitive peoples' speech. I asked him if he knew of an eating house. I added, You'll eat with me. I'd just as soon be with a regular customer in such places. There was a long table with two benches of exactly the same length on either side. Across the table he spoke to me of his life, of his wife, of his animal, then again of his life, of the atrocious life that was his, chiefly because of his character. He asked me if I realized what it meant to be out of doors in all weathers. I learnt there were still some cabmen who spent their day snug and warm inside their cabs on the rank, waiting for a customer to come and rouse them. Such a thing was possible in the past, but nowadays other methods were necessary, if a man was to have a little laid up at the end of his days. I described my situation to him, what I had lost and what I was looking for. We did our best, both of us, to understand, to explain. He understood that I had lost my room and needed another, but all the rest escaped him. He had taken it into his head, whence nothing could ever dislodge it, that I was looking for a furnished room. He took from his pocket an evening paper of the day before or perhaps the day before that again, and proceeded to run through the advertisements, five or six of which he underlined with a tiny pencil, the same that hovered over the likely outsiders. He underlined no doubt those he

would have underlined if he had been in my shoes, or perhaps those
concentrated in the same district, because of his animal. I would only
have confused him by saying that I could tolerate no furniture in
my room except the bed, and that all the other pieces, and even the
very night table, had to be removed before I would consent to set foot
in it. About three o'clock we roused the horse and set off again. The
cabman suggested that I climb up beside him on the seat, but for some
time already I had been dreaming of the inside of the cab and I got
back inside. We visited, methodically I hope, one after another, the
addresses he had underlined. The short winter's day was drawing to a
close. It seems to me sometimes that these are the only days I have
ever known, and especially that most charming moment of all, just before night wipes them out. The addresses he had underlined, or rather
marked with a cross, as common people do, proved fruitless one by
one, and one by one he crossed them out with a diagonal stroke. Later
he showed me the paper, advising me to keep it safe so as to be sure
not to look again where I had already looked in vain. In spite of the
closed windows, the creaking of the cab and the traffic noises, I heard
him singing, all alone aloft on his high seat. He had preferred me to a
funeral, this was a fact which would endure forever. He sang, *She is
far from the land where her young hero,* those are the only words I
remember. At each stop he got down from his seat and helped me get
down from mine. I rang at the door he directed me to and sometimes
I disappeared inside the house. It was a strange feeling, I remember, a
house all about me again, after so long. He waited for me on the sidewalk and helped me climb back into the cab. I was beginning to have
my bellyful of this cabman. He clambered back to his seat and we set
off again. At a certain moment there occurred this. He stopped. I shook
off my torpor and made ready to get down. But he did not come to open
the door and offer me his arm, so that I was obliged to get down by
myself. He was lighting the lamps. I love oil lamps, in spite of their having been, with candles, and if I except the stars, the first lights I ever
knew. I asked him if I might light the second lamp, since he had already
lit the first one himself. He gave me his box of matches, I swung open on
its hinges the little convex glass, lit and closed at once, so that the
wick might burn steady and bright snug in its little house, sheltered
from the wind. I had this joy. We saw nothing, by the light of these
lamps, save the vague outlines of the horse, but the others saw them
from afar, two yellow glows sailing slowly through the air. When the
equipage turned an eye could be seen, red or green as the case might
be, a bossy rhomb, as clear and keen as stained glass.

After we had verified the last address the cabman suggested bringing me to a hotel he knew where I would be comfortable. That makes sense, cabman, hotel, it's plausible. With his recommendation I would want for nothing. Every convenience, he said, with a wink. I place this conversation on the sidewalk, in front of the house from which I had just emerged. I remember, beneath the lamp, the flank of the horse, hollow and damp, and on the handle of the door the cabman's hand in its woollen glove. The roof of the cab was on a level with my neck. I suggested we have a drink. The horse had neither eaten nor drunk all day. I mentioned this to the cabman, who replied that his horse would take no food till it was back in the stable. If it ate anything whatever, during work, were it but an apple or a lump of sugar, it would have stomach pains and colics that would root it to the spot and might even kill it. That was why he was compelled to tie its jaws together with a strap whenever for one reason or another he had to let it out of his sight, so that it would not have to suffer from the kind hearts of the passers-by. After a few drinks the cabman invited me to do his wife and him the honour of spending the night with them. It was not far. Recollecting these emotions, with the celebrated advantage of tranquility, it seems to me he did nothing else, all that day, but turn about his lodgings. They lived above a stable, at the back of a yard. Ideal location, I could have done with it. Having presented me to his wife, extraordinarily full-bottomed, he left us. She was manifestly ill at ease, alone with me. I could understand her, I don't stand on ceremony on these occasions. No reason for this to end or go on. Then let it end. I said I would go down to the stable and go to bed. The cabman protested. I insisted. He drew his wife's attention to the pustule on top of my skull, for I had removed my hat out of civility. You should have that removed, she said. The cabman named a doctor he held in high esteem and who had rid him of an induration of the seat. If he wants to sleep in the stable, said his wife, let him sleep in the stable. The cabman took the lamp from the table and preceded me down the stairs, or rather ladder, which descended to the shed, leaving his wife in the dark. He spread a horse blanket on the ground in a corner on the straw and left me a box of matches in case I needed to see clearly in the night. I don't remember what the horse was doing all this time. Stretched out in the dark I heard the noise it made as it drank, a noise like no other, the sudden gallop of the rats and above me the muffled voices of the cabman and his wife as they criticized me. I held the box of matches in my hand, a big box of safety matches. I got up during the night and struck one. Its brief flame enabled me to locate the cab. I was seized, then abandoned, by the desire to set fire to the stable. I found the cab in the dark, opened the door, the rats poured out, I climbed in. As I settled down I noticed the cab was no longer level, it was inevitable, since the shafts rested on the ground. It was better so, that allowed me to lie well back, with my feet higher than my head on the other seat. Several times during the night I felt the horse looking at me through the window and the breath of its nostrils. Now that it was unharnessed it must have been puzzled by my presence in the cab. I was cold, having forgotten to take the blanket, but not quite enough to go and get it. Through the window of the cab I saw the window of the stable, more and more clearly. I got out of the cab. It was not so dark now in the stable, I saw dimly the manger, the rack, the harness hanging, what else, buckets and brushes. I went to the door but couldn't open it. The horse didn't take its eyes off me. Don't horses ever sleep? It seemed to me the cabman should have tied it, to the manger for example. So I was obliged to leave by the window. It wasn't easy. But what is easy? I went out head first, my hands were flat on the ground of the yard while my legs were still thrashing to get clear of the frame. I remember the tufts of grass on which I pulled with both hands, in my efforts to extricate myself. I should have taken off my greatcoat and thrown it through the window, but that would have meant thinking of it. No sooner had I left the yard than I thought of something. Weariness. I slipped a banknote in the match box, went back to the yard and placed the box on the sill of the window through which I had just come. The horse was at the window. But after I had taken a few steps in the street I returned to the yard and took back my banknote. I left the matches, they were not mine. The horse was still at the window. I was sick and tired of this horse. Dawn was just breaking. I did not know where I was. I made towards the rising sun, towards where I thought it should rise, the quicker to come into the light. I would have liked a sea horizon, or a desert one. When I am abroad in the morning, I go to meet the sun, and in the evening, when I am abroad, I follow it, till I am down among the dead. I don't know why I told this story. I could just as well have told another. Perhaps some other time I'll be able to tell another. Living souls, you will see how alike they are.

—Translated by Richard Seaver
in collaboration with the author

Alberto Moravia

Back to the Sea

One of the leading Italian novelists of this century, Alberto Moravia was born in 1907. His first novel was published when he was in his early twenties, and since then he has become celebrated for Two Adolescents, The Woman of Rome, Two Women, *and, recently,* The Empty Canvas.

The landscape was flat, with wide meadows scattered with soft white daisies. On the horizon the pine wood bounded the meadows with a long, unbroken wall of solid and motionless greenery. The car made its way slowly and as though reluctantly, jolting over the holes in the un-paved road. Through the windscreen Lorenzo could see the mass of the pine wood coming to meet him, as if it were moving – melancholy, mys-terious, hostile. Lorenzo had planned this outing as a way of making things up with his wife. But now, faced by her solid silence, he felt overcome yet again with timidity. However, as they approached the pines he said: 'Here is the pine wood.'

His wife made no reply. He lifted his hand and adjusted the mirror over the windscreen. When they had started out he had tilted it towards her, and during the drive he had done nothing but watch her. She had sat firm and erect, her gloved hand on the door, her coat folded on her knees, her white linen shirt open as far as her breast. Her slender neck rose up from the shirt like a graceful stem. Over her sunburnt face and red mouth her freckles and the soft down on her lip threw a veil of shadowy sensuality. But her eyes, small and black, gazed obstinately ahead, and the upward sweep of her hair from her forehead gave her whole appearance an aggressive, hard look. She had something simian about her, Lorenzo thought; manifest not so much in her features as in her sad, decrepit and innocent expression, like that of some small monkeys. And like a monkey she put up a pretence of offended dignity which he knew she was quite incapable of.

Now that they were approaching the pine wood it appeared less dense than before, with red trunks leaning this way and that as if they were just about to fall against each other. The car left the road and took to a stretch of bare, soft ground over which the wheels bounded gently. The pine wood was deserted; here and there in the shade stood an uninhabited chalet with closed shutters. Then the wood brightened, the air became white and trembling: the sea.

Lorenzo would have liked to announce the sea as he had announced the wood – but his wife's silence seemed even more determined, and she wouldn't be able to resist the temptation of snubbing him – the sight of the sea caused him such genuine delight. So he remained silent and drove over the bare soil. The car stopped, and for a moment they sat motionless in the shadow of the low hood. They couldn't see the sea properly yet, but they could hear it now the engine was switched off, with its varied and diffused murmur in which each wave seemed to have a different tone. 'Shall we get out?' he suggested at last.

His wife opened the door and put out her legs, hindered by the narrowness of her skirt. Lorenzo followed and shut the door. Immediately they felt the wind, strong and warm and fierce, lifting clouds of sand and dust from the rough ground.

'Shall we go down to the sea?'

'Yes; of course.'

They set out across the clearing. The bombardments had ruined much of the promenade; here and there there were wide gaps in the cement paving. There were still a few pillars standing; others had been thrown down and were gradually being covered with sand blown in long tongues as far as the middle of the clearing. When they looked in the direction of the beach they saw that it was criss-crossed all over with barbed-wire entanglements. The wind blew under the barbed wire, smoothing out the sand. The thorny threads of steel, wrapped in a white and furious cloud of dust, stretched away into the distance.

They found a way marked out by poles through the barbed wire to the sea. Lorenzo let his wife go ahead and followed at some distance behind. He did this so as to watch her at his leisure, as he had done earlier in the mirror of the car. After he had managed this manoeuvre, he reflected that perhaps the most pathetic thing about all his misfortunes was his tardy and unforeseen passion for his wife. He had not loved her at first; he had married in a hurry in the interests of his political career. And now that the vacuous and noisy luck which had dazzled him for so many years had come to an end, he had fallen in love with her, when she had no use for his love. Or rather a sort of pungent lust had been kindled in his blood, something shy and awkward as in a boy. As he followed her he found himself watching her with a sad and surly desire that astonished him. She was tall, thin, elegant, boyish, and when her long, strong legs, sturdy in relation to the slimness of her torso, moved clumsily over the uneven sand, they recalled the legs of an awkward foal. Lorenzo paid special attention to those legs on which innumerable hairs were visible through her transparent stockings – black, long hairs which looked as though they had been stuck on to the skin and were flat and lifeless. She didn't have them plucked, as many women do. When she put up her hand to arrange her hair, disordered by the wind, he seemed to make out the blackness of her armpit through the linen shirt and felt profoundly troubled.

They reached the sea. Offshore the wind was pushing up long and sonorous springtime billows, rolling one over the other; but farther out the sea was almost calm, with alternating streaks of turbid green and dark violet. For a while Lorenzo stood beside his wife, looking at the waves. He picked one out as far away as the eye could see – in fact, at its birth – and then followed it as it rose, overturned on the rump of the one ahead of it, and passed on beyond it. As the wave lingered, lost its way in the ebb and died at his feet, his glance leapt back to the sea in search of another. He didn't know why, but he wanted at least one of those innumerable masses of water breaking on the shore to overcome the rivals that held it back and the retarding impact of the backwash; to hurl itself on the shore, pass beyond him and his wife, mount the beach and wreathe with far-flung foam the barbed-wire defences and the clearing. But it was a vain wish, and he suddenly understood why he wanted it so much. As a child, on stormy days, he loved to watch the varied impetus of the waves, and now and again, when he saw a bigger and stronger one spreading quickly up the beach as far as the bathing huts, he used to think ambitiously: 'I shall be like that wave.' He shook his head vigorously to banish the recollection and, turning to his wife, asked: 'Do you like it?'

'The sea?' she said indifferently. 'It's not the first time I've seen it, you know.'

Lorenzo would have liked to explain his feelings – yes, to tell her about his childish fancies; but a sort of hopeless timidity prevented him from speaking. He felt a strong impulse to free himself from his preoccupation and at least seem carefree. He bent down and picked up a stone, so as to throw it as far as he possibly could. He hoped that the violence of the action would cast away his pain as well as the stone. But the stone was deceptive. It was as big as his fist, but light; it was pumice and porous with holes. It fell close to him, floated on the crest of a wave and grounded in the sand at his feet. He felt a sensation of bitterness, as though this was reality's silent answer to all his aspirations. His suffering resembled the pumice stone, and he hadn't the strength to cast it away; it would always come back with the jetsam and black debris that the rough sea vomited on to the shore.

He approached his wife and put his arm round her. He wanted to walk with her along the sea's edge with the health-giving wind blowing against them, in the clamorous solitude of the waves breaking on the shore. But, startled and stubborn, she pushed him off.

'What's the matter with you?'

'Don't you want us to go for a walk?'

'It's too windy.'

'I like the wind,' he said. And he took a few steps along the shore by himself. He felt his behaviour was desperate and unreasonable, like a madman's. His feeling of madness was increased by the crashing of the waves and by the wind blowing into his hair, his eyes. 'I've completely lost my head,' he thought coolly, and he started to go towards a little heap of sand which had formed round some derelict and rusty object.

'What are you doing?' he heard his wife ask angrily. 'Where are you going? There are mines about.'

'What do I care about mines,' he answered with a shrug. He would have liked to add, 'or if I'm blown up,' but was silent out of modesty. He turned to see what his wife was doing. She was still facing the sea, looking bored and undecided. Then she said: 'Don't play the hero; you know you want to live,' with a contempt which wounded him and seemed unfair. He jumped back and took her arm. 'You must believe me when I say that at this moment I don't care a fig about dying; in fact, I'd be glad.' He squeezed her round, firm arm tightly and was depressed to notice the ease with which physical contact turned his despair into desire and made him insincere in spite of himself. She glanced at him crossly: 'Leave me alone ... It's the usual story ... And, any way ...' Then, after a pause, 'Do what you like, but I won't follow you. I haven't the slightest desire to die myself.'

Lorenzo left her and set out purposefully for the little mound. His feet sank, his shoes filled with sand. The mound was no more than fifty yards away; he reached it and discovered it was an old petrol tin. The sea had corroded and rusted it and the wind had filled it three-quarters full of sand. Beyond, the beach stretched on as far as the eye could see, swept by the grazing wind, traversed by delicate barbed-wire entanglements which in the soft whiteness of the sand looked like healed-up scars. He hesitated a moment, dazzled by the reflection of the cloudy sky, and then turned back.

His wife was no longer there. Lorenzo picked his way through the narrow passage of the barbed wire to the clearing. His wife was standing by the car, one hand on the door, the other at her forehead fixing her hair. 'What are we going to do now?' she asked.

'Let's eat,' he suggested in a cheerful voice, though he felt scarcely capable of speaking, let alone being cheerful.

'Where?'

'We can go into the pine wood.' Without waiting for an answer, he took the picnic basket from the back of the car and set out in the direction of the pines. His wife followed.

They crossed the clearing towards the remains of what had once been the local restaurant. In the white, dusty light, upright stumps of half-buried ruins arose out of the convulsed ground — pale outside and coloured inside like decayed teeth. The cement stairway leading to the main hall, in which people used to eat overlooking the sea, mounted one or two steps and then suddenly stopped above a hollowed-out chaos of pieces of ceiling, twisted and rusting iron and blocks of mortar and bricks. The other rooms inside the crumpled walls were recognizable from similar ruins, agglomerated in dusty pulp. They walked round the ruins and he said: 'You remember the last time we were here?'

'No.'

'Two years ago. Things were already going badly, but I didn't want to face up to it. You had a wisp of something round your breast and another round your waist which passed between your legs. You were very brown; you had a little turban round your head. Now,' he went on in an unexpectedly strained voice, 'I realize you're very lovely, but then I didn't seem to see you. I thought about nothing but politics and let all the idiots who followed us around make love to you.'

'And so what?' she asked dryly.

'Nothing.'

Behind the restaurant was a lawn and the rough, dirty grass was mixed with sand. Thick bushes and twisted trees with branches like arms grew on the edge of the lawn. The bombardment had thrown a piece of the café piano into the middle of the lawn: the keyboard with a few white notes and a great hunk of splintered wood looked exactly like an animal's jaw with a few putrefying teeth. The grass all around was scattered with felt hammers. Another part of the instrument, the frame, had been hurled into the fork of a tree. The metal strings hung from it and curled like the pendant tentacles of a grotesque creeper.

Lorenzo searched for a withdrawn spot with a blind and concentrated premeditation as though his purpose were not love but crime. His wife followed some way behind, and he felt she was looking increasingly discontented and hostile. The pine wood was full of little grassy glades unevenly bordered with bushes and undergrowth. At last he thought he had found what he was looking for. 'Let's sit down here,' he said, and slid to the ground.

She remained standing for a moment, looking around. Then slowly, stiffly, contemptuously, she sank on to her thighs and sat, swiftly pulling her dress over her knees. Lorenzo pretended he wasn't looking at her and began to take the food from the basket. There were many packets, big and small, carefully wrapped in white tissue paper of the kind used in fashion shops. And there was a bottle of wine.

'Was it you who packed the basket?'

'No. I got the maid to do it.'

He spread out a napkin on the grass and carefully arranged the eggs, the meat, the cheese and fruit. Then he uncorked the bottle and put the cork back in again.

'Would you like an egg?'

'No.'

'Meat?'

'Give me a roll with a slice of meat.'

Lorenzo took one of the rolls which had already been cut in half and buttered, put in two slices of meat, and handed it to her. She accepted it fastidiously, without thanking him, and ate unwillingly. His head still down and without glancing at her, Lorenzo took a hard-boiled egg and bit at it hungrily, then filled his mouth with buttered bread. He felt a sorry kind of hunger which seemed rather like his desire for his wife. Hunger and lust grew and prospered on his despair, he thought – as if he were only a corpse without life or will and his wants had grown on him in the way hair grows on the beards of the dead. He ate one egg, then another, then a third, hesitated, and then ate the fourth. He enjoyed biting into the elastic whites, and the feeling of the soft yolks as they crumbled between his teeth. He ate energetically and now and again put the bottle to his mouth and took long gulps. After the eggs he turned his attention to the meat; there were two kinds, a roast in large red slices, and cutlets fried with breadcrumbs. Without a glance at his wife he went on eating, and as he ate, despite his emptiness and sadness of spirit, he could feel the turgid vitality swelling in his veins. In view of his despair, this vitality seemed a useless and ironical form of wealth and he felt desolate. At last he lifted his eyes and offered her the bottle without a word. She still had her roll – she had only eaten half of it. She shook her head.

'Aren't you eating?'

'I'm not hungry.'

Lorenzo finished eating, then collected the eggshells and other remains, wrapped them in a piece of paper and threw them as far as he could. He put the half-empty bottle back in the basket. These small actions he performed with deliberate doggedness as though he were tidying up his own disturbed mind rather than the picnic. His wife, who by now had finished her roll, began touching up her face with hand-mirror and puff. 'And now,' she said, 'shall we go?'

'Where?'

'Home.'

'But it's still early.'

'You've seen the sea,' she said unkindly. 'You've had lunch. You don't want to sleep here, do you?'

Lorenzo watched her, not knowing whether to feel infuriated or humiliated by her pig-headed hostility. Then he said in a low voice:

'Listen. I've got to talk to you.'

'Talk to me? Haven't we talked enough already?'

He slid along the grass with an effort and sat beside her.

'I'd like to know what your grievance is.'

'I haven't one. Only I don't see why we have to go on living together, that's all.'

'You no longer feel any affection for me?'

'I never did feel any, and less than ever now.'

'But at one time,' Lorenzo insisted, 'whenever I gave you a present of some money, you used to throw your arms round my neck. You used to hug and kiss me and say you loved me.'

'I liked the presents, of course,' she agreed, obviously annoyed by this reminder of her childish avarice, 'but I didn't love you.'

'It was all a pretence, then?'

'No; not exactly.'

Lorenzo realized that she was being sincere. With women like her, gratitude for gifts closely resembled love: indeed, perhaps that was the only kind of love she was capable of.

'But I—' He looked down. 'Since things have been going badly, I feel for you for the first time in my life, you see ... I don't know how to explain ...'

'Then for heaven's sake don't try to,' she exclaimed mockingly.

'Can't I know what you have against me?'

'Against you?' She was growing angry. 'I have the fact that I don't want to be the wife of a jailbird.'

'I was only in prison for a few days and anyway, it was on political grounds.'

'So you say. But others say there was something else, and ... that you might be locked up again any time.'

Lorenzo noticed a trace of uncertainty in her voice, as if she were repeating something she had heard rather than thought out for herself.

'You're talking about something you know nothing about. I bet that all these years we've been together you never even knew who I was or what I was doing.'

'Don't be absurd.'

'Well then, tell me.'

'You were ...' She hesitated. 'Well, you were someone in control.'

'That's not enough. What was my position?'

'How do I know?' she said scornfully. 'All I know is that everyone referred to you as one of the authorities; but you were always changing; at one time you were one thing, at another time another. I had something else to think about besides your jobs.'

'Yes,' said Lorenzo gently. 'You had Rodolfo, Mario, Gianni, to think about.'

She pretended not to hear the names of her lovers – all of them as young and silly as herself. Lorenzo went on: 'At least you know what has happened since the time when I was an official? Do you?'

He saw her lift her shoulders impatiently. 'There you are. Now you're taking me for a fool. I'm much more intelligent than you think.'

'I don't doubt it in the least, but tell me what has happened.'

'The war came. Fascism came to an end. That's what happened. Now are you satisfied?'

'Fine. And why do you think I lost my career?'

'Because,' she said, unsure, 'now the government has been taken over by the enemies of Fascism?'

'And who are the enemies of Fascism?'

This time she lifted her eyes to heaven, tightened her lips, and said nothing. A kind of rage took hold of Lorenzo. Such ignorance, he thought, was far worse than any mere facile condemnation. It made even his mistakes, not to mention his few merits, fall into a void; there remained no more trace of his life than his footsteps, a little while ago, on the sand along the shore.

'What was Fascism?'

Again the same silence. Abruptly Lorenzo seized her by the arm and shook her. 'Answer, you fiend. Why don't you answer?'

'Leave me alone,' she said sullenly. 'I don't answer because I know you want to tie me up in knots and make me change what I think. I don't want to stay with you any longer, that's all.'

Lorenzo was no longer listening. The contact of that arm had once again aroused his desire. He looked at her skirt stretching tightly over her thighs as she sat; the softness and warmth and weight of her flesh seemed to communicate themselves to the material. At the sight of it, he felt his mind melting away and his breath catching. Nevertheless, he said slowly: 'Don't you realize that you're leaving me at the very time when another woman would stand by me, and for motives you don't even see clearly, for some mere whim or piece of gossip?'

'I realize that many society women don't invite me to their houses any more, or greet me in the street. I've already told Mother that I want to go back to her. That's all; I don't want to stay with you any more.' She stood up.

Lorenzo looked her up and down. She stood erect and scornful, her legs in an ungainly attitude with her overtight skirt and her high heels. He realized that it would be easy to fling her down and disarm her contempt. Those legs of hers, hampered by the tightness of her skirt, were like her character, which was hampered by her silliness. He felt a violent desire to upset her balance. With one thrust of his whole body, he threw himself at her legs and toppled her over on to the grass. She fell headlong and, startled into fury, exclaimed, 'Leave me alone. What's the matter with you?'

Lorenzo didn't answer, but threw himself on her, crushing her under his body. He said, 'I am what I am,' holding his lips against hers as if he wanted to insert each word into her mouth. 'But you're not really any better than me; you're a silly, empty, corrupt girl; as long as it suited you you stayed with me. Well, then, now it doesn't suit you any more, you'll stay with me just the same.'

He saw her look of terror and then she said again, almost in supplication, 'Leave me alone.'

'I won't leave you,' Lorenzo said between his teeth. He knew, because he had proved it in the past, that his wife, for all her fury, would surrender to violence in the end. At a given moment she always seemed to be overtaken by a kind of languor or complicity with the force she was being subjected to, and then she yielded and became passively loving, as though all the previous repulses had been no more than wilful coquetry. That was another aspect of her silliness – the incapacity to carry any feeling, whether hostile or friendly, to its conclusion. And so, when they began struggling, she defending herself and he trying to overcome her defences, Lorenzo suddenly 'saw in her little innocent eyes the tempted, passive and languid look he knew so well. At the same time, he felt her resistance weaken. Then she said in a low voice: 'Stop, I tell you. Someone might see us.' And that was already an invitation to go on.

But suddenly he felt disgusted with his victory. After all, nothing would be altered, even if she did yield. He would get up lovelessly from the body he had enjoyed; she, scornful and untidy, would pull down her crumpled skirt; and with the first words she spoke their disagreement would begin again, but with added feelings of disgust at the meaningless, mechanical coupling. And it wasn't that that he had intended when he brought her out for the day's trip.

With a brusque movement, he left her and drew himself away on the grass. She sat up looking injured and deluded. 'Don't you know that violence gets you nowhere,' she said crossly.

Lorenzo felt like bursting out laughing and answering that on the contrary violence was perhaps the only thing that worked with her. But at the same time he couldn't help recognizing that what she said was true; for what he really needed, violence didn't get anywhere.

Despite this, he said cruelly: 'That doesn't alter the fact that if I'd gone on a bit longer you'd have opened your legs.'

'How vulgar you are,' she said with sincere disgust. She rose to her feet, clambered through the bushes and set out determinedly for the clearing.

Lorenzo stayed sitting on the ground with his eyes on the grass. When he thought over his wife's answers he felt as though he himself no longer knew what he had done or stood for all those years. 'She's right,' he thought. 'It was all an empty dream, a delirium; and now I've woken up.' As he looked back over the past he realized that he couldn't remember anything except his constant cordiality – cordiality to his inferiors, his superiors, his friends, his enemies, to strangers and to his wife. He reflected that in the end his cordiality must have a bad effect, for after so much talking and smiling he now felt incapable of either; as if his tongue had dried up and the corners of his mouth had become sore. In these conditions even an idiot like his wife found her game easy.

He jumped at the distant throb of a car, and paused a moment listening; then, suddenly suspicious, he leapt to his feet and began to run across the pine wood, leaping over the bushes and the uneven ground towards the clearing. When he arrived there, panting, it was only to find it empty. The air was still full of dust raised by the car in which his wife had fled.

It seemed a worthy ending to the day, and he didn't even feel annoyed. He would probably be able to get a lift back on a military truck. At the worst, he would have to walk a couple of miles to the main road; plenty of cars passed along it, and he could easily get a lift.

But as he set out along the path through the pine wood he felt the call of the sea, a longing to go back again to the everlasting motion, the everlasting glamour, before returning to the city. And then he wanted to do something he would never have dared to do in front of his wife, take off his shoes, roll up his trousers, and walk along the sea's edge in the shallow water of the ebb and flow of the waves.

He was aware, too, that he wanted to walk along by the edge of the sea to prove to himself that he didn't care about his wife's flight. But he knew that this wasn't true, and when he sat in the sand to take off his shoes he noticed that his hands were trembling.

He removed his shoes and socks, folded his trousers up to below the knee, and picked his way through the barbed wire to the water's edge. He set out walking in the ebbing and flowing water, with his shoes in hand, his head bowed and eyes lowered.

His attitude was that of thought but he wasn't really thinking. He liked seeing the surf pass over his feet, rise along his legs, form a whirl of water round his ankles, then flow back peevishly, carrying away the sand beneath his feet, tickling like something alive. He liked, too, to keep his gaze down and see only water to right and left, turbid, swirling, sprinkled with white rings of foam. The sea near the shore was full of a black sedge which each wave threw on to the sand and then carried away again in the backwash. There were minute sticks like ebony, oval and smooth scales, tiny wood splinters, myriads of little black objects that the movement of the turbid sandladen water kept in continuous turmoil. The transparent shells of tiny dead crabs, green seaweed and yellow roots put some splash of colour into this carbonized chaff. When the surf ebbed the sedge clung gluttonously to his feet, making an arabesque of black on their shining whiteness. Here and there some flotsam of larger bulk floated in between one wave and the next, in the ground-glass turmoil of the foamy water. He saw something not far away of uncertain colour and shape which made him think of an animal; but as he drew near, overcoming the water's pressure, he discovered that it was the wooden hoof of a woman's orthopaedic shoe. Little shells of pallid amethyst had spread thickly over the toe, making a kind of dense tuft, while the heel was still covered with red cloth. As he was looking at the remains a high foamless billow passed by, rapidly bathing him as far as the groin. He threw the shoe away and retreated nearer to the shore.

He didn't know how long he walked along the beach on the soft and fleeting sand with his feet in the riotous water. But as a result of looking down at the water which broke ceaselessly on his legs and passed beyond towards the unseen shore, he felt a kind of dizziness. He lifted his eyes over the sea and for a moment he imagined he saw it tall and upright like a liquid wall. The sky on the horizon was no more than a streak of vapour. There some sea bird was skimming the skin of the water in distant and dangerous flight which revived the thought of the drunken violence of the wind. Dazed, he nearly fell under the weight of a heavier billow. And the clamour of the waves seemed suddenly to become shriller and fiercer, as though redoubled by the hope of his collapse.

Almost fearfully he turned towards the beach, thinking to get out of the water and sit down for a moment on the dry sand. He had walked a long way. He had left the clearing and the ruins far behind. Here the sand, mounted in dunes and defences, was criss-crossed by barbed wire and stumps which looked like people holding hands with arms outstretched so as to block the way. His attention was attracted by a thick bank of black and shining seaweed underneath which the waves had hollowed out the sand. He jumped as far as this seaweed and, touching the ground with one hand, he leapt on it.

The torrent of seaweed and sand which soared into the air with a thundering echo darkened his eyes to the sky for a moment as he fell back in the whirlpool of the explosion. He thought he was falling headlong forever in a perpetual din of cataract. But silence and immobility followed. He lay on his back in the water; the noise and movement of the sea were singularly sweet and distant under a sky again visible. The water pulled him under by the hair; head down and feet up, his body moved with the passage of a wave, and he saw a large red stain hastening towards the shore with the rings of foam and the black debris. Then another wave came and pulled him under and he closed his eyes.

Translated by Bernard Wall

Cesare Pavese

Suicides

*Cesare Pavese was born in Piedmont, Italy, in 1908 and educated
in Turin. Between 1936 and 1949, he wrote nine novels (and many
short stories), including* The Devil in the Hills, Among Women
Only, The Beautiful Summer, *and 'a historical cycle of my own
times' based upon his political activity against the Fascists. He
died, a suicide, in 1950.*

There are days when everything in the city I live in – the people in the
streets, the traffic, trees – awakens in the morning with a strange
aspect, the same as always yet unrecognizable, like the times when you
look into the mirror and ask: 'who's that?' These for me are the
loveliest days of the year.

On such mornings, whenever I can, I leave the office a little earlier
and go into the streets, mingling with the crowd, and I don't mind
staring at all who pass in the very way, I suspect, that some of them
look at me, for in truth at these moments I have a feeling of assurance
that makes me another man.

I am convinced that I shall obtain from life nothing more precious
perhaps than the revelation of how I may stimulate these moments at
will. One way of making them longer which I have sometimes found
successful is to sit in a new café, glassed-in and bright, and absorb the
noise of all the hurry-scurry and the street, the flare of colours and of
voices, and the peaceful interior moderating all the tumult.

In only a few years I have suffered keen stabs of disappointment
and regret; still, I may say that my most heartfelt prayer is for this
peace, this tranquillity alone. I am not cut out for storms and struggle:
even though there are mornings when I go forth to walk the streets
vibrant with life and my stride may be taken for a challenge, I repeat, I
ask of life no more than that she let herself be observed.

And yet even this modest pleasure sometimes leaves me with a
bitterness which is precisely that of a vice. It wasn't only yesterday

that I realized that in order to live one had to exercise cunning with oneself, and only then with others. I envy the people – they are women mostly – who are able to commit a misdeed or an injustice, or merely to indulge a whim, having contrived beforehand a chain of circumstances so as to give their conduct, in their own eyes, the appearance of being altogether proper. I do not have serious vices – provided this withdrawal from the struggle from lack of confidence, in search of lonely serenity, is not the most serious vice of all – but I do not even know how to handle myself wisely and to hold myself in check when enjoying the little that comes my way.

It sometimes happens, in fact, that I stop in my tracks, glancing about, and ask myself whether I have any right to enjoy my assurance. This occurs especially when my moments out have been rather frequent. Not that I take time off from my work: I provide decently for myself, and support in boarding school an orphaned niece whom the old lady who calls herself my mother doesn't want around the house. But the thing I ask myself is whether – on these ecstatic strolls of mine – I am not ludicrous, ludicrous and disgusting; for I think sometimes that I am not really due my ecstasy.

Or else, as happened the other morning, I need only to be present at some singular scene in a café, which intrigues me from the outset by the normalness of its participants, in order to fall a prey to a guilt-ridden sense of loneliness and to so many bleak memories that the farther they recede the more they reveal to me, in their immutable natures, twisted and terrible meanings.

It was five minutes of play between the young cashier and a customer in a light-coloured topcoat, accompanied by a friend. The young man was shouting that the cashier owed him change from a hundred-lira note and was slamming his fist on the desk top as she pretended to check through her handbag and pockets.

'Young lady, that's certainly no way to treat customers,' he said, winking at his friend, who stood by looking ill at ease. The cashier laughed. The young man then concocted some story about a ride they would take in the elevator of a public bath. Between controlled bursts of laughter they finally decided that they would deposit the money in a bank – once they had it.

'Goodbye, young lady,' he shouted back as he left at last. 'Think of me tonight.'

The cashier, exhilarated and laughing, turned to the waiter: 'What a character!'

I had noticed her on other mornings, and sometimes smiled without looking at her, in moments of abstraction. But my peace is too flimsy, a tissue of nothing. The usual stab of remorse returns.

'We are all sordid, but there's a good-natured sordidness, with a smile, that provokes a smile from others, and there's another sordidness that is lonely and holds people off. The sillier, after all, is not the former.'

It is on such mornings that I am surprised, each time anew, by the thought that what is truly sinful in my life is only silliness. Others may achieve out-and-out evil by design, sure of themselves, taking an interest in their victims and in the sport – and I suspect that a life so spent may afford many satisfactions – but as for myself, I have never done anything but suffer from great bumbling uncertainty, and writhe, when brought into contact with others, in my own stupid cruelty. Because – and there's no solution – it's enough that I give in to that remorse of my loneliness for an instant or so and I think again of Carlotta.

She has been dead for more than a year, and now I know all the routes that my memory of her may take to surprise me. I can, so wishing, even recognize the initial state of mind that announces her appearance, abruptly diverting my thoughts. But I do not always wish it; and even now my remorse provides me with dark corners, new points, that I study with the trepidation of a year ago. I was so tortuously true with her that each of those far-off days stands in my memory not as a fixed thing, but as an elusive face possessing for me the same reality of today.

Not that Carlotta was a mystery. She was, rather, one of those transparently simple souls – pitiful women – who become irritating if they cease for only an instant being themselves and attempt subterfuge or flirtation. But so long as they are simple no one notices them. I have never understood how she could bear to earn her living as a cashier. She had the makings of an ideal sister.

What I have not fathomed, even yet, are my feelings and my behaviour then. What, for instance, should I say of the evening in Carlotta's two-room lodgings when she had put on a velvet dress – an old dress – to receive me, and I told her that I should have preferred her in a bathing suit? It was one of my first visits and I had not even kissed her.

Well, making a shy grimace, Carlotta withdrew into the anteroom and – of all things – actually reappeared in a bathing suit! That evening I took her into my arms and forced her down on to the davenport; but then – the moment it was over – I told her I liked being alone and left, and I did not return for three days; and when I did I addressed her formally.

Thereupon another ridiculous courtship began, consisting of timid confidences on her part and few words on my own. Suddenly I addressed her familiarly, but she resisted. Then I asked her if she had reconciled with her husband. Carlotta began to whimper. 'He never treated me the way you do,' she said.

It was easy to press her head to my chest and caress her and to tell her I loved her; after all, being so alone, couldn't I love a grass widow? And Carlotta let herself go; softly, she confessed that she had loved me from the very beginning, that I struck her as being an extraordinary man, but already, in the short time we had known each other, I had caused her to suffer miserably, and she — she didn't know why — all men treated her the same.

'Blowing hot and cold,' I smiled into her hair: 'that's how you keep love alive.'

Carlotta was sallow, with enormous eyes a little worn with fatigue, and her body was pale too. In the shadows of her bedroom that night, I asked myself if it was because I didn't like her body that I had hurried off the time before.

But even this time I didn't have pity on her: in the middle of the night I dressed and, making no excuses, announced that I had to be going, and went. Carlotta wanted to come along.

'No, I like being alone.'

And, giving her a kiss, I left.

When I met Carlotta I was just emerging from a tempest that had nearly cost me my life; and now, returning to the empty streets, retreating from a woman who loved me, I was possessed by a wry mirth. For quite some time I had had to spend days and nights browbeaten and in a fury on account of a woman's whims.

I am convinced now that no passion is so strong as to alter the nature of one who endures it. One may die of it, but that doesn't change a thing. When the frenzy has passed, one returns to being the decent man or the rogue, the family man or the boy, whatever one was, and proceeds with one's life. Or more precisely: from the ordeal our true nature comes out, and it horrifies us; normality disgusts us; and we would wish even to be dead, the insult is so unspeakable, but we have no one to blame but ourselves. I owe it to that woman if I am reduced to this singular life I lead, from day to day, aimlessly, incapable of securing ties with the world, estranged from my fellows —

estranged even from my mother whom I only just tolerate, and from my niece whom I don't love – I owe it all to her; but might I not have fared better in the end with another woman? With a woman, I mean, capable of humbling me as my nature required?

Nonetheless, at the time, the thought that I had been wronged, that my mistress could be called treacherous, did afford me a measure of comfort. There is a point in suffering when it is inevitable – it is a natural anaesthetic – that one should believe oneself to be suffering unjustly: this brings into force again, according to our most coveted desires, fascination for life; it restores a sense of our worth in the face of things; it is flattering. I had found, and I should have liked, injustice, ingratitude, to be even more unspeakable. I recall – during those interminable days and those evenings of anguish – being aware of a pervasive and secret feeling, like an atmosphere or an irradiance: wonderment that it all happened – that the woman was indeed the woman, that the periods of delirium and stabbing pains were quite what they were, that the sighs, the words, the deeds, that I myself – that it all happened just as it did.

And now here I was, having suffered injustice, repaying, as inevitably happens, not the guilty one, but another.

I would leave Carlotta's little apartment at night satisfied and absent of mind, delighted to be walking alone, retreating from all solicitude, freely enjoying the long avenue, in vague pursuit of the sensations and thoughts of early youth. The simplicity of the night – darkness and street lamps – has always welcomed me with tenderness, and made for the wildest and most precious fantasies, heightening them with its contrasts and magnifying them. There, even the blind rancour I showed towards Carlotta for her eager humility had full rein, freed of a kind of awkwardness which pitying her made me feel when we were together.

But I was not young any longer. And the better to disengage myself from Carlotta, I reconsidered and anatomized her body and her caresses. Crudely, I considered that separated from her husband as she was, still young and without children, she was simply jumping at the chance for whatever outlet she could find in me. But – poor Carlotta – she was too simple a mistress, and it may have been precisely for this that her husband betrayed her.

I remember returning arm in arm with her from the cinema one evening, wandering through the semi-lit streets, when she said to me: 'I'm happy. It's nice going to the movies with you.'

'Did you ever go with your husband?'

Carlotta smiled at me. 'Are you jealous?'

I shrugged. 'In any case, it doesn't change anything.'

'I'm tired,' Carlotta would say, pressing against my arm; 'this good-for-nothing chain that holds us is ruining both his life and mine, and making me respect a name that has brought me nothing but suffering. Divorce ought to be possible, at least when there aren't children.'

I was lulled that evening by my long, warm contact with her, and by desire. 'You have scruples, in other words?'

'Oh, darling,' Carlotta said, 'why aren't you good all the time, like you are this evening? Think, if only I could have a divorce.'

I didn't say anything. Once before when she had mentioned divorce I had burst out: 'Now just look here, can anyone be better off than you? You do whatever you please – and I'll wager he still slips you a little, if it's true it was he who betrayed you.'

'I have never accepted a thing,' Carlotta had replied. 'I've worked from that day on' – and she had looked at me. 'Now that I have you I'd feel as if I were betraying you.'

The evening we went to the movies I shut her up with a kiss. Then I took her to the station café where I bought her a couple of drinks.

We sat like a pair of lovers in the steamy light of the glass panes. I downed quite a few jiggers myself. Presently, in a loud voice, I said to her: 'Carlotta, shall we make a baby tonight?'

Some of the people looked at us because Carlotta, radiant and flushed, closed my mouth with her hand.

I talked and talked. Carlotta talked about the film, making silly remarks – passionately – finding comparisons between us and the characters in it. And I – aware that only by drinking could I love her – I drank.

Outside, the cold was invigorating and we hurried home. I spent the night with her, and waking in the morning I felt her by my side, dishevelled and full of sleep, fumbling to hug me. I did not repulse her; but when I got up my head was aching and Carlotta's repressed joy as she got my coffee, humming to herself, grated on my nerves. Then we had to leave together, but remembering the concierge, Carlotta sent me out first, not without a wifely hug and a kiss behind the door.

My keenest memory of waking that morning is of the boughs of the trees bordering the walk, stark and dripping in the fog, visible through the curtains in the room. The warmth and solicitude inside, and the raw morning air awaiting me, charged my blood; however, I should have liked to be alone, thinking and smoking by myself, imagining an altogether different waking and another mate.

The tenderness that Carlotta extracted from me at such moments was something I reproached myself for the instant I was alone. I underwent moments of fury, scouring my soul to be rid of the slightest memory of her; I made up my mind to be hard and then was even too hard. It must have been apparent that we loved each other out of indolence, out of some vice – for all the reasons except the very one she sought to delude herself about. The memory of her grave, blissful look after the embrace irritated me, noticing it on her face angered me; whereas the only woman on whom I had wanted to see it had never given me that satisfaction.

'If you accept me as I am, fine,' I told her once; 'but get it out of your head that you can ever mean anything to me.'

'Don't you love me?' Carlotta stammered.

'The little bit of love I was capable of I burned out in my youth.'

But there were also times when I lost my temper, having admitted, out of shame or desire, that I did love her a little.

Carlotta would force a smile. 'We're good friends at least, aren't we?'

'Listen,' I told her seriously, 'all this nonsense repels me; we're a man and a woman who are bored; we get on in bed—'

'Oh, yes, that we do!' she said; she clutched my arm, hiding her face. 'I like you, I do like you—'

'—period.'

It was enough to have just one of these exchanges, in which I struck myself as spineless, for me to avoid her for weeks on end; and if she rang me up at the office from her café I told her I was busy. The first time Carlotta tried being angry, I let her spend the evening in torment, while I sat frigid on the davenport – the lampshade cast a white light on her knees – and in the half-light I could sense the contained spasms of her glances. It was I, in the unbearable tension, who finally said: 'Thank me, Signora: you're likely to remember this session more than many others.'

Carlotta didn't stir.

'Why don't you kill me, Signora? If you think you can play the woman with me, you're wasting your time. The flighty one I'll play myself.'

She was breathing heavily.

'Not even your bathing suit,' I said to her, 'will help you this evening ...'

Suddenly Carlotta bounded at me. I saw her black-haired head go through the white light like some hurled object. I thrust out my hands.

But Carlotta collapsed at my knees in tears. I laid a hand on her head two or three times. Then I rose.

'I ought to be crying too, Carlotta. But I know that tears are no use. All this you're going through I've been through myself. I've been on the point of killing myself, and then my nerve failed me. This is the rub: a person so weak as to think of suicide is also too weak to commit it ... Come now, Carlotta, be good.'

'Don't treat me like that ...' she stammered.

'I'm not treating you like anything. But you know I like being alone. If you let me be alone, I'll come back; if not, we'll never see each other again. Look, would you like me to love you?'

Beneath my hand, Carlotta looked up with her swollen face.

'Well, then, you must stop loving me. There's no other way. The hare's the hunter.'

Scenes of this sort shook Carlotta too deeply for her to consider giving me up. But didn't they also denote a fundamental similarity in temperament? At bottom, Carlotta was a simple soul – too simple – and incapable of clearly recognizing it; but certainly she sensed it. She tried – poor creature – to hold me by being light-hearted, and would sometimes say things like 'Such is life!' and 'Poor little me!'

I believe that if at that time she had firmly repulsed me I should have suffered a little. But it wasn't in her power. If I remained away for two evenings running, I found her with sunken eyes. And whenever, on occasion, I took pity on her or was kind, and stopped by her café and asked her to come out with me, she got up flushed and flustered, even more beautiful.

My rancour was not directed at her; rather, at all the restrictions and the enslavement our liaison seemed likely to produce. Since I didn't love her, her smallest claim on me struck me as an outrage. There were days when addressing her in the *tu*-form disgusted and degraded me. Who was this woman clamped on to my arm?

In return, I seemed to experience a rebirth, certain half days, certain hours when, after hurrying through my work, I was able to go out into the cool sun and walk the sunlit streets, unencumbered by her, by anything, feeling satisfied of body, my old sorrow soothed: eager to see, to smell, to feel as I had when I was young. That Carlotta might suffer on my account alleviated my past griefs and made them paltry, and estranged them from me a little, as from a laughable world; and far removed from her, I found myself whole again, more adept. She was the sponge I used to cleanse myself. I thought this often of her.

*   *   *

Some evenings when I talked and talked, engrossed in the game, I was a youngster again and I put my rancour behind me.

'Carlotta,' I would say, 'what is it like to be a lover? It's so long since I was one. All told, it must be a fine thing, I imagine. When all goes well, you enjoy it; when it doesn't, you hope. You live from day to day, they say. What is it like, Carlotta?'

Carlotta would shake her head, smiling.

'Another thing, you have so many wonderful thoughts, Carlotta. Whoever takes love lightly will never be happy like the lover. Unless,' I smiled, 'he sleeps with another woman and then makes game of the lover.'

Carlotta knitted her brows.

'Love is a fine thing,' I concluded. 'And no one escapes it.'

Carlotta served as my public. I was talking to myself, those evenings. It's the pleasantest of talks.

'There is love and there is betrayal. In order really to enjoy love there's also got to be betrayal. This is the thing young boys don't realize. You women learn it earlier. Did you betray your husband?'

Carlotta essayed a cunning smile, going red.

'We boys were stupider. Scrupulously, we fell in love with an actress or schoolmate and offered her our finest thoughts. Except that we never got around to telling them. To my knowledge there wasn't a girl our age who didn't realize that love is a matter of craft. It doesn't seem possible, but boys go to brothels and conclude that the women outside are different. What were you up to at sixteen, Carlotta?'

But Carlotta's thoughts were elsewhere. With her eyes, before answering, she told me that I was hers, and I hated the hardness of the solicitude her glance gave off.

'What were you doing at sixteen?' I asked her again, staring down at the floor.

'Nothing,' she replied gravely. I knew what she was thinking.

Then she asked me to forgive her – she was acting the poor forlorn creature and she knew she hadn't the right – but her glance was enough. 'Do you know you're stupid? For all I care, your husband could take you back!' And off I went with a feeling of relief.

Next day in the office I received a timid telephone call, to which I replied dryly. That evening I saw her again.

Carlotta was amused whenever I talked about my niece who was away at boarding school, and she shook her head with disbelief when I told her that I would rather have shut my mother up in school and lived with the child. She pictured us as two quite different beings, playing at being uncle and niece, but actually having a whole world of secrets and petty grievances to delight and occupy us. She asked me, put out, if the girl were not my daughter.

'Of course. Born when I was sixteen. She decided to be blonde just to spite me. How can one be born blonde? Blondes for me are creatures like monkeys or lions. It must be like always being in the sun, I should imagine.'

Carlotta said: 'I was blonde when I was little.'

'I was bald myself.'

My interest in Carlotta's past, during that final period, was a bored curiosity which from time to time allowed me to forget all she had previously told me. I scanned her as one scans the page of local news in the paper. I delighted in puzzling her with whimsical sallies, I put cruel questions to her and then supplied the answers. I was actually listening to no one but myself.

But Carlotta had seen through me. 'Tell me about yourself,' she would say some evenings, pressing my arm. She knew that only by getting me to talk about myself could she make a friend of me.

'Carlotta, did I ever tell you that a man once killed himself because of me?' I asked her one evening.

She looked at me radiant and half amazed.

'It's nothing to laugh at,' I went on. 'We killed ourselves together – but he actually died. Youthful shenanigans.' Wasn't it curious, I thought suddenly, I had never told a soul, and of all people Carlotta would be the first. 'He was a friend of mine, a fine-looking blond boy. And he really did look a lion. You girls, you don't make friendships like that. At that age you're already too jealous. We were schoolmates, but we always met afterwards, in the evening. We talked in the dirty ways boys will, but we were in love with a woman. She must still be living. She was our first love, Carlotta. We spent our evenings talking about love and death. No one in love has ever been more certain of being understood by his best friend than we were of each other. Jean – his name was Jean – had a bold sadness that used to put me to shame. All by himself he created the melancholy of those evenings we spent walking together through the fog. We didn't believe one could suffer so much—'

'You were in love, too?'

'I suffered for being less melancholy than Jean. Finally I discovered that we might kill ourselves, and I told him. Jean took to the idea slowly, he who was normally so imaginative. We had a revolver between us. We went out to the hills to test it, in case it should explode.

It was Jean who fired. He had always been foolhardy, and I think that if he had stopped loving the woman I should have stopped too. After the test – we were on a barren footpath, halfway up; it was winter – I was still thinking about the force of the shot when Jean put the barrel into his mouth and said: "Some guys do it this way . . ." And the gun went off and killed him.'

Carlotta stared at me horrified.

'I didn't know what to do and ran away.'

Later that evening Carlotta said to me: 'And you really loved that woman?'

'What woman? I loved Jean; I told you.'

'And did you want to kill yourself too?'

'Naturally. It would have been foolish, though. But not doing it was rank cowardice. I'm sorry I didn't.'

Carlotta often returned to the story, and spoke to me of Jean as though she had known him. She had me describe him and asked me what I myself was like then. She wanted to know if I had kept the revolver.

'Don't go killing yourself now. Have you never thought of killing yourself?' So saying, she rested her eyes on me.

'Every time you fall in love you think of it.'

Carlotta didn't even smile. 'Do you think of it still?'

'I think of Jean sometimes.'

At noon, the thought of Carlotta distressed me terribly when, after I had left the office, I passed her café window, hurrying by so as not to have to look in and kid with her a little. I did not go home at noon. I especially liked seating myself alone in an eating house and whiling away that part of an hour I had, with my eyes barely open, smoking. Carlotta, in her chair, would be ringing up change automatically, tilting and nodding her head, smiling and frowning, at times with a customer joking with her.

She was there, in her blue dress, from seven in the morning till four in the afternoon. They paid her four hundred and eighty lire a month. Carlotta liked rushing through the day in a single sitting, and would take lunch, with a big cup of milk, without rising from her place. It would have been an easy job, she told me, except for the way the door banged with all the coming and going. There were times when she felt it like punches on the raw surface of her brain.

Ever since, on entering cafés, I have closed the doors carefully. With me, Carlotta tried to describe the little scenes with the customers, but she could never bring off my way of talking, just as she was never able to get a rise out of me with her sly allusions to the proposals some old goat was making to her.

'Go right ahead,' I told her; 'just don't let me see him. Receive him on odd days. And take care you don't pick up any diseases.'

Carlotta made a wry mouth.

For some days a thought had been gnawing at her. 'Are we in love again, Carlotta?' I said to her one evening.

Carlotta looked at me like a whipped dog. And I lost patience with her again. Those shining glances of hers, that evening, in the half-light of the little room, her squeezing my hand – it all infuriated me. With Carlotta I was forever afraid of being tied down. I hated the very thought of it.

I grew sullen again; surly. But Carlotta had stopped taking my outbursts with her former injured paroxysms. She simply looked at me, without moving, and sometimes when, to comfort her, I reached out to caress her, she would draw back in an affectionate motion.

Which was something I liked even less. Being compelled to court her in order to have her was repugnant to me. But it would not begin without a prelude. Carlotta would start: 'I have a headache ... oh, that door! Let's be good this evening. Talk to me.'

The moment I realized she was really serious, regarding herself as a poor unfortunate, dredging up regrets, my outbursts would end: I simply betrayed her. I relived one of those colourless evenings of the past when, returning from a brothel, I had sat in any wretched, cheap café to rest, neither happy nor sad, muzzy. It seemed only just: one either accepted love with all its hazards or nothing remained but prostitution.

I believed Carlotta's jealousy to be an act, and it amused me. She suffered. But she was too simple a soul to turn it to her gain. Rather, as happens to those who really suffer, it made her ugly. I was sorry, but I would have to have done with her, I felt.

Carlotta saw the blow coming. One evening when we were in bed together, while I was instinctively avoiding conversation, she suddenly thrust me away and curled up towards the wall.

'What's eating you?' I demanded, annoyed.

'If I were to disappear tomorrow,' she said, suddenly turning back, 'would it make any difference to you?'

'I don't know,' I stammered.

'And if I betrayed you?'

'Life itself is a betrayal.'

'And if I returned to my husband?'

She was serious. I shrugged.

'I'm only a poor woman,' Carlotta continued. 'And I'm not able to betray you ... I've seen my husband.'

'What?'

'He came to the café.'

'But didn't he go to America?'

'I don't know,' Carlotta said. 'I saw him at the café.'

She may not have meant to tell me, but it came out that her husband had also come with a woman in a fur coat.

'In that case, you weren't able to talk?'

Carlotta hesitated. 'He came back the next day. He talked to me then, and afterwards saw me home.'

I must confess that I felt uncomfortable. I said softly: 'Here?'

Carlotta clung to me with all her body. 'But I love you,' she whispered. 'You mustn't think—'

'Here?'

'It was nothing, darling. He simply talked about his business. Only, seeing him again I realized how much I love you. He can beg and I won't go back to him.'

'Then he begged you?'

'No. He just said that if he were to marry again he would still marry me.'

'Have you seen him since?'

'He came to the café again, with that woman ...'

That was the last time I spent the night with Carlotta. Without taking leave of her body, without regrets, I stopped ringing her up and stopped visiting her at her flat. I let her telephone me and then wait to meet me in cafés – nor was it every evening: only now and then. Carlotta would come each time and devour me with her eyes, and when we were about to leave her voice would quaver.

'I haven't seen him again,' she whispered one evening.

'You're making a mistake,' I answered; 'you ought to try to get him back.'

It annoyed me that Carlotta missed her husband – as she unquestionably did – and that with such talk she hoped to entice me. That unconsummated love of hers was worth neither her regrets nor my own risks.

One evening I told her over the telephone that I'd call on her. She let me in with a look of disbelief and anxiety. I glanced round the entry hall, a little apprehensive. Carlotta was wearing velvet. And I recall that she had a cold and kept squeezing her handkerchief and pressing it to her red nose.

At once, I saw that she understood. She was quiet and meek, and she answered me with pitiful looks. She let me do all the talking, while she cast furtive glances over the top of her handkerchief. Then she rose and came to me, leaning her body against my face, and I had to place an arm round her.

Softly, in the same tone, she said: 'Won't you come to bed?'

We went to bed, and through all of it I disliked her damp face, inflamed by her cold. At midnight I jumped out of bed and began dressing. Carlotta turned on the light, looking at me for an instant. Then she turned it off and said: 'Yes, go if you wish.' Embarrassed, I stumbled out.

In the days that followed I feared a telephone call, but nothing disturbed me, and I was able to work in peace for weeks on end. And then, one evening, desire for Carlotta took hold of me again, but shame helped me to overcome it. Even so, I knew that if I had rung at that door I would have brought happiness. This certainty I have always had.

I didn't yield; but, the day after, I went by her café. There was a blonde at the cash register. They must have changed hours. But she wasn't there in the evening, either. I thought that perhaps she was ill or that her husband had taken her back. This was not an appealing idea.

But my legs shook when the concierge, with extreme ill grace, fixing me with a hard beady gaze, told me that they had found her in bed a month before, dead, with the gas jets on.

Translated by Ben Johnson

Stanislaw Zieliński

Uncle From Heaven

Stanislaw Zieliński (1917—) gained prominence in post-war Poland with two volumes of short stories, The Old Sabre *(1957) and* The Ship of the Cross-Eyed *(1958), from which 'Uncle from Heaven' is taken. In both volumes, he reveals himself as a first-rate satirist of absurd and ludicrous political conditions. Earlier, he had written several novels (*The Last Fires, *1951;* Poland Still, *1953) and stories about Polish soldiers during the war.*

Since everyone was busy with something, it was decided that I should drop by my aunt's with the birthday cake. Everything was settled before I could even say 'I don't mind a bit'.

'Her birthday's the day after tomorrow. You'll have to hurry.'

'I'll take a plane. I love flying.'

The next day I went off to the airport. I arrived just in time; there was one seat at the booking office. I had never seen Aunt Izabella. I was also curious about the place where my aunt had been living for years. Soon after the take-off, when the plane had gained height and banked on to the right course I glued my nose to the window to see as much as possible on the flight. Absorbed by the fields, woods, rivers, villages, roads, etc, slipping by under the wing I soon lost all sense of time. I had not expected that the earth would look so pretty from the air. I longed for the flight to last until it was dark.

Suddenly I heard the name of the town which was my destination. The attractive stewardess repeated in a slightly irritated voice:

'Who's there for N?'

I smiled at this adorable creature. The stewardess also smiled as she replied.

'You?'

'Yes. I'm flying to my aunt for her birthday. But,' I paused significantly, 'it's not till tomorrow. We've lots of time.'

The stewardess made an encouraging movement of her hand. I took her gesture as an invitation. The passengers were dozing with their noses in their books. No one was paying any attention to us. Adjusting my tie I followed the stewardess to a compartment in the tail. Inside, as soon as the door was shut I asked her openly:

'When did you notice that I loved you? At the airport or after we'd taken off?'

I tried to put my arms round her but the angel slipped out of my ardent embrace with singular ease.

'Now, now.'

Then she handed me a parachute and helped me fasten the straps.

'Hurry up, we're almost over N.'

I surrendered to her attentions meekly. A magnificent, fantastic adventure, such as I had not dreamed of before the flight, loomed ahead of me.

'You're ready to give up your uniform, your plane, your bonus, your pension? I'm touched and indescribably happy. Let's hope auntie won't object and lets our love blossom under her roof. Anyway, aunts! In cases like this, who cares about aunts. We'll manage without Aunt Iza. Are we jumping together or separately? I don't see another parachute.'

The stewardess pulled out a bottle of cognac and poured a stiff drink.

'One for the road.'

I gulped it down. The girl put a hand on my shoulder.

'Now listen carefully, dear. Try to land in the middle of that white circle. Next to it, in that house with the red roof lives our agent, who represents the airlines in N. Hand in the parachute, get a receipt, and then you can go to your aunt's. Aim at the middle of the circle. The agent's an old man, so don't make him run all over the field after you. Don't forget your receipt.'

I listened half-dazed.

'Stand over by the wall. The pilot is throttling down and reducing height. I must open the hatch. We're over N.'

'And you?'

'Don't be silly.'

'It's not fair!' I shouted tearfully and desperately.

'I get all my passengers off in the same way. There's no airport in N. Watch out for the cake!'

The stewardess grabbed me by the collar and threw me out of the plane. Seized by the current of air I fell with a great roaring in my ears. Then the parachute opened, there was a violent jerk and I hung in absolute silence. The plane had disappeared, vanished into thin air.

Slowly I lost height. I felt that the white dome of the parachute was fastened to the clouds and that I would never reach the ground. The rocking, at first hardly noticeable, grew as I fell. I could now make out the ground. I saw the white circle painted on the grass and the house with the red roof. In front of it stood the airline's representative in N. He shouted to me through a megaphone:

'Use the ropes and balance your body. Close your knees and bend your legs. You're too stiff, sir! Would you mind being a bit more elastic?'

Although I tried to balance my body and pulled on the ropes, I overshot the white circle. A light breeze steered me towards some haystacks. I landed on the hay without any serious shocks or abrasions. The grey-haired agent helped untangle me from the ropes and unfastened the straps.

'Good morning,' he said courteously. 'Next time it will go better.'

'This whole business stinks,' I said shaking hands.

'That's the hay.'

'Throwing passengers out with their birthday cakes. Well, I mean to say.'

'N does lie at the crossing of some important lines of communication, it's true, but they all cross very high up over N.'

The agent looked up and smiled at the clouds. His air of benevolence disarmed me and mellowed my mood. How can you be angry with a man who smiles at the calm sky? I folded the parachute and walked over to the little house with its tiled roof. The grey-haired agent pulled up an armchair and, when I was comfortably settled, went to the cupboard.

'Happy landings,' he said pouring cognac into a silver noggin.

I protested spiritedly:

I've had one drink today by myself and look where it got me. I like a drink but only in company.'

'The cognac is company property. It's reserved for arrivals and departures at N. You understand.' The agent spread his hands.

'Departures from N?' I repeated sneeringly. 'Interesting! How do departures from N get to the plane?'

'I don't know. So help me, I've never had a single booking here, though I hang up a new timetable every season in our show-case in the market. There's never been any question of getting aboard.'

'I'm not interested in communications now. I'd like to stand you a cognac. Can I do that?'

'Yes, here's the price list.'

'Well then, two doubles,' I said relieved.

'One and a half,' the agent corrected me. 'The company pays for a normal one for you. A normal is half a double. So you pay for one and a half, and the firm for half.'

'It can go to hell.'

'I'd lose my job, my home and my perks,' he replied dryly and knocked on the unpainted wood.

'I'm sorry ... What are you doing? What now?' I asked because the agent seemed to have forgotten his cognac. The filled glasses stood on the table; the old man was rummaging through some papers in the drawer.

'I have to give you a receipt. I'm looking for the form, the stamp and a new nib.'

Then he carefully examined the form, smoothing the frayed edges with his thumb. Finally with an air of throwing caution to the winds he appended a clumsy signature and stamped it.

'And the cognac?' I asked putting away the receipt.

'I never touch a drop before lunch. I'll tell you what. I'll pour my cognac back in the bottle and drink it later.'

'You can pour mine back, too.'

'Thank you very much, doctor.'

'I'm not a doctor.'

'Oh well, you will be. You've got the right look in your eyes.'

I checked my aunt's address, asked the shortest way and went out. Irritated by the turn affairs had taken, furious at my magnificent adventure which had made such a signal fool of me, I walked off flourishing the box with the birthday cake and swearing briskly until I met some children. They seemed to have appeared from nowhere. I bit my tongue and tried to smile blandly.

'Uncle from heaven,' said a boy.

'I'm not an uncle. I'm the nephew of Miss Izabel. And you,' I addressed a tot staring at the boy as if at a toy, 'wipe your right eye with a ring. Your brow's red. It'll come out in a stye.'

I walked on but had hardly taken a few steps when the boy spoke again.

'He's not an uncle, he's just a clot. You're too little to have a ring. A real clot he is!'

'You horrible brat,' I yelled, 'if I wasn't in a birthday mood, I'd give you a good hiding.'

'I'd rather have a piece of cake,' the boy muttered.

I shook my finger at him, and advised the girl to run home and ask her mother for a boric acid or camomile compress.

'All right, sir. See, he is a doctor, after all,' she whispered to the boy.

'You should follow her example. And if you're good, there'll be cake too.'

'Cake' reminded me of the birthday. I left off my moralizing and walked on looking for my aunt's house. Thanks to the directions given by the grey-haired agent I found it without difficulty. The garden was full of delicate tea roses. I picked the three best. 'I asked some gardeners and in the flower shop about flowers. They told me there weren't any more beautiful flowers in the neighbourhood than yours, auntie.' Having worked out this greeting, I boldly walked up to the door. Vines were trailing over the walls. The door was ajar. I cleared my throat so that it would not dry up at the sight of my aunt. I am easily flustered, and when I am flustered I lose my voice and wheeze as if I was having a fit. I cleared my throat a few more times for assurance. I am not fond of family reunions. My aunt lost her husband in tragic circumstances and though this had happened some time ago, I had no idea how long my aunt's mourning season would last. Holding the birthday cake and flowers, I stood in front of the door with the air of a pallbearer. I felt very sad. I had tears in my eyes and, on the tip of my tongue, there were the most heartfelt expressions of sympathy on account of my uncle and the tragic circumstances in which he had left my aunt. A minute more and I would have burst through the door shouting tearfully: 'Auntie, auntie, how terrible not to have uncle. What are we going to do?' The minute passed. I was still standing on the step. The house was silent. The garden was empty. My tears swelled and then dried. I suddenly felt, without any offence to the dead, that I had had enough of my uncle and my aunt's birthday. The hell with tragic circumstances. I wanted to drop the flowers, fling away the cake, and go wherever the impulse took me. What was all this to do with me? Amazed by my switch of mood, I waited, picking at the stalks of the tea roses. I was struck, neither capable of going away nor of knocking on the door. I was waiting for something; I felt that any moment something was going to happen which would settle the whole business for me. Before the next minute was out I heard a woman's calm voice.

'Filomen, Filomen!' A woman called in the depths of the house. 'Answer me, you red devil!'

'Here I am, auntie.'

'Filomen talks! Good Heavens, my wishes have come true!'

The shout was followed by the sound of footsteps. The door was flung wide open. In the doorway stood my aunt. She looked at me and her face fell.

'Oh, it's you,' she said disappointed. 'I thought Filomen had been learning to talk in secret.'

My aunt glanced away into the garden. In her hand she held a blue saucer of milk. I could not remember a single word of the speech I had prepared. I bit my lips and unsuccessfully tried to hold back the blush that was creeping over my neck, cheeks and ears. Meanwhile the second Filomen had appeared on the path. He walked past me indifferently. He rubbed against my aunt's leg and, disdaining the milk, began wiping his face with his paw.

'Black nose and dark paws,' I mumbled. 'A pure Abyssinian, isn't he?'

'Oh, yes.' Suddenly my aunt furrowed her brow and spoke sharply: 'What's that in your hand?'

'I've brought you a cake, auntie. And condolences, and wishes for lots of happiness from the whole family.'

'Good, good; where did you get those roses?'

'Here, in the garden.'

'That's the last straw! You've stripped "Madame Kriloff"! Tell me, how could you?'

'I'll apologize, auntie,' I said dropping my eyes and lowering my head.

'D'you know how to?'

'I think so, auntie.'

'Well then, come in. Filomen first, of course. I called him Filomen out of affection for your uncle.'

In the room I found myself face to face with a portrait of Uncle Filomen. In this picture, hung in a gold frame, my uncle held himself proudly erect. He had had a gleaming, twirly moustache and flushed cheeks. He had lived on bacon and probably liked black broth, *sucrée*. From his fleshy nose protruded three black hairs. The artist had perpetuated these on my aunt's pleas. Looking at the three hairs, one had the urge to tug them and shout: 'Boo!' For the time being, however, condolences seemed more in place. My aunt was silent, but I could sense expectancy and impatience in her silence. After all if a person takes so much trouble over little things like hairs in the nose, it means that some bond exists.

'I heard that uncle ...,' my voice broke, 'in tragic circumstances, it seems? Probably fell off a tree? Or perhaps he was run over by a tram. That's a horrible sight. I always turn my head away and close my eyes.

A crunch, yells and that "ups-a-daisy" when they lift the car. I quite understand your feelings. It must have made mincemeat out of uncle. I'm sorry, auntie, but they'll be questioning me about it at home: did uncle fall under the first or second car?'

'There aren't any trams here. He died of mushroom poisoning.'

'A toadstool?' I cried enthusiastically. 'One of those red things with white spots? You can't eat toadstools. Dwarves live in them. Everyone knows that.'

My attempt to relieve the atmosphere fell flat. My aunt fixed me with an icy stare.

'Filomen poisoned himself with a black stinkhorn.'

'Oh, that's a great rarity. You can travel half way round the world and not see one.'

'Your uncle wasn't just anybody.'

I lowered my head.

'A black stinkhorn would fell an ox. My uncle is fully exonerated.'

My aunt sighed.

'He got excellent notices. They wrote: "Major mushroom tragedy". There were photographs in the papers and speeches at the funeral.'

Automatically we glanced at my uncle. A sun speck played round the nose of the stinkhorn victim. His left eye rested on my aunt's deep decolletage; the right gazed into the garden through a chink in the curtain. My uncle had an impressive squint. It occurred to me that it was this that had caused the 'major mushroom tragedy'; with his eye on a pinelover he ate a stinkhorn, as the saying goes.

My aunt adjusted her dressing gown. When she spoke there was a distinctly warmer note in her voice.

'Since Filomen's death, I only serve mushrooms as a last resort, when there's nothing else to give visitors.'

The cat raised its head and looked at my aunt through orange eyes.

'Don't interrupt,' muttered Aunt Iza.

I guessed that the time for confessions was approaching. My aunt lowered her eyes and through mascaraed lids stared into a dark corner beyond the bureau.

'I don't know if you know . . .' she said rubbing the end of her nose.

'Someone's knocking, auntie.'

'It's always like that. Someone's always knocking on somebody's door. It's like living in a shop window. You can't have any secrets in the country. I'm coming! I heard! What's going on? Who's that?'

She went out, the heels of her mules tapping. She was back soon.

'It's for you. About camomile compresses. I said the surgery wasn't furnished yet and so the first visit would have to take place in the hall.'

I sat down.

'There's not going to be one. A comedy of errors, that's all.'

'Aren't you the young doctor who flew in this morning?'

'I'm not a doctor. I'm not going to treat anybody.' I repeated stubbornly.

'You've got to be somebody. Everyone here is, or was, at any rate.' She smiled at my uncle and pinched me lightly on the ear. 'Go on, don't keep the woman waiting. We've been without an oculist for years. A good beginning will assure your career. Off you go and be back quickly.'

'Remember, I'm only doing this for you, auntie.'

My aunt thrust out her arms. Thinking she wanted to kiss me on the forehead, I lowered my head. My aunt recoiled and then seized me by the shoulders and pushed me out of the room.

The mother of the girl with the stye was in the hall. Her addressing me as 'doctor' lent me self-confidence and loosened my tongue. In an assured voice I prescribed camomile compresses and yeast three times a day to be taken at each meal. This last advice proved a very happy idea. With the yeast I won her complete confidence.

'You can tell a good doctor by what he tells you to swallow,' she said frankly, 'any old woman can stick plaster on you.'

This blunt observation was followed by a stream of compliments. I listened, a little amused and a little surprised. I had not expected that praise would give me so much pleasure. Finally, not to push matters too far, I made an appointment for her next visit and led her to the door. As she said goodbye, the woman pressed into my hand a note folded in four. I grimaced because I had not seriously considered the question of a fee. The woman mistook the expression of embarrassment on my face. She began to apologize. She explained that that was how much 'the late vet used to take'. She promised that 'my husband will drop in personally later and bring some more'. 'Nothing for it,' I thought, 'I'll have to keep the game up to avoid a scandal.' I nodded absent-mindedly and locked the door after this quick-witted female.

I found my aunt in the armchair, lounging in an effective pose, with her hands behind her neck, her head tilted and legs crossed.

'I heard. You did very well. Just the right tone of voice. A moment's thought, not too long, not too short, just right. Diagnosis convincing, cure simple. It's valuable, too, to be able to take money graciously.'

'Thanks very much, auntie.'

'Come closer. My throat aches. I don't want to shout. She's a smart old bag, I know her well; she came to have a snoop. But you had her up the garden path before she could look round. There'll soon be real patients coming. A rather queer disease has broken out here. I don't know how to call it. People develop some sort of eye trouble. But you'll manage. I'm sure of it.'

The roses – she had put them in a cut glass bowl – threw an interesting shadow on her calves. I leant against the armchair and said softly:

'Maybe, auntie.'

'Don't call me, auntie. It's cold and off-putting. It simply makes me shiver all over. "Auntie" sounds so terribly staid; and I did get married when I was almost a child.'

She moved her foot. Her mule fell onto the carpet. Under the table the cat miaowed sneeringly.

'Filomen, please leave the room. No, dear, I was talking to the cat. Shut the door after Filomen. I sometimes have the feeling that Filomen understands every word and reads my thoughts. Where are you? Here? Good.'

For a long minute we both pretended that we did not hear a knocking at the door. The knocking was polite but forceful and insistent. After a while it was transferred from the door to the closed shutter. Then even my aunt waved her hand.

'People keep interrupting us. We'll have to hang out a board with surgery hours today. This is ridiculous.'

The second patient introduced himself as the husband of the woman who had called a little earlier. He was a man of medium height, average build and unassuming features. Remembering what Izabel had said, I carefully examined the eyes of my visitor. I was looking for the trouble which was the symptom of the disease infecting the neighbourhood. The patient stood with his head hanging. He was clearly avoiding my eyes. I asked about his daughter's stye. He answered with a shrug of his shoulders and asked for a word with me in private. I pointed to a nook in the far corner of the garden.

For a long time I could not understand what it was all about. The patient complained that he was seeing 'too far'. He said that many of his friends were suffering from the same trouble. In theory to diagnose farsightedness seems child's play and hardly justifies a doctor's bill. In practice, however, it ruins the nervous system, since it upsets your peace of mind and forces you to do some quite unprofitable thinking. This complaint has been rife for years. Doctors avoid our town like the plague. Diagnosis has failed and all known forms of treatment have been a flop. Strangely enough, the majority of doctors have died prematurely in mysterious circumstances.

I leaned my head on my hand and examined the man through my fingers. 'A loony,' I thought, emphasizing my conclusion with a serious nodding of my head. Later, when the patient got properly into his stride I decided that the matter had gone beyond the limits of normal lunacy. There was something else here. If I only knew what! 'If I swallowed his bait ("there is money to be made here, and good money at that"),' my thoughts ran on, 'then after a lightning career I'll increase the number of prematurely dead doctors.' Such a fate, though it had its amusing side, since I was a total stranger to medical or veterinary science, would have spoilt my plans for the immediate future. I had promised myself that right after the birthday I would take up a job with the customs which I had wangled through a cousin who had made a hit with the excisement. The desk job could not compete with the position of oculist in N. But my difficulties, should I decide to stay on in N, were symbolized by the black stinkhorn which had finished my uncle. So I racked my brains trying to find a way out of the situation. Unfortunately no solution occurred to me.

The patient stopped talking. He pointed at a young couple walking up the street. Holding hands, the boy and girl passed the garden and turned into the path leading to the wood. When they were out of sight, the patient asked me what I thought the boy and girl were doing at that moment. Without hesitating I answered that the youngsters were kissing under the first tree they came to.

'You're guessing, but I can see. I'll try and describe what I see as exactly as possible.'

The patient closed his eyes and began to talk very fast. His 'farsightedness' forced me to gaze into someone else's future. Anyone affected by this defect of eyesight took part in scenes being played out in some unknown place and at some unknown time. His 'farsightedness' did not disclose the whole future but showed only selected fragments. This was especially irritating and drove one into a helpless rage. For instance my patient could not see what was happening in the nearby wood. Instead he saw the boy and girl at a later stage of their acquaintance when their innocent flirtation had taken on the flush of love. Here is what my patient told me stripped of its unnecessary trimmings.

'In an upstairs room, the girl is waiting for the boy. The sun is shining, the window open, the street full of holiday traffic. In the distance a band is playing. The girl is waiting, she is restless. She winds her watch, then stands in front of the mirror. She adjusts her hair and arranges her negligée to look its most fetching. Time seems to be crawling for the girl, though the appointed hour is still some way off. But the creeping minutes pass. There is the sound of footsteps. Someone is running up the stairs two at a time. The girl flings herself on the divan. She hides her face in a book and, at the sound of a knock, answers absently "Come in, it's open". He knows she's been waiting. She knows he knows but they play this little game and get an added pleasure out of their pretence. They're happy together, that's certain. It's been like this for a long time. How long, we don't know. We don't know how long it's been since that bewitching stroll in the country. Despite the stillness of the weather the atmosphere in the room is stormy. The boy instead of embracing the girl takes a suspicious object out of his pocket. "Take care of this bomb. Put it where it'll go off at the most blissful moment. Here's the safety catch. Click, and it's set." The girl bursts out laughing. Then she becomes serious. She asks reasonably: "Why must we blow ourselves up?" "Because granny isn't in the cupboard," answers the boy and opens the cupboard. The girl gapes: skirts, blouses, dresses. No granny. The girl's beside herself with joy. Enchanted by the boy and his absurd explanation. The boy leans over the bed and tries to stuff the bomb under the mattress. The girl sobers up. With a deft kick, she knocks the bomb out of his hand. It sails out of the window. She couldn't have picked a worse moment. A carriage is just passing under the window with some distinguished visitor. The band stops. You can hear the stamping of scared horses. Then there is an uproar of outraged shouts over which the orders of officers and police whistles slowly make themselves heard. The girl swallows her tears and despite the heat puts on her warm underwear. "The roof, behind the chimney" the boy advises despairingly. The girl smiles sadly. There is the clatter of heavy boots on the stairs. Into the room bursts a crowd of armed men. "There they are, take them!" yells a police officer with his nose dirtied by the blast. "It was me," says the girl firmly. "It was me," cries the boy. But these dramatic protestations are lost among the curses and crashing of overturned furniture. The metallic click of snapped handcuffs closes the scene. The room empties. A policeman stays behind on guard. Then everything fades into a blur.'

The patient raised his head. His eyes, bleary from the disease, gazed at me imploringly.

'You're curious what happened next?' I said.

'Hell, that's just what I want to know. You're a smart one, doctor.'

I lit a cigarette and, blowing a ring, looked in the direction of the wood where the boy and girl were ... I learned later that he had not even kissed her then. They had sat close together on a mouldy tree trunk and counted the clouds drifting across the horizon.

'All right, I'll tell you what happened next and how it came out.

'They were taken out together but locked separately in the dungeons of a powerful fortress. A detailed investigation established that the bomb had been manufactured by some crackpot confectioner who had a weakness for fireworks. The chocolate ball had burst with an enormous bang and, though there had been no casualties, the distinguished visitor had to interrupt his ceremonial drive and change some of his clothing. The interminable questioning brought to light the quite irrelevant as well as the material. The boy, confused by the situation into which he had dragged the girl, mentioned that at the beginning of their friendship the girl had made the following remark: "You better watch out because I'm Post Box No 9". The police officers were jubilant. This "Post Box No 9" taken together with the bomb (albeit a chocolate one) added up to something. There was a stream of the usual questions. If the girl was Post Box No 9 what was concealed in the box? If she was No 9 there must be a No 1, 2, 3, 4, 5, 6, 7 and 8. Where were they? What were their names? "I don't know," the boy answered. Finally under pressure he slipped up again. He said that Post Box No 9 had something to do with a zeppelin factory. The investigation went off on a new tack. A search was begun for a zeppelin factory somehow connected with the Number 9 and post boxes. Before the right works could be found, the Grand Duke arrived on a tour of inspection of the fortress. An inventory was made immediately and presented to him. As a result it was discovered that the dungeons held two persons "imprisoned for a bomb and zeppelins". The Grand Duke looked at the dossier and shouted "Fools!" It turned out that there wasn't a single zeppelin factory in the world. It also transpired that the distinguished visitor wasn't quite as distinguished as he made out, and that later he had more to worry about than a forced change of trousers. The crackpot confectioner has never looked back. His chocolate bombs, with a somewhat smaller charge, now pop off at all official receptions to the delight of the assembled personages. Only the business of the post box has never been cleared up, but this detail was magnanimously waved aside by the Grand Duke. The boy and the girl were brought into his presence. The Grand Duke took them by the hand and personally set them free. The young couple looked at each other, smiled, walked a few paces and sat down on a bench. "You once said that you were Post Box 9. What did you mean by that?" were the boy's first words. "I don't know," she replied, turning her head away, "and I don't suppose I'll ever remember now." There were passers-by in their Sunday best strolling in the street. As they passed the bench, they would remark delightedly: "Look at those two! Grey-haired, snowy-white, but as loving as a pair of doves. Isn't it sweet?"

'Sweet,' repeated the patient. 'Yes, we've been waiting for somebody who'll understand and now we've found him. My congratulations, doctor.'

Taking advantage of his mood, I asked him what my predecessors had prescribed. The patient paused for reflection.

'The biggest idiot, I suppose, was your late uncle. He told us to wear spectacles of ordinary glass. On the windshields – I don't see how you can call them anything else – he pasted those folk cutouts. They were supposed to absorb our attention. If this worked, the farsightedness would disappear from sheer fatigue.'

'Well?'

'Nothing. The cutouts came unstuck when it rained. People kept falling down the stairs and breaking their legs and arms. You can't really object to that black mushroom lark.'

'There's no resemblance between a psychological squint and a squint proper,' I said as if to myself. 'We'll have to use mechanical treatment. Please stand up.'

'But, doctor, no one's ever done this . . .'

'Stand up,' I shouted, 'and not another peep out of you.'

I told him to press his right eye ball with his thumb so that it stared at the ground, and with his index finger to turn his left eye up to the sky.

'It's a bit painful.'

'Never mind. Now walk up the path as far as the gate and back.'

'I keep tripping, doctor.'

'It'll pass.'

After a while I noticed the young couple returning from the wood. I told the patient to look in their direction and describe exactly what he saw.

'The toes of their shoes and a stretch of sky,' he said confused.

'Every day, before meals, you are to exercise your eyes in this way. In a week come back for a check-up. Chin-up, everything's going to be all right. Now, my fee, please.'

He paid up and all but kissed me.

I found my aunt in the hall. She flung her arms round my neck and pulled me into the surgery. A card with large letters was hanging on the wall. In a corner stood a hanger with a white smock, next to it a wash basin and clean towels. On the desk lay a mirror with a hole, a thermometer, a pen and a note pad. I also noticed a huge money-box. My uncle's portrait peeked out from behind a cupboard.

'Some measuring apparatus would come in handy. It makes a good impression.'

'We'll have to make do with a tape measure for the time being. And now ...' My aunt lowered her eyes.

'I'm sorry, Iza, but what about the notice with surgery hours?'

'It's on the gate.'

'Iza!'

'Filomen!'

I stayed on in N. I see two patients a day, and in this way, unhurriedly, I provide adults, children and adolescents with artificial squints. The 'farsightedness' is dying out. I am ridding N and the neighbourhood of faulty vision. The universal goodwill gives me pleasure. I like it when people talk about 'the dear doctor' or the 'good uncle from heaven'. All ideas of custom and excising vanished remarkably quickly. I am very happy in my new role. How my patients had missed a good doctor! Of course, you can't please everybody. There are those who grumble 'it's not the same' or 'we still haven't found our good uncle because an artificial squint doesn't solve the problem.' A funny lot, they are still waiting for their good uncle and here I am in their midst. Even the marmalade Filomen rubs himself against my legs and treats me as one of the family. And my aunt ... My uncle's portrait has been relegated to the attic. In its gilt frame now hangs a coloured photograph of me.

Translated by Edward Rothert

Ilse Aichinger

The Bound Man

Born in 1921, Ilse Aichinger belongs to that group of German authors who reached maturity in the post-war period and whose work has been deeply influenced by the cataclysms of the second world war. Miss Aichinger is best known for her collection of short stories, The Bound Man and Other Stories.

Sunlight on his face woke him, but made him shut his eyes again; it streamed unhindered down the slope, collected itself into rivulets, attracted swarms of flies, which flew low over his forehead, circled, sought to land, and were overtaken by fresh swarms. When he tried to whisk them away, he discovered that he was bound. A thick rope cut into his arms. He dropped them, opened his eyes again, and looked down at himself. His legs were tied all the way up to his thighs; a single length of rope was tied round his ankles, criss-crossed up his legs, and encircled his hips, his chest and his arms. He could not see where it was knotted. He showed no sign of fear or hurry, though he thought he was unable to move, until he discovered that the rope allowed his legs some free play and that round his body it was almost loose. His arms were tied to each other but not to his body, and had some free play too. This made him smile, and it occurred to him that perhaps children had been playing a practical joke on him.

He tried to feel for his knife, but again the rope cut softly into his flesh. He tried again, more cautiously this time, but his pocket was empty. Not only his knife, but the little money that he had on him, as well as his coat, were missing. His shoes had been pulled from his feet and taken too. When he moistened his lips he tasted blood, which had flowed from his temples down his cheeks, his chin, his neck, and under his shirt. His eyes were painful; if he kept them open for long he saw reddish stripes in the sky.

He decided to stand up. He drew his knees up as far as he could, rested his hands on the fresh grass and jerked himself to his feet. An elder branch stroked his cheek, the pain dazzled him, and the rope cut into his flesh. He collapsed to the ground again, half out of his mind with pain, and then tried again. He went on trying until the blood started flowing from his hidden weals. Then he lay still again for a long while and let the sun and the flies do what they liked.

When he awoke for the second time the elder bush had cast its shadow over him, and the coolness stored in it was pouring from between its branches. He must have been hit on the head. Then they must have laid him down carefully, just as a mother lays her baby behind a bush when she goes to work in the fields.

His chances all lay in the amount of free play allowed him by the rope. He dug his elbows into the ground and tested it. As soon as the rope tautened he stopped, and tried again more cautiously. If he had been able to reach the branch over his head he could have used it to drag himself to his feet, but he could not reach it. He laid his head back on the grass, rolled over, and struggled to his knees. He tested the ground with his toes, and then managed to stand up almost without effort.

A few paces away lay the path across the plateau, and in the grass were wild pinks and thistles in bloom. He tried to lift his foot to avoid trampling on them, but the rope round his ankles prevented him. He looked down at himself.

The rope was knotted at his ankles, and ran round his legs in a kind of playful pattern. He carefully bent and tried to loosen it, but, loose though it seemed to be, he could not make it any looser. To avoid treading on the thistles with his bare feet he hopped over them like a bird.

The cracking of a twig made him stop. People in this district were very prone to laughter. He was alarmed by the thought that he was in no position to defend himself. He hopped on until he reached the path. Bright fields stretched far below. He could see no sign of the nearest village, and if he could move no faster than this, night would fall before he reached it.

He tried walking, and discovered that he could put one foot before another if he lifted each foot a definite distance from the ground and then put it down again before the rope tautened. In the same way he could actually swing his arms a little.

After the first step he fell. He fell right across the path, and made the dust fly. He expected this to be a sign for the long-suppressed laughter to break out, but all remained quiet. He was alone. As soon as the dust had settled he got up and went on. He looked down and watched the rope slacken, grow taut, and then slacken again.

When the first glow-worms appeared he managed to look up. He felt in control of himself again, and his impatience to reach the nearest village faded.

Hunger made him light-headed, and he seemed to be going so fast that not even a motorcycle could have overtaken him; alternatively he felt as if he were standing still and that the earth was rushing past him, like a river flowing past a man swimming against the stream. The stream carried branches which had been bent southward by the north wind, stunted young trees, and patches of grass with bright, long-stalked flowers. It ended by submerging the bushes and the young trees, leaving only the sky and the man above water level. The moon had risen, and illuminated the bare, curved summit of the plateau, the path, which was overgrown with young grass, the bound man making his way along it with quick, measured steps, and two hares, which ran across the hill just in front of him and vanished down the slope. Though the nights were still cool at this time of the year, before midnight the bound man lay down at the edge of the escarpment and went to sleep.

In the light of morning the animal-tamer who was camping with his circus in the field outside the village saw the bound man coming down the path, gazing thoughtfully at the ground. The bound man stopped and bent down. He held out one arm to help keep his balance and with the other picked up an empty wine-bottle. Then he straightened himself and stood erect again. He moved slowly, to avoid being cut by the rope, but to the circus proprietor what he did suggested the voluntary limitation of an enormous swiftness of movement. He was enchanted by its extraordinary gracefulness, and while the bound man looked about for a stone on which to break the bottle, so that he could use the splintered neck to cut the rope, the animal-tamer walked across the field and approached him. The first leaps of a young panther had never filled him with such delight.

'Ladies and gentlemen, the bound man!' His very first movements let loose a storm of applause, which out of sheer excitement caused the blood to rush to the cheeks of the animal-tamer standing at the edge of the arena. The bound man rose to his feet. His surprise whenever he did this was like that of a four-footed animal which has managed to stand on its hind legs. He knelt, stood up, jumped, and turned cart wheels. The spectators found it as astonishing as if they had seen a bird which voluntarily remained earthbound, and confined itself to hopping.

The bound man became an enormous draw. His absurd steps and little jumps, his elementary exercises in movement, made the rope dancer superfluous. His fame grew from village to village, but the motions he went through were few and always the same; they were really quite ordinary motions, which he had continually to practise in the daytime in the half-dark tent in order to retain his shackled freedom. In that he remained entirely within the limits set by his rope he was free of it, it did not confine him, but gave him wings and endowed his leaps and jumps with purpose; just as the flights of birds of passage have purpose when they take wing in the warmth of summer and hesitantly make small circles in the sky.

All the children of the neighbourhood started playing the game of 'bound man'. They formed rival gangs, and one day the circus people found a little girl lying bound in a ditch, with a chord tied round her neck so that she could hardly breathe. They released her, and at the end of the performance that night the bound man made a speech. He announced briefly that there was no sense in being tied up in such a way that you could not jump. After that he was regarded as a comedian.

Grass and sunlight, tent pegs driven into the ground and then pulled up again, and on to the next village. 'Ladies and gentlemen, the bound man!' The summer mounted towards its climax. It bent its face deeper over the fish ponds in the hollows, taking delight in its dark reflection, skimmed the surface of the rivers, and made the plain into what it was. Everyone who could walk went to see the bound man.

Many wanted a close-up view of how he was bound. So the circus proprietor announced after each performance that anyone who wanted to satisfy himself that the knots were real and the rope not made of rubber was at liberty to do so. The bound man generally waited for the crowd in the area outside the tent. He laughed or remained serious, and held out his arms for inspection. Many took the opportunity to look him in the face, others gravely tested the rope, tried the knots on his ankles, and wanted to know exactly how the lengths compared with the length of his limbs. They asked him how he had come to be tied up like that, and he answered patiently, always saying the same thing. Yes, he had been tied up, he said, and when he awoke he found that he had been robbed as well. Those who had done it must have been pressed for time, because they had tied him up somewhat too loosely for someone who was not supposed to be able to move and somewhat too tightly for someone who was expected to be able to move. But he did move, people pointed out. Yes, he replied, what else could he do?

Before he went to bed he always sat for a time in front of the fire. When the circus proprietor asked him why he didn't make up a better story he always answered that he hadn't made up that one, and blushed. He preferred staying in the shade.

The difference between him and the other performers was that when the show was over he did not take off his rope. The result was that every movement that he made was worth seeing, and the villagers used to hang about the camp for hours, just for the sake of seeing him get up from in front of the fire and roll himself in his blanket. Sometimes the sky was beginning to lighten when he saw their shadows disappear.

The circus proprietor often remarked that there was no reason why he should not be untied after the evening performance and tied up again next day. He pointed out that the rope dancers, for instance, did not stay on their rope overnight. But no one took the idea of untying him seriously.

For the bound man's fame rested on the fact that he was always bound, that whenever he washed himself he had to wash his clothes too and vice versa, and that his only way of doing so was to jump in the river just as he was every morning when the sun came out, and that he had to be careful not to go too far out for fear of being carried away by the stream.

The proprietor was well aware that what in the last resort protected the bound man from the jealousy of the other performers was his help-lessness; he deliberately left them the pleasure of watching him groping painfully from stone to stone on the river bank every morning with his wet clothes clinging to him. When the proprietor's wife pointed out that even the best clothes would not stand up indefinitely to such treat-ment (and the bound man's clothes were by no means of the best), he replied curtly that it was not going to last for ever. That was his answer to all objections – it was for the summer season only. But when he said this he was not being serious; he was talking like a gambler who has no intention of giving up his vice. In reality he would have been prepared cheerfully to sacrifice his lions and his rope dancers for the bound man.

He proved this on the night when the rope dancers jumped over the fire. Afterwards he was convinced that they did it, not because it was midsummer's day, but because of the bound man, who as usual was lying and watching them with that peculiar smile that might have been real or might have been only the effect of the glow on his face. In any case no one knew anything about him because he never talked about anything that had happened to him before he emerged from the wood that day.

But that evening two of the performers suddenly picked him up by the arms and legs, carried him to the edge of the fire and started playfully swinging him to and fro, while two others held out their arms to catch him on the other side. In the end they threw him, but too short. The two men on the other side drew back – they explained afterwards that they did so the better to take the shock. The result was that the bound man landed at the very edge of the flames and would have been burned if the circus proprietor had not seized his arms and quickly dragged him away to save the rope which was starting to get singed. He was certain that the object had been to burn the rope. He sacked the four men on the spot.

A few nights later the proprietor's wife was awakened by the sound of footsteps on the grass, and went outside just in time to prevent the clown from playing his last practical joke. He was carrying a pair of scissors. When he was asked for an explanation he insisted that he had no intention of taking the bound man's life, but only wanted to cut his rope because he felt sorry for him. He was sacked too.

These antics amused the bound man because he could have freed himself if he had wanted to whenever he liked, but perhaps he wanted to learn a few new jumps first. The children's rhyme: 'We travel with the circus, we travel with the circus' sometimes occurred to him while he lay awake at night. He could hear the voices of spectators on the opposite bank who had been driven too far downstream on the way home. He could see the river gleaming in the moonlight, and the young shoots growing out of the thick tops of the willow trees, and did not think about autumn yet.

The circus proprietor dreaded the danger that sleep involved for the bound man. Attempts were continually made to release him while he slept. The chief culprits were sacked rope dancers, or children who were bribed for the purpose. But measures could be taken to safeguard against these. A much bigger danger was that which he represented to himself. In his dreams he forgot his rope, and was surprised by it when he woke in the darkness of the morning. He would angrily try to get up, but lose his balance and fall back again. The previous evening's applause was forgotten, sleep was still too near, his head and neck too free. He was just the opposite of a hanged man – his neck was the only part of him that was free. You had to make sure that at such moments no knife was within his reach. In the early hours of the morning the circus proprietor sometimes sent his wife to see whether the bound man was all right. If he was asleep, she would bend over him and feel the rope. It had grown hard from dirt and damp. She would test the amount of free play it allowed him, and touch his tender wrists and ankles.

The most varied rumours circulated about the bound man. Some said he had tied himself up and invented the story of having been robbed, and towards the end of the summer that was the general opinion. Others maintained that he had been tied up at his own request, perhaps in league with the circus proprietor. The hesitant way in which he told his story, his habit of breaking off when the talk got round to the attack on him, contributed greatly to these rumours. Those who still believed in the robbery-with-violence story were laughed at. Nobody knew what difficulties the circus proprietor had in keeping the bound man, and how often he said he had had enough and wanted to clear off, for too much of the summer had passed.

Later, however, he stopped talking about clearing off. When the proprietor's wife brought him his food by the river and asked him how long he proposed to remain with them, he did not answer. She thought he had got used, not to being tied up, but to remembering every moment that he was tied up – the only thing that anyone in his position could get used to. She asked him whether he did not think it ridiculous to be tied up all the time, but he answered that he did not. Such a variety of people – clowns, freaks, and comics, to say nothing of elephants and tigers – travelled with circuses that he did not see why a bound man should not travel with a circus too. He told her about the movements he was practising, the new ones he had discovered, and about a new trick that had occurred to him while he was whisking flies from the animals' eyes. He described to her how he always anticipated the effect of the rope and always restrained his movements in such a way as to prevent it from ever tautening; and she knew that there were days when he was hardly aware of the rope, when he jumped down from the wagon and slapped the flanks of the horses in the morning as if he were moving in a dream. She watched him vault over the bars almost without touching them, and saw the sun on his face, and he told her that sometimes he felt as if he were not tied up at all. She answered that if he were prepared to be untied, there would never be any need for him to feel tied up. He agreed that he could be untied whenever he felt like it.

The woman ended by not knowing whether she was more concerned with the man or with the rope that tied him. She told him that he could go on travelling with the circus without his rope, but she did not believe it. For what would be the point of his antics without his rope, and what would he amount to without it? Without his rope he would leave them, and the happy days would be over. She would no longer be able to sit beside him on the stones by the river without arousing suspicion, and she knew that his continued presence, and her conversations with him, of which the rope was the only subject, depended on it. Whenever she agreed that the rope had its advantages, he would start talking about how troublesome it was, and whenever he started talking about its advantages, she would urge him to get rid of it. All this seemed as endless as the summer itself.

At other times she was worried at the thought that she was herself hastening the end by her talk. Sometimes she would get up in the middle of the night and run across the grass to where he slept. She wanted to shake him, wake him up and ask him to keep the rope. But then she would see him lying there; he had thrown off his blanket, and there he lay like a corpse, with his legs outstretched and his arms close together, with the rope tied round them. His clothes had suffered from the heat and the water, but the rope had grown no thinner. She felt that he would go on travelling with the circus until the flesh fell from him and exposed the joints. Next morning she would plead with him more ardently than ever to get rid of his rope.

The increasing coolness of the weather gave her hope. Autumn was coming, and he would not be able to go on jumping into the river with his clothes on much longer. But the thought of losing his rope, about which he had felt indifferent earlier in the season, now depressed him.

The songs of the harvesters filled him with foreboding. 'Summer has gone, summer has gone'. But he realized that soon he would have to change his clothes, and he was certain that when he had been untied it would be impossible to tie him up again in exactly the same way. About this time the proprietor started talking about travelling south that year.

The heat changed without transition into quiet, dry cold, and the fire was kept going all day long. When the bound man jumped down from the wagon he felt the coldness of the grass under his feet. The stalks were bent with ripeness. The horses dreamed on their feet and the wild animals, crouching to leap even in their sleep, seemed to be collecting gloom under their skins which would break out later.

On one of these days a young wolf escaped. The circus proprietor kept quiet about it, to avoid spreading alarm, but the wolf soon started raiding cattle in the neighbourhood. People at first believed that the wolf had been driven to these parts by the prospect of a severe winter, but the circus soon became suspect. The proprietor could not conceal the loss of the animal from his own employees, so the truth was bound to come out before long. The circus people offered the burgomasters of the neighbouring villages their aid in tracking down the beast, but all their efforts were in vain. Eventually the circus was openly blamed for the damage and the danger, and spectators stayed away.

The bound man went on performing before half-empty seats without losing anything of his amazing freedom of movement. During the day he wandered among the surrounding hills under the thin-beaten silver of the autumn sky, and, whenever he could, lay down where the sun shone longest. Soon he found a place which the twilight reached last of all, and when at last it reached him he got up most unwillingly from the withered grass. In coming down the hill he had to pass through a little wood on its southern slope, and one evening he saw the gleam of two little green lights. He knew that they came from no church window, and was not for a moment under any illusion about what they were.

He stopped. The animal came towards him through the thinning foliage. He could make out its shape, the slant of its neck, its tail which swept the ground, and its receding head. If he had not been bound, perhaps he would have tried to run away, but as it was he did not even feel fear. He stood calmly with dangling arms and looked down at the wolf's bristling coat under which the muscles played like his own underneath the rope. He thought the evening wind was still between him and the wolf when the beast sprang. The man took care to obey his rope.

Moving with the deliberate care that he had so often put to the test, he seized the wolf by the throat. Tenderness for a fellow creature arose in him, tenderness for the upright being concealed in the four-footed. In a movement that resembled the drive of a great bird (he felt a sudden awareness that flying would be possible only if one were tied up in a special way) he flung himself at the animal and brought it to the ground. He felt a slight elation at having lost the fatal advantage of free limbs which causes men to be worsted.

The freedom he enjoyed in this struggle was having to adapt every movement of his limbs to the rope that tied him – the freedom of panthers, wolves, and the wild flowers that sway in the evening breeze. He ended up lying obliquely down the slope, clasping the animal's hind legs between his own bare feet and its head between his hands. He felt the gentleness of the faded foliage stroking the backs of his hands, and he felt his own grip almost effortlessly reaching its maximum, and he felt how he was in no way hampered by the rope.

*   *   *

As he left the wood light rain began to fall and obscured the setting sun. He stopped for a while under the trees at the edge of the wood. Beyond the camp and the river he saw the fields where the cattle grazed, and the places where they crossed. Perhaps he would travel south with the circus after all. He laughed softly. It was against all reason. Even if he continued to put up with the sores that covered his joints and opened and bled when he made certain movements, his clothes would not stand up much longer to the friction of the rope.

The circus proprietor's wife tried to persuade her husband to announce the death of the wolf without mentioning that it had been killed by the bound man. She said that even at the time of his greatest popularity people would have refused to believe him capable of it, and in their present angry mood, with the nights getting cooler, they would be more incredulous than ever. The wolf had attacked a group of children at play that day, and nobody would believe that it had really been killed; for the circus proprietor had many wolves, and it was easy enough for him to hang a skin on the rail and allow free entry. But he was not to be dissuaded. He thought that the announcement of the bound man's act would revive the triumphs of the summer.

That evening the bound man's movements were uncertain. He stumbled in one of his jumps, and fell. Before he managed to get up he heard some low whistles and catcalls, rather like birds calling at dawn. He tried to get up too quickly, as he had done once or twice during the summer, with the result that he tautened the rope and fell back again. He lay still to regain his calm, and listened to the boos and catcalls growing into an uproar. 'Well, bound man, and how did you kill the wolf?' they shouted, and: 'Are you the man who killed the wolf?' If he had been one of them, he would not have believed it himself. He thought they had a perfect right to be angry: a circus at this time of year, a bound man, an escaped wolf, and all ending up with this. Some groups of spectators started arguing with others, but the greater part of the audience thought the whole thing a bad joke. By the time he had got to his feet there was such a hubbub that he was barely able to make out individual words.

He saw people surging up all round him, like faded leaves raised by a whirlwind in a circular valley at the centre of which all was yet still. He thought of the golden sunsets of the last few days; and the sepulchral light which lay over the blight of all that he had built up during so many nights, the gold frame which the pious hang round dark, old pictures, this sudden collapse of everything, filled him with anger.

They wanted him to repeat his battle with the wolf. He said that such a thing had no place in a circus performance, and the proprietor declared that he did not keep animals to have them slaughtered in front of an audience. But the mob stormed the ring and forced them towards the cages. The proprietor's wife made her way between the seats to the exit and managed to get round the cages from the other side. She pushed aside the attendant whom the crowd had forced to open a cage door, but the spectators dragged her back and prevented the door from being shut.

'Aren't you the woman who used to lie with him by the river in the summer?' they called out. 'How does he hold you in his arms?' She shouted back at them that they needn't believe in the bound man if they didn't want to, they had never deserved him. Painted clowns were good enough for them.

The bound man felt as if the bursts of laughter were what he had been expecting ever since early May. What had smelt so sweet all through the summer now stank. But, if they insisted, he was ready to take on all the animals in the circus. He had never felt so much at one with his rope.

Gently he pushed the woman aside. Perhaps he would travel south with them after all. He stood in the open doorway of the cage, and he saw the wolf, a strong young animal, rise to its feet, and he heard the proprietor grumbling again about the loss of his exhibits. He clapped his hands to attract the animal's attention, and when it was near enough he turned to slam the cage door. He looked the woman in the face. Suddenly he remembered the proprietor's warning to suspect of murderous intentions anyone near him who had a sharp instrument in his hand. At the same moment he felt the blade on his wrists, as cool as the water of the river in autumn, which during the last few weeks he had been barely able to stand. The rope curled up in a tangle beside him while he struggled free. He pushed the woman back, but there was no point in anything he did now. Had he been insufficiently on his guard against those who wanted to release him, against the sympathy in which they wanted to lull him? Had he lain too long on the river bank? If she had cut the cord at any other moment it would have been better than this.

He stood in the middle of the cage, and rid himself of the rope like a snake discarding its skin. It amused him to see the spectators shrinking back. Did they realize that he had no choice now? Or that fighting the wolf now would prove nothing whatever? At the same time he felt all his blood rush to his feet. He felt suddenly weak.

The rope, which fell at its feet like a snare, angered the wolf more than the entry of a stranger into its cage. It crouched to spring. The man reeled, and grabbed the pistol that hung ready at the side of the cage. Then, before anyone could stop him, he shot the wolf between the eyes. The animal reared, and touched him in falling.

On the way to the river he heard the footsteps of his pursuers – spectators, the rope dancers, the circus proprietor, and the proprietor's wife, who persisted in the chase longer thán anyone else. He hid in a clump of bushes and listened to them hurrying past, and later on streaming in the opposite direction back to the camp. The moon shone on the meadow; in that light its colour was both of growth and of death.

When he came to the river his anger died away. At dawn it seemed to him as if lumps of ice were floating in the water, and as if snow had fallen, obliterating memory.

Translated by Eric Mosbacher

PICADOR outstanding international fiction

The Naked i 6op
edited by Frederick R. Karl and Leo Hamalian
Fictions for the seventies. By twenty-five authors, including Leonard Cohen,
LeRoi Jones, Robert Coover, Carlos Fuentes, James Leo Herlihy, Sylvia
Plath, Ken Kesey.

A Chinese Anthology 5op
edited by Raymond Van Over
A collection of Chinese folktales, fables and parables which, by any standard,
can be termed definitive. It captures the elements which comprise the spirit
of Chinese culture – intensity of imagination, wit and humour, human
concern.

Cannon Shot and Glass Beads 6op
Modern Black writing edited by George Lamming
An anthology of the finest Black writing of our time, from Africa,
Afro-America and the Caribbean.

A Personal Anthology 45p
Jorge Luis Borges
South America's major prose-writer makes his own selection of the pieces on
which he would like his reputation to rest.

The Aleph and Other Stories 5op
Jorge Luis Borges
The most comprehensive collection of his work available in English.
It contains a long, specially written autobiographical essay as well as a
brilliant selection of fiction.

Gentlemen Prefer Blondes　40p
Anita Loos
The sparkling modern classic about a not-so-dumb gold-digging blonde.
'I reclined on a sofa reading *Gentlemen Prefer Blondes* for three
days. I am putting the piece in place of honour' – James Joyce

The Third Policeman　50p
Flann O'Brien
Wildly funny and chillingly macabre; the most extraordinary murder thriller
ever written. 'Even with *Ulysses* and *Finnegans Wake* behind him, James
Joyce might have been envious' – *Observer*

Murphy　50p
Samuel Beckett
Brilliant tragi-comic novel of an Irishman's adventures in London, by the
Nobel Prizewinner.

More Pricks than Kicks　50p
Samuel Beckett
His first and most light-hearted novel. The adventures of a student in Dublin
are explored by 'one of the greatest prose writers of the century'
– *Times Literary Supplement*

The Exploits of the Incomparable Mulla Nasrudin　40p
Idries Shah, *with drawings by* Richard Williams
A collection of stories about Nasrudin (an international folk hero of
medieval origin but timeless appeal) which illustrate the philosophical
teachings of the Sufis.

Rosshalde 40p
Hermann Hesse
The story of an artist's journey to self-discovery. By the Nobel Prizewinner who is perhaps the most influential novelist of our time.

Klingsor's Last Summer 50p
Hermann Hesse
The work which Hesse called 'my revolutionary book'. Written in the same period as *Siddhartha*, these novellas describe a time of immense emotional turmoil, of heightened pain, pleasure and perception in the lives of three characters.

Siddhartha 40p
Hermann Hesse
Hermann Hesse's greatest masterpiece. A profoundly moving love story and the account of a lifetime's quest for spiritual fulfilment.

If the War Goes On 50p
Hermann Hesse
The faith in salvation via the 'Inward Way', so familiar to readers of Hesse's fiction, is here expressed in his reflections on war and peace, on politics and the individual.

Knulp 40p
Hermann Hesse
The story of the loves and the wanderings of a vagabond whose role in life is to bring 'a little nostalgia for freedom' into the lives of ordinary men.